No Fences in Alaska

GLEN SOBEY

Black Rose Writing | Texas

First printing

ISBN: 978-1-68433-297-7
PUBLISHED BY BLACK ROSE WRITING
www.blackrosewriting.com

Printed in the United States of America
Suggested Retail Price (SRP) $21.95

No Fences in Alaska is printed in Calluna
Cover design by Cherie Chapman @ ccbookdesign

To all those who can be the parents and grandparents their kids need and will love them for what they are, not what they want them to be

And to all my grandkids:
Kyra, Lily, Jonas, Samantha, Jane, Bella, Desmin, Carolyn, and Brian

May you find Cooper when you need him

No Fences in Alaska

"No fences in Alaska, sweetheart.
Never let them build one around you."

—Cooper Lyons

Chapter One

Harper's plan was beautifully wicked: go to Trish's house to work on a school project and then spend the night, sneak out of her bedroom window, meet Zachary on the corner, and party all night at his place. His real 21st birthday was Saturday, but he wanted a pre-party celebration with her. Trish would let her back in the next morning, and Harper would drive them both to school. A full night with Zachary, some smack, and a case of beer. She couldn't wait. And she'd bring a little something back for Trish. She smiled at herself knowingly in the mirror as she hummed and curled her lashes. Of all the times she had been with him, this would be the first she could spend the entire night.

"Where are you going, Harper?" asked Alex, her 11-year-old sister, who had her face behind a hand mirror, working on her lips. They shared a bedroom. Not the best arrangement for Harper's escapades, but Alex was now her confidante.

"To spend the night with Trish." Harper smiled at her through the dresser mirror.

"Uh-huh. Don't think so." Alex smiled, her top lip bright red. "Is he cute?"

"Oh my God, you wouldn't believe!" Cute was an understatement when it came to Zachary. He was gorgeous, ripped, and tall, with the softest lips that matched hers perfectly.

Alex giggled, shaking her thick, curly bangs over her huge eyes.

"Isn't that my lipstick?" asked Harper.

"You said I could use it. Besides, you don't use red anymore."

No, she didn't use red anymore, not since boys in her class taunted her with "hot lips" and especially "horny lips." Harper didn't want her sister to experience that.

"It's OK for dress-up at home," said Harper, "but use something more subtle for school."

Alex rolled her eyes.

They rarely fought. Alex admired everything about Harper and always provided support when their parents pulled theirs, sometimes dragging Alex into arguments she hadn't started. Little Jack, who slept down the hall, never experienced such falls from grace. He was the angel of the family, and he knew it.

Harper admired her outfit in the mirror: tight, white shorts that she had cut off an extra few inches. She admired her long legs, which she tried to show off as much as she could get away with. They were her best feature. Her hot-pink top was strapless, coming just to her ribs to reveal her stomach and her rose-colored stud belly ring. Her eyeliner enhanced the blue in her hazel eyes. Her long nails made her fingers look tantalizingly sensuous, and she could just imagine how good they'd look running down Zachary's chest. Harper turned and struck her most alluring pose—lips partly open in a circle, one hand behind her head lifting her hair, her other hand hooked into the band of her shorts, pulling them down slightly.

"Am I hot?" she purred.

"On fire!" said Alex.

"Hopefully Zachary thinks so." She turned around and added more gloss to her lips.

Alex finished her bottom lip and practiced her pucker. "How long before I look like you?"

Harper stopped and frowned at her sister in the mirror. Alex's side of the room was full of dolls on shelves and princess posters. She even had a *Frozen* bedspread. Where Harper's side was bare except for the bottles of makeup, brushes, nail polish, and lip-gloss crammed onto shelves on either side of her dresser mirror. Her shocked parents had removed all her "entirely inappropriate" posters last month—shirtless guys with bulging pecs gripping beautiful, barely dressed women. They even made her toss her adult romance novel collection—over two hundred books—because they had caught Alex reading one.

Four years ago, when Harper's side looked similar to Alex's, a friend of her 16-year-old brother Chris opened her bedroom door "by mistake." Luke wore only boxer shorts and was gorgeous with a toned figure like a runner, messy blonde hair and blue eyes. Harper froze, standing before her mirror in a bra and panties; a dark red blush covered her face and spread to her chest.

Luke gasped and stared.

"How old are you?" he asked, a bulge forming in his shorts.

"Twelve," said Harper, snapping out of her shock and covering herself with her pillow.

"Wow! You look eighteen at least."

Harper stared at his shorts. Part of her wanted to shove him out of the room and lock her door. But another part of her, a darker part, was curious and wanted him to come closer. He noticed and smiled, more of a sneer, and it unsettled her.

"Too bad you're only twelve," he teased and left.

The next time Luke visited, he spent the night with Chris and happened to mistake doors again. Harper tried very hard not to look or act twelve during her first make-out experience. She didn't know if she really liked or wanted him or if she just wanted the experience that she had heard so many older girls murmuring about. What was the big deal about a kiss? What did it feel like?

And it was nothing like she imagined.

There was lust and thrill, but there was also fear and guilt. While the kiss and the way he touched her made her feel alive, it didn't feel right.

Then her brother walked in and all hell broke loose.

Later, Luke claimed the horny little girl attacked him, forcing him to accommodate her inexperienced efforts. Chris punched him a few times, and her father never looked at her the same way again. She didn't know what hurt more, Luke's accusations or that her father had believed him.

However, it wasn't the damage to her moral reputation that bothered her, but her lack of experience, which she quickly gained during the next few years, doing everything except intercourse. At the time she still thought it was important to preserve her virginity. Or at least her parents and the church did. Every other act was fair game, as far as she was concerned. Boys her age were like matches against a flamethrower. Though some tried to keep up with her, they inevitably scampered away, calling her names, trying to shame her to hide their own hang-ups. So she looked elsewhere and found Zachary.

Now she stared at her sister, still very much a little girl, and didn't want the same future for her. Lying. Secret parties. Drugs and alcohol. Unrestricted sex with a college guy. That was Harper's life, not her little sister's.

"Hey, Earth to Harper!" shouted Alex. "How long before I look like you?"

"You don't want to look like me, Alex," Harper said, grabbing a tissue, intent on wiping the make-up from her sister's lips. "Just be you."

Alex stood and moved away. "Are you kidding? You were hot at twelve, and I've done everything at least a year sooner than you did, according to Mom. I should have boobs any day now. I can't wait!" She shoved a stuffed animal under her pajama shirt against her chest, stood, pushed out her "boobs," and lifted her shirt past her hip. "Am I hot?" She puckered her full red lips and lifted her hair over her head until it hung seductively over her face.

Harper's jaw dropped. Maybe she needed to hide more of her secrets from Alex, but Harper already felt so isolated and lonely in her own house. Harper realized she was staring at her sister, wide-eyed and open-mouthed. She tried to smile.

"You should see your face!" Alex flopped onto her bed in a heap of giggles.

Harper heard her phone ring down the hall and ran to the bathroom where she had left it.

"Hey, Zachary," she whispered as she closed the door.

"Hey, Lovebug. Plan still a go?"

She turned on the sink faucets and walked toward the tub to ensure no eavesdroppers could catch anything. "I'll be at the corner in about ten minutes. I'm bringing a hot birthday present for you. Something to change into," she groaned softly, "and then out of."

"I like the out of part," he replied huskily.

"Won't be long. I'll see all of you soon."

She ran back to the bedroom to finish dressing, leaving the door open. She had met Zachary through Trish's brother, Larry; both were in college. Harper was a sophomore in high school, visiting Trish when the young men stopped by. Zachary made his interest in her obvious. He told her he loved her large hazel eyes and golden-brown hair, and her strong nose with the little uplift at the end. And, of course, her figure of generous curves in all the right places. But her lips were his favorite part: full, pouty, shiny with burnt orange gloss. She gave him her number, and the secret dates began. Her parents would never approve of Zachary, and the secrecy made their meetings even more intoxicating.

• • • • •

From the top of the stairs, Greg looked at his sixteen-year-old daughter standing in front of her dresser mirror and gasped in horror. The decision to confront her about the missing twenties from his wallet left his brain. Her long hair piled on top of her head, cut-off shirt and shorts, and flat sandals revealed as much flesh as possible, an image he couldn't believe his daughter wanted to project. Why would she want to look like that? A little smear of pink and white was all that kept her from total nudity.

He watched her slip on a baggy, long-sleeved shirt, buttoned to her neck to hide her real outfit, then dab perfume on her chest. When she wiped a streak along the inside of each long thigh, his shock turned to anger.

Greg stomped down the hall toward her open bedroom door. "What the hell are you doing?"

Harper kept staring at herself in the mirror, adding more rings to her ears. "I'm going over to Trish's." She shoved her phone into her shirt pocket, grabbed her overnight bag from her bed, and tried to move past him, but he held out his arm against the doorframe to stop her. She tried to shoulder past him, but she couldn't budge him.

He wouldn't let his daughter go anywhere looking like that. Did she think he was stupid? As if she'd dress like that for Trish. She shouldn't ever dress like that. Period.

"Who are you really meeting?" he asked, his face reddening.

"I already told you. We're working on a school project." She tried to walk through him but bounced off. "Can you move?"

He gently grabbed her shoulders. "Harper—"

She shoved off his hold. "Don't touch me! I'm going, and you're making me late!"

"For what? If you were just going to hang out at Trish's, she wouldn't mind. Tell me one good reason for putting perfume on your legs."

"You watched me?"

"As if I wanted to see that." He matched her tone of disgust. "What is going on with you, Harper?"

Harper pulled out her phone and punched out a text with her thumb. Greg took a deep breath to try to compose himself.

"Who are you texting?" he asked.

"Trish. I'm spending the night at her house. I already told you. Now please get out of my way."

"She's going to see Trish, Dad," said Alex. "I heard her call her just a minute ago."

Harper glanced at Alex, who nodded back.

Greg looked at his younger daughter and was astounded again. He noticed her red lips. Great. Harper was corrupting Alex. He wouldn't let Alex become Harper 2.0.

"Give me your phone!" he demanded, holding out his hand to Harper. He didn't know who she was texting, but he was sure it was another bad influence in her life. Damn it, he wouldn't see her end up like he was in high school or worse, like Heather, his dead sister. He had to stop this now.

"It's my phone!" Harper ran to the other side of the room and fumbled to turn on the camera.

"I pay for it! Give me the phone!"

Just as Harper lifted the phone to start the video, Greg yanked it out of her hand. Harper pulled on his arms as he held the phone up out of her reach, trying to see her latest text. But he already knew she'd called him a pervert for watching her dress.

Two weeks ago, he and Harper had argued about the clothes she planned to wear to school. After he made her put a bra on under her tank top, she sent a note to her friends: "My dad keeps staring at my boobs!" Kids talked to parents, and a few had called him. He was just as stunned and disgusted by her accusations as they were. He couldn't believe Harper hated him so much as to subject him to that. Now he'd have to deal with the awkwardness again, all because his daughter had found the one weapon she could use to challenge his authority. He had no idea how they had gotten here. Why couldn't she see he was doing this to protect her?

"Give me my phone!" Harper raked her nails down his arm.

"Damn you!" Greg saw drops of blood ooze on his forearm.

"Dad!" yelled Alex. "Just let her go!"

"Natalie!" Greg yelled for his wife as he leaned out of the doorway. "I need you up here!" Then he slammed Harper's door shut.

"Get out of my room!" yelled Harper. "What's wrong with you?"

Greg sat against the door inside her bedroom. Harper twisted the handle above his head and pulled, but the door wouldn't open. She put her foot against the wall and pulled the handle, bending the door against Greg's body. He pushed his back toward the frame and snapped the door closed.

Natalie knocked quietly from the other side. "Greg? What's going on?"

"You're not leaving," Greg ground out to Harper. "I want to know who you were planning to meet. And why you think it's appropriate to wear those clothes and wipe perfume on your legs. Why your legs, for God's sake?"

Greg was horrified. He suspected she was acting a little wild around boys, especially now that she attended a public school, but he'd tried to deny the clear signs of sex and drug use. They'd both been missing cash during the past few months. A week ago, Natalie had found the bag of marijuana in Harper's car, which she claimed belonged to someone else, as well as the sensuous rubbing oils. Their daughter was a liar and up to no good. They needed to clamp down hard on her, but he didn't want to admit the truth. He couldn't believe his own daughter was following the same path as Heather, a victim of drugs, alcohol, and liberal parenting. He had tried so hard to make his house different from his parents', yet the same problems arose. What was causing this?

"Get away from the door!" Harper kicked at her father's legs, but he grabbed her foot and pushed her back.

She stumbled and picked up a bottle of nail polish from her dresser and whipped it at him. He blocked it with his large forearm. She threw another, and it smashed into his temple, just missing his eye.

"Dammit!" he yelled.

"Just let her leave!" Alex yelled. "I can't stand this!"

"Let me go," Harper warned, ready to throw another bottle.

"You're not going anywhere," said Greg, "until you tell me who you're meeting and what you plan to do tonight."

"I'm not telling you anything!" She threw the bottle against the door, breaking the top, splattering red polish on his shirt and neck.

"You throw anything else at me and I'm calling the police," said Greg, hoping the threat would be enough to subdue her.

Harper stormed to a window and jerked it up. "I'll jump out if you don't move! Don't think I won't!"

Cold swept through his veins, cooling his skin and his temper. She was such a good liar he couldn't tell if she was serious or if this was just another one of her antics. "You'll die if you jump."

"Then you'd have to explain why your daughter killed herself."

An idea flashed in Greg's mind. A way to protect himself, get professional help for Harper, and have time to figure out what to do with her. He wouldn't lose her like this.

"Natalie," Greg shouted, "call the police and tell them our daughter is threatening to kill herself."

"What?" Natalie panicked and banged on the door.

"She's going to jump out the window. Call the police!"

Harper huffed in disbelief. "You're calling the police? Such a dork." Harper tore off the window screen and tossed it outside. She straddled the windowsill. "What's it going to be Daddy-O? A bloody splat on your driveway or an open door?"

He raised a brow. "Up to you. But you're not leaving the house tonight."

"Aren't you going to stop her?" Alex asked him breathlessly. "Please don't, Harper." She ran over to her sister, crying, and pulled her arm. "Please."

"I know you don't like hearing this, Alex. I sure didn't like hearing him tear into Chris when I was your age." She glowered at him. He returned her glare, undeterred. "They tore into him until he couldn't wait to get out of here. He'd rather join the Army and get shot at in Afghanistan than live under this roof."

He wasn't going to rise to her bait. "Your brother turned out to be a fine young man," said Greg. "He knows we're proud of him."

"Only after he left your house. You never said anything good about him when he lived here. He couldn't wait to leave." She spit her words at him. "Just like me!"

Greg remembered all the fights he had with Chris, how they could never seem to just talk. God, was he destined to go through the same thing with Harper? How could he stop this?

Harper climbed back inside, and Greg hid his sigh of relief. Alex hugged her tightly. Harper kissed her head and led her back to her bed. "Don't worry, Alex. He'll probably care more for you than he does for me."

She sat at her desk, while Alex chewed her fingernails on the bed. She watched him for a minute, and he could see the wheels turning. She spoke calmly, "Dad, I need to call someone."

"Who?" Greg snarled.

"Please. Just let me have my phone. I'll even change my clothes if that's what you want." She smiled sweetly.

He wasn't buying it.

His eyes narrowed. "Who are you meeting?"

Her face dropped and she exploded. "None of your damned business!" She leapt off the chair and closed her hands into fists.

"It is my business. You're my daughter, and I pay for the phone with the money you don't steal from me!"

"Damn it! I need to leave!" Her face was bright red and her eyes took on a sheen.

Good, he was getting to her. "What's wrong?" asked Greg. "Are you out of marijuana? Or are you hooked on something stronger?"

She scoffed. "As if you care."

"I do care. Very much. That's why I'm not letting you leave." Why couldn't she see that?

"Yeah, you cared so much about me that you kicked me out of your precious school last year."

"Because you had beer on a volleyball trip!" he shot back, exasperated. He was Headmaster of The Cross Academy, founded by Natalie's parents, John and Zoe, who had made a fortune in various Christian businesses.

"I didn't buy it! The other girls gave it to me. I told you a hundred times. They told you the same thing!"

"And that's supposed to make it OK? You should've turned them in. As soon as they gave you the beer, you should have told the coach."

Her eyes shot daggers. "That would've made you proud, wouldn't it? Rather than disgusted and embarrassed!"

"That's what a respectful daughter would have done."

"And one who would have no friends. No social life."

"And this is your social life?" He motioned to her outfit. "Dressing like a slut to sneak off to a party or some guy?"

The flicker of pain across her face punched him square in the gut. But the words were out, and there was no taking them back.

"So now I'm a slut?" her voice quivered. "Then why don't you kick me out of the house? I would love to leave."

"We could make that happen, young lady. But tonight, you are telling the truth. Who are you meeting?"

"Greg!" Natalie banged on the door. "They're on their way!"

"God, I hate you!" she bellowed, throwing her hands up.

"Regardless of what you may think, I care for you," said Greg.

"Then care enough to stop me."

She climbed through the window and stuck both legs out. Alex screamed. Greg jumped to his feet.

"That's concrete beneath your window with nothing to break your fall," Greg informed her as he cautiously crossed the room. "The least you'll end up with is a broken leg, but you could crack your skull."

"I don't care!" she threw over her shoulder.

"Harper, please!" shouted Alex, leaping off her bed.

Sirens grew louder as a patrol car roared up their street.

"The only reason you'd care if I jumped," said Harper, "is that you'd have to explain why the great Godly Greg's daughter wanted to kill herself. Oops! Not so Godly after all. I forgot about your annotated Bible that Chris found in the garage. The one you used in college. The one with 'BS' written in all the margins. And your research paper revealing the Bible as nothing but lies. Let's not forget that gem!"

Here it comes. He kicked himself every day for not tossing out all of his college books and papers. Chris had found the crate in the garage during his senior year, which had added fuel to the ongoing fire between them. Natalie was especially unhappy with Greg at the time. She knew he wasn't religious when she met him, but she didn't know he'd actually hated religion. The rift between them took months to mend.

Fortunately, Natalie's parents never found out.

Harper scooted out farther and leaned forward.

Alex shrieked again and ran to her sister, grabbing a handful of her shirt and pulling her back in.

"Please, Harper. Don't!" Tears poured from her eyes. She looked back at Greg. "Dad, please stop her!"

Greg froze. He knew she wouldn't jump, that she was just manipulating him to get her way. Always the drama queen. But he also worried if he got too close, she just might scoot farther away and slip. Did she despise him so much that she'd rather fall out a window than let him hold her?

Harper climbed back inside. "Notice that our father didn't move, Alex. Guess that claim of caring about me was as false as he considered the Bible during his college days."

"I was raised in a Godless house, as you very well know. I wrote that paper long before I met your mother and found Jesus Christ."

"And her parents' money," she smirked.

Greg could have punched that smug smile right off her face, but he prayed quickly for patience. He was the spiritual and moral leader of his family. His kids were supposed to fear their father as they feared God. His job was to keep his school and house protected from the world's evils and not subject to drugs, sex, and selfish indulgence. Now his daughter was defying him in front of Alex. He couldn't tolerate this.

Greg inhaled deeply. "Harper, you can lash out at me all you want, but you aren't leaving this house tonight. I'm through playing games."

"So am I." Harper opened a drawer and pulled out a large pocketknife. With the blade pressed against her forearm, she walked slowly toward Greg.

"Open the door or I bleed," said Harper.

Alex ran towards her.

"Stay away, Alex!" Harper said.

Alex stopped.

"I don't want you hurt!" Harper pressed the blade harder against her left arm while glaring at Greg. "Last chance. Move or I cut."

"The police are here," shouted Natalie through the door.

A heavy knock followed her words, and a man's muffled voice ordered. "Please open the door, sir."

Greg stood, his legs quivering. She was bluffing. She had to be. "Put the knife down, Harper."

"Move away and let me go to Trish's," she said firmly.

"You are not leaving this house!"

Harper ripped the blade up her forearm and screamed, "I hate you!"

"Oh, my God!" Greg breathed. He opened the door.

Everyone looked at Harper holding up her bloody arm with emotions that ranged from stunned to determined.

"I'll do it again if you don't let me go." Harper moved the blade toward her arm.

Two officers, a tall man and a stocky female, strode into the bedroom. The female wore latex gloves, smiled at Harper, and placed one hand around her cut arm and the other around her hand holding the knife.

Claire's eyes locked onto Harper's with sympathy. "I'm Officer Claire. Let me help you, Harper."

Greg stood there in bewilderment. She'd so easily done what Greg couldn't—show genuine concern without anger.

Harper panted. "I need to leave!"

"We want to help you," Claire told her with a reassuring smile. "Let us take a look at your arm. OK?"

Harper relaxed a little, and Claire took the knife.

"This is Officer Robert." She nodded to her partner.

Robert had a large shaved head and a big smile, which produced thick wrinkles in his forehead. Harper stared blankly at him. "Got too much skin up here," he chuckled and patted his head. "Hey, I like all those earrings. Where'd you get them?" he asked as he put on gloves.

"At the Ear Shop in the mall. It's a kiosk."

"Great. I'll tell my daughter about it," said Robert. "Let me see your arm, Harper." He turned toward Natalie. "Can you get me a towel or bandage, please?"

Natalie ran out of the room and shortly returned with a towel and handed it to the officer, who then dabbed the blood off Harper's arm.

Greg went to Alex who had covered her head with a pillow at some point during this madness. He sat on the bed and put his arm around her. "You OK, Alex?"

Alex removed the pillow and seethed. "Go away!"

Greg tried to rub her back.

"Go away!" She shook off his hand. "Mom!"

Greg stood and looked at Natalie, who moved to Alex's bed.

"I'll get some bandages," Greg said to the officers seated on either side of Harper on her bed. He returned with the first-aid kit and handed it to Claire.

"Why did you cut yourself, Harper?" asked Claire, taking out a roll of gauze and sterile tape.

"Because my father wouldn't let me leave." Tears trailed down Harper's cheeks.

"Did you threaten to jump out the window?" Claire asked as she dressed the superficial wound that was already clotting.

"Yes."

"Would you have done it?"

She hesitated, meeting Greg's eyes. Her lip pursed. "Yes."

"Did you worry about hurting yourself?"

Harper rolled her eyes. "I didn't care. I want to leave. Please don't make me stay here. I'll cut my other arm if I have to stay with him." She waved at Greg.

Greg stopped breathing. This didn't sound like manipulation. She was serious.

The officers glanced at each other. Robert nodded to Claire.

"We have a good place for you to go, Harper. We'll take you there."

They helped her stand up.

"Where?" Harper's eyes watched them carefully. "I just want to see Trish."

"Maybe she can visit you at the hospital."

Harper looked stricken. "Hospital? I don't need a hospital." She tried to pull her arms away from the officers.

Greg wasn't sure this was the right course of action either. Had he pushed her to do this? Or did she really need help? He just didn't know.

"You tried to hurt yourself, Harper," said Claire, gently, smiling. "We know some good doctors who will help you."

"I'm fine now," said Harper. All the make-up on her face couldn't hide how pale she went.

"We know you are, but we need to take you to the hospital," said Robert.

"Why? Everything's OK. It's just a little cut."

When Greg glanced his way, Robert beckoned him aside. "Pack some clothes for Harper and meet us at the Behavioral Hospital at the Medical Complex."

"You threatened to kill yourself," said Claire. "We need to make sure you don't hurt yourself again."

Harper struggled against Claire's grip on her arms.

"Harper." Claire's tone remained amiable. "If you struggle, I'll have to handcuff you, and I don't want to do that. You've been through enough already."

"I need to go to Trish's house!" She broke away from Claire and grabbed her overnight bag. Claire gently but firmly took her arm and led her out of the room. Harper glared at her parents as she walked past them into the hallway. "You're having me locked up? I'll never forgive you for this. Never!"

Alex ran toward the bedroom door. "I want to hug her! Harper!"

Greg caught her with an arm around her waist, securing her to his side. Natalie bent down and hugged Alex's shoulders.

"We'll get to see her soon," said Natalie.

"I love you, Alex!" shouted Harper as she descended the stairs, past all the children's portraits, professionally posed in ornate chairs with hand painted enhancements, when each child was four years old. Then up the foyer past the living room and the baby grand piano Harper had been forced to play until she refused at fourteen. And past the placards of scripture and crosses decorating all the walls.

Greg stood rooted at the top of the stairs with Natalie and a teary-eyed Alex.

Harper turned at the front doorway and looked around her, pointing at placards on the walls. "'Bless this house.' 'Love Never Fails.' Oh, and my favorite, 'Family is Everything.'" Harper let out a broken sounding laugh that wrenched Greg's heart. "I never realized these sayings were supposed to be jokes. Very funny!"

She kept laughing as Claire and Robert led her through the door.

Greg was the first to move, coming downstairs to gaze out the windows framing his front door, trying to see if anyone was watching his house or the patrol car. With its lights blinking, it almost begged his neighbors to come outside and look. He watched his daughter walking toward the patrol car. Should he have done something differently? He'd called the police without thinking it through. *Stupid.*

Alex broke away from Natalie, ran down the hall, and slammed her bedroom door.

Greg sighed. He knew his anger had caused this. Stomping up the stairs to blast his daughter for stealing from his wallet. Again. Then he saw her clothes and knew what she was about to do. He'd seen his sister do the same thing countless times.

The patrol car pulled away. Harper didn't even look out the window at him. She didn't look back even once as the car strolled down the street or even as it turned the corner.

Part of him wanted to run after the car, beg them to stop, to let her go. But he didn't move.

Maybe someone at the hospital could help her.

He never could.

Chapter Two

Cooper Lyons removed his pistol from its leather holster and wondered if he had the courage to use it on himself.

"A .44 magnum is the only pistol that can take down a grizzly." The salesman's words echoed in Cooper's mind as he stared down the four-inch barrel. He'd bought it when he first moved to Alaska sixteen years ago for protection against bears. At the time, that was its only purpose. Since then he'd mainly shot it at the firing range in his hometown of Anders Fork, Alaska, though he'd carried the heavy Mountain Gun while walking among grizzlies and polar bears all over the state during his various teaching jobs and visits to wildernesses.

He considered the irony of its purchase for protection and its final use for his own death. He hoped that when the time came he wouldn't forget why his finger was on the trigger.

He'd often forgotten something a few seconds after trying to fix it in his head: which tool he needed to fetch or what he was looking for in the pantry. Websites, however, said such lapses were normal.

But when he started hallucinating a few weeks ago, he decided to see a doctor in Fairbanks.

After driving the eighty miles to town, Dr. Johns' nurse, Hannah, fussed at him because he hadn't come by for a physical since he retired from teaching two years ago.

"Have my numbers changed?" asked Cooper as he stepped off the scale.

"No, they haven't. They never do."

"Then you didn't miss anything," he chuckled.

"But your ponytail is longer and maybe a little whiter, so something's happening." Hannah smiled. They had known each other for years. "Tell me about these episodes you mentioned."

"A few weeks ago, I was walking my year-old retriever toward the river park, something I do two or three times a day. I had just emerged from the trees into an open field covered in dandelions. I stopped to admire the view when Snowball saw something and tore off, pulling me down before yanking the leash out of my hand. I looked up and thought I saw snowflakes drifting all around me. I tried to remember which month it was and couldn't figure out why snow would be falling.

"Then a large white dog ran toward me like a fullback. I thought it was going to attack me, so I tried to run away. I slipped, and the dog started licking my face. After a few seconds I realized it was Snowball.

"I sat up and saw the poplar pollen floating over the field like it always does this time of year. Always reminded me of miniature paratroopers. That was my snow—just a bunch of cotton floating in the breeze, trying to find a place to plant its seeds.

"A week later, I was tilling the dirt in my raised planters, getting them ready for the vegetables I'd been raising inside for the past few weeks. All of a sudden, I was staring at my arms sticking out of the dirt, wondering what had happened to my hands. Then I looked at my house and saw the housewrap where I hadn't finished installing the siding last summer. I wondered why Tyvek had put his name all over my walls."

Hannah stared at him, concern pinching her lips and wrinkled brow. Her pen was still poised over her clipboard. "I'm real sorry, Cooper. Do you have any family nearby?"

Cooper thought about his son, Greg, his grandkids, and his ex-wife, Rachel, back in San Antonio. A pain tightened in his throat as he thought of Heather, the daughter he lost seventeen years ago. He tried to speak, but coughed. After swallowing, he said, "No. They're all back in Texas."

"Maybe you should see them," she advised, not knowing what she was asking of him.

Cooper closed his eyes, trying to stop the tears from running down his face. *That wouldn't be possible. They wouldn't want anything to do with me.* But out loud he said, "Maybe."

After tests and images, Dr. Johns told Cooper he might have been experiencing dementia episodes, which are possibly indicators of early-onset Alzheimer's.

Though he'd expected the diagnosis, hearing it confirmed sent a wave of helplessness and despair through him. What would happen to his puppy and kitty? With no kids to fill his days after retirement, he thought he needed new pets before he got too old to handle a puppy or kitten. Now at 65, he might be.

Who would take care of them as his mind continued to fail? His heart ached over thoughts of having more episodes where he wouldn't recognize them. They were all he had left, and soon even they'd be gone, against his will. Frustration chased away his pain, and he exhaled heavily. Why did it have to come to this?

"My mother-in-law had that," said Cooper. "She died after several very difficult years in a nursing home. Still no cure, is there?"

"Not yet," said Johns. "But we have better medicines."

Cooper looked at Dr. Johns and raised his eyebrows. "No bullshit, Doc."

"We can't stop it, but sometimes we can slow it down and reduce the memory lapses."

So, he was destined to a gradual disappearance from his life, just like his mother-in-law.

No way. He couldn't do that.

He wouldn't.

He drove home through the hills west of Fairbanks, providing amazing views of the Alaska Range and Denali, all blazing in the sun, still increasing its time above the horizon every day. He stared numbly through his bug-smeared windshield, his mind still reeling. Would he have time to finish his latest novel? He'd self-published his first two books, but a small company in Texas had recently offered to publish his newest book next spring. Would he be around for the release? Would he be able to read his own book?

He came home to a crazed Snowball, nearly tackling him when he opened the front door. His seven-month-old kitten, Houdini, a long-haired forest cat, escaped outside.

"Dammit, Houdini! Get your ass back here!" He chased the cat across the yard, with Snowball in pursuit, forcing the kitty to run faster, until he reached a swampy area. Houdini hesitated at stepping into the water, and Cooper scooped him up.

"Crazy cat!" Cooper berated. "Don't you know we got lynx and owls out here?"

Back inside the house, he opened the bag the nurses had given him and removed a labeled weekly pill sorter and a whiteboard calendar to stick onto his fridge, with three appointments already written in.

A sense of dread washed over him. This was going to be his life now. And what was the point really? None of these pills were going to save him from the inevitable end. Nothing could.

He sighed, cleared a space on his crowded counter, and set down the sorter. He removed three bottles of pills from a bag then looked at an old photo of Heather taped to the top of the fridge door. She looked so happy and innocent in tenth grade, but even then she was popping every pill she could get her hands on. Now he could see the sadness in her eyes, even as she dazzled everyone with her smile.

The rest of the door was covered with his grandkids' pictures: Chris, Harper, Alex, and Jack, along with his son, Greg, and his daughter-in-law, Natalie. He'd never met Alex and Jack, and Harper and Chris he hadn't seen in ten years. The photos were sent each Christmas with no message, other than the implied one of, "This is what your bad behavior prevents you from seeing." Natalie must have insisted on this cruel ritual each year. His son wouldn't have bothered.

Each year, Cooper sent Christmas gift cards to each child along with a handwritten note—"Hope to see you someday"—his phone number, address, website, and email. He'd never heard anything from them. Maybe Greg had tossed the notes and just given them the money.

A picture of Rachel, his wife of twenty-five years who divorced him sixteen years ago, was fastened above the icemaker. The photo was old, taken when she was 48. He didn't have anything more recent. They hadn't had any contact since the divorce.

He couldn't find a place to put the calendar without removing photos, so he tossed it outside into the yard and slammed the door. He didn't want pills or appointments, which ultimately would do nothing except slow the disease's progress—maybe.

He still split his own wood and shoveled the snow from his driveway and went backpacking each summer. Whatever pains his body threw at him, he could handle. And he hadn't yet found his limit of emotional pain: he'd lost his only daughter to drugs and alcohol and his family to his own stupidity, three of his village students had killed themselves, and he knew so many other sad stories about young girls and babies. Yet he'd survived.

But he had never confronted losing his mind before.

He never thought, mere days later, he'd be staring down at a pistol in his hand. He returned it to the backpack he always kept hanging by the door, ready to grab if he had reason to believe a bear or wolf was in the area.

The pistol had a different purpose now.

Could he end things on his own terms, or would he acquiesce to becoming a vegetable?

Cooper walked back into the kitchen where Houdini had jumped onto the counter to demand his food. He fluffed and shook his long tail at the cabinets, arched his striped back, opened his mouth to emit a plaintive plea, then followed Cooper as he fetched a can of food.

Cooper sighed. "I should never have bought you or Snowball." The dog heard his name and jumped up, ready to be fed. "No, it's not your time for food." The dog plopped onto the floor, head on his paws, looking offended. "What am I going to do with you two?"

He considered calling his son, whom he hadn't heard from in years. Maybe they could actually talk without screaming at each other. Maybe Greg could pretend to be concerned about his dying father. He'd had one visit from Greg, Natalie, and their two eldest kids ten years ago. They'd spent a week being happy tourists in Seward before father and son had argued, dragging up old, painful memories and making bitter accusations. Since then, nothing.

He wouldn't even answer the phone if I called, he thought.

Cooper stared at the one photo he had from that trip, taped to the side of the fridge by the coffee pot. He had dropped to one knee and put his arm around six-year-old Harper as they smiled at the stranger holding his camera. He'd asked the nice lady quickly, unexpectedly, just after Cooper had dropped off his family at the airport, before Greg and Natalie could stomp away. They'd promised to send copies of their trip photos, but never did.

He remembered Harper staring out through a window on a tour boat at the men shouting at each other, having no idea she had started the tirade. Harper loved to sing loudly, with passion, and in front of anyone at any time. She'd stood on a table belting out a song to the other passengers on their boat to see Northwestern Glacier. Such spunk! And what a big voice. Too big, according to her parents, and ill-timed.

He wondered if she still sang so easily. It would be nice to hear her sing again.

Chapter Three

Harper soon realized how big of a mistake she'd made when Claire and Robert left her at the hospital along with a report about her suicide attempt.

The entry nurse searched Harper's bag, removing several potentially dangerous items: a belt, an underwire bra, all of her earrings and studs, nail polish remover, and shoelaces. Another female nurse, who performed a quick search of her body cavities, forced her to pee into a cup while she watched.

"Sorry, but we need to make sure no drugs are brought in here," she explained at Harper's questioning look.

The nurse then gave her flannel sleep pants and a loose t-shirt to wear.

She completed a quick survey and an interview with a counselor, both obviously aimed at determining her level of suicide risk. Harper minimized what had happened. The entire episode had been a misunderstanding, aggravated by her father. She'd never thought about suicide and didn't attempt suicide that night. She merely wanted to hook up with her boyfriend on his birthday and would've done anything to make her father let her leave.

Zachary was going to think she stood him up. Now what would he do? He always made her feel special, but she knew he was very popular, and everywhere they went, other girls smiled at him and knew his name, maybe knowing even more than that. Some would look at her then raise their eyebrows at Zachary, almost saying, "Really?" She'd told him that she'd be with him in ten minutes, and then she disappeared without any contact. Would he care, or just find someone else to celebrate with?

She hated her Dad for doing this to her. None of this would have happened if he could just mind his own business. He was always bent on trying to ruin her fun and her happiness.

She would never forgive him for this.

A nurse took Harper to a room and introduced her to Mia, her roommate, who looked about as thrilled to meet her as Harper was to be there. Both of Mia's arms were heavily bandaged, and her eyes barely opened as she sat in her bed staring straight ahead from a dark, oval face framed by long, wavy black hair. The nurse left, casting the room into uncomfortable silence.

"Hey," said Harper, shifting her weight from foot to foot.

Mia stared at her, maybe even glared, then turned toward the wall.

Harper collapsed onto her bed and let the tears flow onto her sheets. How could her parents have put her here? How did she deserve to be strip-searched and forced to room with the likes of Mia?

She had to get out of here.

After a few minutes, she stood and put her remaining clothes and personal items into a drawer. She held the red satin bag containing the outfit she chose for Zachary to her heart, kissed it, and put it in the back of her drawer under a shirt. Soon she'd be reunited with him. She'd find a way.

The commons room was overseen by a friendly nurse who greeted Harper and showed her what was available. A TV played an animated movie, some shelves contained a limited number of books and magazines, various board games sat on a table, and water was available from a plastic cooler and paper cups. The place smelled like disinfectant masked by an orange-scented candle. Swirling cream and orange paint covered the walls, which blended with multi-colored beanbags, light green soft chairs, and lavender sofas.

A few of the girls in the room gazed her way, stared, even chuckled, but most didn't pay any attention to her. She sat at the end of a sofa and blinked the moisture from her eyes, trying to keep from crying. Another girl had propped her head on the opposite sofa arm, clutching a blanket, her feet inches from Harper's legs. The girl shivered and cried constantly. Harper noticed several girls who had heavily bandaged wrists, including one who pulled her chair closer to Harper's end of the sofa.

"My name is Sky." She reached out her hand with the bandage. Harper stared at it, unsure whether shaking hands would hurt the girl or not.

"It's OK. Just don't pull or twist." The girl winked.

Harper squeezed her hand very lightly. "I'm Harper."

"You look like you came from a party. I like your perfume." Sky was a wisp in her baggy clothes. One had to look hard to see a body beneath the material. She smiled and repeatedly opened her eyes very wide, accentuating her beady black irises with a half-inch of white around them.

Harper realized her face was still covered in make-up. "Never got to go. Daddy blocked the door."

"So what did you do?"

"Threatened to jump out the window then cut my arm."

Sky observed the small bandage on Harper's arm and her lips curled. "Not much of a cut."

Harper shrugged her shoulder. "I wasn't trying to kill myself. I just wanted to meet my boyfriend."

"And your father called the police?" She arched a brow. "Bet he'll regret that."

"Why?"

"Because mine did. Very embarrassing to explain to family and friends why your daughter is in lockdown. The first time I scarfed down a bunch of Benadryl, my parents took me to the emergency clinic. I had to wait for hours in a lobby full of disgusting, noisy people. Then when the doctor finally examined me, he sent me home. So the next time I took pills, they called the police because they didn't want to waste twelve hours again. But then they had to have a therapy session with me besides having to come up with excuses about where I was for their friends. So they got me out early."

"Why are you back?"

She held up her arm. "Because I gave them no choice. Almost bled to death. Now they have to engage and listen to me. No more excuses. They just have to deal with me. I get to watch them squirm during our sessions. Worth losing a little blood over." She smiled and winked.

Harper wondered if her parents would be forced to attend a session with her. Would she want that? Would she tell them how hurt and angry she felt when she had to leave their school? Would she tell them about the drugs and parties and Zachary? That she needed it all to escape living under Godly Greg's roof? Would they listen to her then?

"You might want to remove that tiny bandage," Sky suggested.

Harper's brow furrowed. "Why?"

"To prevent ridicule. They'll call you Scratch or worse. I'd stick with the jumping out the window story, if I were you."

Harper looked around the room, stupefied. She thought her incident was serious, beyond reconciliation. Yet this room was full of girls who'd really tried to kill themselves.

"Do you want to know her story?" asked Sky referring to the girl crying on the sofa. "She slit her wrist in front of a webcam. People watched and cheered her on, then she stopped, and they booed." Sky nodded to a curly-haired blonde sitting by the games. "That girl over there with the bandages around her neck? She tried to hang herself while live streaming on Facebook. The rope broke. People made fun of her online for days."

Harper open and closed her mouth, struggling over what to say or how to respond. She didn't know what she would've done if her Dad had acted that way, or even her Mom and Alex. She was pleased to see their fear and worry, that's what she wanted to see. A reaction. For them to finally see her, really see her.

Is that what all of the girls here wanted? To be seen? Cared about? Heard?

Chimes sounded as the clock hit ten. All the girls stood up and headed for their rooms.

Sky waved over her shoulder. "See you tomorrow, Harper."

Harper returned to her room to find Mia holding up a pair of sheer panties she'd pulled from Harper's red satin bag.

She glared at Harper and spat, "*Puta!*"

Harper lunged toward her. "Stay out of my stuff!"

"You touch me and I scream," Mia snarled. "I'll rip off a bandage and say you attacked me."

Harper stopped short, several feet away from her. "What do you want?"

Mia pulled the top out, also sheer with a feathery fringe. "Are you a whore?"

Harper bristled. Why couldn't they have roomed her with someone like Sky?

She wouldn't be in this room if her father hadn't ordered her mom to call the police. What kind of father does that to her daughter during an argument? Well, Sky's did, and they regretted it, she said. Maybe he would, too.

"No, I was going to see my boyfriend tonight," she growled and crossed her arms. "I bought that outfit for him. Why do you care anyway?"

"ICE deported my father a month ago. My mother was kidnapped in a *guerra de bandas*. Some men captured me. I was raped and forced to be a *puta* to pay her ransom." She held the outfit to her body, as if checking whether it would fit her. "They made me wear these clothes all the time. And one day, I just couldn't do it anymore. I couldn't be used by them anymore. So, I sliced my wrists, intending to die on the street before my john picked me up. He found me and sent me here. I'm finally free of them." She blinked and met Harper's gaze and shook her outfit. "Why does your boyfriend want you to wear this?"

Harper was unsure what to say. She knew she didn't belong here. Her story was nothing compared to these other girls'. How would Mia react if she told her she bought the outfit as a tease for Zachary? That she could've prevented the entire incident at her house by backing down to her father and staying home. She'd been scared to death of falling out of that window. Now, she was trapped in a hospital with girls who'd given up on life for reasons she couldn't imagine, much less endure, and all she'd wanted to do was spend the night with Zachary under a warm blanket of heroin. She had to find a way to get out and to fit in until her escape.

She remembered what Sky had told her and decided to make up a story. She didn't feel like suffering through more ridicule. "My boyfriend gives me heroin for sex," Harper lied as tears gathered in her eyes. "I'm an addict. He forced me to buy those clothes. I was supposed to entertain his friends after him. My father stopped me from going. I knew if I didn't show up at his party, he'd find a way to hurt my little sister, so I tried to jump out of my upstairs window, but my sister stopped me. I tried to slice my arm, but the police stopped me before I did any real damage." Harper pulled off her bandage and showed Mia her arm. "I know it's pathetic, but I tried."

Mia studied Harper's arm and the tears streaming down her face. "*Lo lamento mucho*," said Mia softy. "I'm sorry." She walked towards Harper, holding out the clothes.

"I don't want them," said Harper, shaking her head. "I wish I were home with my sister, Alex. She's probably scared in our room and can't sleep." She wondered how Alex was coping with all of this, and once again the simmer of anger surfaced that she couldn't even call her to see. She hoped her parents felt as guilty for putting her here as she felt about subjecting Alex to her lifestyle. Watching Alex try to look hot tonight had really hit her hard. She needed to somehow steer Alex away from all of this.

Mia dropped the clothes in the trash and sat next to Harper.

"How old is Alex?"

"Eleven."

"Old enough to learn to deal with crap. Maybe she's tougher than you think. I was six when I saw my first shooting. Cried for a long time, but then realized I had to toughen up if I was going to make it."

Is she serious? Harper sent her a look of disbelief. "She's just a little girl. I don't want her to have to toughen up because of me."

"Then you need to get home. When you talk to Valerie tomorrow—she's one of the counselors—you need to tell her the truth about your boyfriend and the danger to your sister. And tell her you want to speak to your father. She'll know you aren't lying because no one here except me wants to see their parents. Well, not true. Crazy Sky wants to see hers twice a week, so she can torment them. She's got the weirdest eyes!"

"She kept making them really big and winking at me." Harper demonstrated, and Mia laughed.

"Hey, I'm sorry I got angry with you," Mia grinned sheepishly. "A girl's gotta have her guard up around here."

"That's OK. Thanks for talking to me."

Mia smiled and walked back to her bed. She picked up the Bible on her nightstand and started reading. Harper went to the bathroom to wash her face. Looking at herself in the mirror as the layers came off, she cried again.

Was she a *puta*?

Did she love Zachary, or did she love the experience of him, which usually included heroin? He'd introduced her to the drug with admonitions about avoiding addiction. He'd told her that he never used more than once every three days, that he never injected, and that his supplier made sure the smack was pure and not contaminated with anything else. He claimed he'd go a week without using just to prove he could, but she wasn't sure that was true. The past two times she met him, he was already high. She had never used without him, and the only cravings she felt were for him and his body. The smack was frosting.

She kept replaying the movie of what happened in her bedroom tonight, trying to find what started it all. If she'd simply closed her bedroom door after talking to Zachary, her father never would've seen her real clothes or seen her put perfume on her legs to smell good for Zachary. He seemed to come unhinged at that. He claimed he cared about her, but he never pulled her away from the window. He had stopped a few feet from her. Why?

Harper couldn't remember a time when he'd been proud of her or praised her for anything, at least in the last few years.

He was angry when she quit playing the piano. She'd wanted to learn more popular songs, but she was restricted to hymns and classical. Her state test scores were nearly perfect, but all they produced was criticism of her grades. "With your brains, you should be making A's in every class with no problem."

She was too interested in boys, and they were certainly too interested in her. Dad had made it clear he wanted her to focus more on academics, sports, and the church and lay off the make-up. But she was beautiful, with or without enhancements. She couldn't help how she looked. Besides, Zachary and his friends made her feel special and wanted, unlike her parents or her teachers.

She scored in the top tenth percentile on her PSAT in October. She was congratulated by her teachers who all added comments about her lack of effort in their classes. Which were all boring. When would she ever use what she learned in any of them? Was it her fault that nothing they taught appealed to her? Sex with Zachary, beer, smack, and joints were so much better.

Or did she feel that way because they were secret and forbidden?

She enjoyed the moments and looked forward to them, but afterward she felt empty and even ashamed.

She thought about what she would say to Valerie tomorrow. On the one hand, she needed to get out of there. On the other, she needed someone to talk to—honestly, for a change.

The next morning, she ate breakfast with plastic utensils and shared her story: addict, evil boyfriend, forced to have sex, threats to her sister and that she was trying to leave her house to get her drugs and save her sister.

Sky smiled, widened her eyes, and winked a few times. "Much better," she praised.

At ten o'clock she met with Valerie, a very top-heavy, short-waisted woman with long, skinny legs and tiny feet who seemed imminently unstable while standing. Harper couldn't help but gape at her.

"You're probably wondering why I'm not a runway model, aren't you?" she asked with a wry smile as she sat gracefully into a chair. "Your drug test was negative. Your survey score and interview last night indicate no suicidal ideation. So, either you're the healthiest young woman in the building, or you're quite intelligent and figured out the purpose of each of our questions. Which is it?"

Harper realized both options were traps. "Neither one. I answered every question as honestly as I could."

They locked eyes, both slightly smiling.

"I'm sure you did," said Valerie in a placid tone. "Your father has called a few times this morning. He wants to pick you up as soon as possible. He said it was his fault the argument escalated as much as it did and that you were not suicidal. Is he correct?"

Harper gasped. "I've never heard him say anything was his fault."

"Really?" Valerie clicked her pen and scribbled on her notepad. "Whose fault is it usually?"

"Mine. Or Chris' when he lived with us. Sometimes Alex's, but never Jack's."

"So your father is infallible like the Pope?" She belly laughed while taking notes.

"I think he's embarrassed about where I am and how it will reflect on him."

She gave a slow nod, looking pleased. "Very insightful. We've had several parents call the morning after. At any time last night did you intend to harm yourself?"

"Just enough to get him to move away from the door. I wasn't trying to kill myself."

"Has anyone in your family committed suicide or attempted suicide?

"My aunt died from a drug overdose. At least that's what Dad says." He didn't like to talk about Aunt Heather. If she were still alive, maybe Harper would've had someone to talk to who understood about heroin and Zachary and all the things happening at home.

"His sister?"

"Yeah. She died the year before I was born. He's told us several times he'd kill us if we ever used drugs or drank alcohol before twenty-one."

"The threat obviously worked on you." She smiled while shaking her head. "You use drugs, which you hide, along with your boyfriend, who gives you the drugs, most likely. And you've been sexually active for how long?"

Harper paused. "Is everything I say confidential?"

"Yes, dear," she assured her. "I am here to help you."

"When I was twelve. With one of my brother's friends."

Valerie scribbled on her clipboard. "Did he rape you?"

"No. We...did a lot, but didn't go all the way."

"You were twelve, and he was how old?

"Sixteen."

She met Harper's gaze, intently. "That makes it rape in Texas. At twelve you're not old enough to give consent to have sex. That boy took advantage of you. Do you understand?"

"Yes." Harper averted her gaze. "But I didn't then."

"Exactly." She pointed her pen at Harper. "That's the point of the law. And do your parents know about this?"

"Not really."

Valerie's brows rose. "Explain 'not really.'"

Harper played with a wrinkle in her pants. "The first time he stayed at our house, he barged into my room and saw me in my underwear. He said I looked good, but then he left. The next time he stayed, I came out of the bathroom in a robe, walking to my room. Luke came out of my brother's room, just by chance. I purposely bumped into him and opened my robe. I didn't know my father was watching from the top of the stairs. Dad didn't see skin or anything, so I could deny opening the robe on purpose, but he let me have it a few minutes later in my room."

"Explain 'let me have it.'" Valerie's eyes narrowed slightly.

Harper shrugged a shoulder as she wrung her hands in her lap. "Called me a slut, fussed at me, said I was going to get raped if I acted like that around boys."

She wrote some more, and Harper wished she could see what she was writing. "Typical male attitude: Girls are raped because they act or dress inappropriately. Do you have intercourse with your current boyfriend?"

"Yes."

"Was he the first?"

"Yes."

"And what made him special?"

What didn't make Zachary special? Harper fought to keep from grinning. "He's gorgeous. He thinks I'm extremely hot."

Valerie smiled and lifted her brows. "Do you think you're hot?"

"Not right now, but when I'm fixed up, I think I look pretty good."

"Suffice it to say, I never felt as confident in my appearance. Men tend to like a large chest," she pointed at her top, "but not stuck onto toothpicks," as she kicked out her very thin legs.

Harper coughed a laugh and covered her mouth. "I'm sorry."

"I hoped you would laugh. Too many of the girls here can't laugh anymore. So, that's a good sign. My point is every man with working eyeballs is going to think you are beautiful. You might want to pay attention to the ones who see something more to admire in you than your looks. Do you understand?"

"Yes."

"OK. What else makes your boyfriend special?"

"He's in college. He likes to party. He's got cool tattoos. We...." Harper took a steadying breath. "We use heroin together."

Valerie pulled her notepad to her chest. "That's very dangerous, Harper. Did he offer you heroin before you had sex?"

"We messed around before that, but we smoked it before we had intercourse."

"Do you think that could be why he gave it to you?"

Harper would never forget that night in his truck over two months ago. It was the night that changed everything for her.

"Are you a virgin?" Zachary asked as she sat on his lap in the backseat.

For some reason she wondered if he would laugh at her. "Yes."

He shot her a sly grin. "What are you waiting for?"

"Somebody very special."

"I have something special for you." He turned and opened up the center console.

"What?"

He held up a tiny red balloon tied into a knot.

"Why is that special?" she asked, almost giggling.

"I'll show you."

They smoked, and she'd never felt so tingly, so amazingly aroused. He was her very special someone that night. She wondered if she would've made love to him without the smack. Maybe, but during that first smack experience, he couldn't have kept her off him if he'd tried. The flamethrower had found a volcano.

"When is the last time you used heroin?" asked Valerie.

"Maybe two weeks ago. Just once. My boyfriend's very strict about how often we use."

"How old is he?"

"Twenty. He'll be twenty-one on Saturday."

"And your first sexual experience was with a sixteen-year-old when you were twelve. Do you see a pattern here?"

"So, I like older guys."

"Harper, you're sixteen. You're using drugs and having sex with a twenty-year-old. Where do you think this will lead to?"

"I don't know. Probably not a good place." Her stomach sank.

"You're on a self-destructive path, and I think you know this. You seem very bright, but you use your intellect only to manipulate your parents and males. So why keep doing this?"

Why? "Because there's nothing else?"

Valerie smiled and gently reached for Harper's hand. "There is something else. You just haven't found it yet. You need to look for it. Please. This hospital is full of girls who wouldn't or couldn't find something else, and now their lives are broken, many beyond repair. You still have a choice, Harper. Find something to pique your interest besides an orgasm."

Harper flinched and almost pulled her hand away. No adult had ever used that word with her.

"Yes, it feels good," said Valerie, "but it doesn't last very long and, frankly, with all the stimulatory aids you can buy now, it's very easy to obtain." She let go of her hand. "You'll be happy when you find something that's hard to get but makes you want it so bad you'll endure almost anything, including boredom, to get it."

"Like what?" Her eyes moistened, and her throat started aching.

"Maybe trying to help broken teens find their way. That's what hooked me. You have to search for your own interest, and I'll tell you a secret: it's not hanging between a man's legs or cooking in a spoon under your nose. Is that clear?"

"Yes, ma'am."

"When is the last time you can remember your father praising you or showing affection toward you?"

Harper suppressed the urge to roll her eyes. "A long time. I think he's worried I'll turn out like his sister."

"Sounds like he has some unresolved guilt regarding her."

"He's always blamed his father. He lives in Alaska. We haven't seen or heard from him since I was six."

"For what does he blame your grandfather?"

"For not being strict enough as a parent. And especially for not raising them in the church. My parents are very religious. He's the headmaster of The Cross Academy."

Valerie put away her clipboard and pen. "You will go home today, Harper, back to the very complicated family dynamics of your home. What you do about it from here is your choice." Valerie stood. "Well, I enjoyed talking to you, Harper."

Harper stood and shook her hand.

"And I hope there's not a next time. Gather your things. I'll call your father."

Harper went to her room and found it empty. She'd hoped to say goodbye to Mia. While changing into jeans and a knit shirt, she remembered the outfit she'd bought for Zachary and looked into the trashcan. There it was. Part of her said to leave it. Mia and Valerie were right. But another part wanted to see the look on Zachary's face when she emerged from the bathroom at his house dressed in that.

Mia had not pulled out everything. Her white thigh-highs were still rolled inside. She picked the top and panties out of the trash and quickly pushed everything into the bag, which she hid inside a pair of shorts. She then retrieved all of her checked items from the entry station, including her underwire bra. As she put it on in the bathroom, she considered how something meant to enhance your looks could also be used to kill yourself. Who would've thought?

Chapter Four

That morning, Greg reset the passcodes for Harper's phone and computer and downloaded monitoring software onto both. Once her phone's data had been restored, he scrolled through her texts and found the message Harper had sent to a group of friends the night before: *Dad just watched me dress. Such a pervert.*

His jaw clenched. He couldn't help feeling angry, but he knew underneath it was hurt. He always used anger to hide his feelings. It was better to lash out than cry. But here he was, searching through his daughter's computer, hoping he wouldn't find other signs of her hatred toward him. Did she really hate him, or was she lashing out for the same reason—to hide her pain? He had to do a better job of controlling his anger.

He looked for any other texts to indicate whom she'd planned to meet, but he found nothing. He found an unknown number in the call log from last night, just before he argued with Harper. She'd probably forgotten to delete it from her list. He thought about calling it to see who answered, but whoever answered would know the call came from Harper's phone even if he hung up. If he spoke and demanded to know who he was, he'd have another fight with Harper. He decided he'd wait and let the software do its thing. Of course, she would know that something had changed on her devices, because she'd have to reset her passcode, but maybe that would make her more cautious. A long shot, but he'd try anything at this point to try and keep her safe.

Natalie drove the kids to TCA by herself and would tell colleagues Greg would be late because of a doctor's appointment. Before Greg left he received a call from a parent, questioning the nature of the text Harper had sent her daughter last night. She had threatened to speak to the Board. Greg took Harper's car and drove to the hospital, wondering how he could keep his job and where he would find another one, thinking about what he would say to Harper. He had to get her on his side.

He found her sitting on a sofa outside the entry station. Her body was turned away from the door, her jaw clenched as she flipped through a magazine. He remembered when she used to be excited to see him and yell, "Daddy!" But that hadn't happened for a long time and too many arguments ago.

She glanced at him then turned back to her magazine.

"Are you ready?" Greg asked her.

She flipped two pages before she answered. "For what?"

"To get out of here."

"I'm not sure. You wanted me here last night, and now you don't." She looked up at him then. "Why?"

He sighed wearily. Of course, she wouldn't make this easy. "I think we both know you don't belong here. We both acted hastily the other night. I'm sorry for making the call, but I'm not sorry they stopped you."

She looked away, her face hardening. "Yeah. *They* stopped me."

He ignored the jab. He didn't want to argue. He just wanted to get her to school and as far away from this place and the memory of last night as he could. He signed papers at the desk, and they left the building.

As they entered the car, Harper asked, "Where are we going?"

"School. You're late. I already called."

"Did you tell them I was at the hospital? Maybe I can do an oral report for extra credit."

"You might try not being a smartass for once." He backed out of the parking spot, almost hitting a passing car.

"Not trying to be. Just need to know what I'm supposed to say when I'm asked."

Greg drove out of the lot and headed for the expressway. Before Greg expelled Harper last October, she had her provisional license and drove to the Academy when her behavior warranted a reward. If she didn't drive, she rode with her siblings. But after her expulsion, plans had to change. Greg didn't want her to attend the nearest public high school because he feared its reputation for drugs and fights on or near campus, even though bus service was available. They enrolled her in, what they considered to be, an excellent school miles away, which meant Harper had to drive herself. The school was too far away for them to drive her and then get to work. Without realizing it, they had removed an important leverage they had to keep her in check, a decision he already regretted.

Greg fought through traffic to exit onto 1604. For several minutes, the car moved a few feet at a time, and neither of them spoke. Heat waves shimmered above the cars ahead of them. Harper's leg bounced repeatedly, and every few seconds he'd see her shoot him a look.

"What was it like being with teenage girls who had tried to commit suicide?" asked Harper out loud, waving her hand. "Hm. Well, it was a shock and very sad. My roommate wanted to die so she could escape being a sex slave. Another girl had been there once before, but her parents got her out quickly because they were embarrassed. What would they tell their friends? But she cut herself seriously this time and got back in."

Greg slammed on the brakes to keep from hitting the car in front of him.

"I know you're angry with me for calling the police," said Greg, "but I seriously didn't know what to do. I thought they'd show up and scare you enough that you'd back down. I didn't expect you to cut yourself."

"I didn't either." She glanced at him quickly then turned toward the window.

Greg noticed a couple of tears on her cheek and softened. Damn it. He didn't want to argue. "How is the cut?"

She rolled up her sleeve revealing the hairline cut that had already scabbed over. "It's better. Compared to what the other girls did to themselves, it's nothing."

"I'm sorry you had to experience that." He hoped Harper would accept that apology. He knew she'd be surprised at hearing it.

"Actually, the experience opened my eyes to a lot of things. I had a good talk with one of the counselors this morning."

"Good," he replied apprehensively.

"She said we have very complicated family dynamics."

No shit. "Really? This conclusion is based on which source of information?"

"I left out ninety percent."

He frowned. "Did you tell her about using drugs and keeping secrets from us?"

"I was totally honest with her."

Somehow he doubted that. "Very good parsing of words to avoid admitting anything."

"She gave me good advice," she said sweetly. He didn't like that tone. "And asked me when the last time was that you said anything good about me. I couldn't remember. But I'm sure I'm forgetting something. When was that, Daddy?"

When was the last time you did something I would be proud of?

Greg clenched his jaw and shook his head.

He had rehearsed what he wanted to say during the drive to the hospital. He had decided to pull in his horns and try to be kind and understanding, even though he was still mad as hell at her. So far, this conversation hadn't gone as he'd hoped.

"Harper, I work at a school with kids. About the worst rumor for any teacher is that he might be a pervert. I don't think you believe I am and that you sent a text last night and that other a week ago in anger without realizing how harmful those statements would be to me. A parent already called me this morning. You need to help fix the problem you caused."

Her head snapped around. "I caused?"

"Did I watch you dress? No. I saw you put perfume on your legs and cover your real outfit with a long shirt. We both know you weren't going to Trish's for an innocent sleepover. I caught you in that lie and kept you from meeting whoever used that unknown number last night, and you got mad."

"I got mad? You went ballistic!"

"Yes, I did. Please let me know how you react when your sixteen-year-old daughter does the same to you. Would you want Alex to do the same?"

Harper said nothing for a few seconds while she looked out the window. "No."

"Alex looks up to you more than you know. You have to consider what actions of yours you want her to copy."

The car was silent for several minutes.

"What do you want me to do about the messages I sent?" asked Harper.

Maybe I got through to her. "Send a note to your friends and write a letter I can show to my Board members."

"OK."

"But Harper, no matter what you write, some will always wonder whether I am a pervert. You used a label that is impossible to entirely erase.

My sister did something similar to my father, and it always haunted him. Even Grandma worried at times if it was true."

Greg exited the highway then crawled through the merging of cars to the traffic light. He looked at Harper and hoped she would apologize and swear never to make that accusation again.

"Aunt Heather has haunted this family from the beginning," said Harper. "You've been scared for years that I'll turn out like she did." Harper looked at Greg. "And maybe because of that fear, you raised me and Chris, but especially me, in a way that almost guaranteed we would. Starting with threatening to murder us if you caught us using drugs. Why would we ever talk to you after hearing that?"

"By anything you mean using drugs, having sex, and drinking?"

"Anything. Like why school sucks. Like why I understand some of what those girls at the hospital feel. Like why I worry about Chris getting shot. Anything."

He ignored the ache in his chest. He would've loved to have Harper show more candor about those worries. For them to have real talks instead of so many words said in anger and hurt. But…"Right now, Harper, I don't know whether anything you say is true or not. How many lies have you told us recently? How can two people have a conversation when one lies all the time?"

"Easily. Because I tell you what you want to hear."

Greg pulled into a parking spot outside the school. He reached into the backseat for Harper's school backpack and handed it to her.

"Your phone and computer are in there. I'll pick you up this afternoon. If you have a chance, please send me the message about your texts before you send it out."

He walked with her to the front desk. When the secretary asked for the reason for Harper's tardiness, Greg paused.

"Medical appointment," he told her.

She raised a brow. "Do you have a doctor's note?"

"No. They didn't give me one. Sorry."

"I need to see a note."

"You don't believe me?" asked Greg. "I'm her father."

"I'm sorry, Mr. Lyons. It's school policy."

Harper pulled her shirt back and showed the lady her forearm. "I spent the night at the Behavioral Hospital because I tried to slice my arm last night. But they realized that this cut is only a scratch, and there's nothing wrong with me, so they released me this morning." Harper sneered at him. "I'm totally fine. Aren't I, Daddy?"

He could have strangled her.

The secretary shot him a questioning look before opening a drawer beside her. "OK, but please bring a note next time." She gave Harper a pass.

"Thanks. See ya." Harper saluted her dad as she left the room and joined the other students moving through the halls.

Greg looked back at the secretary, who glanced at her papers. "Do you have a daughter?" he asked.

"Not yet."

"Don't." He hurried out to his car and rushed back to his school.

Chapter Five

Harper knew her father had reset her phone when he mentioned the unknown caller in the car. She wasn't sure what else he had done or could do. She'd have to make sure that any future texts or calls from Zachary were deleted immediately. She opened her computer in class and realized it had been reset as well, and a strange little icon was near the Wi-Fi and Bluetooth icons. When she clicked on it, a box appeared asking for a password with the username greglyons@gmail.com. Unbelievable. He'd installed something to monitor her computer, which meant he'd probably done the same to her phone. So now she'd be spied on continuously and lose all privacy. Great. As if her night weren't bad enough, her father had to go and make things worse. Shocker.

She's have to buy a new phone as soon as she got her car back. Until then, she'd be creative.

While the teacher droned on, Harper thought about her conversation with Dad in the car. They'd come close to connecting, but so many barriers still remained, and she knew she had built at least half of them. She did feel guilty about her damning texts to her friends, so she wrote the message that would save Dad's reputation—keeping it formal and intelligent. Maybe he'd actually be impressed.

I mistakenly called my father a pervert last night, claiming he watched me dress. He did not. A week before that, I claimed my father stared at my breasts, but he did not. In both cases I was dressed inappropriately and became angry when he admonished me. I apologize for my actions and hope you do not hold my father responsible or accuse him in any way.

This note sounded like a kid was ordered to write it, but it was probably what he wanted. Then she thought of another approach.

I spent last night at the Behavioral Hospital among girls who had tried to end their lives through cuts, hanging, and pills. My ticket there was provided by my parents who thought I needed a jolt of reality to obtain my compliance and obedience. What they got instead was my awareness of the deep pain many girls endure for as long as they can until they see no option but to end their lives. At least two of the girls streamed their suicide on social media, only to be ridiculed when they didn't die.

Compared to their difficulties, my complaints against my father last night were selfish and petty. I'd threatened to jump out of my window, and I cut my arm to force him to allow me to spend the night with my friend. To get my way, I called my father a pervert and sent that message to my friends, similar to another message I had sent a week before.

I dishonored the genuine suffering in that hospital by disguising my peevish anger as a serious threat to my life. In the future when I think I'm upset with myself or my parents, I will weigh my feelings against the girl who lay beside me on a couch, shivering and crying with a deeply cut wrist, or my roommate who'd lost both parents and was forced to be a prostitute until she sought escape with a knife cutting both of her arms.

I can't imagine anything in my life causing me as much pain as they have endured. Until that time, I'll try not to overreact to my relatively small aches and pains again.

She genuinely enjoyed writing that version. Honest, deeply felt, and compassionate towards the girls, which the act of writing about them had defined. She could think of nothing she'd written which meant as much to her. But Daddy would want the first version. She sent both to him with the text:

Written on my bugged computer and sent to my equally bugged phone, then to you. Please tell me which version you prefer and how you want me to send it.

At lunch she found Trish sitting with her friends.

"What happened?" asked Trish.

"Dad called the cops who put me in a suicide hospital," said Harper. "Then he got embarrassed and took me out this morning. Welcome to my family!"

All the girls stared at her with opened mouths.

"Did you try to kill yourself?" asked Trish, her eyes trailing down Harper's arm with concern.

"Kinda." She showed her cut. "But it was a half-assed effort."

No one called it a scratch. One girl claimed she was going to throw up and left the table.

"Shouldn't you have stitches or a bandage or something?" asked Trish, her hands half covering her eyes.

"Yeah, but I ripped it off last night, so the other girls wouldn't call me Scratch."

"Your parents sent you there?" asked Trish. "What creeps!"

Harper's phone dinged with a message from Greg.

The first one is fine. I've already printed it out, and your mother signed your name. I needed something to show the staff today. I'll try to get there by four.

So am I supposed to send the first version to my friends? Harper thought. They'd laugh at it. Since he didn't make himself clear about which to send to her friends, she decided to send them the second version.

Before the end of next period, Harper had received many comments from her friends about her message, several negative about her father for sending her to the hospital, but most responding to the girls' problems and Harper's sympathy for them. A few complimented her writing. None of them thought her father had forced her to write this note.

At the beginning of English, her last class of the day, she saw Trish holding her phone so the teacher could read it. After she removed her glasses, the teacher looked at Harper and waved her to the front.

"Very good writing, Harper. I'm touched. Your writing is clear, profound, and poignant. I wish you'd put as much effort and talent into your assignments as you did with this." She smiled.

I would if you'd give me something worthwhile to write about. "Thanks," said Harper then returned to her seat.

At four, Greg pulled up to her on the sidewalk, opened the passenger door from inside, and pushed it toward her.

"Get in!" shouted Greg.

"What's the matter with you?" asked Harper as she buckled up and closed her door.

"I told you the first version was fine. Why did you send the second version?"

"You didn't say to send the first version to my friends. I thought you wanted the first one for your parents and Board members. You weren't clear."

"I was perfectly clear! Now I'm getting calls about how I sent you to that hospital!"

Then you shouldn't have sent me. You're just like Sky's parents. "My English teacher loved it! She praised me for it! That's the first time all year she's said anything good about my writing."

"Your teacher knows? You showed it to your teacher?"

Greg gunned the car too much and spun his tires. Several students pointed at him. He slowed down and eased into the long line of cars exiting the school. Neither one said anything to each other all the way home.

Harper was angry and hurt. She knew her father would object to the second version, but he should've said something good about it. Then she remembered what she wrote. Compared to Mia's problems, Harper's were almost nothing. But the constant irritation of little things, like picking a scab, would eventually draw blood just as surely as a deep cut.

Greg pulled into their driveway. "Do you think we can have a pleasant evening with no yelling? Your mother had a hard night dealing with Alex."

Harper panicked. "What's wrong with Alex?"

"She threw tantrums about you leaving. She wanted to see you."

Harper gave him a baffled look. "So I should tell her how great the place was and how glad I was you sent me there?"

"Please, Harper. Can we try to be pleasant?"

"Sure. I'll just pretend like everything is OK in the Lyons' house. You've already said I lie all the time."

She grabbed her pack and her overnight bag from the backseat and crossed the yard, taking the front steps two at a time and hip-bumped the front door open.

"Harper!" yelled Alex. "You're home!" She ran down the stairs and leaped into Harper's arms.

"Hey, little sis." Harper felt little arms hugging her left leg and saw Jack's smiling face looking up at her.

"Hey, Jack." Harper hugged him with her left arm.

"Are you OK?" asked Alex.

Greg entered the house as Natalie walked into the foyer.

"That's the first time anyone in this family has asked me that all day."

"How are you?" asked Natalie.

"OK," said Harper, looking at her mother, who smiled and said nothing else.

Her little brother and sister kept squeezing her while her parents stood on either side of her watching the love fest. After a minute more of her parents' silence, Harper put Alex down.

"I'm going upstairs to put my things away."

"You two need to finish your homework," said Natalie, moving them back into the kitchen where their books and papers lay scattered on the table.

"Dad, how are you holding up?" asked Harper, flashing him a hard smile as she started walking up the stairs.

Greg watched her for a couple of seconds. "Fine. How about yourself?"

"Never better. See you at dinner."

Harper threw her bags onto the floor and collapsed on her bed. Her father hated her, and her mother lived in a dream world.

She wanted to call Zachary, who must hate her by now. She imagined him waiting at the corner, and waiting some more, then leaving. Thinking what? She stood him up? Why hadn't he called her since then? How would she ever see him again?

She opened her door a crack to see if anyone was there, then walked to Alex's side of the room, as far from the door as possible while she punched in his number. His phone rang then went to voicemail. "Leave a message."

"Zachary, this is Harper. I'm so sorry about last night. I tried so hard to get out of the house, but my dad was an asshole. He called the cops, and I had to spend the night in a hospital. He's bugged my phone, so don't call me. I'll get a new phone tomorrow and send you the number." She needed to convince him she was worth the wait. "I still have that new outfit. The sheer one. Hope you still want to see me in it." She sighed seductively. "Love you. Bye."

She deleted the call from *Recents* then looked through all of her messages, responding while feeling her dad watching over her shoulder.

A guy she'd never heard of claimed he got her Snapchat handle from a friend and wanted to take her to his cool cabin. He described his amazing personality and athletic prowess then asked her for nudes. How many times had this happened to her? And to her friends? How would her father react? She blocked the guy and unpacked her bags.

Alex came in to tell Harper dinner was ready.

"I missed you," said Alex, hugging her.

"I missed you, too." Harper kissed her forehead.

"Where were you? Where did they take you?"

She fluffed up her hair. "To a hospital for teenage girls who had tried to hurt themselves."

"Was it bad?"

"Not too bad." She opened a drawer and slipped in some clothes. "The other girls hurt themselves much more than I did."

"And Dad got you out this morning?"

Harper shoved Zachary's outfit to the back of her drawer. "Yeah. I think he got embarrassed about having his daughter in that place."

Alex sat on Harper's bed, clenching her jaw. "I hate him."

Harper moved next to her. "No, you don't. We both got carried away and wouldn't back down." She put her arm around her sister. "I'm sorry I put you through that."

"You're not angry?"

"Sure I am. The only ones who seem to be happy I'm home are you and Jack."

They both heard Natalie call from downstairs that dinner was ready.

"Would you ever hurt yourself for real?" asked Alex, softly. "Would you have jumped?"

"I was scared to jump. I don't think I could ever do that."

"I love you, Harper." She clutched her sister.

"I love you, too, Alex."

Natalie called again. They both left the room and walked downstairs to find her parents and Jack holding hands around the table, waiting for the girls to join their prayer circle. Both girls hesitated for a second and looked at each other. *How awkward is this going to be?* They trudged to their places, Harper next to her father, holding Alex's hand. Jack and Alex hooked pinkies.

"Harper, could you say the blessing?" asked her dad.

Harper knew he would ask her. He wanted affirmation of his authority and a clear signal of her intent to be obedient. His eyes fixed on her as he gently held her hand.

"Certainly." They all bowed their heads. "Lord, thank you for this food before us. We thank you for our family and the love we share for each other.

A—"

"That some of us share for each other," Alex interjected. She squeezed Harper's hand. "Amen."

Greg's eyes jerked open as he let go of Harper's hand. "Some of us?"

"Jack and I missed Harper," said Alex, "but you and Mom didn't."

Greg frowned at Harper. "Did you tell her to say that?"

"No."

"You two were up there talking about something for several minutes." His eyes narrowed with suspicion. "You planned this, didn't you?"

"We didn't plan anything," said Alex. "You and Mom weren't happy to see Harper. It was obvious."

"We're very glad Harper is home," Natalie assured her. "Let's eat before our food is cold." She sat down.

"The only reason she's home is because you were embarrassed," shouted Alex.

"Alex," said Harper calmly. "You don't have to fight my battles."

Alex wasn't deterred. "You think holding hands and saying a stupid prayer is going to hide how everyone feels?"

"Go to your room, young lady!" shouted Greg, cords tightening in his neck.

Alex glared at him. Harper knew that look because she had glared exactly the same way at him last night.

"Why can't you ever talk to us?" asked Harper. "We should talk as a family about what happened. You just order everyone around!"

"Straight from your counselor's mouth!" shouted Greg.

"Can't we eat our dinner?" pleaded Natalie. "Greg, please."

"I don't want to eat with him," said Alex, stomping out of the kitchen and up the stairs.

"I had nothing to do with this," said Harper.

"You had everything to do with it!" shouted Greg.

"I'm not hungry. Alex needs me." Harper turned to leave the room.

"No, she doesn't. We're moving you out of her room," said Greg.

"What?" Harper balked. A cold wave flooded her stomach.

"Your mother and I agreed that you should move into Jack's room, and he'll share with Alex."

"No way!" Jack's nose scrunched. "I don't want to share with Alex! Gross!"

Harper's chest pounded. "Why?"

Greg pointed at Harper. "Because you're not a good influence. One of you is enough for this family."

"No!" screamed Alex from the top of the stairs. "I want Harper!" Alex ran down the stairs, back to Harper. "You can't move her out!" She grabbed Harper's hand.

"Stop!" Natalie jumped up from her chair. "Everyone needs to stop right now!"

Harper had never heard her mother raise her voice before, especially at her father. Jack and Alex stood wide-eyed and silent, staring at her.

"Greg, we don't need to talk about this now. We haven't decided anything yet. No one is moving tonight or anytime soon. Please, let's just sit down and eat."

After an awkward pause, everyone sat down.

"Harper, would you please pass the potatoes?" asked Natalie.

"Sure," said Harper.

During the rest of the meal, no one spoke. The only noises were the sounds of chewing and swallowing or the scrape and clatter of utensils. Every moment festered with a stifling subtext. Harper could barely stand the painful masquerade. How would she endure this ritual every evening? She couldn't. She would have to do something to preserve her sanity and her siblings' childhood, such that it was.

She'd pretend, deflect notice, regain her parents' trust and gain some freedom, then decide what to do.

Chapter Six

"I can't stand living here!" shouted Alex just as Harper closed their bedroom door. "Can't we just run away? I'd live anywhere, even under a bridge if I could get away from him." She picked up her doll from her bed and threw it against the wall. "How can Mom stand him?"

"We don't need to run away," Harper said, taking her next victim from her hands and setting it back on her bed. "We have each other. We'll get through this."

"Promise me you won't leave me again."

"I promise."

"Snuggle with me?"

"Sure." Harper climbed into bed with Alex, humming a tune while stroking her face. Finally, Alex fell asleep.

Later that night while Harper went to the kitchen for ice cream, she heard her parents arguing behind their bedroom door down the hall. Only once before had she heard them yell at each other—when Chris found Greg's college Bible and paper. Harper knocked tentatively.

Natalie opened the door, her eyes widening at seeing Harper.

"Can I come in?"

"Certainly," said Natalie, stepping back to let her through, wiping her eyes. Greg sat on the bed in his t-shirt.

"Alex finally got to sleep," said Harper. "I'm sorry for everything. It's my fault you're yelling at each other. It's my fault that Alex wants to run away from home."

"She wants to run away?" Natalie gasped. The look of horror on her mother's face stung. She hadn't looked at her that way when the police were taking her away. Would they even miss her if she were gone?

"Look, if I had a place to go, I'd leave, too. This is too painful for everyone. If I have to eat another dinner like tonight's, I'll go nuts. I just want to tell you that I'll try my best to be civil and not make you angry. I know you've bugged my phone and computer, and I hate that, but you're the parents, so I'll have to live with it. I'll try to earn your trust."

Natalie shot a surprised look to Greg, indicating to Harper that she didn't know what he'd done.

"I won't talk about our family problems to my friends and try to not embarrass you anymore. I'll not allow Alex to talk bad about you and I'll change the subject if she brings up running away. I don't know what else I can do."

Natalie rushed toward Harper and hugged her. "That's all we can ask. We'll try to be better parents." She looked back at Greg.

He and Harper locked eyes, and his calculating expression made her wonder if he had any real sympathy for her.

"Yeah. Thanks, Harper. I appreciate everything you said. I'll try not to get so angry." He sounded wary, suspicious that she was manipulating them again.

Natalie held her shoulders and gave her a warm smile. Harper had no doubt that in her own way, her mother loved her, even if it was an earlier or incomplete version.

"OK. Thanks. I hope tomorrow we'll all feel a little less awkward. Goodnight." Harper turned back down the hall for her room. Could she really do this every day? Something needed to change, and it sure wasn't going to be her parents. Maybe running away wasn't such a bad option. But where would she go? Zachary's? Trish's? Those weren't far enough out of her parent's reach that she wouldn't end up being dragged back. She sighed, wearily. God, was she trapped here until graduation? Could she survive another three years under this roof?

At breakfast, Greg gave her the keys to her car. "I know you won't mind driving yourself this morning."

"Not at all," Harper said, trying not to sound too enthusiastic. "Thanks, Daddy."

Alex rolled her eyes at Harper then bent back over her bowl of cereal.

On her way home from school that afternoon, she bought a prepaid phone with money she'd stolen from her parents over the past several months. She'd wanted to get a job as a hostess or waitress at a nearby restaurant, but Dad had said no. "All the staff does in restaurants is hook up with each other and do drugs. That's how my sister got started." And no allowance because, "Why should we pay you for doing things you're supposed to do?"

What was left besides stealing from her parents?

She needed to talk to Zachary.

Hey, Zachary! I bought this phone just for you. I can't stand not being with you! Things are crazy at my house, but I might be able to get out to see you in a few days. Love you!

Zachary responded right away.

Hey, Lovebug! I'm having a big party at my house next Sunday. Would love for u to come—lots! Haha! Until then I want to fantasize about kissing your luscious body—all of it! Send me some new pics to make that easier. Mmmmmm! Can't wait to see the real thing!

Overjoyed he was still interested in her, she stopped at Starbucks and ran inside the bathroom where she shot several photos in various stages of undress through the mirror, along with the message, *I still want to show you my new outfit.*

It was so much easier to continue the joyful family ruse, knowing that Zachary still wanted her. She had stood him up, and yet he still wanted to see her. That had to be proof that he really cared about her.

During the next several days, Dad was polite but aloof, Mom smiled in her dream world of family bliss, and Alex at first felt betrayed that Harper had joined the dark side but finally returned to her little girl world of dolls and princess books. Even Harper found herself ignoring the awkwardness and pretense within their house, even forgetting that her father was monitoring her phone.

One night, Harper received lots of messages from one of her casual friends at school on her regular phone. Diane complained about her boyfriend getting a hand job from his ex at the mall. She asked for opinions about whether she should take him back despite his lapse and the video his friends shot of the event, now circulating along with lots of comments.

Votes for taking him back were almost even with dumping him. Harper was about to type *Give him another chance* when she considered what she would do if Zachary had done the same to her. Had he waited for her during the last week? She wanted to believe he had. He seemed so eager to see her on Sunday.

A few minutes later, her dad appeared at her bedroom door.

"You should put that away for the night," he said through a stone face.

She remembered her phone was bugged. *Crap!* How could she live with him passing judgment on everything she did? She pasted on a smile. "Yes, Daddy."

"Now," he growled. He waited until she put the phone down. He said nothing else. No "good-night" or "thanks for being better around the house." Nothing. The fact that the civility and occasional smiles during the past few days had been merely a ruse hit her, like a sucker punch to the gut.

Harper saw such a look of disgust in his face. She believed he would've erased her from his life and all of his memories if he could.

She knew then that her father would be nothing more than her overseer; an unblinking eye watching over her shoulder, ready to pounce at anything he considered wrong, which was everything she was. Her parents could never talk to her about anything she needed to talk about.

She certainly couldn't talk about Zachary, whom she craved, along with the heroin and pot he always provided. The anticipation of meeting him at the upcoming party was intoxicating: the sex, the drugs, and the illicit contact. She played through every possible iteration of their meeting and lovemaking, some coy and teasing, but most ending with each devouring the other. Now that she realized there was no hope of reconciliation between her and her father, she plunged into fantasizing about Zachary, each time leaving her more ecstatic and breathless.

Harper's next plan had to work. She'd spent several days convincing her parents she needed more conservative clothes, claiming to be embarrassed wearing the ones she had. Harper wanted to go to the mall with Julie, who still attended TCA and was known as a wholesome girl. Julie sang in the church choir and helped with Sunday school for the younger kids.

Julie's parents, however, didn't know about her secret boyfriend. The girls would go to the mall Sunday afternoon, find their guys, then meet back in four hours, shop quickly and return home.

Both sets of parents checked with each other before granting their consent. Greg and Natalie had a lengthy, serious talk with Harper, telling her they wanted to give her this chance, that they would trust her, and they expected her to appreciate their trust. They told her they wanted to believe in their daughter again.

Harper knew that all their sentiments came from her mother. Her father would just as soon lock her in her room.

Julie found her boyfriend in the candy shop. He left, and she followed at a distance until they reached his car. Julie had told her they were going to the movies to find a dark corner to make out in.

Harper found Zachary in the food court. She ran to him with a shriek, nearly knocking him down as she barreled into him and hugged him. He kissed her in front of everyone and said, "God, I missed you."

"I missed you too! I don't think I could've waited another day."

She hooked his arm, and they walked out of the court.

"You're even more beautiful than I remembered," he said as he opened the door to his car. "A very important part of me has been aching to see you again." He pulled her to him, squeezing her butt.

Harper laughed and pushed herself into him, feeling heat flood her body. He bit her neck a little too hard and growled.

She flinched. "Ouch!"

He leered. "You bring out the animal in me."

She sat and rubbed her neck quickly as he walked around the car. For the briefest of moments, doubt flashed through her mind, but she decided he just couldn't control how badly he wanted her.

They drove to Zachary's house, a three-story old Victorian near the university. His wealthy, very connected father had bought it for him. Zachary rented out rooms to friends, which, along with his drug business, made him quite a bit of money. They nearly ran upstairs to his bedroom on the top floor, lavishly decorated in a rustic Texas style: leather, horns, wrought iron, and skinned logs. She pulled her red satin bag out of her purse and asked, "When should I model this for you?"

"After we smoke this." He put a crystal of heroin into a darkened spoon and held a lighter underneath. They sucked the burning smack through straws until they both collapsed in rapture. She was consumed with overwhelming desire. Every nerve tingled and begged to be touched, but he lay back, grinning at her. "Make me groan." He threw his arms out onto the floor.

Removing her shirt, she crawled on top of him, stroking him, teasing him. He writhed and giggled but never touched her back.

·w her off? He was proud and lucky to have her. That was something ad would never say.

achary bit her lip. She yelped softly then kissed him back, vaguely ; his beautiful face in front of hers.

'es?"

'es," she purred. "Anything for you."

le led her out of the room then down the stairs. She heard guys :ling and growling. Some girls laughed while others leered. Phones ed taking pictures until they reached the first floor.

'hey danced, drank beer, and got wild along with everyone else. After a ninutes, Harper no longer felt embarrassed and ground her hips against ary's. Music thumped through the walls and floors as guys convinced e girls to battle-strip for free cocaine.

Zachary gawked at one girl's performance and drifted away from per.

She started to go after him, but somebody offered her his joint.

She could feel warmth at her back and snuggled in closer to Zachary. : body ached in all the best ways, and her lip throbbed, probably from hary's devouring kisses. The scent of cinnamon engulfed her as an arm pped around her bare hip. Cinnamon? That's not what Zachary smelled :. *What the...?* She jerked up, seeing a strange man lying passed out beside r on a bed she'd never seen before. Her heart jackknifed in her chest. *Who he? Where is Zachary?* She tried to remember, but her head pounded.

She stood and saw several people sprawled out on the floor and rniture. She stumbled outside the room and saw a couple sharing a joint. here was her phone? Her heart skipped a beat as she stumbled upstairs d into Zachary's bathroom, finding her clothes piled on the floor. She tore rough them until she found her phone and noticed the time—8 o'clock. ie'd left the mall almost five hours ago.

Crap!

She changed her clothes as quickly as she could. As she slid on her shirt, ie caught a glimpse of herself in the mirror over the sink and paused at the ght of her swollen lip still oozing blood and bite marks on her neck. She pplied make-up and lipstick until her face and neck looked somewhat ormal. She tried to stuff all of her outfit back into the little bag but couldn't orce all the pieces in.

"I have something to show you." She slipped off him
bathroom. She emerged in a few minutes in her sheer
highs and found him naked, sprawled out on his chair.

He sat up, his hazy eyes sharpening as they raked over

She slinked over to him, doing a little spin for him to se
she asked as she gently dragged her nails down his legs.

"Isn't that obvious?" he said huskily, leaning in closer.
her lips.

She attacked and made sure the next several minute
intense in Zachary's life.

Afterward, she lay on top of him as he panted for breath.
She had won him back, despite her difficult parents.

Suddenly he pushed her off of him. "Get up. I want to s
guys."

"What?" What did he mean? "Why?"

He pulled on his shorts and t-shirt. "Fix yourself up," he
want to show you off."

Harper was confused, still dizzy and floating. He pulled h
and roughly straightened her outfit. *Not like this!* She hugged
turned away.

"My hair..."

"It looks great. Wild like you are." He turned her toward him
her neck then slapped her butt. He sent her a dark grin. "You we
Can't believe how lucky I am." He bit her neck harder, causin
whimper.

He grasped her hand and started to lead her out of his room.

Harper panicked as she neared the door and dug in her hee
him stop. "I can't go out like this." *Are you serious?*

"Why not?" he purred in her ear. "I'm proud of you. I want all
to be green with envy." He tugged on her.

She pulled back. Why was he doing this? "Zachary! I'm... ner
you sure?"

He lit a joint, took a hit, and offered it to her. "You look amazi
a hit." She did. "Take another," he coaxed, and she did. "You're t
beautiful girl in the world, and you're mine. I can't believe how luck

She felt dizzy, almost giddy. He wanted her. He thought
beautiful. Zachary made her feel like she belonged. Had anyone ever

She growled in frustration before yelling, "Zachary!"

She found him downstairs in the kitchen with a girl sitting on his lap, who couldn't be older than fifteen. She wore only a cut-off cheerleader t-shirt from Harper's school. Harper vaguely remembered seeing her in the halls. Wasn't she a freshman? How the hell did Zachary know her? *And why is she sitting on his lap and not me?*

"Hey, Harper," said the girl with a little wave and giggle.

"I need to leave," Harper told Zachary, ignoring the girl. Her head was spinning, confused from the drugs still in her system and Zachary's desertion.

He squeezed the girl's hips, and she stood, smiling at Harper.

"C'mon, then." He waved for her to follow him as he grabbed a set of keys from off the counter.

He walked quickly out to his black Lexus, cooking in the heat. The blazing sun made the pounding in Harper's head worsen. She winced as she climbed into his car, and got blasted by the unbearable heat inside that made it hard to breathe.

She looked at him. "Zachary, who was that girl?"

"Nobody." He turned toward her and grinned but it didn't touch his eyes. "Just a girl. Don't even know her name."

"She's younger than me. She was naked on your lap."

He laughed. "Don't be so dramatic. She had on a shirt."

"You know what I mean." Was she angry? Should she be? Her head was still foggy.

He headed for the highway, taking it north until it crossed 1604, where he went west toward the mall. He said nothing as he whipped into gaps between cars. Harper crossed her arms, holding herself, to refrain from holding onto the dashboard.

Trying not to whimper, Harper asked. "Why did you leave me?"

He shrugged like it was no big thing. "I thought you left me."

"The last thing I remember is you walking away from me toward the stripper." *Why did he even do that?* She closed her eyes, just wanting this nightmare to be over.

"Maybe, but when I came back you were having fun with Levi. Or maybe Levi was having fun with you. Whole thing's kinda fuzzy." He turned up the music and rapped his hands on the wheel.

Panic churned her gut. Could that possibly be true? Could she have jumped in bed with a random guy? Had she been that high? She remembered someone giving her a joint as Zachary walked away from her.

"And who did you end up with?" she asked, tears forming in her eyes.

He smiled. "Don't remember. Guess we were both too wasted." He stopped the car by the curb next to one of the mall entrances.

"We're here."

"Zachary, I..." Sobs stuck in her throat.

"Don't worry about it. We're not engaged or anything." He gave her a wry grin, and dropped a zip-lock bag containing five balloons onto her lap. "For you. A token of my appreciation. You were amazing. And don't lose that outfit!" He then reached over and pulled the handle to open her door. "You better hurry."

As soon as she exited the car, Zachary pulled away from the curb, barely waiting long enough for her to close the door. She ran toward the fountain where she saw Julie talking on her phone. Harper bumped into an older woman.

"So sorry," said Harper. The lady stared at her.

Harper realized she was still carrying the zip-lock in her hand, so she stuffed it into her purse. Harper had to sit down. She needed something to drink.

"Sorry, Mom," said Julie, her eyes widening when she spotted Harper. "We caught a movie. We'll leave here in about thirty minutes. OK. Love you!"

"Sorry," Harper panted. "I'm so sorry."

A young boy walking with his mother pointed at Harper and laughed. Harper wished the ground could just open up and swallow her right there. How was she going to hide this from her parents?

"You look like crap," said Julie, her brown eyes full of concern. "I hope he was worth it." The corner of her mouth twitched. "Mine was."

Harper's grin was watery. "Tell me all about it in the car." Anything to get her mind of the last few hours.

"I think your story will be more interesting." Julie pointed toward Harper's shorts and raised her brows.

Harper looked down and mentally slapped herself. They weren't buttoned! She quickly fastened them. Harper looked up at Julie and tried to keep her chin from quivering. She almost blurted out the truth but clenched her teeth and turned her head. Mia's words about being forced to wear those clothes flashed in her head, as well as the lie she had told about her boyfriend giving her drugs for sex and wanting her to entertain his friends.

She hadn't lied after all.

She stifled a sob.

"You OK?" Julie searched her eyes, frowning.

"Sure," Harper heard herself say. "Just dehydrated."

"Hurry. We can grab a few things at Kohl's then leave."

Harper stumbled around the store, grabbing items without caring. She took them to a dressing room, looked in the mirror, *really* looked. Her eyes watered, as a sob caught in her throat. Her hair was matted, and she had beer stains on her top.

Her stomach flipped, and a wave of nausea hit her. She raced out of the room and ran to the restrooms outside of the store.

Her puke barely made it into a stopped-up toilet. She realized she hadn't eaten in hours.

A cockroach skittered from behind the toilet.

Harper screamed and stomped on it. The bug exploded with a horrid pop. After frantically checking the walls around her and the ceiling for other roaches, she scrambled out of the stall.

At the mirror, she redid her make-up and tried to smile. It was fake, just like everything else: the lies she'd told her parents, the happiness she'd felt with Zachary, the rush of warmth at the first whiff of burning heroin, her value to anyone. She carefully dabbed a tear with a tissue and hurried back to the dressing room.

After buying the clothes, she changed into one of the new outfits, not even paying attention what she put on and stuffing her old clothes in the trash. She chugged an iced coffee before joining Julie.

On the way back to her house, Julie told her about the movie, so Harper could fake it, though Julie had seen little of the film herself. The two girls laughed and giggled as they walked up to Harper's front door—Harper's idea. The girls would seem so delighted with each other that Natalie wouldn't think to question her daughter before she ran up to her bedroom. Because of the laughter, Harper could cover her mouth, hiding her swollen lip from her mother.

After tossing the bags onto her bed and rushing to the bathroom, she threw up again. She'd never been one to puke after drinking. She looked at herself in the mirror and tried to keep her panic from exploding out of her head. Was she sick from the party, or from something else?

She tried to remember her last period and realized it should've happened two weeks ago, but it hadn't. Her periods began when she turned twelve. They were irregular, long, and very painful. The doctor had told her parents that birth control pills would help her condition, but they'd refused. No twelve-year-old of theirs was going to take contraceptives. She'd bought her own just a few weeks ago.

Back in her room, Alex smiled amiably at her. "Did you see him?"

"Who?"

"Your boyfriend. The one who's gorgeous!"

The thought of Zachary made her queasy again. "No. I didn't."

"Really?" she teased, her grin turning sly.

"I said no!" Harper bellowed.

Alex flinched.

"I'm sorry, Alex." Cold sweat pooled in her armpits.

Alex watched her remove all her new clothes from the bags and toss them onto her bed.

"You bought those?" Alex picked through them in disgust. "You don't even like purple. What were you thinking?" Alex held up a white dress shirt and purple, pleated pants with cuffs. "Are you kidding me?"

Everything came crashing down. Harper collapsed onto her bed and cried. She was such a fool, a total loser. She'd threatened to jump out her window to see him? She was nothing but a sex toy to him. When Alex asked her what was wrong, Harper claimed she must have eaten something bad at the food court.

Later that night, she snorted the contents of a balloon in the bathroom and forgot.

No memories.

No worries.

Fake and wonderful.

Chapter Seven

Harper couldn't concentrate in any of her classes the next day. The effects of the party should've disappeared by then, but she still felt queasy. Her stomach churned all morning. She decided she needed to go by a clinic after school even though her parents would wonder why she was late coming home.

"What happened to your lip?" asked Trish at lunch.

"Had a nightmare and must've hit myself." Harper covered her mouth. "Is it that obvious?"

"Not as bad as that outfit you're wearing. Where did you get that?"

Harper wore the white shirt and purple pleated pants Alex scoffed at last night. "I bought clothes my mother wants me to wear." Harper laughed. "Keeps the peace at home."

"Hey, Harper," asked Trish while looking around to make sure no one heard, "you don't happen to have any...?"

Harper's shoulders sagged. "Sure, Trish. Come by my car after school."

Her eyes lit up. "You're the best!"

Harper picked at her food. The noise in the cafeteria was deafening. Every chair scrape and slurp from Trish's straw assaulted her ears. The room spun around her until she staggered to the bathroom and puked.

That afternoon she slept through a test and made a fool of herself faking an oral report on The Great Depression. Teachers chastised her, and classmates snickered.

In English, Harper learned that she hadn't turned in a personal narrative essay due last week. Mrs. Connolly told her she could still turn one in for half credit and suggested that she could write about her experience at the hospital.

Harper opened her computer and realized that whatever she wrote would go to her father. She hesitated, thinking he would not like her telling others more about that night. Then she thought, *Screw him!* She tried to type, but all she could see was Mia holding up her sexy outfit and hear her words about being a sex slave. God, was she Zachary's sex slave, just something to make him feel good before he tossed her away? Harper cried and put her head on her desk.

Trish noticed. "Hey, Harper. You OK?"

Someone else said, "Maybe she needs to go to that hospital again."

After school, she gave Trish a balloon.

Trish stuffed it into her purse. "What do I owe you?"

"Nothing."

Trish shook her head, riffling through some bills in her wallet. "At least let me pay what you had to pay."

Waking up under a strange guy and seeing a freshman cheerleader smiling on Zachary's lap flashed through her mind. "You wouldn't want to do that. Be careful, Trish."

Harper crawled through traffic for the next thirty minutes. Whether everyone moved slower than usual that day or whether she was desperate to get to the clinic, she didn't know. By the time she turned off the highway into the clinic parking lot, she had cursed and blared her horn a dozen times.

She peed in a cup in the bathroom, then sat in the lobby along with other nervous girls and women. The test confirmed that she was pregnant. She had been for eight weeks.

Can my life get anymore messed up right now? She wished she could jump into a time machine and go back to the day she let Zachary screw her and slap herself.

A nurse in her early twenties took her into a small room and closed the door. She pulled up a chair so her knees almost touched Harper's. "My name is Gwinn. Harper, are you surprised by these results?"

"No." Harper's chin quivered. "I was hoping I might just be sick, but..."

She raised a brow. "Do you have a boyfriend?"

She wiped a tear. "Not a good one."

"Does he have any idea you're pregnant?" Gwinn handed her a tissue.

Harper locked eyes with Gwinn's and a new horror hit her. What would Zachary say? God, what would he do? She stared at the floor. "No. He won't be happy about it." Hell, she wasn't even happy about it.

"Do your parents know?" the nurse spoke softly.

Panic took her breath away. "No. You can't tell them. They can't ever know."

She nodded, grabbing a clipboard from the counter. "Let me explain your options."

Options? Harper had no options. She was sixteen and pregnant, and her parents would kill her when they found out.

Gwinn told her that Texas required minors to obtain parental consent or permission by a judge, which required evidence of past sexual abuse from a parent or potential danger to her. Her parents would never agree to an abortion, and the judge would deny her request—she simply didn't meet the qualifications.

What could she do? Give birth and have the baby adopted, the whole time being subjected to even more disdain from her parents? That'd be unbearable. She could tell Zachary and hope he wanted their child, but that seemed unrealistic. She wasn't even sure he really wanted *her* at this point.

Before she left the parking lot, she decided to call Zachary. It was the right thing to do. He deserved to know. And who else could she really tell? Trish? Half the school would know by the next morning.

Her hands could barely hold the phone she was so nervous.

"Hey, Lovebug," he greeted. His tone deepened. "I was just thinking about you."

"I was just thinking about you, too," her voice quivered. Tears dripped off her chin. She wiped her nose on her sleeve.

"You sound awful. Are you sick?"

"No, not sick. I'm...I'm pregnant, Zachary. With your baby. I just left the clinic."

Please be kind, she thought, but she knew what was coming.

"How do you know it's mine?"

The condescension in his voice irritated her.

"Who else's would it be?" Harper barked. "You were my first, Zachary, and only until last night. I didn't take pills until a month ago. The clinic says I'm about eight weeks along."

There was a moment's pause before his voice exploded through the receiver. "You're such an idiot! I thought you were taking pills the whole time."

"Well, I wasn't. I had no reason to take them before I met you. I'd just turned sixteen."

"You're only sixteen?" he repeated dumbly. "Damn it!"

Her brow furrowed. *Is he for real?* "You knew my age, Zachary! You just didn't care, and neither did I."

There was another pause before he said, "So when can you get an abortion?"

"What?" Her head spun. She had barely had enough time to process that she was pregnant, let alone think of what to do now. That Zachary could talk so casually about it made her wonder if this wasn't the first time he'd ever received this kind of news.

"How soon can you get an abortion, Harper? I'm not getting stuck with a kid now."

Harper covered the speaker as she convulsed in tears. She tried to catch her breath, but all she could do was cough.

Zachary's voice blared through the speaker, "Harper, get back into the clinic and make an appointment!"

She ended the call and tossed the phone onto the passenger seat. She had no idea what to do, but an abortion was not an option. At least not with her parents and the laws in Texas.

She couldn't raise the baby on her own, and she couldn't bear the thought of reliving her stupidity and Zachary's indifference every time she held her child.

And Alex. How much more of a bad influence could she be for her sister? If there was any hope for Alex to turn out normal, Harper had to leave.

She had to find some other place to go.

But where?

Harper eased back into traffic and fought her way home, racing from stoplight to stoplight, past one gated community after another. Before she punched in the entry code, she looked up through the crooked oak limbs to the milky white, cloudless sky, like a lid holding the heat in, baking her hometown of two million people. Even this far away from the highway, the air stank of exhaust, while the roar of cars racing home filled her ears.

The gate opened, and she drove into the oak forest of her neighborhood, full of short gnarly trees afraid to stand tall in this heat.

She remembered a family trip to Alaska ten years ago to see her grandfather, where the trees were tall and it was cool even in July. The skies were deep blue or swirled with layers of beautifully colored clouds. She hadn't seen him since.

Another plan pecked at her brain. What were the abortion laws in Alaska? Could he give her permission? She pulled over to the curb. A car behind her honked twice while driving past. She tapped her phone.

After some Googling, she discovered that no parental consent was required in Alaska. How could she get up there? She had some money but not enough to buy a ticket. She surely couldn't ask her other grandparents. Driving would cost more, and she didn't have a passport to drive through Canada.

How could she force her parents to send her to him—without knowing she was pregnant? They must hate him because they never talked about him and never visited. They'd never willingly agree to send her to see him.

What if something more than texts calling her father pervert made the rounds of students and parents?

Maybe photos.

She considered options as she drove through her neighborhood until she saw the thick, low limb in her front yard. It looked like a witch's finger extending from the house, curled at the end, beckoning little kids inside. Great for Halloween scares and laughs. But now she knew what could really happen: kids go in and come out screwed up, drug-using, suicidal, pregnant teens, walking around half-naked in a house full of horny, college guys.

After checking her face once again in the visor mirror, she exited her car and walked in the front door. She hurried into the living room and opened the second drawer on the left in the china cabinet. Underneath years-old Christmas greetings, she found several small folded notecards. She had discovered the stash two years ago when she saw her mother open cards from Grandpa in Alaska and hide the messages in the drawer before handing out their Amazon gift cards. It hardly mattered then. Now it was everything. It was a lifeline.

She pulled one out and stuffed it into her pocket just as her mother entered the room.

"Why are you late?" barked Natalie.

Harper had never heard that tone before. What was wrong with her? "Traffic was terrible. Two wrecks on 281."

"You didn't stop anywhere? Or see anyone?"

She tried to act offended. "No, Mom. Where would I stop, and who would I meet? For all I know, you can track my car, too." Harper started up the stairs.

"Don't be smart with me," her Mom yelled after her. "You're thirty minutes late. Shall I check to see if there were two wrecks reported on your route home?"

Harper stopped at the landing and looked back, confused at her mother's tone. *Even she is starting to hate me.* "Whatever you want to do." She ran up the remaining steps and fled down the hall.

Alone in her room, Harper turned sideways, pulled up her shirt, and peered at her stomach in her mirror. Had she gained any weight?

Two quick knocks at the door had her scrambling to pull her shirt back down. As her parents entered her room, Harper walked quickly to the window, with her back to the door.

"We need to talk," barked Greg.

Great. What have I done now? Harper continued to gaze outside.

"Please, move away from the window and talk with us," said Natalie.

"Don't worry. I'm not going to jump," she remarked dryly.

"Harper, please sit down," said Greg, doing a bad job of trying to sound calm and reasonable. He sat on Harper's bed.

She turned from the window and folded her arms. "What's up?"

"We received your grades today," Natalie informed her, as she sat beside her husband.

That wasn't what Harper expected. "What grades? Finals don't start for two days."

"The school sent a report of your current grades. You're failing everything except PE and art," said Natalie.

"Unless you ace your finals," said Greg, "you'll be in summer school."

Grades? What else can go wrong? "Fat chance of that. Look, I'm exhausted. I have homework." Harper sat at her desk and rummaged through her pack, not for anything in particular, but she had to block them out. She had enough to worry about right now.

"Julie's father called me today," said Greg with a weird look on his face and a glint in his eyes that made her nervous. "A friend of his told him he saw Julie yesterday with a strange boy enter a movie theatre, miles away from the mall."

She shrugged. "Maybe the friend made a mistake."

"She confessed to her parents last night." Greg's nostrils flared.

She tightened her eyes. "Really? Did they threaten to send her to the hospital?"

"Stop it!" said Natalie. "Stop blaming us for what happened that night. You were the one threatening to jump out the window."

"And used a knife. Do you hate us that much?" asked Greg.

"Of course, it's about you." She showed them her tiny scar. "It'll always be a reminder to me that even attempted suicide wouldn't make you care."

"It was manipulation, not suicide." Greg glared at Harper, who glared back.

"Whatever it was, it hurt my grades. So I need to study. *Alone*."

"Where did you go when Julie left the mall?" asked Greg. "Who did you meet?"

"Here comes the 'Who?' attack. Again. Didn't meet anyone. Watched the same movie at the mall. Can't imagine why Julie didn't want to take me with her." Harper kept digging in her bag, and then realized what wasn't there.

Her phone.

Her *secret* phone.

She stopped breathing. Where did she have it last? She searched her brain. The car. She left it in her car.

She stood. "Look, I left my book in the car. I need to get it."

"Your book, or your phone?" said Greg, as he pulled her phone out of his front pocket and shook it.

Harper smiled while her heart pounded in her chest. "Not my phone," she lied and pulled her other phone out of her back pocket and held it up. "This one's mine."

"This was in your front seat," said Greg.

She narrowed her eyes. "Maybe Trish left it there. She sat in my car for a few minutes after school."

He wasn't buying it. "Key in the passcode, young lady. This is your phone."

Harper laughed harshly. "And your proof? If that was my secret phone, I wouldn't leave it in the front seat."

The phone buzzed in Greg's hand. All three looked at it and saw Zachary's name and number appear on the screen.

Can nothing ever go my way, just once? Harper groaned inwardly.

"Who is Zachary?" asked Greg.

"Don't know a Zachary," said Harper. "Must be a wrong number."

Greg accepted the call and snarled into the phone. "Who is this?"

"Where's Harper?" Harper heard Zachary ask.

Greg took the phone away from his ear and sneered at his daughter. "You want to talk with Zachary?"

As Harper lunged for her phone, her elbow smashed into her mother's face. Natalie screamed. Greg twisted around, shoving his wife's back for leverage, trying to catch Harper.

"What are you doing?" Natalie cried at them both.

Harper slammed the door behind her, barely hearing Greg say, "I'm sorry, Natalie," as she ran down the stairs and out the front door. She raced to her car and started it up. She backed out of her driveway just as Greg ran out of the house. Before Harper switched gears to drive forward, she locked eyes with him as he mouthed the words, "Damn you," then looked back toward the open door like he heard something. He jerked his head back at Harper, glared at her, and ran back inside.

For a moment, she still didn't move, almost wishing he'd run back out of the house to her car and stand in front of it, crying, pleading with her to stay.

But he didn't.

She stepped on the accelerator, breathing a little easier with every house that passed, carrying her farther away from a place she called home, but had never felt like it.

She would never see him again.

Chapter Eight

Harper nearly sideswiped a car as she veered into traffic and headed back toward the highway. She had her real phone and her backpack, but she'd left the family phone on her bed. Her parents now had no way to contact her.

At the overpass, Harper saw the traffic backed up and crawling on the highway, so she kept driving north to find somewhere she could hide. Her parents would surely call the police and report her missing.

What was she going to do? How could she go back home? They'd take her car and ground her forever, even before knowing about her pregnancy. She wiped her eyes and tried to concentrate. She didn't want to add a wreck or ticket to her growing list of troubles.

After driving for miles, she found a tiny restaurant she'd never seen before called Rafael's. It was bright pink with a Modelo sign flashing in the window, surrounded by painted cactus. When was the last time she ate? She thought she'd driven far enough that her dad couldn't find her—assuming he even tried to look. She parked in back and walked into the building only to feel dizzy.

A young waitress came by as Harper grabbed the back of a nearby booth. The waitress looked at her, surprised, and said, "Aren't you Harper? Mr. Lyons' daughter?"

Harper's stomach flipped. How could anyone know her here?

The girl looked vaguely familiar, a little shorter than Harper with large brown eyes nestled under perfectly arched eyebrows.

"I'm Ariana. I graduated from TCA." She smiled. "We had PE together last year. You were in ninth grade."

"Oh. Hi." Harper could feel the sweat beading on her forehead as her stomach gurgled. She had a vague memory of knowing this girl, but her brain was as fogged as her guts were churning.

Ariana's grin faded. "Are you sick?"

"Maybe. Where's your restroom?"

"This way." Ariana held Harper's arm and helped her walk down the hallway.

"Thanks."

Harper retched but nothing came out. She wet paper towels, wiped her face, and looked at herself in the mirror. Her face was pale, haggard, and sweaty. After a minute more of trying to calm down, she opened the door and found Ariana waiting for her.

"You OK?"

"Think so. Dry heaves."

"Flu or something else?"

Harper stared at her face and remembered the short ponytail she always wore while they ran laps around the gym. "I remember you. You work here?" Harper put her hand on her stomach and noticed Ariana watch her.

"My parents own the restaurant. I've waited tables here since I was fifteen." She paused while looking intently at Harper's face. "What's wrong?"

"I left my house. I can't go back. I just started driving." A tear ran down her cheek, and she placed a hand on her stomach. "Please don't tell anyone I'm here."

"Who would I tell?" Ariana glanced at her hand on her stomach. "What's happened?"

Harper quickly dropped her hand and looked into Ariana's eyes. *She knows.* "Just learned I'm pregnant." Harper sniffed and wiped her nose. "My parents don't know."

"Here. Come sit down, and I'll get you some water."Ariana led her to an empty booth. "I'll be back in a second. Ice? Lemon?"

"Yes." Ariana walked away.

Zachary called again, but she dismissed it. She didn't need more criticism and yelling. She had no more doubts about Zachary's feelings for her, or lack of them. She reached in her pocket for a tissue and pulled out a wad, which included Grandpa's Christmas card. She opened it and looked at his phone number, address, email, and website. Punching in cooperlyons.net, she found his site where he had two books for sale and some music.

Several favorable review blurbs were listed under each novel:

"The tension and conflict grip the reader from the opening line."

"Lyons' compassion for troubled teens warms the heart."

"Lyons compels his readers to confront the significant moral issues of our time."

He wrote books and songs? Why had she never known this?

She listened to a song about a girl determined to bounce back after being used by a male. *Story sounds familiar*, she thought. The melody was catchy, and the lyrics were powerfully sung by a woman.

You knocked me down
But I'm not out baby,
I'm off the ground
And on my feet

Ariana returned with the water.

"Thanks."

"Like the song. Who's the singer?" asked Ariana, sliding into the booth with her.

"Don't know. But my grandfather wrote the song."

Ariana bent closer to the phone. "Really? Cool."

"He lives in Alaska. I visited him when I was six." Harper's eyes brightened. She remembered feeling happy then.

Ariana removed the paper from the straw and stuck it into the glass. "I've always wanted to go to Alaska!" She moved the glass closer to Harper, who took a sip.

"Thanks. I'm going to see him soon."

"Lucky! Does your grandfather know?"

"No. He and my dad had a big argument the last time they saw each other. I'm not sure Grandpa will want to get involved with me if he knows I'm pregnant. Not sure if he'd even want me."

Ariana patted Harper's hand. "Bet he will. Does the father know?"

"You mean my asshole ex-boyfriend? Yeah, he knows. He wants me to get an abortion." Harper slumped down in her seat.

"What do you want?"

"I can't have a baby, especially not his. My parents already hate me. I just can't."

Ariana moved closer and spoke quietly. "My cousin got pregnant. She got an abortion, and her parents kicked her out." Ariana looked around the restaurant. "She stayed with me for a while. My parents never knew."

Harper sat up. "Was she a minor? Did she need a judge's permission?"

"No. She's eighteen. Why?"

"Because I'm sixteen. I can't get permission from my parents or a judge."

"Your dad is still Headmaster?"

"Yeah."

Ariana nodded. "Guess he'd be pretty pissed if he knew."

Understatement. Harper ripped a napkin into little pieces. "He'd kill me."

"You aren't going back?"

"No." She wadded up the pieces and threw the ball against the facing seat.

Ariana looked around then said quietly, "You can stay with me if you want. I have an apartment upstairs."

Harper felt a surge of hope. "You sure?"

Ariana patted her hand and smiled. "Yeah. Think about it." She stood up. "You want something to eat?"

"Yes. Nachos. *Compuesta.*"

"OK."

"And thanks for helping me."

"*De nada.*"

Someone from another table called Ariana, and she walked over.

Harper considered her options again. Parents? No. Mom's parents, Zoe and John? Double no. They traveled all the time and were stricter than her father. After the Academy opened and Dad was appointed Headmaster, Dad changed. John was the "fear God" and "burn in hell" kind of guy. Their family changed churches, and Dad began to yell more at Harper. She had liked their previous pastor, a kind-hearted man who preached about God's love and forgiveness. Their new pastor was John on steroids—God's law, heathens everywhere, a literal Bible with no ambiguity, and obvious political opinions.

Rachel, her grandma and Cooper's former wife, took care of her very old, very sick father. Harper used to see Grandma on Sundays, even PawPaw. They'd take them to church then out for brunch. But now she couldn't leave the house. Grandma was sweet, but she couldn't deal with Harper's problems right now.

Cooper was her only option, but he was almost a blank to her. Other than receiving gift cards once a year and vague memories of being with him in Alaska ten years ago, she knew nothing about him. He'd never visited San Antonio after he moved to Alaska. No pictures of him appeared in their house. The argument between him and Dad must have been horrible to produce such a long separation, but now that she'd experienced a horrible argument with her father, she sympathized with Grandpa more. He may have had an affair and run away to escape a scandal of some sort, but knowing her father, she had to believe the fault lay more with him than with her grandfather.

He was her only option.

She punched in his number and listened to the ringing on the other end. No one answered. She tried again.

"This is Cooper," said a gruff and deep baritone.

"Hi, Grandpa!" She hoped she sounded cheery. "This is Harper."

"Who? Who is this?"

Her grin slipped off her face. *Will he remember me?* "This is Harper. Greg's daughter. Your son's daughter."

"Harper...? Well, hello there, Harper! How are you? My God, I haven't seen you for a whole bunch of years." He had a big, jolly voice and seemed thrilled to talk to her. This encouraged her and eased her nerves a bit.

"Ten years, Grandpa. I was six when we visited you."

"I know. Been a long time. I kept hoping maybe one of you would call or send me an email or something."

Guilt lanced her. Harper wanted to say she'd hoped he would visit, but in truth the only time she'd given him a passing thought was on Christmas when the gift cards were passed out.

"I started sending notes with my address and phone number a few years ago, along with the cards," he said.

She felt horrible. "We never got them, Grandpa. Mom hid them in a drawer." She didn't tell him she pulled one out two years ago and tossed it back in. She felt ashamed. He had wanted to hear from his grandkids, but she only cared when she needed help.

"Guess I didn't realize how angry they were with me." He sighed. "I should've flown down there and knocked on the door."

She heard years of hurt and regret in his voice.

"It's not your fault, Grandpa. We let you send us money and never asked questions. I'm so sorry."

"I'm sorry, too, Harper. But I'm talking to you now, and it's really good to hear your voice. How's your family?"

She glanced around the restaurant. "I'm kinda separated from them right now."

"Sorry to hear that. What happened?"

"I...I left before they kicked me out. They're pretty angry with me."

"Why?"

"Pretty much everything. Grades, boys..." She paused, wondering if she should trust him.

"Anything else?" he asked gently.

If not him, then who? she thought. "Drugs."

"Did your dad ever tell you about his sister, Heather?"

Harper saw a nearby man frowning at her. She turned away and huddled closer to the phone. "A little. He's afraid I'm going to be like her."

"Are you?" he asked gently.

"I hope not, but I'm getting worried." She swallowed and tried to stifle the whimper in her voice.

"Where are you?"

"I'm sitting by myself in a restaurant, waiting for nachos."

"Real nachos, or bagged chips and fake cheese sauce?" he asked with an edge of excitement.

"Mexican restaurant nachos."

"God, I miss Mexican food! Nothing like Mexican food from South Texas. If they had a decent Mexican restaurant up here, I'd be in absolute heaven. That's about the only thing I miss in Texas. Well, except for you and your brother, and you got two other siblings now."

Harper smiled. *Maybe this will work.* "That's right. Alex and Jack."

"I know. I got all your photos on my fridge. Looking at them right now."

Harper felt sorry for him. He'd put up all their pictures, but none of them had bothered with his. They'd never sent him anything, never even talked about him.

"So, why are you calling me, Harper?"

She looked around to see if anyone noticed her, then quietly said, "I ran out of the house and needed someone to talk to."

"Your parents don't know where you are?"

"No."

"Do they know you're calling me?"

"No."

"Don't think your father's going to be too happy when he finds out."

Her heart stopped. *Will he call Dad?*

"I'm sorry you're having problems, Harper." She waited for the "But I'll have to check with your parents first." Instead, she heard a kind, gentle voice say, "What can I do for you?"

The dam broke in Harper's eyes. She clutched a napkin to her face. After a few failed attempts to speak, she said, "I...I don't know. I'm really messed up."

"I'm so sorry, Harper. Guess you've tried talking to your parents?"

"Yeah, but we're at war right now. I just can't go home." She rubbed her face and tried to breathe. "I don't know where to go."

"What about Rachel? Doesn't she still live down there?"

"She spends all her time with PawPaw who's dying."

"Really? Well, I wouldn't know anything about that. You must be desperate to call me. I've hardly been a decent grandparent to you. Wait. Hold on a second." She heard a click as he put the phone down.

Harper heard him yell in the background. "Snowball, stop wrestling with that kitty! OK. You're OK. Now calm down a little, you big galoot. I'm on the phone."

"Harper? You still there?" asked Cooper.

"Yes, Grandpa. What was that about?"

"I've got a rambunctious puppy that plays too rough with my kitten. The cat holds his own, but sometimes his whole head disappears inside Snowball's mouth. However, they do seem to love each other." He chuckled. "So where were we? Oh yeah. So you're by yourself in a Mexican restaurant and you could think of no one else to call except your grandfather whom you've only seen once in ten years. Sounds bad. But on my end, that sounds good. At least I didn't scare the dickens out of you when you visited. Must've made a decent impression on you. Of course, you were only six. Kind of easy to fool a six-year-old."

Harper enjoyed his voice. It was loud but kind and genuine.

"Not quite as easy to fool a sixteen-year-old, I imagine."

"Actually," said Harper, "I've been fooled a lot recently."

He lowered his voice and spoke slowly. "Everybody gets fooled, Harper. No shame in that. The trick is whether you bounce or crash afterward."

She took several deep breaths.

"Feel like I've crashed pretty hard, Grandpa." Tears flooded her eyes again. "I don't think I'll ever get up again."

"Give it time. You'll find a way. And call me Cooper or Coop. That's what all my friends call me, at least to my face. Think I need to earn being your Grandpa before you call me that."

"OK, Cooper." She wiped her eyes with a napkin.

"How can I help you, Harper?"

She covered one side of her face with her arm. "Can I visit you?"

"Would your parents let you?"

"I don't know. I might not give them a choice."

"You're welcome here at any time, but please don't run away from home, Harper. Don't want you getting into trouble you can't get out of. I can't just take you away. Somehow you need to talk to your parents and get their permission. Your dad has enough complaints about me already."

"I think he's got more complaints about me."

"Well, maybe we can get back into his good graces together," he said encouragingly. "When does your school let out?"

"Doesn't matter, Grandpa, um, Cooper. I'm failing everything now. I need to get away, to start over."

"Alaska is a great place to start over, but it's not an easy place. Got to work hard at it. I'll sure help you if you can get up here."

A slight smile formed on her lips. She liked this man. "Thanks, Cooper. Wish we could have spent more time together before now."

"Me, too, sweetheart. The older you get, the more regrets you build up. Are you going back home tonight?'

"Don't think so. I will tomorrow. Maybe."

"Do you have somewhere safe to stay tonight?"

"Yes." She hesitated. Should she tell him about Ariana? What if he talked to Dad and mentioned her name? He might know where her restaurant was. "With a friend of mine."

"Please be careful. I'll worry until I talk to you again. Is this a good number?"

"For a while. I'll probably have another number soon."

"Harper, listen. I'll do anything I can to help you. Just know I'll always try my best."

"Thanks, Cooper." She felt warmth spread through her body.

"Do you still sing?"

Harper was confused. Why would he ask her about singing? "Sing?"

"Yeah. You were a heck of a singer when you were six. I still remember that big voice of yours."

"Just a little to myself in the car. I forgot I used to sing to anyone." She remembered the boat trip and singing on a table. And then her parents yelling at her for standing on the table. She couldn't remember singing to anyone after that.

"Well, maybe you'll feel like singing out loud up here. Big sky and big country everywhere you look. Need a big voice just to be heard!" He laughed. "You may not know this, but I write songs."

"I know. I listened to one on your website. I loved it!"

"Really? I'm glad, Harper. I'd sure love to hear you sing one of them."

"That'd be cool! I'd love to."

Ariana came by with the nachos.

"And Ariana loved your song, too."

"It was great!" shouted Ariana. "And I want to go to Alaska, too!"

"I'd love to have you visit," shouted Cooper.

Several people in the restaurant turned toward both girls. They smiled back. Ariana left quickly toward another table.

"Hello? Cooper?"

"I'm here, Harper. You sure you have a safe place to stay tonight?"

"Yes."

"And talk to me tomorrow? Please?"

"I will."

"Great. Well, I got to get back to planting my vegetables."

"This late?"

"Twenty-four hours of sunlight this time of year. Got to put these puppies in the ground. Take care of yourself, Harper."

"I'll be up there soon."

She ended the call. It had been years since she felt so comfortable talking to anyone in her family. Cooper listened and didn't judge her. He seemed to really care about her.

Harper took a bite of the nachos, felt sick, then ran to the bathroom, but found it occupied. She pushed open a back door and barely made it out of the building before throwing up near the dumpster. Grabbing her knees, she heaved a few more times, then gasped for breath.

Hurried footsteps on gravel pounded from behind her.

Ariana pulled her hair back from her face. "Hey, let me take you upstairs to my apartment. You can clean up and rest. I'll bring you some food when I get off in another hour."

"Thank you."

Ariana helped her up the stairs, unlocked her apartment door, and led her inside. Harper looked around the small kitchen/living room. Dirty dishes sat on the counter, clothes were strewn about on the floor, most of the sofa cushions were awry, and several textbooks lay in a heap on the kitchen table.

"Wasn't expecting visitors," said Ariana sheepishly. "Sorry about the mess."

"This is a mess I can deal with. Is it OK if I straighten things up until you're done downstairs?"

"Sure, if you feel up to it."

Harper pulled cash from her pocket and held it out to Ariana. "Here. For the nachos."

"No," said Ariana. "You clean this mess, and we're even."

Harper stuffed the bills back into her pocket. "Will your parents mind me staying here tonight?"

"They won't know. Just like yours won't know. During PE, I always heard guys talking about you, saying how pretty you were. Staring at you all the time. You seemed to enjoy it. I wished several times I could be you for just one day, but then I thought how horrible it must have been to go to school where your father was the Headmaster. That must have sucked."

Harper thought about the last few months—the expulsion, the drugs, Zachary, Mia, her pregnancy. "Don't think you'd want to be me now. I know I don't."

Ariana wiped a tear from Harper's cheek. "I'll be back as soon as I can."

"Not too soon. It's going to take me a while to clean this junk pile up." She laughed. "Go. You've got customers."

Ariana squeezed her hand and left. Harper went to the sink and started cleaning dishes, all the time wishing it was that easy to clean up her life.

Chapter Nine

Some tears zigzagged down Cooper's cheeks until his beard swallowed them. He stroked Houdini's back and tail as the kitty purred on his lap. Snowball drank from his bowl, sounding like rocks tossed in a lake with each lap. Cooper still held his phone in the other hand as he sat at his kitchen table. He remembered another phone call from a desperate girl many years ago—his daughter, Heather.

Cooper was washing dishes while Rachel worked on her crossword puzzle behind him. The phone rang, and he answered.

"Hey, Pops. Need a favor." Her tone was happy, but Cooper recognized the edge underneath. She wanted something.

"I can't send you money, Heather."

"I just need a little bit," she whined. "Greg said he'd give me $50. If you do the same, I can pay my rent for this shithole of a room for another week."

"Aren't you making money at the restaurant?"

"Sure. Lots, but someone broke into my place and stole my stash. Rent's due tomorrow."

Rachel watched Cooper who held his hand over the phone while he whispered, "She needs $50." Rachel shook her head. He told Heather, "Tell you what. Let me call Greg first."

"You don't believe me?" she snarled. "What the hell?"

"The last time you said Greg was sending you money, he said you told him we were. You're lying to both of us. You're just going to buy drugs. We don't want to help you kill yourself."

"Some parents you are!"

After a click, the line disconnected, ending the call.

Variations of this scene had happened over and over.

Though both Cooper and Rachel had raised Heather, Greg cast most of his blame on Cooper for his sister's life of drug abuse and untimely death. At one point, Heather claimed Cooper had abused her in her youth, but could never pinpoint an event or age when it happened. There had to be a reason Heather was so screwed up, right? Cooper knew she wanted an excuse for her misery, but the charge fueled his anger at her and raised doubts about him from his wife, Greg, and her friends. Sexual abuse of children was possibly the worst rumor for a teacher to manage.

Cooper imagined that Greg must have struggled watching his own daughter become wild and defiant, especially since he'd seen it happen before with his sister. Cooper knew his son would be furious when he learned of their conversation and Harper's desire to visit.

And, really, how could Cooper help her? What could he do for her that he hadn't tried with Heather? He didn't know the girl. All he had were posed and staged Christmas photos. If he ran into her at a store, he might not recognize her without help.

Cooper knew how Greg would've responded if Harper had called him from the restaurant because he'd done the same with Heather: "Which boy are you with now? How can you be failing everything? Every word out of your mouth is a lie!" Parents and their kids always developed resentments, jealousies, and anger over meaningless slights because they were so close, so raw in their emotions, so quick to judge. Maybe being distant all these years would help.

He felt a connection to her because they were family, but whatever baggage they brought to the relationship would stay in the background, at least at the start.

Cooper put Houdini down and rubbed Snowball's ears. One phone call had changed his life. He feared trying and failing again. But now that she'd called, he cared. If she never came up, he'd still worry. How could he not?

But then, there was his doctor's report. What was he going to do?

He put on his gloves, opened the door for Snowball while holding back Houdini—the kitty had escaped too many times, desperate to catch a bird—and pushed the wheelbarrow to one of his raised garden beds. He wanted to plant his tomatoes and zucchinis and maybe some cabbage. Maybe that would keep him from thinking about Harper.

• • • • •

Harper would tell Cooper about all her problems, but not about the pregnancy. She didn't know his opinion about abortion and worried he'd feel obligated to tell her parents. Waiting until she'd been in Alaska for a few weeks, and she wouldn't be able to hide it anymore, then telling Cooper seemed the best plan. After all, she was only eight weeks along. She had plenty of time to work it out.

If she were going to Alaska, she needed a stash of heroin from Zachary to sell to pay for the abortion. She'd spent most of her money on her phone, negligee, and other clothes for Zachary and needed another source. She couldn't steal from Cooper. She already felt bad enough about using him.

Zachary was a minor dealer who received his supply through the mail from a friend in Harlingen. One day he'd driven her to a post office past Spring Branch where he kept a mailbox. He picked up a package and drove them back to his house where they walked the three flights of stairs to his bedroom.

This had been the second time she'd seen his room. Texas, or a mythical version of it, jumped at her from all sides: three sets of mounted longhorns, several types of spurs hanging on the walls, and deer rugs on the floor.

"Did you buy all of this?"

"No. My dad's decorator did this. You should see our ranch in the Hill Country. I shot the deer, though." He put the package on the floor, whipped out a pocketknife, and cut the seams. From under parchment paper, he pulled out pastries—*pan dulce* and *buñuelos*—took a bite and offered them to Harper who knelt beside him.

"Oh, that's good!" said Harper. "And the smell is amazing."

"Exactly," said Zachary. "These and lots of Bounce sheets hide the odor."

"Of what?"

He placed the pastries on the paper on the floor and moved the packing peanuts until he found the zip-lock bags full of heroin: balloons and baggies.

"My friend at the border pays cash for the stamp and always uses a fake return address. He claims that the peanuts scattered throughout the crate will hide the balloons if the package is scanned. I send him cash every couple of weeks. I always use that little post office. Never been caught."

"That's cool." She thought his life was thrilling.

He raised his brows. "Want to know how to smuggle drugs onto a plane?"

"Stick them into a pastry?"

"The scanner would catch it." He licked off some sugar pieces stuck to her cheek and lips. "Girls have the advantage over guys. They can bring double the amount." He smiled.

Harper looked at him, confused until he pulled a condom out of his wallet.

Harper's eyes widened and she laughed. "Are you kidding me?"

"Nope. Fill this up, tie it off, get lubricant, and shove it in."

Harper replayed that day and what had happened afterward on one of the rugs. The condom was right there, but neither one cared about using it.

Maybe that was the time I got pregnant, Harper thought.

When she'd finished cleaning Ariana's kitchen, she Googled Texas laws for assault and sex with minors. She needed leverage over Zachary. Before meeting him, she had smoked weed occasionally with friends from school, but the heroin started with him, along with sex. She thought he was a hot college guy and was thrilled with his attention. After all, he said he loved her many times. She realized now she was just fresh meat to him. He'd used her; now she'd use him to help her plan.

But, God, it hurt.

She felt stupid and worthless. She was no good to her sister and couldn't possibly be good for a baby.

After ten minutes of research, she called him.

"Hey," barked Zachary, "what the hell happened?"

Showtime. "My father answered the phone earlier. Sorry. I ran away from the house but found a friend who will give me a place to stay tonight. I'm sorry for how I acted at the clinic. I'd just heard the news and was in shock."

She hoped she wasn't laying it on too thick.

"I made an appointment for next week. Finals are coming up, so I can't have the procedure now. They charge $350, and I don't have the money." She paused to swallow her anger at him and at herself for pretending to beg. "Is there any way you can give me some smack to sell at school? I could probably sell enough to pay the fee."

After a pause, Zachary said, "I can't give them to you, but I can sell them to you at my price."

Not a chance. She added a little edge to her voice. "Do you expect me to pay the entire bill?"

"Why can't your parents pay for it?"

"My father is the Headmaster of a Christian school. They'll never agree to an abortion. I have to obtain a judge's permission before I can have it done without their consent."

"You'll get one?" The way his voice perked up sickened her.

"Yes. I already made the appointment. I can show you the reminder from the clinic when I pick up the smack."

"How do I know you weren't screwing another guy? You were quick to jump in bed with Levi last night."

Harper paused and tried to control herself. "I didn't jump in bed with anyone. For all I know, he raped me." Her anger boiled over at him. Why had she ever thought he cared about her? "I should report you to the police for statutory rape. I'm sixteen; you're twenty-one. The law in Texas defines more than a three-year difference as assault. Check it out if you don't believe me. Do you want a paternity test, Zachary? Your call."

She waited several seconds.

"OK. Come by my house tomorrow morning, and I'll give you enough to pay the bill once you sell everything."

She didn't know whether to feel proud of herself for being able to manipulate him, or disgusted that she needed to. Either way, she wanted to take him for as much as possible. Who knew what lay ahead of her. "Maybe throw in some extra for me? I'm going to need it, Zachary. I know that neither of us cared about my age when we started our relationship, but you took advantage of me. You paraded me around your house in a negligee. It'd be easy to get pictures of you walking me around. You should've known better. I don't think a judge would be very kind to you."

"Fine," he barked. "I'll give you extra, but we can't see each other after this. All you bitches want is money and drugs!"

The line disconnected.

She put her phone down. She didn't feel pride in making him agree. Only disgust and shame and hurt.

• • • • •

Greg had given Natalie an ice pack for her cheek, then called the police. He couldn't understand why they'd refused to look for his daughter. He told them she was missing, and they said not for long enough. She'd stolen the car, but it was the car she always drove. She'd likely come back later that evening. He worried she may hurt herself again. Harper was a good liar. She could make anyone believe anything she wanted. Yes, but, her counselor determined she wasn't a threat to herself.

He hesitated to call any of his friends for fear of spreading the news of their family problems. She'd already caused too many rumors about him. He didn't want to end up like his father with his reputation ruined and forced to flee thousands of miles away to escape it. He thought about driving around town to look for her, but she wouldn't be foolish enough to go to her usual hangouts. And there was still a chance she'd come back, wasn't there? He wanted to be home if she did.

But he couldn't sit around and do nothing without going crazy, so he convinced Natalie to help him search through Harper's things. He wanted to know more about his daughter and see how far she'd really fallen. He hoped not far enough that she was completely out of their reach. He didn't want to lose her. Not like this.

"Where's Harper?" asked Alex as Greg and Natalie entered her bedroom. She had been playing with a friend next door when Harper came home then left.

"We don't know," said Natalie.

"Why did she leave? What did you do to her?"

"She was late coming home, which meant she went somewhere she wasn't supposed to go," said Greg, "or met Zachary. You know about Zachary, don't you?"

Alex folded her arms across her chest. "Never heard that name before."

"Really. Thought you two were best friends," Greg baited her. "I can't believe she wouldn't have told you about her boyfriend."

"I asked her if she met him at the mall, and she said no. She even got angry at me for asking."

"Thought you didn't know anything about a boyfriend," Greg deadpanned.

"I didn't say that. I said I didn't know anyone named Zachary. She's never mentioned that name before."

"What has she mentioned?" Greg's voice hardened. "Did you know she was meeting him yesterday?"

"No."

"You're lying. Tell the truth, damn it! Why do both of my daughters have to be liars?" Greg fumed. He went to Harper's dresser and pulled out drawers.

Natalie sat down beside Alex. "Your sister is having secret meetings and probably using drugs. Do you know anything about that?"

Alex looked at Natalie like she was crazy. "Harper doesn't do drugs."

"I discovered a bag of marijuana in her car a few weeks ago."

"That was probably someone else's. Harper doesn't do drugs," Alex repeated firmly.

Greg pulled out another drawer, dumped it, and raked through its contents on Harper's bedspread.

"What are you looking for?" asked Alex.

"Money your sister has stolen from us. Drugs. Photos. You name it. Something that will tell me how the hell she got like this, how we all got to this point." He pulled out another drawer, this one containing Harper's underwear.

He remembered the night when his parents had finally decided to go through Heather's things after she hadn't come home from a party. They'd asked Greg what he knew, but he'd lied to them. At the time, he thought he was covering for his sister and being a cool brother. They went through every bit of her clothing, lifted the mattress, and examined the underside of drawers and shelves. They eventually found a journal where she wrote about screwing guys and taking LSD. But that was before cell phones. Did kids even write anything down anymore?

Alex walked over to Harper's bed as Greg flipped through clothes and examined the drawer. He held up a bustier. *Why in the hell did she have that?*

"Find what you were looking for?" Alex deadpanned as she put her hands on her hips.

"Did you know she had this?" He grabbed a pair of sheer panties. "Or this?"

Alex glared at him with hatred. "We don't model our underwear for each other."

Greg stopped and stared at his daughter. He'd lost her, too.

"Take your homework and get out of this room," he ordered.

The two stared at each other for several seconds. Finally, Alex grabbed her backpack and left, slamming the door behind her. Greg tossed the underwear toward Natalie. "Can you take care of these? I'll look through the closet."

Natalie went through Harper's underwear, removing pieces, while Greg rummaged in the closet. He found a couple of what appeared to be old balloons he thought were trash in the back corner, but left them there. He sat on Harper's bed with his head in his hands.

Natalie sat next to him. "We're losing them, Greg."

Greg replayed Alex's comments to him in her bedroom and the look in her eyes. The same look he'd seen in Harper's eyes a few years ago and many times since. "As long as Harper lives here, we've lost."

"Where do you think she is?"

He snorted. "Maybe a crack house on the west side. That's where my sister was when Dad picked her up one night. Another time he found her in some guy's apartment a few miles from our house. Another time she was unconscious in her car in a Walmart parking lot. The list goes on and on."

"Should we have done something differently?" asked Natalie.

He stood up and absently picked up bottles of nail polish and tubes of lipstick from Harper's dresser. "Sure. I should've caught everything sooner. I should've listened to you months ago."

"You didn't want to believe Harper could act like your sister. I can understand that."

"And now Alex. She's going to turn out the same way." He leaned against the dresser, facing her. "How did you escape all this? Did you ever rebel?"

"Once. When I was eleven." She looked away. "At that time, we were poor and lived in a tiny place in the country. I spoke back to my father. He slapped me so hard I fell to the ground. Then he dragged me out of the house where I cried for about an hour. My mother came out with a Bible full of sticky notes and told me, 'When you think you deserve to live with us again, come to the door.'

"Every note identified a verse about respecting and honoring parents or being punished by God. I read them all. Finally, I went to the door and asked for forgiveness. My father asked me to repeat Deuteronomy 5:16. I fumbled with the Bible trying to find the verse. 'Memorize them,' he said through the door, 'or you can't come back.' I was out all night, hungry, bitten by bugs, but I memorized the verses and passed his inquisition on the porch the next morning. I never challenged him again."

Greg remembered a conversation with Natalie's father just after being named Headmaster four years ago. They were walking around the courtyard as workers were planting bushes and laying paving stone.

"I will probably regret giving you this job, Greg."

Greg stopped, his heart skipping a beat as fear roiled his stomach. He smiled to hide his shock. "Why is that, sir?"

"Because you're too soft. Just like Natalie. I did not put a half million dollars of my own money and more from my friends into a school that harbors delinquents. If the children who attend this school are not obviously better behaved and more sincere in their religious beliefs than the riff-raff who attend the public schools, then what's the point of The Cross Academy? You make sure that our kids learn the Bible, fear God, and fear you. I don't want any of our parents worried that one of their child's friends is a bad influence. Get rid of any bad influence. No hesitation. Parents will pay our tuition to keep their kids away from drugs, sex, alcohol, and heathens. You understand me, Greg? No hesitation. No exceptions."

"Yes, sir."

Had he only known then that Harper would become one of those "no exceptions."

"Should we have done that?" asked Greg.

With anger that surprised him, she stood. "No! God is love, not fear of punishment. If I'd walked to the road that night and left them, he wouldn't have missed me. I don't want our kids to doubt our love for them."

"It may be too late for me and Harper," he said slowly.

Natalie held his hand.

During the past four years, Greg had tried his best to run a tight ship at school and at home, but his efforts had little effect on Chris, now Harper, and probably Alex. Or the effect was not what he had intended. What was he doing wrong? Why did it keep ending up like this? He was losing everything. He looked around Harper's ransacked room. Maybe he had already lost it.

"I'm worried about her, Greg," said Natalie through tears.

"I am, too, sweetheart. I am, too."

•   •   •   •   •

Ariana brought up food when she returned later in the evening. "Oh, my gosh, we can actually sit down at my table and eat! Thank you!"

"It didn't take long. Took my mind off everything. I put your textbooks on that chair. You're going to college?"

"Yeah, for education. I have class tomorrow at 8:30. Ugh! I'm going to be a kindergarten teacher. I want the kids before they turn into devils."

"Like me?"

Her eyes softened. "Don't be so hard on yourself."

Harper tried to climb in bed about 11:30 while Ariana sat at her table doing homework. At midnight, Harper went to the bathroom. She hadn't puked in a few hours, but she felt antsy and couldn't sleep. She had a craving to snort smack but was worried about being caught and worried she had the craving. She'd used yesterday and was scared that she wanted to use again so soon. Zachary had told her he always waited three days—his rules. But Zachary was an ass. Who cared what his rules were? As she removed the balloon from her pocket, she heard a light knock on the door and opened it to find Ariana.

"You OK, Harper?" she asked.

"Can't sleep."

Ariana smiled and took Harper's hand. They climbed through the window to a balcony on the backside of the restaurant. Ariana lit a joint, took a hit, and passed it to Harper, who took a deep drag and mellowed. She could still hear cars rushing down the highway and barely see stars or the moon through the ozone haze, but everything seemed better.

"How are you going to convince your parents to send you to Alaska?"

"I will be very mean to them."

Ariana lifted her eyebrows. "Why would that work?"

"Because Daddy can't afford to have a wild daughter and keep his job. He'll choose his job over me any day. I'm going back to my house tomorrow morning to set up a camera in my bedroom and take some pics of me sleeping like someone shot them secretly. I'll flash my ass and boobs, then send them to my parents with a note that I found them on my father's phone. I'll threaten to send the pics to his board members and to students unless he buys me a ticket."

Ariana blurted out a laugh. "That is very, very mean." She passed the joint.

"Yup." Harper pulled a long toke. "He'll pay money to send me away from him rather than lose his job. I want to make sure he realizes that."

"Why go home for the photos? What if one of them is there?"

"I was thinking the pics had to be realistic, like he really did it when I slept in my bed. But on second thought, who cares? No one will believe my story anyway, least of all my parents. But he'll agree to the ticket because he won't want to deal with more problems at school. You want to be my photographer?"

"You want me to photograph your ass?" She laughed.

"Yes. And boobs."

"OK, but I'd better finish this first." She shook her joint.

After a few more minutes and several tokes, their heads seemed to drift above their bodies, smiling at nothing. They struggled to climb back into Ariana's room and collapsed in giggles when they stumbled into Ariana's sofa, arms and legs intertwined. After catching their breath and stifling another round of laughter, they set the scene.

Harper wore one of Ariana's baggy t-shirts and pretended to be asleep, half covered with sheets. While Ariana shot photos, Harper pulled up the shirt, exposing her butt, then another revealing more, then another. She changed into a long, buttoned shirt that just happened to come undone during her twisting and turning during a restless sleep. By the time they finished, they collapsed from laughing so hard. They went through the photos together and laughed again—several showed Harper smiling in her "sleep."

Harper picked out five of the best and cropped them to remove as much of the bed as possible.

"You know, these are kind of creepy," said Ariana. "They look real. What if someone actually did this?"

Harper thought about all the photos she'd sent Zachary and the ones that guys surely took of her at his house. And the hand-job video. And all the photos her friends had sent to others.

"People have done worse," said Harper. "Thanks, Ariana. Glad I found you today."

"*De nada.*"

They smiled at each other, turned over, and fell asleep.

Chapter Ten

The girls struggled to wake up the next morning. Ariana offered Harper some clothes for the day.

Harper waved her off. "No need. I'm going by my house to pack my things."

"You sure?"

"I'll scope it out before I go inside."

The two girls looked at each other. "If you need a place to stay tonight, come back."

"You just want someone to keep your apartment clean."

"No. Well, yes, but I think we could be good friends."

Harper had never had a real girlfriend, someone to hang with and talk to. Someone to share problems with and do fun things together without guys complicating everything. She and Trish had never been like that.

"I think so, too." They hugged each other.

"If Alaska doesn't work out, give me a call," Ariana said.

"Thanks."

Harper drove to the clinic. She made an appointment for next Monday, the weekend after the finals. She asked for proof of an appointment so she could show her boyfriend.

They gave her a note and reminded her that state law required a parent's or judge's permission for the procedure since she was a minor. Harper also asked for medicine to stop her puking. She paid for a bottle and took one pill before leaving the clinic.

While sitting in her car in the parking lot, Harper tried to call Cooper.

After several tries, he answered.

"Huh? Who's calling?" he slurred.

"Hey, Cooper! It's me, Harper." Apprehension filled her. "Did I call at a bad time?"

"It's 5:30 in the morning, Harper. I'm three hours earlier than you."

"Oh, my God. Sorry! You want me to call back later?"

"It's OK. What's up?"

"I was wondering if I can fly up tomorrow?"

"Tomorrow? So soon? Have you talked to your parents?"

"Not yet, but I'm sure they'll buy me a ticket for tonight or tomorrow." *Please say yes!*

"You can come up anytime your parents say you can."

She breathed a sigh of relief. *They'll agree. Don't you worry.*

"I'm sure Greg will call me," said Cooper. "Should I admit we talked or not?"

Feeling hopeful this plan would work, she said, "Yes, we did."

"OK, just so you know, he'll be pissed that I didn't call him after speaking with you last night. I'm sure he's worried sick."

"I think he'll be angrier at me than you."

"Not a contest I want either of us to win. How long do you want to stay?"

Should she lie and say just for a week? Or tell the truth and say "forever"? "As long as you'll have me, Cooper. I don't plan on coming back here." She listened to silence for several seconds, holding her breath. Would he change his mind?

"That's a big decision, Harper."

"I know, but that's my plan."

"Well, let's leave the departure date open for now."

He didn't say no! She breathed deeply and smiled.

"You may hate my cooking, who knows?" He chuckled.

"We'll make it work, Cooper. I'll call you later."

"OK. Give me a couple of hours at least. I'm going to feed Houdini, let Snowball out, then try to get back to sleep. Ouch! Snowball, get your big paws off my leg! Hell, I guess I'm up whether I like it or not. Take care of yourself, Harper."

Harper texted Zachary that she was on her way then drove out of the parking lot and headed toward the house where she'd lost so much. She was so frustrated with herself for believing Zachary and for allowing him to get her pregnant. She'd spent too many hours feeling sorry for herself; now it was time to get off the ground and fix her life.

She parked in front of his house and got out of her car. Beer bottles and food wrappers littered the old porch. His door was open, so she walked right in and found Zachary hunched over a bowl eating cereal in the kitchen. His hair was a mess and his face was dirty. He picked at a sore on his cheek. How did she ever think this guy was desirable?

He lifted his face out of the bowl and leered at her. "Something to eat?" He slurred his words, and milk dribbled off his chin.

"No, thanks. I'd just puke it up. I'll be glad when this morning sickness is done."

He sat up and scratched his chest. "Next week, right?"

"Monday. Here's proof of our little mistake." She gave him a printout of the pregnancy results. "And proof that any connection between us will be destroyed next week." She gave him the appointment reminder.

He lifted a bag from the seat next to him and pushed it to the center of the table.

"There's a hundred in there. Nope. Sorry. Only ninety-nine." He laughed. "I smoked one this morning. Got bored waiting for you."

What a jerk!

She went to grab the bag, but he held on to it.

"You will show me a receipt after it's done." An order, not a request.

"I'll take a photo of the receipt and text it to you. You can hang it from one of your longhorns as a souvenir."

She picked up the bag and turned to leave. He shot out of his seat and grabbed her hand. She tried to yank it away, but he squeezed tighter and twisted her wrist. Gritting her teeth, she glared at him over her shoulder and tried not to yelp. She refused to squirm, staring directly into his bloodshot eyes.

"That hurts," she growled. She couldn't keep her chin from quivering

He twisted his mouth in a sneer and warned, "You'll have more than a bruised wrist if you screw me over."

She never realized how evil Zachary could be. Panting, she forced her lips into a smile. "You're just adding to the charges I can file." With as much hatred as she could muster, she roared, "Let go!"

He shoved her arm away. "I'm not a bad guy, Harper. I'm helping you out, aren't I?"

"You're an asshole." She hurried out before he could see her cry.

At Home Depot she bought a couple of plastic crates, packing peanuts, and duct tape. At a grocery store she bought a new backpack, condoms, lubricant, and latex gloves. She drove to her neighborhood, then by her street to look at her house. Seeing no cars in the driveway or anyone outside the other houses, she drove back to her house, opened the garage, and drove inside. She waited for the garage door to close before leaving the car, just in case any nosey neighbors were watching.

She carried all the items upstairs to her bedroom. She put on the gloves and opened Zachary's drug bag. She wanted to ensure the TSA drug detector would find no residue on her hands or carry-on. One zip-lock contained balloons; the other, baggies. She removed a few balloons to take with her on the plane and divided up the rest, along with her bag of pot, inside several zip-lock bags. She replaced her gloves, grabbed her jacket, sweaters, and shoes, placed them on the bottom of each crate, then added the drug bags, packing peanuts, Bounce sheets, then more shoes and clothes.

After fastening the crate lids with several strips of tape looped around the entire crate, she wrote, "Cooper Lyons, General Delivery, Anders Fork, AK 99744." She hesitated when trying to think up a fake return address. Seemed easier to write one she knew. She wrote Zachary's address on the top left corner. If the crates were inspected, the cops would trace them back to him. It'd serve him right.

After replacing her gloves, she emptied her old pack on the bed, decided what she wanted to take, and threw the items into her suitcase. In her new pack she put her computer, headphones, make-up, toiletries, contact lenses, saline solution, the remaining condoms, and tampons. At some point she'd have periods again. The condom she had removed from the box held ten balloons, two joints, and a quarter length of a soda straw. She didn't want anything remotely resembling drug paraphernalia in her pack.

After tying off the end and rubbing it with lubricant, she pushed it into her vagina—it was a little more difficult than Zachary had implied—and hoped the very awkward feeling would soon disappear. But the awkward juxtaposition of a condom full of drugs and her uterus with a growing fetus would stay with her forever.

Replacing her gloves again, she removed her clothes then opened her drawers to get new ones.

They went through my clothes!

They had removed all of her special underwear and some of her shirts and shorts. *Like that would fix what's wrong in this house.*

She picked out clothes for the plane and threw everything else into her suitcase. She looked at herself in the mirror.

This room had been her refuge for sixteen years, and she realized she might never see it again. Oddly, she felt no pain leaving the room. Leaving Alex, though, was killing her.

It was only three nights ago that Alex woke up at midnight, scared from a bad dream.

She sat right up and said, "He's almost here!"

"Who's almost here?" Harper was sitting up in bed, texting Trish.

Her eyes widened. "Him! Him!"

Harper put down her phone and moved over to Alex's bed. "You had a dream. No one is coming. Lie down and snuggle with me."

Alex stared at her sister. "You sure?"

"Yes." Harper patted the space beside her. "Lie down."

Alex scooted under the covers, and they fell asleep, Harper spooning Alex's back.

Who would comfort Alex now? How could she leave Alex to cope with her parents by herself? Because she loved her. Harper knew she couldn't help being a bad influence on her sister, who wanted too badly to be like Harper. She'd never forget Alex lifting her pajama shirt, stuffing a pillow underneath, and asking if she was hot. She should want to be like almost anyone else. Harper couldn't bear the thought of her sister experiencing Zachary's party.

She grabbed a red lipstick from the dresser and wrote, "I love you, Alex!" on the mirror. She did the same for Jack in his room: "Love you, Bro!" She took a few photos of Alex's side of the room with her phone, and grabbed her remaining stash of money—built up from saving cash presents and stealing from her parents—through the slit in her box spring, hidden by the mattress sham.

After being in the house for no more than thirty minutes, she drove north to the Spring Branch post office and mailed the crates to her grandfather, paying cash. There'd be no credit card receipt to track or serve as proof of who mailed it. Zachary had taught her well.

After buying another phone to hide her main number from her parents, she found a McDonalds where she bought ice cream and a coffee. She sat, took a bite and sip, held her new phone, and prepared to send the least revealing photo to Mom and Dad. She felt weird sending such photos to her parents, but overcoming that taboo would give them no choice. After the initial horror and struggle to look or turn away, they'd realize they could do nothing except follow her demands. This stunt would brand her as cruel and irretrievable. But she had no other option because she couldn't talk to her parents about the vortex her life had become. She was sure Dad would choose to send her away rather than lose his job. The choice was his to make.

Hope this works, she thought.

She texted: *I found photos on my father's phone a few days ago. I can't believe he did this to me! I am parked outside a police station trying to decide if I should report this. Please help me!*

That's how I'll start the message I'll send to your board members, including Grandpa and Grandma, and parents and students. I'll send several photos to them today unless you buy me a plane ticket to Fairbanks, Alaska. An Alaska Airlines flight leaves this evening at 7:05. I've already packed my bag. Cooper, my grandpa, knows I am coming to live with him. If you don't text me a confirmation number and itinerary by noon, I'll send photos to the board. By 1:00, I'll send them to every parent I know. You can imagine their reaction! I won't live with you anymore. I need my Grandpa.

She pressed the send arrow and waited for hell's gates to open.

Chapter Eleven

Greg emerged through his office door, staring at his phone. He'd read Harper's message, twice. Fear pumped through every one of his arteries, and he struggled to breathe.

"Greg!" Natalie screamed as she ran toward him, having just returned from waiting at Harper's school to see if their daughter would appear.

Students and staff stared at her as she hurried toward the main office.

"Natalie, please stop crying. Stop it!" He hustled her into his office and shut the door.

"Harper's dead!" cried Natalie.

"Did you read the text?" asked Greg. "Look again. Read what she wrote."

After a few seconds of staring at Harper's message, she looked up. "That's not her bed. Where do you think she was when she took these? Zachary's? We need to find out where he lives."

"She won't be there. She's trying to get to my father's. With our car, she could drive there if we don't give her the ticket. And who knows what the hell she'll do to get money for the gas to make the trip." Since when were Harper and his father so close? He didn't even know she'd been speaking with him. Why didn't his father tell him?

Both their phones dinged. Harper had sent the next photo with another message.

Your time is running out.

This one was more revealing with a button up shirt, a few buttons popped.

"Damn it!" yelled Greg. "How can she blackmail us like this?"

"Can't we prove that someone else took these?"

"It won't matter. If she sends these to anyone, especially your parents, and claims I did it, I'm toast. I'm barely hanging onto this job as it is, and I'd never get another one in a school."

"What are we going to do?" Her skin was ashen.

"I'll call Dad first and find out how the hell he's involved in this." He scrolled through his contacts and realized he didn't have his father's number. He hadn't spoken to his dad in ten years, and now he was taking Harper away from him? *Damn him!* He went to his computer and Googled Cooper's name until he found a number with a 907 area code and punched it in.

• • • • •

Cooper had decided he couldn't go back to bed after Harper's early call. If she flew in tomorrow, he'd have to get the house ready. He decided to finish planting his garden but leave the flowers for both of them to plant together. And then he'd try to clean up inside.

The sun sizzled through his shirt. Even though it was only seventy degrees outside, the Alaskan sun on a clear day caused his head and back to explode with sweat. The aroma of rich soil in the sun lifted like an earthy incense into his nostrils. He knew that his planters would be overflowing with greenery, accented by yellow zucchini and tomato flowers in two weeks.

He had just gathered soil around a cucumber plant and was pushing a labeling stick into the dirt when he heard a ringing. He wondered where the sound came from. Snowball put his big paws on the edge of the planter and sniffed the plants. Cooper stared at him, confused, and clueless.

The ringing started again, so he tossed his trowel into the dirt and hurried toward the house, thinking he still had the old landline. Snowball must have thought Cooper wanted to play because he ran around him, barking. Then he lifted his paws onto Cooper's chest with his big pink tongue hanging out the side of his mouth.

Cooper stopped. After another few seconds, he pushed Snowball down. "Get off me, Snowball."

Another episode.

The ringing started again, and he felt the vibration in his back pocket.

He grabbed his phone.

"Hello? Harper, is that you?"

"How long have you been talking to my daughter?" a male voice snapped.

"What? Who is this?"

"Greg. Your son."

"Well, hello, Greg, my son. How have you been?" Cooper sat down on a deck chair. "Thought I'd hear from you today."

"Are you behind this?" Greg growled.

"Behind what?"

"Her plan to go to Alaska! To ruin my career!"

"Greg, let's all calm down and start over." Snowball chased last winter's leaves swirling around the yard. "Harper called me yesterday. That was the first time I've heard her voice in ten years. She told me she'd run away and that her life had crashed and burned. She asked to come visit me. I told her sure, but she needed to talk to you and Natalie first. Then she called me this morning and asked about flying here tomorrow."

"You should've called me yesterday! We worried all night about her."

"I thought about it, but I didn't know where she was. And to tell the truth, I wasn't looking forward to being yelled at." He wiped his brow with his sleeve. "I'm sorry, Greg. I should've called."

"Do you know where she is now?"

"No idea. She called a few hours ago and said she'd fly up here tonight. Has she talked to you?"

Cooper heard Greg's phone ding.

"Damn it!" yelled Greg. "Natalie, use my computer and find a flight to Fairbanks."

Cooper heard scuffling in the background.

"What's going on, Greg?" asked Cooper.

"She's sending us revealing pictures of herself and claiming that I took them while she slept in her bed. She's going to send them to my board members, which include Natalie's parents, unless we buy a plane ticket for tonight."

Oh, no. And now I'm a part of this. "I had no idea that was her plan, Greg. I know this is tearing you and Natalie to pieces."

"I think you suggested this to her. You gave her the idea! You know all about being accused of inappropriate behavior!"

Cooper wiped his neck and took a breath. "I do, which is why I wouldn't have suggested anything like this to Harper. I know how destructive it is. She's being horribly cruel to both of you. If you try to defend yourself, you'll just dig a deeper hole. She must be desperate and angry. If she'd asked you to send her up here, would you have considered it?"

"Not a chance!"

"Then that's why she's doing this. She could see no alternative. I don't see any options for you. Send her up, Greg. I think I can help her."

"She's a thief, a liar, using drugs, screwing who knows who, and smart as hell when she wants to be! You think you can handle that better than we can?"

"She's not giving you another chance to try. I'm sure you've tried your best with her, but kids have their own minds and decide to do things for their own reasons. Your sister sure did."

Greg exploded, "Harper's not going to be like her!" After a long pause, he spoke more quietly, "Dad, I never thought I'd be in this position with my own daughter."

Cooper heard "Dad," and his eyes brimmed. He never thought he'd speak to his son again, much less be called Dad.

Cooper tried to soothe him. He knew how his son felt. "I know, Greg, and I'm so sorry this is happening to you. I don't have quick answers about what to do with her, but maybe a change of scenery and getting out of that rat-race of a city will help. Please send her up here."

"For how long?" Greg sounded defeated.

"As long as it takes. She told me this morning she wants to stay up here. I'm sure that will change, but she can't think of another option. Can you?"

Greg lashed out. "You still smoking dope with your students?"

Cooper sighed and counted to three. He'd almost lashed back at Greg. Why was everyone's first instinct to cause pain in others when they felt pain?

"I never did that, Greg, and I think you know it."

"Well, that was the rumor."

"I'm sure it was. Just like rumors kids are spreading about you and Harper. I taught for fourteen years in four schools up here, received great evaluations, and never had any problems with staff or kids. I retired two years ago in case you're interested."

"What if she spreads rumors about you?"

"Let her. If she's not happy here, she can leave anytime. She's in trouble and she's scared. She's in pain. I'm not going to be her parent. I'm going to be her friend and help her find something to live for."

"And let her do anything she wants. Great!"

"Please, Greg. I know you're angry with her and with me. The same reason you and I can't talk to each other without getting into a fight is the same reason she can't live with you right now. I've done nothing to be a grandparent to her. Let me try now."

Cooper heard Natalie in the background. "There's space on a flight leaving tonight at 7:05. It arrives in Fairbanks at 2:11 am."

"2:11 am?" Greg asked Cooper. "Is that OK?"

"Sure. Most flights get here late at night or early in the morning." But Cooper did feel a flutter of worry. Driving to the airport at two and then driving back wasn't an issue two months ago. But now, he didn't have the confidence he could drive there and back without running off the road. He thought maybe he should say something about his condition but stifled the thought. He needed Harper, maybe more than she needed him. He had to take this chance.

"The ticket costs $850," said Natalie.

"My God! Book the flight," said Greg. "Then send Harper the confirmation number."

"Thanks, Greg," said Cooper.

But he still had doubts. How fair was it to Harper to stick her with a forgetful old man? No, more than that. A demented old man. About as fair as him having to help a wild, drugged up teen. He chuckled. Maybe they could argue about who got the worst hand. Or maybe it was the best hand for either of them. It all depended on how it was played.

"I know you think everything happens for a reason," said Cooper, "that God is in control. I think things just happen, and our responses define the reason. Harper made a plan that seems cruel and heartless, but maybe it'll be the best plan she ever made or lead to the best. No one tries to make a bad plan. We think they're the best thing for us at the time."

"What's your plan?" asked Greg.

"Used to be to write three more novels and twenty more songs before I died. Now my plan is helping Harper."

"You write novels?" Greg muttered in disbelief.

"Sure do."

"What will you do with her?"

"Hopefully have some fun. I have flowers to plant and a garden to tend to. And she'll love my pets. I want to take her hiking and camping and fishing. See if she wants to learn music. Maybe sing again. Mainly, I want her excited about something in life besides drugs and sex."

"What about school? She'll miss her finals, and she's failing."

"So what? She'll die unless something changes. School and grades mean nothing compared to that. She can always get a GED."

"Natalie?" asked Greg.

"Yes," said Natalie.

"All right. She's yours for the time being."

"Thanks, Greg."

"We'll want to stay in touch, talk to you and talk to her if she allows it. Now that she's in charge. You know she's manipulating all of us, don't you?"

"She sure is. And doing a hell of a job. She just needs to direct that intelligence and determination in another direction. I'll try my best with her."

"We wish you luck. And, Dad, thanks."

"You're welcome, son. Means a lot to me." And for the first time in many years, he actually felt like a dad, someone who could come through in the clutch.

"Natalie will send you the itinerary."

"OK. I'll text you sometime tomorrow to let you know she's arrived." He ended the call and stood up, feeling hopeful and excited. He clapped his hands at Snowball, who ran up to him, beating Cooper's leg with his long tail. "You're going to have someone new to play with, Sonny Boy. Hope she likes you."

Snowball cocked his head. Cooper then realized he'd just called Snowball by his previous dog's name. He sat down on the deck.

"Sorry, Snowball."

• • • • •

Greg had just talked to his father for the first time in ten years. During those years Greg had blamed him for Heather's death and his own failures with his kids. He thought his dad's bad influence and even his bad genes had prevented him from being a better parent, one that Natalie's father would be proud of. Now he was entrusting the fate of his daughter to his father. How could he straighten her out? Greg had no idea.

At least with her in Alaska there was less chance she could destroy their home. And what would he do with her if she had stayed? Lock her up? Yell at her even more? His Dad had come out of nowhere, eager to offer his help. Maybe he wanted to have a family again. Maybe something good could come of this.

His father wrote books? And songs? *What the hell?*

"Did you send something to Harper?" Greg asked Natalie.

"Just did."

Their phones dinged.

Thanks, guys, texted Harper. *Guess I won't send you the next photo. Was the best one. Very revealing. I'll save it in case you show up at the airport.*

I'll park the car on the bottom level of the garage, as close to rows G or H as I can and leave the parking ticket on the floor. You have another key. Pick it up tomorrow. If I see either of you at the airport, I'll send all the photos.

I knew you'd choose your job over me, Daddy.

Greg gritted his teeth and shoved his phone into his pocket. *Could they ever just talk to each other?*

Natalie stood, crying. "She's going tonight? We can't even say good-bye?"

"Guess not." He pulled Natalie into his chest.

"Greg, she can send those photos any time. Tomorrow. A week from now. Anytime."

"I know."

She pushed back, looking up to his face. "Is this ever going to end?"

Greg stared out the window. "Up to her and Dad now." He felt Natalie's chest heaving against his. "We'll get through this." He patted her back. *Would they?* His shoulders slumped.

Someone banged repeatedly on the door. "Mr. Lyons? Are you all right?"

Natalie broke away and tried to straighten her hair while Greg fixed his tie.

"What will we tell everyone?" asked Natalie.

"We'll tell everyone that my grandfather fell at home and my mother was worried, but everything is fine now."

"What will we tell Alex and Jack?"

"That Harper is visiting her grandpa. What else?"

Greg opened the door and faced several very concerned faces. He and Natalie smiled.

Chapter Twelve

Harper checked the confirmation number and found her reservation. So, it was done. And well before noon. Something to be proud of? Not really. Part of her felt like a bitch for being so mean and manipulative, but another part felt angry that her parents had forced her to go this route. Last year she had tried to talk to her father about the beer incident on the volleyball trip. She was honest with him, even narced on one of her friends. Yet the result was the same as if she'd lied. She could've claimed one girl put the beer in her bag without her knowledge, but she had told the truth. She knew it was there but didn't want to rat on her friends. And where did that get her?

But there was also the issue of the strip video.

For away games, the visiting teams stayed in classrooms of the school they were playing. This was a tournament weekend, so several teams played, including boys. Guys and girls texted each other throughout the night even though all devices were supposed to be turned off at eleven. Some cute guys from another team asked the girls for nude photos.

Marcy and Fran, who'd brought the beer, texted back: *Sure!*

"What about you, Harper?" teased Marcy. "You game?"

"I don't think Headmaster's daughters do that," said Fran to Marcy.

Having her dad as Headmaster sucked. She was treated differently because of him. "This daughter does," said Harper, "but not for those guys. I have higher standards."

Marcy laughed. "Oh, really? What if they looked like him?" She showed Harper a picture of Nick Robinson. "Or him?" Then one of Shawn Mendes. Both girls growled.

Dorks, Harper thought. She personally loved Chris Hemsworth's body, but she played along. "Then I'd send them a strip video."

"Let's go!" giggled Fran.

They went to the bathroom where Harper took teasing photos of the girls, cropped later to hide the most significant parts. During the shoot, they'd been playing music. Harper and the girls started dancing, which turned into a competition. Finally, Marcy conceded. "Girl, you got some moves. Did I tell you I have Nick Robinson's Snapchat?"

"No, you didn't," laughed Harper.

Fran turned up the volume.

"Time to strip!" shouted Marcy. "Or are you all talk and no action?"

Harper hesitated.

"Like I thought," scoffed Fran. "Headmaster's daughters don't do anything bad."

She'd never live it down if she didn't strip, so she raised her arms above her head and wiggled her hips to the beat.

"Go, girl!"

The girls whooped and hollered, egging her on. They shot the dance with both their phones. Later, they had fun editing the video, blurring some areas, but the result was very provocative.

Marcy and Fran sent their photos to the boys. The edited video was completed on Harper's phone where it stayed. Later that night, the coach caught Marcy and Fran using their phones and drinking beer. When she checked their phones, she saw the photos sent to the boys and the videos of Harper. She took everything to Greg when they returned from the tournament. During the expulsion meetings with parents, Greg never mentioned the photos or the video. He must've never told Natalie, because she never said anything to Harper. But he did bring it up with Harper privately in his office after school.

"You plan to be a stripper?" Greg yelled.

She gasped. *Did he watch?* "We were having fun in the bathroom, Dad. What was the harm? None of us sent a video. I edited what they shot and hid all the bad stuff."

"What did you plan to do with it?" Greg snarled.

She felt like someone had punched her sternum. "Keep it. Show it to my girlfriends. I have no intention of showing it to guys."

"Really? Just like you didn't intend to open your robe in front of Luke when you were twelve!"

How did he know? "I didn't open it!"

"You are a slutty, beer-drinking, boy-chasing liar!"

Harper covered her head with her arms and pulled herself into a ball.

"And a wannabe stripper! I've never been more ashamed of anyone in my life!"

Harper fought to keep the tears from pooling in her eyes. "I didn't drink beer. I didn't send nude photos. I'm not guilty of anything except being your daughter! You have no idea how hard that is at your school!" She begged him to understand her perspective.

"You participated. You helped those girls break the rules. You had a bottle in your pack. Even if I wanted to, I couldn't let you stay at the Academy. I have to follow the rules."

"Even if you wanted to?" she huffed. What did he take her for? "You never wanted me at your precious school. I'm just an embarrassment to you."

He met her gaze levelly. "Yes, you are."

Pain wrapped around her chest like a vise, making it hard to breathe. Harper fought the pain and turned it into anger. She hated him. War had been declared. She wanted to hurt him back. "How much did you watch?"

Greg's eyes opened wide. "None of it. Your coach told me about them."

She noticed the fear and was thrilled. She pounced. "How much, Daddy? And what about the nudes of the girls? Must have been fun for you." She walked towards him, and by God, he moved away from her. She had power over him. "There's a reason you didn't want to talk about this part of the incident at the hearing. Why?"

Harper had found a way to get back at her father. She'd never let him hurt her again.

Now as she sat in the McDonalds, she looked around at the other customers: young families, a few teens, a couple of older men. She knew they'd call her a thug or an evil extortionist if they knew how she'd manipulated her parents. She knew she'd been cruel, not just to them, but to those who'd really been abused by their fathers. It was still too easy to dismiss a female's assault claims, and her lies had made it easier. Would her father believe one of her friends if they claimed to have been bullied, or worse? Probably not.

But she'd found the only way to escape without running away and putting herself in danger. What else was she supposed to do? Hang out at truck stops until she found a nice guy to drive her? Or an asshole who wanted something in return, most likely. At least now that she'd be staying with Cooper, her parents wouldn't have to worry about her being attacked or killed in a strange place.

After finishing her ice cream, she left the restaurant, stomped on a roach before it reached the ivy by the sidewalk, entered her car, and counted her cash. Only eighty dollars remained. Her nausea had calmed, so the pills must have worked. She decided to grab something to eat closer to the airport, then check in early. The sooner she was through security, the better, and once at the gate, her parents couldn't do anything to stop her trip.

She found a Starbucks not far from the airport entrance to use the internet and kill time. She sipped on a Frappuccino and nibbled on a sandwich as she listened to more of Cooper's songs, finding herself humming his tunes and mouthing his lyrics. Each song had a strong beat, often syncopated. Even slow melodies had a fast background. A couple were raunchy blues, but many of the lyrics were beautiful poetry. Several were love songs. He even had two duets.

One song—"The Girl You Used to Be"— was so sad, full of heartache about a teen leaving home, getting into trouble, and wishing she could be a little girl again. Was it about Heather, the aunt she never knew? It could soon be about her. She wondered whether Heather was ever pregnant. Maybe Cooper could write another song about a young girl finding her way to a better life. That was the plan—make a good life for herself with her Grandpa in Alaska. What was the alternative?

She felt queasy, but thought she could keep her food down and decided to leave. A wet wall of heat slammed into her as soon as she opened the door to walk to the car. The asphalt burned through her sandals. Sweat erupted from her face and chest, and her bare legs stuck to the seat when she climbed into her car. She felt faint as the AC blew hot air onto her face for the first few seconds. Finally, the air turned cold, and she could breathe again. She wouldn't miss the heat or the humidity or the roaches.

She drove toward the airport through heavy traffic. The parking garage was stifling, but she was lucky to find an empty spot near the ramp to the terminal. Once inside, she felt cool and perused the map to find Alaska Airlines.

After checking her bag, she entered the long line through security. Her nervousness increased with every step she took forward. She chewed her gum faster, and worried that she'd draw more attention to herself. Finally, she approached the counter.

"Going to Alaska?" said the TSA agent checking her boarding pass.

"Yup! Going to see my grandpa. He writes songs and books and has a dog and a cat!" Harper grinned so wide it made her cheeks ache. She'd act as girly as possible, smacking gum. Maybe blow a bubble or two. Why would anyone suspect such a hyped-up happy girl would be carrying drugs?

The agent nodded and returned her pass.

Harper bubbled as she tossed her belongings into the trays and pushed them over the rollers. Her hands shook so much she thought everyone would notice. The agent waved her into the scanner, looking her up and down. Was he checking her out, or did he suspect something? Her mouth went dry. She lifted her arms and spread her legs and thought she felt slippage in her pants. She closed her legs.

"Not yet," said the agent sternly. "Put your feet on the yellow shoes."

Oh no! Did he sound angry? Harper spread her legs again and waited for what seemed like an hour, her heart pounding in her chest.

"OK," said the agent.

She bounded out, and the agent held out her hand while she checked the screen.

"Do you have something in your back pocket?" she asked.

Harper paled instantly. Did the condom slip down? Would they frisk her? She reached toward her pockets and found her second phone. She pulled it out and showed it to the agent.

"Oops! Sorry. I'm so sorry! I forgot I had two phones!" She tried to look as cute as she could and smile.

The agent was not amused and waved her to the side while her phone went through the scanner. She apologized a few more times as she gathered her things, then walked toward her gate. Finding a bathroom nearby, she ducked into a stall and collapsed onto the toilet seat, breathing heavily. She took some toilet paper and blotted the sweat on her forehead, making the paper break apart. After a couple of minutes, she stood and removed the condom, dumping the balloons into her pack. She'd done it! At least this half. Maybe the crates would arrive soon with no problems. Until then, the worry would continue to gnaw at her. How could anyone be a drug mule for a living?

After finding a seat near the gate, she looked back at the concourse, searching faces. She knew she had threatened her parents about coming to the airport, but she thought they might try to do something.

The gate attendant called her row for boarding. She stood, got in line, then handed her boarding pass to the lady. Just before she walked into the jetway, she looked back one more time.

Nobody had come. There was no last-minute attempt to take her home.

Some tiny part of her hidden behind the calloused façade wanted desperately for her parents to have tried something—rash, foolish—but prove they cared. That same part had wanted her father to pull her off the windowsill, grab the knife, and just hold her days ago. Just once she wanted him to love her more than himself—more than his job, the hurt pride, and accusations and shame.

But they didn't, and Harper couldn't help but believe their love wasn't strong enough. She knew she would've grabbed Alex in a similar situation and fought off everyone. Harper would've died trying.

But they didn't.

Chapter Thirteen

"Where did you send her?" screamed Alex from the top of the stairs.

Natalie and Greg hadn't mentioned Harper to the kids on their way home, so they couldn't understand how Alex knew. They both walked upstairs and found the lipstick messages on the mirrors. *She had to get in one last shot*, thought Greg. He didn't want to see those notes from her every day. And it didn't escape him that she hadn't left such sentiments on his or Natalie's mirror. She certainly didn't love them.

"Natalie, get a towel, please," said Greg as he went to Jack and tried to calm him down. Natalie brought a towel from the bathroom and wiped off Jack's mirror.

"No!" Jack yelled.

Greg picked him up. "It's got to come off at some point, Jack. You don't want lipstick on your mirror forever, do you?"

They all walked into Alex's room. Alex looked at the smeared towel in Natalie's hand and screamed again. "No! You can't erase it!" She jumped onto the dresser. "That stays until she comes back. Where is she?" Alex held out her arms and stood in front of the mirror like a sentry.

"Alex," said Natalie, "you need to calm down and move away from the dresser."

"No! Where is she?"

"Do what your mother says, Alex!" barked Greg.

"She went to visit your grandfather in Alaska," said Natalie.

Alex glowered at him. "Why? Did you force her to go?"

"This was her choice. We wanted her to stay," answered Natalie. "Please, get down before you fall."

"They erased mine!" cried Jack.

"You erased his?" Alex shouted. "How could you?"

"Get down from there!" yelled Greg, as he grabbed for her arm.

Alex yanked it away. "You touch me and I'll tell everyone in school that you beat me, and that you erased the last message from my sister." Alex glared at her parents with the same anger and hatred they'd seen on Harper's face a month ago. Greg couldn't believe how much of Harper he already saw in her.

"I want to go to Alaska, too."

Maybe I should send all of my kids to Alaska, thought Greg. Both Alex and Jack would tell their friends tomorrow about Harper, and he wouldn't be able to control what Alex said. He would talk to them at dinner, try to make this sound like a plan between their Grandpa and him to help Harper, but Alex knew that Harper ran away. Who knows what Harper had told her during the past several months? Somehow everything would get out and eventually to Natalie's parents.

John wasn't happy last fall when Harper was expelled. Her wildness reflected poorly on Greg's parenting, and therefore his leadership of the school. It also affected John's reputation. His granddaughter had been expelled from the school he founded! And he knew about the photos and the video. He'd talked to the coach about the incident, making sure Greg was acting in the school's best interest. John agreed that the beer should be the focus of the expulsion—the school didn't need more embarrassment about its students' behavior—but he couldn't believe that Harper was such a hellcat.

"Have you seen these videos?" John had asked, glaring at Greg as he held the girls' phones.

As if he would want to see his daughter acting provocatively. He'd unfortunately caught some of her antics at home and was scarred enough from that. "No. I trusted Coach Henley's assessment and didn't feel the need to."

"You should!" he shouted. "My sixteen-year-old granddaughter is an accomplished stripper. She could get a job at The Palace tonight!" John looked at Greg and slowly shook his head. "The men would tip her 50s and 100s! You've done a great job raising her!"

Evidently not, thought Greg.

"You need to control that girl. Just because she's out of our school doesn't mean she won't affect your reputation and your ability to lead our students."

He was sure John was going to fire him. Greg knew the chances of losing his job were increasing, and he couldn't shake the nagging thought that it might be best if he did.

He remembered the warning his mom had given him about taking the job: "Don't work for John and force your kids to attend a school you lead."

But he had ignored her. The raise in salary had been too tempting.

As he thought about past events, he realized that so many problems with his kids started when he became Headmaster. It was difficult being both a father and the head of their school. He acted too much like a boss to them and wondered if that had become the cause for their rebellion. Compounding the past four years was the edict John had given him: be strict, no exceptions. This from the guy who would've disowned his only daughter if she hadn't memorized the Bible verses on obedience and punishment he'd marked.

The axe was going to fall. The question was when?

• • • • •

The air-conditioning in the jetway couldn't thwart the heat. Perspiration hid the tears on Harper's cheeks as she shuffled through in the middle of a long line of passengers. She wondered whether she would ever see her parents or home or siblings again. Her phone rang. She glanced at the ID, her heart deflating a bit at not seeing the words Mom or Dad on the screen. Even if they wouldn't call, she'd hoped maybe Alex would've stolen one of their phones to call her. Didn't anyone miss her?

"Cooper?" she greeted, willing her voice to be steady.

"Hey, Harper! What do you like to eat and drink? I'm at a store in Healy. Thought I'd pick up some things you like."

The thoughtful gesture eased some of the tightness in her throat. "I could use a beer right now. It's really hot."

"Where are you?" asked Cooper.

"Trying to get on the plane where I hope the AC works." Her voice lowered. "Cooper, you don't have to get me anything special."

"You're my guest. You can have anything you want."

Harper decided to test him. "OK. Corona Light, Diet Coke, sweet iced tea, jerky, turkey lunchmeat. Got that?"

"Almost. Dropped my pen. OK. Turkey lunchmeat. Got it."

The line moved more quickly for a moment then stopped.

"And the beer?" Right then, Harper could think of nothing better than drinking a beer with her grandfather, out on the porch while watching his garden grow.

"Whatever you want, Harper. I also have some good Alaskan beer. What else?"

She couldn't believe he was being so cool about this. How did this man raise her father? Or was he testing her right back? Baffled, she said, "Tostitos, guacamole dip, pretzels."

"And for breakfast?"

"I don't usually eat breakfast."

She entered the plane and walked down the aisle.

"I make great breakfasts. All kinds of tacos, French toast, omelets. You need to try my *huevos rancheros*."

She laughed. "I thought you missed Mexican food."

"I do! I can't make it as good as Texas, but mine's still pretty good. I'd go crazy without a fajita every once in a while."

Me, too. Harper smiled at something they had in common and slid into her seat, a middle in the 30th row.

"All of that sounds great for breakfast," said Harper. "Oh, get me Golden Grahams, please."

"OK. Anything you don't eat?"

"I don't like sushi or oysters."

"Neither do I. By the way, what are you wearing?"

The question was innocently asked, but for a second, Harper's mind flashed back to the scene with her father three weeks ago when she left with the cops. She wore similar clothes today, though her shirt was longer and tied at her waist.

She pushed the thoughts away. "Too much! It's hot as hell in this plane."

"Did you pack a jacket?"

"Yeah."

"Are you wearing shorts?"

"Yes."

"It's been in the high 40s, low 50s the last few nights. You got some jeans in your suitcase?"

"Yes, but I can't remember what feeling the cold is like! It'd be wonderful to shiver instead of sweat. Don't worry about me. I'd love to be cold for a change."

"OK, Harper, but don't say I didn't warn you. It's gonna feel different up here."

She closed her eyes and tried to imagine his house in the woods. "I hope so, Cooper. I really hope so." She remembered sitting in the front seat with this man while he drove to the airport when she was six. He'd made her laugh and feel so special, like she was the most important girl in the world. She'd loved him so much. And then...nothing. He disappeared. Why?

"Just a few more hours, Harper. Looking forward to seeing you. And I'm bringing Snowball and Houdini. They know something special is happening, and they've been crazy all day. If I left them here, they'd just tear up the place."

"Can't wait to see all of you. Thanks, Cooper."

Harper smiled, lifted her face toward the air vent, and closed her eyes. She was finally free, ready to start something new and fresh. Things were going to work out.

"Where you headed?" a sultry male voice said into her left ear, interrupting her peaceful moment.

Harper turned her head. A well-built young man in a tight nylon t-shirt sat next to her in the aisle seat. Harper would've thought he was hot a few days ago, but after Zachary, she felt no interest in guys at the moment, especially ones full of themselves and on the prowl.

He turned toward her. "Myself, I'm going back home for the summer. Olympia. Ever been there?"

Harper ignored him and turned her head toward the window.

"Haven't I seen you before?"

Harper told herself not to panic even as her heart skipped. She kept her eyes closed but moved her head back toward the vent.

"Does that line usually work for you?" she asked.

"Not a line. I'm a sophomore at Trinity University. I thought I saw you on campus. Name's Ted, by the way."

She didn't know him or recognize him at all. But it was possible this guy had seen her. Trinity was Zachary's school, and he'd walked her around campus a couple of times.

"I'm sure it wasn't me." She'd ignore him and deny anything he said, and maybe he'd leave her alone and disappear in Seattle.

She pulled out her laptop and earphones and listened to Cooper's songs as the plane readied to take off.

If Ted said anything else, she didn't hear it.

The woman to her right let out an obnoxious snort in her sleep, making Harper jump.

The flight attendant approached her, asking if she wanted a drink. Glancing sideways, she tried to sneak a look at Ted's face. He was playing a game on his phone.

Had she ever seen him before?

Harper ordered a Diet Coke. Ted held out his ID and asked for two Jack Daniel's.

Soon after the attendants pushed the drink cart farther down the aisle, Harper felt Ted nudge her arm. He palmed one of the bottles onto her tray.

"Yours if you want it," he said.

"I don't."

"Tell me if you change your mind. Couple of my friends thought they recognized you."

"How?" She glared at him. "You took a picture of me? When?"

"When you pretended to ignore me. Anyway, they said you were at a party on Sunday. Thought you might have been one of the strippers. Not the girl who won, but still." He laughed and poured his whiskey into his Coke.

Harper had to get away from this guy. She wouldn't be stuck beside him for the next three hours. "Couldn't have been me. I've never lost a stripping contest." Ted gaped at her; Harper cocked one eyebrow and smiled. "On second thought, I'd like that bottle." She held out her hand, and he palmed the bottle into hers, lingering a little.

Harper flipped down the window lady's tray and put her Diet Coke down. She flipped up her tray and grabbed her pack from under the seat.

"Excuse me, Ted. I need to use the restroom."

"Sure thing."

She walked to the back of the plane and found a flight attendant.

"The creep I'm sitting next to gave me one of his Jack Daniel's bottles." She held out the bottle. "I'm sixteen. Now he's harassing me. Can you move me to another seat?"

"Sure, wait here." The attendant took the bottle and strode down the aisle until she found an empty seat by the wing, then signaled Harper to walk over. When Harper passed Ted, he stood.

"Where are you going?" he asked.

"To my seat."

"Your seat's here."

"Not anymore," Harper said sweetly.

A few minutes later she stole a glance backward and saw two attendants talking to Ted at the back of the plane. She smiled to herself as another attendant came up to her. She ordered a fruit and cheese platter and took another nausea pill.

If Ted had friends at the party, would he know Zachary? What did it matter? She'd be in Alaska in a few hours. Zachary would find out she was gone before next Monday. Trish would ask questions, find out from someone where she went, or even ask her brother to ask Zachary. She guessed he'd know within two or three days. So what? Nothing to worry about. What could he do? Fly to Alaska to retrieve his smack? She doubted he would. The ticket would cost more than the drugs were worth.

Speaking of which, she could use a hit.

She counted the days since the party. Two and a half. Not quite three, but she'd like to disappear into a cloud right now. She hoped living in Alaska away from creeps like Ted and Zachary would make her lose interest in smack, but for now she needed something to help her sleep.

She dropped her napkin and stole a look back as she picked it up. Ted was asleep, sprawled across her old seat. She grabbed her pack and cup and walked back to the restroom. Inside, she pulled out a balloon, the straw, and saline solution. After mixing the brew in the cup, she stared at it before inserting the straw.

Valerie's comment flashed into her mind: "That's very dangerous, Harper."

But she needed to sleep. After this one time, she wouldn't do it anymore.

She snorted the liquid into her nose. The wave would drown her a few minutes after she sat back down, and float her into Seattle.

Chapter Fourteen

Cooper unpacked his groceries and fed his pets. As they ate, he looked around his house. The light poured in from the west side, highlighting the tangles of dust, hair, and spider webs hugging the screens on his windows. Globs of dust hung from the ceiling fan's blades, meaning the tops were covered by a mat of dirt. When had he turned into such a slob? Probably because he was desperate to finish his book before he couldn't. Cleaning things had slipped down his totem pole of priorities.

But Harper was coming, and she shouldn't live in a dustbin. He had several hours before he planned to leave his house at midnight to drive to Fairbanks.

Houdini jumped onto the table and sniffed at his soup. He scooted his feet under his belly and darted his long pink tongue into the bowl.

"You already had yours, kitty."

He raked his fingers down Houdini's back, causing the kitten to arch its fluffy tail over its back, which undulated against Cooper's hand. Houdini revved his purring motor into high gear, the loudest cat he had ever heard. Cooper stroked the kitten with one hand while he spooned in his soup with the other.

He fetched some rags, wet them, then rubbed down the fan blades. He wiped pollen off his red oak windowsills and trim and then his table, picking up the Scrabble pieces as he went. Did Harper like to play any games? He used to play by himself every night until he realized he was wasting time that he soon wouldn't have.

As he dropped the lid onto the game box, he remembered a phone call from Heather when he was still married to Rachel. She had wanted to come home for a visit.

"I sure would like to have a breakfast taco and one of Mom's coffeecakes."

"We're both really busy right now, Heather. I've got play rehearsals, and your mother has the History Day Competition coming up," he lied to her, and she probably knew it. In truth, they didn't want her stealing from them again.

"You can make time for Scrabble, can't you? No one I know will play with me. Maybe you can beat me for once." She laughed.

"I'd like to try, but maybe some other time. OK?"

"Sure, Pops. When I have another day off, I'll call you." She sounded hurt and disappointed, and even then he regretted saying no.

What if they had left town and gone camping like they used to do when she was much younger? They could've gone to the mountains where they could be away from everything. But this time let her drink with them, even smoke her pot without having to hide or be yelled at. Just accepted her and loved her and tried to have fun together.

Maybe their relationship could've transcended the yelling and blaming if they'd accepted her as she was. Cooper believed now that their daughter wanted love and friendship to the end, but they'd rejected her. Self-preservation, they'd told themselves. But Heather died, and much of Cooper and Rachel had died along with her, as well as their relationship.

He'd let too many stupid things interfere with showing his love for his daughter until she doubted it existed. And the most painful realization was that he and Rachel had stopped loving what she had become—an addict. After that ugly shell died, the immense love they had for their daughter, the one who'd always existed despite the shell, flooded back, drowning them. She was gone, and they could never show their love again.

When Harper arrived, if there was only an addict to love, then Cooper would love the addict. And try his best to help her, to say yes as much as he could, to encourage her. He never wanted his last word to anyone he loved to be "no" ever again.

But in the meantime, he had cleaning to do.

• • • • •

Harper wanted to get as far away as possible from Ted once they landed in Seattle. She hurried up the jetway, checked the flight board, and then ran down the steps to the subway connecting terminals. Barely slipping through the closing doors, she held a pole while the train took her to N terminal where she trotted to a bathroom and sat inside a stall for ten minutes. After taking her time washing her face, she walked outside and carefully looked for Ted. He should've gone to baggage claim, but she worried he might follow her as payback for her complaint about the bottle.

She found her gate and sat down to check for messages. Ariana had sent a selfie and texted, *Miss you!* Harper sent a selfie back and told her where she was, apologizing for not seeing her again before she left.

Harper texted Cooper. *Just arrived in Seattle. Will text before takeoff. Finally feel a little cold!*

She had an hour and a half before boarding. She wanted to walk around and maybe grab a coffee, but she was worried Ted might be lurking somewhere. *So stupid*, she thought. She could deal with him if she had to.

As she looked at planes moving outside the glass wall, she saw his reflection standing behind her.

"Harper Lyons," said Ted.

She leapt up and faced him. "You dick! Get out of here before I call security."

"Security?" He was amused by the threat. "Maybe security would like to check your pack. Call. I'll tell him you tried to sell me a balloon. One of *Zachary's* balloons. You're supposed to be selling for him, aren't you?"

Ted sneered, and she glared back, unblinkingly.

"Lot of the guys recognized your picture, even though you have so many more clothes on now. They sent me some of you dancing. Love the negligee. Especially the thigh-highs. Want to see them?" He held his phone up with a picture of her on the screen.

Harper wanted to run, but she wouldn't give him the satisfaction.

He smirked. "Word is you'll do anything for drugs and beer. You're just a piece of ass, Harper Lyons. Zachary's slut. You know, he got bored with you and gave you to Levi that night. Look at your clothes. Why would anyone think any differently? Yet you got offended when I offered you a drink." He took a piece of gum from his pocket, and stuck it in his mouth.

"That's actually pretty funny." He chewed open-mouthed, looking down his nose at her.

Just a piece of ass? she thought. What good was she? An idiot who allowed herself to be hooked by a college guy looking for sex, using drugs as bait. Just a piece of ass, a pregnant piece. And soon she wouldn't even be that. She was a nothing.

"Leave me alone!" She wouldn't let him see her cry.

"No problem. With all the guys you've been with, I don't want anything to do with you. I'm going." He took a few steps away, then stopped. "Oh. Zachary says you'd better make that appointment on Monday."

That a-hole! She had to strike back. "I'm not even pregnant," Harper scoffed, hoping she could keep from crying a little longer. She didn't want Ted walking away, thinking he got the best of her. "It was just a lie to get freebies for my trip. He was so easy to fool." She smiled, hoping her lie would piss Zachary off.

"Freebies? Nothing's free. How many times did he screw you? And for what? A few balloons? Pretty cheap, if you ask me. You're just a whore, girl. Nothin' but a whore." He walked away, then stopped. "I'll give him the good news about not being a daddy." Ted strutted into the crowd.

She watched until he disappeared, then collapsed into a seat, her arms clasped above her head.

After crying and wiping her face, she looked around the terminal and saw hundreds of people moving onto planes, reading papers and thumbing phones, watching CNN on the monitors—all of them with more meaningful lives than hers. People with jobs, students who didn't fail in school, athletes with matching clothes, and families who actually cared for each other. She tried to find another teenage girl sitting by herself. Was there anyone else as stupid and alone as she was?

Her eyes drifted around the concourse, then to a man in his twenties wearing a Seattle University t-shirt, drinking a coffee, staring at her. He smiled. She looked away, hoping he'd move elsewhere. After a minute, she glanced back in his direction and saw his Birkenstocks next to her pack.

"Can I get you something? Maybe a coffee?" he asked.

"No, thanks." She stood up, ready to strike.

His eyes moved slowly down her body as he stood directly in front of her. His hair was spiked up, and he wore a silver loop in his left ear. Harper could tell by his cocky grin that he thought he was a babe magnet. "You flying to Alaska like that? Who's the lucky guy?"

Harper yanked her shirt down to her waist and held her pack in front of her shorts, to hide her legs. "My grandfather, you asshole."

She swung her arm to the right as she darted to the left, causing him to stumble, and kept walking away from the gate toward the stores and restaurants. After a few minutes, she found a place selling Seattle sweatpants and bought a pair. Nothing matched in her outfit, but she didn't care. Maybe if she covered up, guys would leave her alone for the next few hours.

She walked back to her gate and found a row of seats in front of the windows. Harper opened her computer and found one of Cooper's songs she had listened to earlier—"I Will Not Bleed."

The message was defiance:

You knocked me down,
but I'm not out, baby.
I'm off the ground and on my feet.

She listened several times and tried to imagine herself punching out those sentiments. With her eyes closed, she could see herself on a stage holding a microphone in the spotlight.

The one thing I will remember
is love is never free.
The next time I love
I will not bleed.
I will not bleed.

In her mind she belted out that song and could feel her head vibrate.

The song ended. She saw herself bowing and smiling as the crowd screamed. The applause seemed so real. She opened her eyes and saw a family sitting in the next row clapping their hands.

"That was great!" said the woman.

Harper was perplexed. "What was?"

"Your singing," said the man. "What a voice! Are you a singer?"

Harper saw others smiling at her, nodding their heads. She must have sung out loud. "Not really."

"Well, you should be. What song was that?" asked the woman.

The gate attendant called Harper's section to board.

"Something my grandfather wrote," said Harper as she stood.

"It's very good."

"I'll tell him you said so. I'm going to meet him in Fairbanks."

They nodded at her as she backed away. *Wow! They liked my singing.*

The line moved past the counter and into the jetway. Harper remembered putting on shows when she was little, using the toy karaoke machine, a Christmas gift from her parents. She remembered everyone on one level of a tour boat clapping for her, actually standing and cheering. She wondered when she had stopped singing and why.

Harper took her seat on the plane. A mother across the aisle fed her baby under a blanket. Two kids behind her kicked the back of her seat. A grandfather stood in his aisle holding a restless baby, humming in her tiny ear, while a young woman (maybe the mother?) removed a bag from the overhead bin. The older man let the woman slip back into his aisle. The grandfather held up the baby in front of him and made funny faces. Then he blew raspberries on the baby's neck until the baby giggled. Soon, she squealed as he lifted her high.

Harper almost squealed along with her and wondered if Cooper had ever done the same with her.

Chapter Fifteen

Cooper had cleaned every drawer in the downstairs bedroom, wiped down the blinds, and washed the sheets after discovering vole droppings under the pillows. *Must have happened before I got Houdini*, he thought. No vole was safe in the house now.

He made a sandwich and packed drinks and snacks into a small ice chest in case she was hungry or thirsty after her flight. One of his old jackets and pair of sweats hung by the door, in case she got cold.

He looked around his house, trying to find anything amiss. Harper was surely used to better surroundings without drywall tape sagging from the ceiling or creaky, slanted floors. Maybe Harper had already realized that the shell was less important than the warmth of the core inside. He hoped so.

Snowball lay by the door, ensuring that Cooper wouldn't leave without him.

Nearby, Houdini gorged on his tuna and salmon dinner, his sixth meal of the day.

Snowball seemed to be pouting.

"You can't understand why he gets six meals while you only get three, can you, boy?" Cooper teased.

Cooper poured coffee into one of his thermal cups, grabbed the food and clothes, and started the truck. Snowball ran to the passenger door and waited to jump in. Houdini purred in Cooper's arms as he carried him outside and placed him in his lap. Snowball always rode shotgun.

The trip to town usually took eighty minutes. At this time of day, however, and it was still very much day at this time of year, he could cut that time by five or ten. The sun would set in thirty minutes, but no one would notice any absence of light, just a deeper saturation of colors while the sun scooted just below the horizon a few degrees, before popping up again in two and a half hours. Cooper always wore his sunglasses outside during the summer.

During the drive he sipped his coffee, noticing that his cup was a souvenir from the Kenai Fjords tour he took with Greg's family. He'd bought it for Harper because she could get free refills of hot chocolate. They'd figured out she had to drink at least six hot chocolates to cover the cost of the cup. She'd drunk nine before they returned to the dock.

Cooper had met Greg, Natalie, and kids in Anchorage ten years ago and driven them to Seward where they spent a week fishing, hiking, watching whales and sea lions, and photographing glaciers. The trip had gone well for the most part; no one mentioned the divorce or the scandal in Texas.

Then the boat trip on the last day changed everything.

Chris and Harper wanted to sit outside on the bow, while Greg and Natalie wanted to stay inside out of the wind. Cooper volunteered to watch them. The boat was large with three decks and lots of stairs. Most of the inside seating consisted of long booths with tables in between. The kids found everywhere to go in the first thirty minutes, then visited them all at least twenty more times during the trip.

Cooper had a blast chasing them down and enjoying their excitement. He put them on his shoulders to help them see the wildlife, when the crowds were thick along the rails. They loved seeing a humpback breach and puffins skimming the waves. They even got to hold a piece of glacial ice.

During one long stretch of the trip when many tourists on the lower deck slept, the kids wanted another hot chocolate, so Cooper took them to the galley.

"Why is everybody sleeping?" asked Harper, sipping her cup.

"They're tired," said Cooper. "It's been a long day."

"They're missing everything! I'll wake them up!"

She put down her drink, climbed onto a table, stomped her foot, and yelled, "Wake up, everybody!" She started singing a very loud, fast version of *You Are My Sunshine* punctuated by dance moves. For a six-year-old kid, her voice was clear and bright. Her smile was infectious, and before the end, many sang the chorus with her.

Chris groaned and disappeared around the corner.

Harper hit her last note and did a curtsey on the table while many stood and clapped.

Cooper whistled and yelled, "Encore! Encore!"

Harper beamed at the crowd.

"What's going on?" asked Greg, surprising them from behind. Natalie and Chris followed. "You were supposed to get your drinks and come right back."

"She wanted to wake them up, so she sang to them!" said Cooper, proudly. "You should have heard her. She was amazing!"

Greg grabbed Harper, put her onto the floor with a thud, and held her hand while he pulled her away.

Someone said, "What's wrong with him?"

The rest of the family followed him to their seats upstairs.

"Harper, you can't jump up on tables!" said Greg. "People eat food there. Do you understand?"

Her face turned red, and she looked at the floor.

"You allowed her to stand on a table?" asked Natalie, shooting Cooper a dubious look.

Cooper chuckled. "She's pretty quick."

"It's not funny, Dad."

"Oh, what's the harm? They loved her!" said Cooper. "She's got a hell of a voice for a six-year-old. She's a natural singer. Harper's got amazing spirit. She wasn't afraid at all. Just stood up there and belted it out. God, I wish I had recorded it."

"She jumped onto a table where people were sitting, sleeping even, and you allowed her to sing a song? Did you even try to stop her?" asked Greg.

Natalie knelt, held Harper's shoulders, and looked her in the eyes. "Do not jump on tables. Do you understand?"

"Yes, Mommy."

She'd been so happy a few minutes ago, and now she wouldn't drag her eyes from the floor. Cooper ached for her.

"And ask permission before you start singing in public," Natalie added.

"OK," said Harper. "Can we go outside now?"

"No," said Greg. "You both sit down. You've run around enough for the day."

"Grandpa was with us," said Harper, grabbing Cooper's hand.

Greg looked at his father. "Stay in your seats." Greg jerked his head to signal he wanted to speak to Cooper outside. "Natalie, stay with the kids, please."

Both men walked outside to the rail. Greg stood straight, his back to the wind, facing his father.

"We're trying to raise our kids with some discipline," Greg reprimanded, slowly, like he was talking to a child. "I know you don't agree with that approach. This whole trip you have allowed the kids to do anything they've wanted."

Cooper rested his foot on a cleat and leaned on the rail with his elbows, looking out to sea. "They're kids, Greg. They're on vacation." He tried to take deep breaths while he hoped a whale would breach to disrupt this conversation. He knew where this was headed.

Greg folded his arms across his chest and glared at Cooper. "Please don't patronize me. I know exactly what you were doing. You know we have rules in our house, and yet you disregard them. Then, they come back to us and complain about following the rules they're used to. You should respect how we raise our children. We don't want wild kids."

Cooper turned to face Greg. "And I'll make them wild?"

Cooper knew what was coming. An overwhelming sadness began to grow inside him like a cramp in his gut, but he also felt anger. Greg blamed him for Heather's death while never acknowledging any personal responsibility with her drug use. His son had given Heather her first drugs! He fought to keep both feelings in-check while he started to walk away. He should just walk away.

"Yes, you will!" shouted Greg, following his father. "You've done it before, with me and Heather. You can't help yourself because you have no self-restraint." He stopped Cooper and put his face in front of his. "It's why you're by yourself in Alaska." Greg turned toward the bow and moved into the wind a few steps.

"You turned out all right!" Cooper shouted from behind him.

Greg turned around. "Not because of you."

"OK, in spite of me, you turned out all right." Cooper moved toward his son. "Why is that? Because you made your own choices. I don't think parents can make choices for their kids. Parents are supposed to give their kids confidence and knowledge enough to make their own choices. You found God and Natalie! Those were your choices, and they seem to have been good ones for you!"

Greg moved toward his father. "You haven't the slightest idea what 'finding God' means. You disdain the whole idea of God."

Cooper shook his head. Their old nemesis—religion. "No, I don't. I respect those who can believe. I'm glad you find comfort in your belief. I tried, but my head wouldn't let me."

Sneering, Greg folded his arms and shook his head at his father. "You've said many times that 'anyone with a brain can't believe that bullshit.' You raised me on that."

"Well, I was wrong. You're smart as hell, and you believe. That's great for you. I don't criticize you for going to church."

"Then let me raise my kids my way. Don't interfere!" Greg moved to the rail on the other side.

Cooper followed slowly, trying to find the right words to stop this. "I've had fun with my grandkids who I haven't seen in six years. I think they've had fun with me. Find a person downstairs who didn't enjoy the hell out of Harper's performance."

Greg began to walk back toward the door near his family, but Cooper grabbed his arm. "She has confidence and spirit, Greg. Don't quash them!"

"So did Heather!" He jerked his arm free. "She always wanted to be in the spotlight. She was always looking for fun. Parents are supposed to set limits." Greg walked to the door.

Cooper followed. "And because I didn't, Heather died. Is that it? Exposure to me will cause your kids to be like Heather, your sister, who you knew was sneaking out of the house for years, who you knew was meeting guys and smoking pot, and yet you did nothing about it, including telling me. You did it with her! You have a lot of unresolved guilt yourself. So go ahead and blame your father instead, because he's an easy target!"

Greg's face reddened and cords bulged in his neck. "You raised us. I didn't!"

"Along with your mother!"

"Who divorced you for cheating on her! And smoking weed with your students!"

"I did not smoke with students!" That old claim still haunted him, still churned his guts when he heard it.

"The cops said the theatre reeked of pot during your rehearsal!"

"Kids were smoking outside, and the wind blew it in when they opened the doors."

Greg shook his head and laughed. "Do you know how stupid that sounds? You're a joke. You had to run all the way to Alaska to find a job in a stinking village because no one else would hire you. You had to haul your own crap in a bucket to a lagoon every day."

"As did everyone else in the village, which has kids that need some education. A lot of good people work in those villages. They're not jokes. They were happy to have me."

"I'm sure they were. Those places are full of sex offenders, drug addicts, alcoholics, and old men running from something or somebody."

He reached out to hold Greg's arms and felt his son tense. "You think forcing your kids to obey all your rules and going to church twice a week will make them angels? All you'll do is create rebels."

"No, being around you will make them rebels." He pushed his father's hands away. "I think you've been around them too much already." Greg glared at his father. "This trip was Natalie's idea. 'For the kids' sake,' she said. But we've made a mistake. For their sake we should keep them as far away from you as possible."

Cooper knew this statement was coming, but it still sucked his breath away. He watched Greg open the door, walk through, and slam it behind him. He would have groaned, but he had no breath to make a sound. Finally, he gasped.

Cooper saw Harper leaning against the window glass, staring at him. She smiled and waved. He waved back, then wiped a tear from his eye. He turned around and walked to the bow, feeling the wind crash into him, hoping it would purge all of his memories and regrets. He knew Greg was serious, not just said in anger. He would never bring his family to Alaska again.

That night he drove them to Anchorage to catch their flight back to Texas. Greg and Natalie said nothing in the backseat, cloying the air with their anger and resentment. Chris sat between them. Greg must have said something to him about Cooper after the boat trip because he wouldn't say much to his grandfather anymore.

Harper sat in the front seat next to Cooper, leaning against him while she talked about all the fun things they'd done. He tried to pretend that this drive wouldn't be his last with them and wanted to squeeze every moment of conversation with Harper for the tiniest bits of love and happiness to store in his memory. He knew these would be all he'd have left of her.

After pulling up to the curb at the airport, he quickly offered his camera to a passing lady who very kindly took a picture of Harper and him.

Cooper tried to hug Chris, but he stiffened and wouldn't hug him back.

Cooper smiled and shook hands with Natalie and Greg. "Thanks for coming. You're welcome back any time." They smiled, but said nothing back.

"Let's go, kids," said Greg.

Both started to follow their parents, but Harper turned around and broke away.

Cooper dropped to his knees and hugged Harper again. "Don't stop singing, Harper. Ever. Your voice can make the world a better place."

"OK, Grandpa. I love you."

That was the last time he had heard her voice until yesterday.

Chapter Sixteen

Cooper walked into the terminal and into a crowd. Another plane had landed about twenty minutes ago, so people were gathering around the carousel, wheeling away luggage, hugging each other, and being greeted by Princess Tours. He saw two Japanese women posing in front of a long selfie stick with the Yellow Jenny airplane hanging from the ceiling in the background.

I should send her a selfie, he chuckled. He took out his phone and realized he'd never taken a picture of himself. He held the camera at arm's length, smiled, but saw only the wall in front of him through the camera. He looked at the camera, trying to figure out what to do, then saw a teenage girl waiting next to him, looking up the stairs at the passengers walking down.

"Excuse me," said Cooper. "I'm trying to take a selfie for my granddaughter, but can't seem to..."

She smiled, took the phone, showed him how to press the camera button to turn the camera around, then pressed it again. "I'll take one for you."

"Thanks." He fluffed out his gray-white shoulder-length hair, put on his San Antonio Spurs 2014 Championship ball cap, then smiled. "How do I look?"

"Like a skinny Santa Claus. Like every Alaskan grandpa should look." She snapped the picture and handed his phone back.

"Thanks."

He sent the photo to Harper and texted: *No, that's not Santa Claus. That is the quintessential Alaskan grandpa. Since there might be other old farts down here, I'm wearing my Spurs hat to hide my teary eyes. Can't wait to see you, Harper.*

• • • • •

After sleeping for what seemed like only ten minutes, Harper woke as the plane groaned its last descent. The last thing she remembered was being kicked by the kids behind her and hearing a symphony of babies crying.

She looked out the window and was surprised at the light, appearing like late afternoon in Texas. Just below the plane, thick ribbons of water and gravel wove in and out of each other, impossibly tangled. Someone in the row in front of her said, "That's the Tanana River." She saw a few houses and a farm, but otherwise it seemed the world was covered in trees.

When the plane landed, she unlocked her phone and saw the time—a little after 2:00 am. Wow!

After a short taxi, her plane pulled into the gate, and a message dinged.

She opened Cooper's text and saw a photo he'd sent, waiting for her in the terminal. Her throat tightened as her eyes flooded. The memory of seeing him through the window on the tour boat flashed into her mind, his hair whipping around in the wind as he and her father yelled at each other. She knew something bad was happening, so she smiled to make him feel better. Now maybe they could both smile together.

She read his message and texted back. *Will be there in a few minutes. Always wanted to meet Santa Claus!*

She took another nausea pill and stopped at the bathroom. Looking at the mirror, she saw a very tired girl with ratted hair and smeared make-up. She washed her face and brushed her hair, trying to remove the ugly past that had brought her here. She so wanted to enter a new world where someone loved her, the real her, and where she could love back fully, unconditionally. *Please let me find that here with Cooper.*

A pregnant woman emerged from a stall, hanging very low and large. She smiled at Harper. "Thought the plane would never land. I had to go for the last twenty minutes. I'm lucky I didn't pee in my pants."

"How far along are you?" asked Harper, pointing at her belly.

"Maybe tonight," she laughed. "Feels extra heavy. But supposed to be another five weeks." She washed her hands, fluffed her hair, and looked in the mirror. She wore no make-up, and her eyebrows were a little bristly. "I was in Dallas for a week. Besides being hot as hell, all my sisters talked about were shoes, handbags, and Bobbi Brown make-up. God, I'm glad I'm back in Alaska." She patted her tummy. "C'mon baby girl, we're back home. Let's go see Daddy." She shuffled slowly out the door.

Harper had tried not to think of her pregnancy, but the plane was full of babies and kids and at least one pregnant woman. She thought Cooper could accept all her obvious faults, but she couldn't tell him about her pregnancy. It was still a condition to her, not a child. The harsh facts of its creation hid the innocence of its life, too much a symbol of her failures, which drowned her mind, suppressing any hope of self-worth. She tried not to think about half the reason she flew there—like the state's consent laws. She never wanted Cooper to think she had used him.

She needed him to love her. What other family did she have?

She wanted only to be Cooper's granddaughter.

She joined the crowd moving toward the escalator, then saw him standing on the main floor behind the glass wall etched with a sweeping mountain scene, watching for her. He smiled and waved. She squealed, ran down the stairs and through the door, jumping into his arms.

"Cooper!"

His lips spread into a wide grin. "Harper! God, it's good to see you."

His chin rested on top of her head, each trying to squeeze hope for a better life from the other. His tears dripped into her hair; hers onto his old flannel shirt.

They pulled apart. "Didn't realize how much I'd missed you," he said, not bothering to wipe his tears.

"I should've come back sooner. I should've forced them to send me," she blubbered, using his shirt to wipe her face. "I'm so sorry. I must look like crap."

He chuckled and threw his arm around her. "First thing you got to learn about Alaskans is that we don't care how we look. The sooner you take that to heart, the happier you'll be. What you see is all you're going to get, is my motto. And tomorrow I'll probably look worse, so get over it."

Harper chuckled as they walked toward the luggage carousel, her arms still clutched around his waist. She couldn't remember the last time an adult in her family had hugged her. God, it felt good!

Bags tumbled onto the rotating track: car seats, military duffel bags, ice chests, all kinds of boxes covered in duct tape, and some luggage.

"That's mine!" She broke away to grab it, pulled up the handle, and joined him again.

"My truck is right across the road." He guided her through the crowd and out the sliding door.

"How can it be so light outside?" asked Harper, stopping at the curb and shading her eyes.

Cooper chuckled. "The sun set two hours ago."

They walked through the crosswalk to the birch trees bordering the parking area.

"Then why isn't it dark?"

"Because the sun never dips far below the horizon. Always light an hour and a half before sunrise and after sunset. At this time of year, the sun sets for just two and a half hours, so we've got 24 hours of light now, from middle of May through most of July."

"How do you sleep?"

"Wait for winter!"

They headed toward an old black pick-up with extended cab and a camper shell. A big white dog sat in the driver's seat like he owned it. A black and gray, long-haired tabby cat lay curled on the dashboard.

"Prepare to be loved! Snowball is an English Cream Golden Retriever. He's very, very friendly. He'll lick every part of your face."

Snowball put his paws on the window, wagged his tail, and smiled at Harper with his mouth open and pink tongue hanging between his bottom canines. Cooper opened the door, and he jumped out, running around Harper, before lifting his paws onto her shoulders. Harper giggled and hugged the big dog, who licked her cheeks and lips.

She rubbed his ears with both hands. "Snowball! You are the cutest dog I've ever seen!"

Cooper tossed her bag into the truck bed. "You might want to sit in back with Snowball. He makes an awful good pillow if you want to lie down. There's a cooler back there with food and drinks if you want any."

Snowball jumped into the backseat, and Harper climbed in after him, only to be mugged by the dog until her hair flopped in tangles over her face. She paused to fix it but got distracted by a wide panting grin moving left and right, opposite the motion of his tail swinging behind, his large brown eyes fixed on hers. *All this dog wants is to be loved and to love someone else*, she thought. *What everybody wants. Such a simple thing.* She laughed, almost a girlish giggle, in spite of herself, as the retriever dragged his large pink tongue across her mouth. Harper squealed in delight.

Harper could not remember feeling such happiness without the aid of drugs. Why had she never had a dog?

"You might get a little hair on you," Cooper deadpanned.

"I don't care. I love him!"

Cooper merged onto the highway. As they left town, Harper saw a short valley with hundreds of logs on the left, plywood shacks and old trailers on the right, a distillery, a bar advertising bands and movies, and a cannabis shop. Yesterday, the idea of legal weed would have thrilled her. But now she didn't care. She hugged Snowball and peered out the window, excited to see her new world: fresh, unknown, and full of promise.

The road climbed into the hills where trees formed a wall on both sides with occasional glimpses of mountains to the left. A double-tandem truck passed them heading back toward town. Otherwise, the road was empty. Snowball's heavy head lay sideways on her lap while Houdini purred at her feet.

"Does anyone live out here?"

"Lots do. There are houses and cabins all along the highway. Just can't see them from the road. Moose," said Cooper as he decelerated. "Up ahead on the right."

Harper looked out the window and saw a big male walking slowly from the gravel shoulder into the brush. She had never seen a live moose. The bull's body was massive and humped, elevated like a joke on top of four very tall, skinny legs. His small, velvety rack seemed to balance a ridiculously long nose, which he held high, almost aloof. With unexpected grace, he pranced into the forest.

"A lot of moose get killed on the roads. You really have to watch for them," said Cooper. "The previous owner of my house hit a moose one night. Killed his wife."

"That's horrible. I know people hit deer in Texas, but they don't usually die."

"A big deer weighs a hundred pounds. A big moose weighs twelve hundred. Your car would prefer a deer."

After a few more minutes, Cooper slowed and pulled into the Parks Monument turnout. He opened Harper's door and hooked a leash onto

Snowball, who jumped onto the pavement, looking for a place to pee.

"I always stop here for Snowball and the view." He turned and looked at her. "Don't let Houdini escape."

Harper nodded and climbed out.

Cooper handed her a jacket. "You might want this. Kind of windy."

Harper wrapped it around her shoulders, feeling the cold, and moved closer to the edge. "This is beautiful!" She overlooked a sweeping terrain of trees and a river with tall, snow-covered mountains in the distance. Low clouds hung in the foothills, accentuating the height of the peaks behind.

Cooper stood with shirtsleeves rolled up and arms outstretched. "What don't you see? And haven't seen since we've been driving?" he asked.

"What haven't I seen?"

"Sometimes you need to know what you can't see to understand what you can see," he said cryptically. "Just think what you haven't seen on the side of the road that you see everywhere all the time in Texas."

Harper thought then realized what he meant. "Fences."

"That's right. No fences in Alaska. Find one stretch of highway in the Lower 48 that's not in a park without a fence on both sides of the road. You can't. You could travel the length and breadth of this entire state without having to jump over a fence. That's the definition of freedom to me. Most of the state can't be reached except by boat or plane or snow machine in the winter. Alaska is more than twice the size of Texas yet has only five percent of the roads Texas does. I'm lucky to live on the road system."

"I like the mountains. I remember seeing ones like this the last time, but they weren't as tall."

"How much of that trip do you remember?" he asked, gently.

"Not much really. Mostly just standing on a table and singing, then getting reprimanded by my dad. Like that was anything new. I've been trying to remember more of it recently."

He stood in front of her and held her hands. "I told you to keep singing. Why did you stop?"

"My parents didn't want me to perform, except in the church choir. That wasn't really what I wanted. They've gotten pretty good at taking things I like and twisting them into things I've come to hate." A small smile played along her lips. "Though I did sing at the airport in Seattle, but I didn't know it. I was listening to one of your songs and didn't realize I sang out loud until a bunch of people applauded."

"Really?" Cooper seemed genuinely surprised.

"Yes, one lady told me to tell you she liked your song."

"Maybe what she liked was your voice. I want to hear it again. Maybe tomorrow?"

He looked at her with such eagerness, such happiness. No one else had ever cared about hearing her sing. "I'd love to."

"I have a microphone and amp at the house," said Cooper. "Actually have a small studio. I'll show you tomorrow."

"OK. Your songs are good, Cooper. Did you ever try to sell them?"

"I tried several times. Most were part of my books. Sold a few hundred of those."

"I read the first few chapters online."

"I've got copies at home."

He smiled at her for a few seconds then unbuckled the leash and opened the door for Snowball. Harper climbed in after him, and the dog acted like he hadn't seen her in hours—sniffing and licking her, wagging his tail, and hopping on her.

"Here. Take Houdini," said Cooper, handing back the kitten. "When Snowball calms down, put Houdini in his litter box on the floorboard." He merged back onto the highway.

"He's so soft!" she said stroking his back. Houdini felt like a warm cloud. His eyes were huge, but he closed them as soon as she scratched the large white ruff around his neck.

Harper put Houdini into his litter box. Snowball laid his big head on her lap. She lightly stroked his floppy mouth and the hair under his neck as she looked outside.

She felt so comfortable, so peaceful, with no worries at all. She saw herself standing on a table, singing to a bunch of people smiling at her. She closed her eyes and sang the chorus of *You Are My Sunshine.*

Just before she laid her head down on Snowball, she heard Cooper say, "That was beautiful, Harper. I've waited so long to hear that again."

Through the fog of sleep, she heard Cooper call to her. "Harper, we're home."

She stretched, as did Snowball, on his back with four paws reaching for the ceiling. She yawned until she thought her jaws would never shut again. Home? She hoped it would be different than her other home: no painful history, no stress, no regrets.

Cooper grabbed Houdini and opened his door. Harper stepped onto the gravel driveway and looked at the house, which was bigger than she'd expected. Two stories with large, painted window casements, accented with an unusual tile/mortar design along the bottom two feet.

"It's pretty out here."

The sun had turned the northeastern sky magenta, red, and yellow. Forty-foot spruce and poplar trees swayed in the breeze.

Harper listened and heard nothing. "I don't hear traffic or sirens. I don't smell exhaust. I don't see lights glaring everywhere. I can hear the wind blowing through the leaves. How amazing is that?"

Snowball lifted his leg against one of the trees then trotted over to the garage where he sniffed at garbage strewn across the grass.

"What happened to your trash cans?" Harper gawked at the mess as she walked towards them.

Cooper noticed his cans knocked over and torn plastic bags scattered about. He walked away from the truck and found bags pulled back into the trees. "Must be a bear," he said.

She stumbled. *Say what?*

"A bear? There are bears out here?" She rushed to the front door.

He shot her the most peculiar look. "This is Alaska. Bears are everywhere, but usually not around the house. Don't worry about it. I'll deal with it later today."

She was definitely not in the city anymore.

Cooper opened the door and set Houdini on the floor. Snowball ran in and drank water like he'd been crossing a desert for days.

Harper saw stained and varnished wood everywhere—oak cabinets and table, oak windowsills, refinished furniture, shelves full of books—pots and pans hanging from the ceiling above a wooden table. In another room she saw a large wood stove perched on a raised tiled platform and stacked wood in an iron box. The house was full of rich, warm colors. And though she noticed the mismatched wooden planks and slightly sagging ceiling, the place felt homey.

"I love this. I think I'll stay." She saw the photos on the refrigerator, set her pack on the floor, and draped her jacket on a chair. She walked over to the fridge, reaching out to touch some of the photos.

"Oh, my God." She covered her mouth and had trouble breathing. "All our Christmas pictures. And Grandma." All these pictures of them and she didn't have a single picture of him. She felt ashamed. He'd wanted to see them all these years.

Then she pointed to a young girl's photo. "Is this Heather?"

"Yes." His brows rose. "Have you never seen a picture of her?"

She blinked tears out of her eyes. "No. There are no pictures of you or Heather in my parents' house." She couldn't believe she'd never asked why.

She looked at Cooper and saw the confusion on his face. "None?"

Harper shook her head. "Did you always have our pictures on the door?"

"Always."

Harper hugged him. "Cooper, I'm so sorry. Why has Dad been so angry with you?"

"He blames me for her death and all that happened to her. I think he's ashamed of his sister and has been afraid that his kids would follow in her footsteps. Or in his, for that matter."

"I don't understand." Did her father think cutting his side of the family out of their lives would protect them? And yet, here she was, following her aunt's footsteps, hoping this man could save her.

His eyes softened. "Don't worry about it tonight. Get some rest. You look dead on your feet."

He took her suitcase to the end of the hall and set it on her bed. "Bathroom's right there. There's plenty of room in the dresser for your clothes."

Harper looked around the small bedroom, one wall covered with beaded pine, two big windows and thick curtains, a double-bed with an iron headboard. "I love this."

"My house is your house, Harper. Anything you want in the kitchen, take it. I want you to feel comfortable here and safe, despite the bear. Do you smoke?"

Harper hesitated. *Here comes the lecture on drugs.* She tried not to look worried.

"Cigarettes," Cooper clarified.

"No."

"If you want to smoke anything, go outside or on the screened-in porch. That's my only rule."

Anything? She doubted pot would be OK.

"You don't have to hide anything from me. Whatever you want to do, you can do it here. I'm not going to judge you. I don't want you to use drugs, but I'm not going to prevent you from using them. I hope you'll find other things you want to do more, but if you don't, then you don't. I'm always on your side." He looked so kindly toward her. "Always."

"Thank you." Harper hugged him. Cooper patted her back, then Harper pulled him hard against her, burying her face in his chest as she cried. *How could this man be any more loving toward me?* She would try so hard to keep his trust.

"I'm glad you're here, Harper."

"So am I."

Snowball wagged his tail and jumped onto her bed.

"Turncoat!" said Cooper. "First female sleeps in this house and you want to jump in bed with her. At least Houdini will stay with me."

The kitty jumped onto Harper's dresser, shook his tail at the mirror, stretched out, then purred. Harper laughed.

"Both of you are traitors!" He rubbed Snowball's ears and stroked Houdini's back. "But I'm glad you love Harper. Just remember who feeds you. Good-night, Harper."

"Good-night, Cooper."

Cooper walked away.

Harper pushed the suitcase against the wall, climbed onto the bed covers, and curled around Snowball's back. As soon as she closed her eyes, she fell asleep.

• • • • •

Is she there? texted Greg. *You were supposed to call me.*

Cooper texted back. *She's fine. Been awake all night. Call later.*

Greg texted back, but Cooper turned off his phone and dropped it in his pocket. Cooper returned to Harper's room a few minutes later to check on her. She was sound asleep, lying on her side, almost smiling. Houdini had curled into the crook of her legs. Snowball snored softly with Harper's arm draped across his chest. She looked so young, yet he knew she'd already experienced more pain than any sixteen-year-old should have to. But he hoped she wasn't broken.

Later in his bed, Cooper thought about Heather as a little girl. She had loved kittens and puppies, bringing home any stray she found. They all had loved her back, but at some point, the pets weren't enough, and she chased the boys, easy conquests, which she viewed as affirmations of her self-worth for a little while until the victories became preordained. The game was always rigged in her favor.

Good grades, awards, and praise from teachers never seemed to satisfy her for more than a fleeting moment. She had smiled after being presented with a trophy amidst loud applause, but behind that smile was the question: "Is this all there is?"

She, like Cooper, was never satisfied with mere existence. Surely life had to mean more than a moderate progression from one minute to the next—following rules, fitting in, gaining the praise of others, sleeping, then doing it all again the next day.

In her youth, when Cooper and Rachel took the kids on hiking trips, Heather couldn't stay on a trail. She leapt from rock to rock, cut across switchbacks when no one was looking, and snuck out of her tent at night to climb rocks in the moonlight, just to do it. Trails and rules were for other people—the sheep, the boring, the suck-ups.

"You need to be more careful, Heather," he'd said many times, smiling at her, unable to hide his admiration for her spunk.

"I'm always careful, Pops." She smiled back. "Don't worry."

Danger lured her. Risk defined her life. The possibility of her losing her life made it all the more exciting and desirable.

Both had wanted a larger purpose for their lives, but when they couldn't find it, they fell into traps: Heather with her drugs, and Cooper bending rules all his life, eventually succumbing to a secret affair with its constant, intoxicating danger.

If they could've climbed the most difficult mountains or become zealous missionaries or lawyers fighting for the oppressed, then maybe they could have found fulfillment in their lives. But they'd never heard those callings, or the siren sounded too old and spent when they needed heat.

Cooper finally found the all-consuming passion of creation. He wrote books and music. Rather than accept the life he had or saw in others, he'd create his own where events had purpose and meaning, and endings weren't random. And writing music provided the most engrossing feeling: a breathless, sustained gasping of thought and emotion until words and notes and rhythm danced together in joy or aching sadness.

Though he'd found only moderate financial success with these efforts, he'd finally found some peace with himself. The rush of creativity was now the goal of his life, which was why his growing dementia terrorized him. He could accept the failings of his body, but not of his mind where his greatest needs lived. He'd sooner kill it than exist as a breathing, nourished, unthinking husk.

He wondered how similar Heather and Harper were. Though he didn't know all the details of her struggles, he'd heard the same desperation in her voice on the phone as he'd heard from Heather. He thought he knew what Harper needed. The trick was how to encourage her to pursue it. He had to make a plan.

Chapter Seventeen

Harper awoke to the tickle of Snowball's whiskers against her neck and his wet nose in her ear. She turned over and saw the puppy sitting on the floor with his paws on her bed. She rubbed his face and jiggled the soft folds of his neck. "What do you want, boy?"

He walked out of the room, down the hall. Harper shoved her feet into her shoes and followed to find him standing by the door. "You need to go outside?"

Snowball wagged his tail. Harper looked around and saw no sign of Cooper. "OK, just don't run off." She opened the door and followed him out. A breath of cool breeze greeted her as she stood on the steps, squinting in the bright sunlight.

Snowball lifted his leg against a tree at the back of the house, then sniffed around the garbage. Harper found a dog Frisbee on the driveway. "Here you go, Snowball. Fetch!" She threw it toward the deck at the back of the house. Snowball took off, picked up the toy, then saw a rabbit leap into the woods. He galloped after it and disappeared in a second. Harper walked quickly toward the trees. She had no idea how far the puppy would run or what restrictions, if any, Cooper put on him. She didn't want him getting lost on her first morning there.

"Snowball! Where are you?" shouted Harper.

A flash of white crossed the trail behind a shed.

"Snowball! Come here, boy!" She clapped her hands and walked after him, calling his name, trying not to sound frantic.

The air felt colder as she made her way deeper into the trees. She clasped her shoulders and looked wildly in each direction, stumbling over rocks and running into branches. The trail curved back and forth away from the house.

"Snowball?" She saw piles of dead wood and grass clippings on either side, a rusted car door and an old tricycle, but no Snowball. She turned around and could not see the house through the trees. She looked for anything white in every direction.

"Snowball!" She had lost him.

The chill in her gut spread as she turned around again calling his name.

Suddenly Snowball barreled through the trees back toward the house. She smiled, took a few deep breaths, then turned to walk back down the trail.

A loud woof sounded to her right.

She stopped. She'd never heard such a sound. Not like a dog. More clipped and explosive. Her shoulders tightened.

She heard another woof, then heavy breathing, followed by a weird staccato clicking.

This wasn't a sound from a small animal. She took another few steps, slowly, quietly. She heard it again, along with a grunt, and remembered the bear in the garbage. "Crap," she said through gritted teeth.

"Cooper! Cooper!" she yelled, her voice more shrill than she'd intended.

She backed up on the trail, peering into the woods, and jerked around to look behind her. "Cooper!" She still couldn't see the house.

"Harper! Where are you?" shouted Cooper through the trees.

Harper was afraid to shout back. She'd pinpointed the direction of the sound—to her right, between her and the house.

"Harper!"

She waited, hoping Cooper would appear on the trail. Finally, she saw him trotting toward her, holding a large, silver pistol.

"Here," she said as calmly as she could and took a few more steps, her heart pounding in her throat. She waved her arms and pointed to her right as she licked her lips. Her mouth was so dry.

They both heard the next woof. Cooper picked up a rock and threw it toward the trees to his left. "Get outta here, you sonofabitch!" He threw another rock and growled as he walked toward Harper, who started to run toward him.

"Don't run!" He held out his hand, and she stopped. "Throw some rocks and yell!" He grabbed another rock and threw it. He banged a stick on a tree.

Harper found a rock and tossed it into the trees.

"Yell, Harper! Don't let that bear think you're scared of him!" He walked off the trail into the trees banging his stick and growling.

Harper threw another rock. "Leave, you asshole!"

"There you go! Tell him what to do!"

Harper picked up a thick stick and banged the trees as she followed Cooper, both of them screaming and banging tree trunks until their sticks disintegrated. Harper could feel shards of wood hitting her face. Branches grabbed her hair, but she yanked it free. She screamed, "Get out of here!" and felt more angry and violent than she ever had before. Such a release! "Out, you asshole! Grrrr!"

They heard grunts then something crashing through the willows away from them.

Harper threw one more rock. "That scared the crap out of me!" She bent over, trying to catch her breath.

Cooper laughed. "Think you did the same to that bear." He gave her a side hug. "Welcome, to Alaska, Harper. You passed your first test. I'm proud of you."

Proud of me?

"You didn't run away. You went after him. You did good, girl. Real good. You should stand up to black bears and fight back. But walk away from grizzlies as you wave your arms and talk to them. Don't run from either one."

She swallowed passed the lump in her throat. He was proud of her over something so simple as banging sticks against trees. Her dad would never have said that. He would've yelled at her for being out in the woods or doing something reckless, somehow making this situation her fault. "So what was that one? We couldn't see it."

"Black bears usually stay in trees." He returned the pistol to its leather holster.

"Do I need to carry a gun just to walk outside?" She'd never seen a pistol so close.

"No. First bear I've seen around the house in years. Besides, I've barely used this thing since I've lived in Alaska. Guess it makes me more willing to woof and growl back at them if I wave it around. And keeps my pee inside rather than flooding my pants." He laughed. "Though at my age, that happens even without the bear."

Harper felt her stomach twist and knew another round of morning sickness was about to strike. "Speaking of which, I really need to pee," as she ran to the deck and into the house.

Harper missed the toilet with the first spasm of puking. She collapsed on her knees and managed to put her head through the lid for the second spasm. Her stomach lurched halfway up her chest as she coughed out bile. After spitting into the water several times, she flushed and sat back on her calves and breathed. She'd forgotten to take her pills that morning.

When was she going to tell Cooper? And when would she have the abortion? It had to be soon. She needed to start over.

"You OK?" Cooper yelled as he opened the door off the deck.

"Fine!" Harper lurched to shut the bathroom door and soon heard Snowball's paws scratching outside. Grabbing the door handle, she pulled herself up and tried to fight her dizziness.

He whistled for the dog. "C'mon, Snowball. Leave the girl alone for a few minutes."

Harper turned on the bath water and wiped up her vomit. After washing her face, she opened the door and heard Cooper talking on his phone in another room. She rushed to grab some clothes, soap, her pills, and a hairdryer from her room then went back to the bathroom where she looked at herself in the fogging mirror.

A few twigs and spruce needles stuck in her tangled hair. One of her sleeves was ripped, and her cheek was scratched. Just a few hours in Alaska and she'd slept with a dog, cussed out a bear, run screaming through the trees, and got praised by her grandfather. She pulled off her shirt and posed like Wonder Woman. Though "strong woman" weren't the first words she thought, she knew the potential was there. She picked at two broken nails.

Alaska seemed to demand toughness and strength. Maybe she'd start exercising. Maybe in another two weeks she'd see some muscles. Obviously, this wasn't a place for soft and squeezable.

She felt happy stepping into the shower, ready to wash off Texas and Zachary and her parents and explore something new, something fresh, something different. She looked forward to the rest of the day. When was the last time she looked forward to anything that didn't include a party, a guy, or a drug?

She hummed softly, sending happy notes through the steam.

• • • • •

Twenty minutes later Cooper heard a hairdryer from inside the bathroom. He knocked on the door. "What do you order at Starbucks?"

"What?" The hairdryer clicked off.

"What kind of coffee drink do you order from Starbucks?" he repeated.

She stuck her head out of the door. "Is there one close by?"

"Got one right here in the kitchen. What do you order?"

"Hazelnut latte. Extra hot."

"Got it."

"Cool." She closed the door.

Cooper hummed as he moved around the kitchen. He had fried bacon and sausage, made some sausage gravy, and baked biscuits. He tamped down the coffee in the holder and turned on his espresso machine. He loved making himself lattes in the morning but making one for someone else was special. He hadn't treated anyone else since he provided drinks for the horribly boring teacher in-services all the village teachers had to attend on several Saturday mornings throughout the year. He never thought he'd make one for his grandchildren.

He steamed the milk until the pitcher hurt his hand. He set down an Alaskan coffee cup and hesitated. Which syrup did she want?

He knocked again. "Hey, Harper. Did you want vanilla, caramel, or hazelnut?"

"Hazelnut. Three squirts."

"OK." He walked back to the kitchen and stared at the empty cup. He couldn't remember what she'd said. *Dammit!* He grabbed the vanilla bottle and put in two squirts, added the coffee, then poured the milk, leaving room for a large dollop of froth on top.

Harper emerged from the bathroom, filling the air with tangerine body wash. Her long fluffy hair hung over her tank top, which barely met a pair of loose nylon boxers "That shower felt good."

"You're definitely going to improve the smell in this house. Snowball can get pretty rank." He handed her the latte. "Hope you like it."

"Kinda fancy. Lattes in the middle of nowhere." She took a sip.

"Good?"

"It is. You didn't have hazelnut?"

I can't even make a simple coffee drink. "Oh, I do. Just thought you said vanilla." He grabbed the hazelnut bottle and handed it to her. Harper smiled and added a couple of squirts.

"This is really good, Cooper. Do I get one of these every morning?"

"If you want. I always make myself one. Do you like cheese in your scrambled eggs?"

"No. But I do like a little cream if you have it."

"Sure do. I'll put it in right now." He removed the half & half bottle from the fridge and poured a little into a bowl containing the whipped eggs. "I locked up Snowball in the screen room, so he wouldn't scratch on the door while you showered. He can't stand to be left out of the action."

"I'll go see him." Harper left the kitchen. After a few seconds, he heard her squeal, then what must have been Snowball jumping on and off the sofa.

Cooper got the shredded cheese out of the fridge and put it on the counter. The butter had just melted in the skillet when he poured the eggs. He scraped them around with the spatula as he added salt and pepper, then picked up the bag of cheese. He paused. He couldn't remember. Cheese or no cheese?

Harper bolted into the kitchen, chased by Snowball.

"You did say cheese, didn't you?"

Harper looked at Cooper while holding the dog's paws off her chest. "No cheese."

"OK. No cheese." He put the bag back on the counter.

He saw Harper watch him for a few seconds. "You OK?" she asked.

"Never better." His heart skipped a beat. "I hope you like them a little runny."

"Sure. That's fine. Let me help you."

Cooper saw her look and knew what she might be thinking. A wave of fear rushed into his stomach. He didn't want her to know the truth yet. Maybe later. "Grab the plates and let's eat!" He carried plates and bowls to the table and made a big fuss about folding napkins and lining up utensils on either side of each plate.

"You have hot sauce?" asked Harper.

"In the fridge. There's Cholula and Pace."

Harper found the bottles and took them to the table. Cooper still saw that odd look on her face. "Dig in!"

Harper sipped her coffee while Cooper gobbled his food. "Why don't you write things down, so you don't forget them?"

He stared at her for a second. He couldn't pretend any longer. "Probably because I would forget where the paper and pencil are, then start looking for them, then forget what I was looking for."

Harper smiled. "Can't be that bad."

He'd debated with himself when he should tell her: up front so she wouldn't be shocked or try like hell to keep it hidden until something happened, hopefully minor, so she wouldn't get scared and leave. He had hoped they could have a few days without an incident, but no such luck.

"It is that bad and getting worse." He saw the shock in her eyes and looked down at Houdini, stroking his back.

"Have you seen a doctor?" she asked softly.

"Yup. He gave me prescriptions. I'm supposed to go back for more testing. I'm sorry, Harper. I'm just falling apart. I should've told you, but I keep hoping it'll go away. I didn't know it was you yelling outside this morning. I saw a teenage girl in my yard and couldn't figure out why. At least for several seconds. That's pretty bad."

"You just woke up. You had a long night. I forget things, too."

"I hope not too often! We can't afford both of us being senile." He tried to laugh.

"You're helping me, so I'll help you. Especially if you keep feeding me like this!" She smiled. "You have a writing pad or sticky notes?"

"I'm an old teacher. Of course I have sticky notes!" He opened a drawer and pulled out several notepads and a pen.

"So, I'll write things down for you and stick these where you'll see them. I'll be your personal assistant." She reached out to his hand and squeezed it. "Don't worry, Cooper. You'll be fine." She wrote on a note and stuck it on a cabinet door by the espresso machine. "'Three squirts of hazelnut. No cheese in eggs.' Easy." He appreciated her desire to help, but felt more depressed. Maybe he'd end up with sticky notes all over the house: his name, his pets' names, maybe even reminders to get dressed.

Houdini jumped onto the table and licked at the eggs. Snowball put his blocky head onto the table waiting for handouts.

"Get your face out of the eggs, kitty." Cooper picked up Houdini and held him like a baby on his back along one arm while he rubbed Houdini's face and ears with his other hand. "Houdini loves this. Other cats would shred you to pieces if you tried it, but this little guy loves it." The purring was almost deafening. Cooper put a few eggs into a small bowl and put Houdini down beside it. He gobbled them in a few seconds. Harper tossed chunks of eggs into Snowball's mouth, along with a piece of bacon.

"My parents would freak if they saw animals at their table." She fed Snowball a chunk of biscuit dipped in gravy, barely removing her fingers before his teeth clamped down. "You don't believe in training, do you?"

"Nope, other than doing their business outside. Don't do to them what I wouldn't like done to me."

"The Golden Rule?"

"Yup. Same for raising kids. Your father decided that liberal idea contributed to his and Heather's rebellion. So he's tried a different method." Cooper winked. "And here you are."

"Ha!" Harper guffawed and launched a piece of biscuit onto the table. She picked it up and tossed it to Snowball. "Maybe you're passing down a rebel gene to all of us so no matter how we're raised, we rebel. It's still your fault, but for different reasons." They both laughed.

"I'm glad you're not a freak about table manners," said Harper. "At my parents' house, we are constantly reminded how to eat, how to sit, and how to leave the table. I got to the point I'd barely eat at the table, so I could leave quickly then get food out of the fridge later on."

And for similar reasons, you hid your drug use and meetings with boys because you couldn't feel comfortable talking to them, he thought. He'd made similar mistakes with Heather.

"By the way your father texted me after you fell asleep last night. He'll probably call later."

"Tell him I chased a bear and made out with a dog." She smeared gravy on her lips and bent down. Snowball exfoliated her face as Harper giggled.

"He never does that to me," said Cooper. "Must be the beard."

Harper added more gravy, turning her face from side to side as the dog's tongue dragged over both cheeks and her lips. "I love this dog!"

"The feeling's mutual."

Two nearby rifle shots echoed against the walls of the house, startling her.

"What's that?" asked Harper ducking behind the table.

"Digger shot the bear!"

"Digger?"

"A friend of mine. I told him it'd likely come out near A Street. He must've found it. You won't have to worry about him anymore."

"He shot it?"

"What else would he do with it? Bear meat's not bad. I like it battered and fried. He'll sell the coat. You'll see your bear when we go to the post office later."

Harper shuddered. "I think I'll need to work up to that. Thanks for starting me off with bacon and sausage."

They ate vigorously. Harper actually gobbled her food, licking her fingers, while occasionally offering bites to Snowball. Cooper smacked his food and slurped his coffee. Houdini leapt from the table to the window, chasing a fly.

They ate until two biscuits sat alone on a plate. Both stared at them for a full minute.

Harper shook her head. "Don't think I can eat anymore."

"Me neither. I could crawl right back into bed."

"Mmmm, that would be nice. But I want to go back outside and explore my new home."

"OK, let's clean this up, then I'll drive you around our little town. When we get back, we have a bunch of flowers to plant."

"Deal." She held some dishes and did her best to look stupefied. "Uh, what are we going to do again?"

Cooper looked at her and smiled. He couldn't help but admire her spunk, even if it had been misdirected recently. "You're a smartass, aren't you?"

She smiled. "My middle name."

"My condition is serious, you do realize."

"Not as serious now that you have me. You'll be fine. I'll make sure of it."

I'd love to believe you, Harper.

Chapter Eighteen

Cooper called Snowball to jump into the backseat so Harper could take the front. "He's not happy you're taking his seat." As soon as Snowball jumped in, he reached over the seat to snorfle Harper's ear. Cooper loved the sound of Harper's giggling. She'd seemed so unhappy when he spoke to her in San Antonio.

Harper got on her knees and reached back to rub Snowball as Cooper backed up, then turned down the long driveway.

"Got to learn to share, Snowball," said Harper, reaching over to scratch his ear. "Next time I'll ride back there with you." She let the dog lick her face.

The truck bounced over a pothole, knocking Harper almost over the seat. She yelped as Snowball put his paws on her back.

"You OK?" asked Cooper.

"Yeah." She got her knees back on the seat.

Cooper noticed Harper's shorts hiked up on her butt pointing toward the windshield. He shook his head.

"Harper, if I drive too much farther with your butt flashing through this windshield, I'm going to be followed by half the guys in this town, and the other half are going to whistle as I drive by."

She turned from the dog. "Then the guys in this town need to grow up. I'm just hugging Snowball."

Cooper laughed. "No one ever accused our males of being mature. You might have to teach them a little."

"Male and mature shouldn't be in the same sentence. They're all a bunch of horny kids." She turned around and flopped into the seat. "Besides, I'm not trying to attract anybody. Just wearing shorts to feel comfortable. Other people need to get over their hang-ups."

"If you say so." He chuckled. *Such spunk!*

"I've got no make-up on, and the only reason I chose these clothes is because they're comfortable. I don't care what anyone else thinks. I feel wonderful!" She stuck her head out the window and yelled, "Woo hoo! I'm in Alaska!"

Cooper laughed. He was so glad she liked being there. He worried she'd find everything boring with no malls or fast food restaurants.

As they turned onto D Street, Harper saw a man and a boy walking on the side of the road wearing old Army jackets and carrying assault weapons. The boy looked to be in middle school. Cooper waved, and they waved back.

"Is that legal?" asked Harper.

"Sure is. Dan gave Billy an AK 47 for his 13th birthday. They might be coming back from the shooting range at the park."

"They would've been surrounded by a SWAT team in my neighborhood."

"Dan's got about twenty guns in his house, including a machine gun. A SWAT team wouldn't stand a chance. He's an ex-Army Ranger." He saw Harper frowning. *Welcome to Alaska*, he thought.

Cooper stopped in front of a faded blue plywood house with uneven roofs. An older man with a full beard hiding his mouth stretched a bearskin on a sheet of plywood while a younger man used a saw on the carcass.

"Come on. Let's take a look."

Harper shook her head. "I'm not very fond of blood."

"All the more reason to take a look. Stand up to your fears, just like you did this morning."

Harper nodded.

Cooper and Harper exited the truck. Both men stopped what they were doing and stared at Harper. The older man's eyes widened as his jaw went slack, where the younger man's lips stretched into a smug grin as he nodded his head.

"This is Digger and his son Tommy," said Cooper. "This is my granddaughter, Harper, from Texas. That bear woofed at her this morning." He hoped that was enough warning to those two to stop leering at his granddaughter.

Tommy eyed her long legs. "I can see why. Think I'd woof, too." He laughed and looked at the other men like he'd told the best joke.

Cooper shot a harsh look at the boy and almost said something, but Harper picked up a piece of two-by-four from the ground. Cooper wondered if she'd swing it at him.

"I chased it off with a stick about this size." She slapped the board a few times against her hand as she stared hard at Tommy. "I don't like being woofed at."

Tommy held up his hands and backed away, chuckling. "No problem."

Harper tossed the board to the ground and strode back to the truck, slamming the door closed. Cooper turned back toward the men, swelling with pride. *That's my granddaughter!*

Digger raised his eyebrows.

"Like they say, 'Don't mess with Texas.'" Cooper smiled. "You're doing a good job on that skin, Digger."

"Thanks. I'll send Tommy over with a couple of steaks."

"Might be better if I dropped by later on. I wouldn't want Tommy to get hurt." Tommy looked up as Cooper got back in his truck, chuckling. He waved at both as he drove away.

"Give me five, tough girl." Cooper held out his hand. Harper slapped it.

"What a dick!" she said.

"Yes, he always has been full of himself. But you made your point. Is that how you treated the guys in San Antonio?"

She slumped in her seat. "No. I was a wuss, begging for approval."

"So, how'd that work out for you?"

"You know the answer." Harper bit off the fake nail on her thumb and spit it out the window.

"See, you've already learned something, and you haven't been here for a day."

"I should've come up here a long time ago. Maybe if I had..."

Cooper wondered what Harper had gone through. She'd told him almost nothing.

"Maybe you came at just the right time," said Cooper. "I don't think the timing matters as much as how you treat the experience. You decide whether an event means anything to you or not. For instance, your episode with Tommy won't change him at all, except he probably won't get near you if you're carrying a two by four." He chuckled. "But you won't forget it. I don't think you'll ever hope for a whistle or woof again."

Cooper stopped at an intersection and shot her a glance. She looked like a little girl, chewing on her finger.

"A few months ago," said Cooper, "in a town south of here, six men in their 20s were arrested for sexual assault of several girls 13 to 15 years of age. The men gave the girls drugs at parties in exchange for sex. One girl was locked in a car trunk for several hours during February 'cause she wouldn't cooperate and suffered from frostbite. Even after that incident, a couple of the girls kept sending photos and explicit messages to the men during school. Most of the girls never complained about the men. Does that kind of thing happen in Texas?"

"Happened to me," said Harper. "Not exactly the same, but close enough."

And there it was. His worst fears realized. "Why?"

"I loved the attention, and I was bored. Sneaking out to parties and using drugs was exciting. I'm sure those girls felt the same way. Guys know what to say to make you feel special. One guy I thought actually cared about me, but it was all for show, to get what he wanted." Harper stared out her window, tears welling in her eyes. "At the time you think you're life is so much better because of him, then you realize you're actually nothing to him." She looked at Cooper. "Absolutely nothing. And then you wonder, 'What else is there?'"

Cooper had seen that look before—a mask of defiance with so much hurt around the edges. Harper showed more hurt, though, than Heather. And truthfully his stomach ached more because his granddaughter had experienced such pain. *Why does life have to hurt so much?*

He'd often asked himself the same question: What else is there? Why endure the daily boredom just to experience one supposedly exciting event on the weekend?

"Everyone's got to answer the same questions," said Cooper. "What's the point of living? What can I get excited about?"

A couple of tears slid down her cheeks. "What's the answer?"

"That, my dear granddaughter, is what you're up here to find out. And it's not *the* answer; it's *your* answer. Now let's go see Maddie and get my mail."

He pulled into a small parking lot in front of a blue painted building with clumps of wild irises and rhubarb in front.

Harper opened the door and hopped out. "Should I lock it?"

Cooper laughed. "Who would take it?"

She followed him up the stairs and through an arctic entry to a foyer with a hand-painted map of the town on the wall. Harper stared at it. "Where are we?"

He put his finger on the edge of the map near a pond. "Right there. Near the edge of civilization, as opposed to here"—his voice increased in volume—"where there is no civilization." He laughed and strode into the post office. "Isn't that right, Maddie?" Cooper opened his box, pulled out his mail, and carried his yellow card to the window.

"Who're you yelling at, you big oaf?" A tall, very thin woman with short gray hair and a big smile walked into view behind the counter.

"Like I said," he chuckled to Harper, "no civility. Hey, Maddie. What ya got for me?"

Maddie pulled a package off the shelf. "Something from Cabella's." She plopped the package on the counter and scanned the label.

"Must be my new sandals." He gestured to Harper. "Maddie, this is Harper, my granddaughter from Texas."

"Well, hello, Harper." She offered her hand. "Nice to meet you." Her smile revealed crooked teeth she cared nothing about hiding. Harper shook her hand. "From Texas? Up for a visit? Didn't think this old coot had relatives."

"I'm living with him for as long as I can."

"She means as long as I feed her my famous breakfasts," said Cooper.

"Which no one has ever eaten, at least not that I've heard. Famous, my ass!" laughed Maddie.

Harper hooked arms with Cooper. "He made me biscuits and gravy, scrambled eggs, and a plateful of bacon and sausage! It was amazing. And a hazelnut latte!"

"Latte, huh? All Ralph makes me is burnt Folger's," said Maddie. "Maybe I should come visit you in the morning." She put her hand on Cooper's and smiled.

He yanked his hand away. "None of that, woman. Got to act respectable in front of my granddaughter. I'm the paragon of morality and healthy living to her."

"Oh, my God! Harper, run for your life!" Maddie cackled while Cooper and Harper laughed.

Three laughing teens barged in: a boy carrying a letter, and a boy/girl couple hanging onto each other.

"Hey, Maddie," said one of the boys. "Need a stamp." He slapped two quarters on the counter.

"Wait your turn, Kevin. Can't you see I got other customers?"

Kevin turned and noticed Cooper in a daze, and then his bloodshot eyes shifted to Harper and widened. "Whoa! Who's that?"

The other boy disentangled himself from the girl and looked at Harper, mouth open, his eyes bulging out of their sockets. The girl tried to pull him back to her while she sneered at Harper.

Stoned out of their minds, Cooper thought.

"Aren't you supposed to be in class?" asked Maddie.

"Lunch break," said Kevin.

"Which was over five minutes ago," said Maddie.

"It's Dooley's class. He's usually late himself," said Kevin.

"We're done," said Cooper. "Give the boy a stamp. See you later, Maddie."

The other boy asked Harper, "Are you going to school here?"

"Maybe next fall." Harper walked over to the girl with long blonde hair, a cut-off sweatshirt, and floral leggings and held out her hand. "Hey, I'm Harper."

"Hi. I'm Kenzie." She seemed on guard, ready to launch a come-back or even a slug.

"Kenzie will be watching my pets while we go to the park this Friday," said Cooper.

"Cool. See you Friday, Kenzie." She smiled.

"OK," said Kenzie.

Just as they closed the doors to the truck, the kids burst out of the building and ran toward the school, giggling about nothing. Kevin actually pretended to be an airplane flying across the parking lot.

"You know they're stoned, don't you?" asked Harper.

"They walk home for lunch, share a joint, and come back stoned every afternoon. Many of my students did the same in the villages. I don't know how many times I tried to tell parents their kids were smoking weed. Not one ever believed me. They just don't want to believe that about their kid."

"Is Kenzie the only person you can get to stay with Snowball and Houdini?"

"Yes. She's done it before."

"I'll talk with her before we leave."

• • • • •

Harper knew what would happen because she would've done the same. Invite her boyfriend over and party all night. Smoke weed or whatever and forget about the pets. She'd have to explain the new rules to Kenzie because nothing had better happen to Snowball or Houdini.

Had she been so obvious when she was stoned? She had to have been. How could her teachers and parents not have known? Maybe because they didn't want to know. The truth that their kids were living secret lives was too scary to consider, so most didn't unless the truth slammed them in the face.

Cooper drove by the school—a one-story tan building with an elementary wing on one side and a high school on the other.

"Oh, my God, what's that on the wall?" asked Harper.

Cooper laughed. "That's the school mascot. A grizzly. I always thought it looked like a fat dog taking a dump with his right paw raised to say 'Hi.'"

"Looks like he's scratching his balls to me." Harper howled in laughter.

"Never thought of that."

"I left the Rangers at Smithson Valley for a crapping, ball-scratching grizzly? How will I ever face my friends?" She laughed until she couldn't breathe. Snowball stuck his head over the seat, worried about Harper. She grabbed his neck. "I'm OK, big fella. Haven't you ever seen a girl laugh before?"

"Actually, I don't think he has. When's the last time you laughed this hard?"

Every memory of laughing she could muster up happened while using drugs. At least recently. "Seems like years."

Cooper turned off the main road and drove down A Street.

"Where are we going?"

"I thought I'd show you the town."

Harper saw abandoned and burnt out houses. Some may have been occupied, but she couldn't tell. She saw a couple of houses with kids playing in yards full of swing sets, sagging trampolines, dead cars, trailers, and woodpiles. Broken appliances and snow machines rusted in a few yards, overgrown by grass and willows. One house was a half dome completely covered in foam with no windows.

"How does anyone live in that?" asked Harper.

"Nobody does now, but it's supposed to be OK inside."

"No windows?"

"Gets pretty cold here in the winter. Windows leak. And that spray-on foam is a great insulator. People do what they can to stay warm."

"Looks like crap," said Harper. "Almost every house here is a shack in the middle of a junkyard."

Cooper smiled. "One man's junk is another man's treasure. I don't know how many times I've used scraps of wood or old bolts or doorknobs to fix something around my house. I live miles from a store and more miles from a repairman, so I have to fix everything myself. It's easier to hang onto things and make do rather than go to town every time you need something. And a lot less expensive."

"Why doesn't your house and yard look like these?"

"Probably because I lived with your grandmother for twenty-six years and then lived in armpit villages for fourteen more. I decided I wanted to see flowers and vegetables, green grass, and different colors of wood and remember what they looked like during the six-month winter. And Snowball sure looks pretty with his long white hair prancing around my green yard during the summer."

Snowball heard his name, clambered over the front seat, and leaned against Harper, who hugged him. "He looks pretty anywhere."

"Who invited you?" asked Cooper.

Snowball walked over to Cooper and stuck his tongue in his ear.

"Well, thank you! That's the first attention I've had since Harper arrived. Glad to see I'm not totally forgotten."

"Snowball," said Harper with a sly grin on her face. She patted her leg. The dog turned around and put his head on her lap. Harper laughed and rubbed his ears. "Love you, Snowball."

Cooper smiled. "You're stealing my dog from me."

"No, I'm not. He's perfectly free to choose who he wants to be with."

"Like you were free to choose anything in San Antonio?"

She frowned. Was he going to criticize her? "What do you mean?"

"That dog loves to please. It's bred into his genes. If he desired independence, he'd still be a wolf. He loves you because you love him back. If you decide you don't like being covered in hair, or bothered when you eat, or pushed out of your bed and reject him, how would he feel?"

"He'd be sad, but I'd never do that," she said as she hugged him, relieved that she had misinterpreted Cooper's tone.

"But if you did, he'd find someone else to please, namely me. And if I rejected him, he'd run away and find someone else to love him."

He stopped the truck in the middle of the road and looked at Harper, who held his gaze.

"Sound familiar?" he asked. "I know you love Snowball, but would you want to be Snowball?"

"How would I...?" And then she realized what he was saying. She had been expelled by her father. She found someone else to love her, which didn't turn out the way she had hoped. She ran away and found Cooper.

Her eyes widened as she looked at Cooper. Snowball moaned as she scratched the top of his head on her lap. How good he must feel right now. Would she ever feel such contentment? Why wouldn't she want to be cuddled like him?

She'd be entirely dependent on someone else for happiness. She realized the hand that stroked could just as easily strike. Happiness shouldn't be so fragile, so controlled by someone else's mood. She had to be happy with herself first. Then there was something meaningful to share. But should your happiness depend on whether another person loved you?

Or the quality of the smack you bought? She realized the drugs and sex were substitutes for something else, but what was that something? And if she couldn't find it, what was wrong with getting wasted every once in a while?

She had tried that, and what came of it? Lots of tears and a growing regret inside her.

"You lived in a prison down there," said Cooper. "Your parents taught you to obey them or be punished. Now you're up here with me, and I'll love you no matter what you do. You're perfectly free to do anything you want. Make your own choices. I already told you that. The question you have to ask is what being free actually means to you. What do you want to do?" He looked deeply into Harper's eyes. "What do you genuinely care about?"

I don't know, she thought.

"When I came up here years ago, I thought the same things you did. This state was one big junk pile. Everyone was lazy and couldn't drag their butts to the junkyard and dump their crap. But then I realized how much freedom I had up here. I could walk anywhere for miles without running into a fence!

I could build anything I wanted on my house without asking permission. I could dress however it pleased me. I could shoot a bear or take his picture or watch him eat."

He shot her a wry grin. "But freedom is also messy and dangerous. The room I build could collapse on me. The stove I install could burn my house down. I'm free to do what I want, but I have to accept my own failure.

"And if you want freedom for yourself, you have to grant it to others. So if a father and son want to walk around carrying assault rifles, they can. If your neighbor wants to search for aliens and builds two huge radio dishes in his yard, then he can. And if I decide I've had enough of being old and can't find anything I want to live for, then I die."

Harper gasped in a breath and stared at Cooper.

"I love Snowball to death, but I will not be Snowball. Sorry to preach at you." He started driving again. "I feel like I'm in such a hurry and want to make sure I tell you everything. Not sure why."

But Harper knew why, and the not-so-cryptic sentence echoed through her head the whole way home: *And if I decide I've had enough of being old and can't find anything I want to live for, then I die.*

Freedom to live also meant freedom to die. How could you accept one without the other? Cooper didn't plan on allowing his disease to run its course.

Chapter Nineteen

During the drive home, Harper ran all his words through her mind several times. Had he intended to tell her his plans, or did he think she wouldn't understand the subtext? Could he have meant something else? Maybe he meant a life without purpose wasn't worth living. Period. Others had said that without advocating suicide if a purpose couldn't be found.

But Cooper wasn't like those others. His brain was dying, and he was in a hurry. And she knew why he was in such a hurry.

Cooper stopped in the driveway and opened his door. "Let's plant some flowers."

Harper noticed the wild roses growing along the edges of the yard, full of magenta and light pink petals. Plump purple lupine and delicate bluebells hiding in the shadows.

"Your yard is already full of flowers," said Harper. "Why do you want to plant more?"

"Because the ones I plant will last all summer; wildflowers die off in a couple of weeks. They remind me of the inevitability of death. As soon as they reach the height of beauty, they start to die, way too soon. At my age, I don't want to be reminded of how everything rushes to die. So I plant mine and enjoy them all summer."

His outlook eased some of her tension and made her feel better. He hated death and didn't want to be reminded of it. Maybe she had misinterpreted what he said before.

Snowball jumped out of the truck and barreled toward the trees chasing a rabbit. Even if he caught it, he wouldn't harm it. He just wanted to play.

Cooper led Harper to a small back room in his house containing three tall metal shelving units with grow lights. Each shelf overflowed with colors: magenta and pink petunias, yellow and orange marigolds, green pads of nasturtium, purple and red snapdragons, and pale blue bacopa.

Harper couldn't believe what she saw. "You grew these?"

"From seeds. Started in early April, along with my vegetables."

"They're beautiful."

"Wait till you see them in two weeks. Help me carry the flower trays outside."

After twenty minutes, they'd grouped trays of flowers on the deck. Cooper placed a snapdragon in the center of a flower box, surrounded it with marigolds and petunias, and then added a couple of bacopas along the edges.

"Don't want to crowd them. They'll overflow the box in a few weeks. Think you can do that?" asked Cooper.

"Not sure. Maybe you should do another one." Harper grinned.

"Off your butt and get to work, young lady." He tossed her gloves.

"OK. OK. Just kidding!" They both laughed.

"You plant those three containers, and I'll start on the ones in front."

For the next hour they planted and watered while Snowball lay in the shade, chewing on a stick. When the sun popped from behind clouds, it heated the air quickly, but compared to the heat in Texas, this was heaven.

After an hour, Cooper collapsed on a deck chair. "It's hot out here!"

Cooper had unbuttoned his shirt, revealing a mound of white chest hair pushing out of his scooped-neck t-shirt.

"Are you kidding?" scoffed Harper. "This is fall weather in San Antonio. People would be wearing jackets. Must be a hundred degrees there today."

"After being here a month, you'll wonder how anyone lives in such a hell hole. Anything over seventy-five will seem stifling to you."

"If you say so."

"And ten below will seem like a warm front in winter."

She gaped at him. "Below what? Zero? Are you kidding?"

"Speaking of cold, do an old man a favor and grab me a beer."

"Sure." Harper walked to the kitchen where Houdini attacked her leg, flopped onto his back, then jumped onto the counter. She scratched his back while he purred. She found a can of cat food in the pantry and dumped the contents into a bowl, which the kitty immediately assaulted.

Before she opened the refrigerator, she looked at all the photos. A history of her family for the past ten years stared back at her. Harper noticed the evolution of her expression and where she stood or who she sat next to. As a young girl, she stood between her parents and beamed. In the latest, she stood away from her parents and barely smiled.

Rachel and Heather looked so similar: a radiant smile, big brown eyes with a little hint of sadness, full lips, and definitive cheekbones. She recognized Heather's expression, because she had practiced the same one: "I know you like what you see. Come and get it if you dare."

A little gasp of pain escaped her mouth as she thought of Cooper looking at these pictures every day with no hope of seeing any of them, all as inaccessible as Heather. And now he knew neither his nor Heather's picture filled any corner of her parents' house, not to be forgotten, but never to be known.

Her pregnancy flashed into her consciousness. Whatever grew inside her would also never be known if she carried out her plans. But what else could she do? She had no means or way to raise a kid. She couldn't even tell anyone about it.

She opened the fridge and found a bottle of Alaskan Amber and Corona Light, opened them both, and carried them to the deck.

"Wasn't sure which one you wanted," said Harper, "so I brought them both."

"I'll take the Amber." She handed him the bottle and sat down across from him.

"Cheers." Harper offered her bottle toward him.

"Cheers." They clinked and both pulled a long drink.

"I never had the chance to drink a beer with my grandfather," said Cooper. "When did you drink your first?"

"In middle school when my parents were out of the house and then later on at sleepovers. I don't know any of my friends who haven't had a beer."

"When I was a teen, my parents could share their wine or beer with me at restaurants. Even order me one. Don't know when that practice stopped, but it allowed kids the opportunity to drink in front of their parents instead of hiding it from them."

"Did you still sneak drinks with your friends?"

"Sure, but I wasn't crazy with it."

"Did you let my father drink with you?" she asked before taking a sip.

He nodded. "Both him and Heather, but then Heather started down her path, and I got rid of all alcohol in the house." He looked off into the yard. "It was too late, but the idea was to show that booze was bad. I did everything wrong with her. Has Greg said anything to you about Heather?"

"Some. She was a drug addict and died. He used her as an example of what not to do when Chris and I were young." She took a sip. "He threatened that if he ever caught us smoking or drinking or using drugs he wouldn't hesitate to throw us out of the house."

"Good old Greg. Always so sure he was right about everything. The quickest way to make something desirable is to say it's forbidden. So tell me. Did Chris smoke and drink?"

"Sure he did. He and my parents had horrible fights during high school. They told him he'd amount to nothing. He was lazy and had no discipline, but then he enlisted in the Army and loved it. He even graduated first in boot camp. Now they're very proud of him."

"Where I'm sure he smokes and drinks."

"Sure. He gave me my first joint when I was thirteen. My parents never knew."

"Greg should," he said with some bitterness, "because he provided Heather's first joint. And her first snort of cocaine. At least that's what she told me." Cooper drained his beer.

Dad was certainly different before he became her dad. She had suspected as much but hearing it confirmed shocked her. All the more reason for him to talk to her rather than scream. He was as afraid she'd turn into him as a teen as he was scared she'd become Heather.

"Would you mind?" He held out his empty bottle.

"I'd be glad to." She took his bottle.

On her way to the kitchen, Harper thought about all the secrets everyone kept. So much remained unsaid within families. Would her life have been different if her father had told her the complete truth about him and Heather? Would she have listened to him then, rather than tune out his threats to never use drugs and alcohol? If she ever had kids, would she tell them the truth or try to hide it like every other parent did? The odds seemed to be in favor of doing the same thing even though it never worked.

And what did it mean to work? What was the goal? For the kid to never drink or use drugs? Or to hide their use effectively and still get the grades and recognition parents expected? Was the goal of complete avoidance realistic? Would you even want a kid who always did what she was told to do? How did anyone raise a kid? How would she?

As much as she tried to forget her underlying situation and focus on Cooper, she felt the imminent catastrophe waiting along the edge of her mind, becoming heavier and more urgent.

She grabbed two bottles of beer and opened them. She knew she could drink a beer anytime she wanted to in Cooper's house. She could snort smack or smoke a joint. Would she be more or less likely to get wasted now? Or find Kenzie and go drinking? Why would she want to? The secret thrill was gone, as was the trap of living a lie. Once she started lying, she felt she could never stop.

What she wanted was to drink and talk with her grandfather. She opened the deck door and heard a phone ringing. Cooper stood scratching his ear, blankly staring at the trees, making no effort to answer his phone.

"Cooper? Cooper? What's wrong?"

He turned and looked at her, confused.

"I brought you a beer." He stared at her. "Hey. It's me. Harper."

She tried to hand it to him, but he turned back toward the trees.

"What's that sound?" he asked vaguely.

"Your phone, Cooper. Your phone is ringing." Her chest felt heavy. *Oh, no!*

He stared at her, still pulling at his ear. She reached around him and pulled his phone out of his back pocket. She saw "Greg" and his phone number on the screen then dismissed the call.

"Hey, Cooper, why don't you sit down?" She led him to a chair and helped him sit. "I brought you a beer." She put it on the table and held his hand. "Maybe you should go slow with that one."

"Why do you say that?"

"Because you seemed a little foggy when I came back."

"Was I...?"

"I think so." She held out his phone. "Dad called, but I dismissed it."

He sighed. "I'm sorry."

She rubbed the back of his head. "No need to be. You OK now?"

He breathed deep a few times then shook his head back and forth.

"You kinda look like Snowball," laughed Harper.

He pushed his long hair back and smiled. "Who do you think taught him to do it?"

The phone rang again. Cooper picked it up and winked. He punched the speaker button.

"Hello, Greg. How are you doing?"

"Why'd you hang up on me?"

"Did I? Sorry about that. Must have done a butt hang-up. What can I do for you?"

"You know why I called," Greg snapped. "How's my daughter?"

"She's fine. We just planted all my flowers, and now we're sitting on the deck. She even brought me a beer." He winked at Harper. "She's a great kid. Thanks for sending her up here."

Cooper and Harper waited for a response, but none came. "Are you still there, Greg?"

"Yeah. So she had no problems getting there?"

"None she wasn't able to handle."

"Tell him about the bear," said Harper, a little too loud.

"Bear? What bear?" asked Greg.

"Wasn't a big deal." He shot her a playful scowl. "She chased a black bear through the forest. She threw rocks and screamed like a banshee. You should have heard her."

Harper sat down and laughed.

"What?" blurted Greg.

"Then we had one of my famous breakfasts. You remember, don't you, Greg? I used to make them for you every morning."

"Let's get back to the bear," Greg deadpanned.

"You have bears in your yard?" shouted Natalie. "I want to speak with Harper!"

Cooper held out the phone to Harper.

Harper could imagine the expression on her mother's face. She shouted, "I'm fine, Mom. The bear ran away after I growled at it!"

"Everything's fine," said Cooper. "We're having a great time. Going hiking in the park this weekend."

"Can I speak with her?" asked Greg.

Cooper offered her the phone and raised his eyebrows. Harper shook her head. She wasn't ready to talk to him yet.

"Afraid she just ran off chasing Snowball. He took off after a rabbit," said Cooper. "And don't worry about the bear. It's the first one I've seen here in years. Your daughter is an amazing young woman, Greg. Brave and kind but tough when she needs to be. Perfect for Alaska." He held Harper's eyes. "I'm very happy she came to see me."

Harper lifted her bottle to Cooper, who returned the gesture. They both drank.

"Like we had a choice," said Greg.

"Whatever the reason, it's been good for both of us."

"Her little sister wants to talk to her."

Cooper held out the phone and mouthed, "Your sister." Harper nodded.

"Harper!" shouted Cooper, pretending to call her back from the yard. "Come here! Your sister wants to talk to you!" Harper stifled her laugh. "Here she is."

Harper took the phone. "Alex?"

"Harper! I miss you!"

"Miss you, too, sweetie." She did miss her. So much.

"When are you coming home?"

"Don't know. Not for a while."

"Why? It's so boring without you. Can I come up?"

"Maybe later this summer. If Dad will send you."

"Mom said maybe we could all visit."

Harper paced around the deck. How could she live without seeing her sister? "We'll see, Alex."

"That always means 'No,'" she whined.

"Not always. It could happen. Let's just wait a while, then we can talk about it." She tried to think of a way Alex could fly up without her parents. If her mother and father visited, she'd go back to doing everything she'd done at home. They'd never treat her like Cooper did.

"I miss you, too!" shouted Jack.

"Hi, Jack! Be nice to Alex."

"Tell her to be nice to me. She's so bossy!"

"I am not!" shouted Alex.

"Harper, are you OK?" asked Natalie, who had grabbed the phone. Harper could hear Greg fussing at her siblings in the background.

"Yes, Mom. I've never been better. Seriously. Look, I'm going to give you back to Cooper." She handed the phone back, sat down, and drained the rest of her beer.

"Natalie?" said Cooper.

"Seems a little too exciting up there for the first day. Are you sure you can do this?"

"We're going to take it one day at a time."

"I don't want my daughter hurt."

Harper considered the irony of that comment. She'd fled from pain they'd caused, but she was sure her mother was sincere, just oblivious or too deferential to her dad. Neither one helped her.

"I'll keep her safe, Natalie."

"Please take care of her."

"We're both taking care of each other. She'll be fine. We need to start dinner now, so I'd better go."

"OK. Good-bye."

Cooper disconnected.

"He was shouting at Alex and Jack," said Harper, slamming the bottle onto the table. "Why? What did they do wrong?"

"Acting like a brother and sister. Greg and Heather used to fight with each other all the time at that age."

"I was afraid I was a bad influence on Alex. It's one of the reasons why I left her." She turned away, staring into the woods.

Cooper went to her. "You'll be a great role model before all of this is done." He held her shoulders from behind. "She'll be proud to call you sister."

Harper turned toward him. "I hope so." Her eyes searched his face. "When I came back with the beers, you didn't recognize me. You didn't know your phone was ringing."

"I'm sorry." He turned away.

"I wasn't blaming you." She stopped him and went to face him. "How often does that happen?"

"Once every few days." She looked into his eyes. He looked to the side. "Maybe a little more often."

Her hands shook as they reached for his arms. "What would've happened if I hadn't been here?"

He shrugged. "I would've snapped out of it eventually. Always have."

"You could've fallen off the deck, or Snowball could've run off."

"A lot of things could have happened, but they didn't. At least not yet."

"Are you scared?" she asked lowly.

"Yeah, I'm scared. Scared of putting you through this." He pushed a chair and shook his head. "I didn't want to bother you with my problems."

"I was selfish to give you mine, but you took me in to save me." She hugged him. "I'll save you, too."

"I don't want to be a vegetable, Harper. I don't want to get stuck with no way out." He pushed her hair out of her face while a tear ran down his cheek. "I've seen old people with this condition staring at nothing all day. I'll shoot myself before I let that happen."

"Don't say that." He did not plan to fight the disease or allow it to attack him at will. He'd kill himself before it stole his mind entirely. She couldn't process that. She'd just gotten him back; she couldn't lose him. Not again. She regretted all those years she could have known him, years and time they couldn't get back. "I will not leave you," said Harper. "I'll get you back, no matter what it takes."

He held her shoulders and his eyes hardened. "And if you can't, you got to promise me you won't let me stay that way. No one should have to live like that."

She saw the intensity of his gaze, the pleading. She knew what he was asking. Her chin quivered and her eyes dripped tears. How could he ask that of her? She grasped him as hard as she could.

"Promise me," he said.

"I promise."

Chapter Twenty

Harper stood beside Cooper as he opened his grill and flipped the flank steak. "Looks good!" said Harper.

"Should be. I marinated this meat for a day in Amber beer, home grown cilantro, fajita seasoning, and hot pepper flakes. Yum!"

A few geese flew by, their tiny heads pulling their fat bodies at the end of long necks, squawking at the effort.

Harper carried the hose to each planter box and watered the newly planted flowers while Snowball stalked a squirrel.

Harper hadn't said much since her promise to Cooper. She realized he needed her more than she had needed him. She'd wanted him to save her life, while he needed someone to end his, if necessary. Or at least help him escape what he considered worse than death.

She had to get an abortion—soon. She didn't want her problem adding to his burden. She felt horrible that one of her reasons for coming to Alaska was because its laws didn't require adult permission for the procedure. She did not want him to wonder about the sincerity of her feelings for him. Would she have visited him if he'd lived in one of the thirty-seven states requiring parental approval or notification? She couldn't honestly answer that question and didn't want him to worry about her answer. He had enough to worry about, so much more than she did. He could blank out at any moment or forget who she was. How did that compare with her problems?

She felt like a "Scratch" again at the hospital, there due to a technicality but not belonging. She rolled the hose back up on the spool and watched

Cooper bend over the grill, disappearing in a cloud of smoke, then close the cover and back away.

She had to take care of her problem to help him with his. But how? She needed to make an appointment and get to Fairbanks to have it done. How could she do that without him taking her? Would he let her drive the truck by herself to Fairbanks—to do what? What possible reason could she give that would require him to stay home?

She needed money to pay for the procedure. Could she really sell drugs in this town to kids like Kenzie? It would've been easy to find buyers at her previous school. And she wouldn't have felt bad about selling, though she was reluctant to give a balloon to Trish. But here? She'd have to sneak around, go to parties, be very careful and hope Cooper never found out. Or take advantage of Cooper's tolerance and not hide anything. Would he really tolerate her dealing? Even if he did, she would know how much it would hurt him. She couldn't do that to him. Maybe she could ask Kenzie who she bought from and he could buy her stash all at once.

Maybe it would be better to simply tell Cooper and ask him to pay for the abortion. But what would she do with the drugs? She wished she had never asked Zachary for anything.

"When will we go to Fairbanks again?" she asked.

"Not sure. Next week sometime. Why?" He poked at the meat.

"I think I need different clothes for Alaska." All of her warm stuff was in those crates. If they went to town for clothes, maybe she could find a way to get to a clinic.

"You sure do." He closed the grill. "We're going backpacking this weekend." He clapped his hands while a huge grin spread across his face.

She frowned and waved her hands. "Backpacking? I don't even know what that is."

"We hike to the middle of nowhere and pitch a tent," he said gleefully.

She put her hands on her hips and leaned toward him. "And why will this be fun?"

"You'll see. You don't know what you've missed all your life." He picked up his beer and took a sip.

She moved around to face him. "OK, so don't I need clothes for this adventure?"

"Yup. I already talked to Isabelle at the Mountain Shop down at the Gulch. She'll give me a discount."

"Where's the Gulch?"

Cooper sat down on the bench next to his grill. "Just outside of Denali Park about thirty-five miles south of here. Bunch of tourist shops, restaurants, and hotels. We'll be there Friday. We'll get your gear then go into the park on Saturday morning. Don't worry about it. I've got everything planned." Smoke poured out of the grill. He jumped up. "You'll have a blast."

So no trip to a clinic until next week? What was she going to do?

He opened the lid, and smoke billowed. She could see flames leaping up through the grill. "Do you like your fajitas medium rare or burnt?"

She laughed. "Nothing in between?"

He poked at the meat somewhere behind the flames and smoke. "Doesn't appear to be. I like them medium rare. If you don't, I'm sure there'll be some crispy parts. Let's eat!"

He grabbed the slabs of meat with tongs and tossed them into a pan.

"C'mon, Snowball!" yelled Cooper. "Fajitas!"

"These are really good," said Harper, gazing at her plate of fajita scraps, pico de gallo and guacamole smears. "How can you possibly miss Taco Cabana when you make better Mexican food than they do?"

"Because they make it *for* me. Cheap," said Cooper patting his stomach. Houdini licked at a dollop of guacamole then leapt straight up to snag a fly with his paw. It escaped and flew toward the window. Houdini launched himself from Harper's placemat, pushing her food and beer into her lap. She jumped up, her legs dripping with foam and guacamole, a few pieces of tomato stuck to her face. Houdini jumped up the window, snagged the fly, and ate it on the windowsill.

Cooper laughed while Harper wiped herself.

"Houdini, what the hell? All because of a fly? Was it worth it?"

"It was to him," said Cooper. "He can be lazy as hell doing nothing all day but eat, sleep, and bathe himself. Then a fly appears, and he leaps halfway to the ceiling like an Olympic athlete to catch it. There's a lesson there if you look for it."

Harper thought. "You can do amazing things if you find your fly. Like writing novels."

"Or singing." Cooper chuckled. "You've got a helluva brain in your head, Harper."

"And a helluva mess on my legs. Think I'll go change." Harper went to her bedroom and stripped off her clothes. While she looked for a shirt and pants, she found her phone, totally dead. She hadn't charged it last night and had forgotten about it all day. When was the last day she hadn't used her phone? *Why would I care who texted me?* she thought. She finished dressing, then plugged in the phone before she went to the bathroom to wash her face.

• • • • •

Cooper cleaned the plates in the sink. Houdini wove around his legs, purring, shaking his tail, trying to get Cooper's attention. Cooper dutifully scooped a can of food into a bowl and set it on the floor.

He needed to teach Harper how to shoot the pistol. She'd probably never seen one, much less fired it. He was blanking out too often. What would happen if he had an episode while they hiked? He grabbed the daypack from the mudroom and set it on the table. He removed his Mountain Gun from its holster and thought of all the times he'd carried its dead weight in his belt or jacket or pack as he moved through supposedly dangerous territory. Its presence reduced his worry, so he could enjoy his hike and the scenery, but he'd never needed it. He'd rarely removed the pistol from its holster except at the shooting range or at home to clean it.

It was like so many other things in life that someone claimed were absolutely necessary, like oxygen. But Cooper knew what he could live without if forced to: his family, his grandkids, Rachel. He had cut that part of his heart away. Even the photos on the fridge became mere photos.

What had become essential was his passion for writing and composing. But now he would soon be unable to create, and he couldn't imagine living in that lonely void again.

Now he needed Harper, he needed this gun, and he needed her to learn to use it.

"Cooper! What are you doing?" She seemed scared to death.

"Nothing to be scared of. You need to learn to shoot this thing."

"Why?" She approached the table.

"Because we're going into Sections 6 and 7 in two days, which are full of bears. If I blank out, you need to know how to shoot it."

"You said you've never had to use it."

"That's true, but there's always a first time. Sit down. Alaskan women know their way around guns."

She sat down next to him. "This is a Smith & Wesson Mountain Gun. It's a heavy sonofabitch." He gave it to her. "Here. Hold it."

Her eyes opened wide as she held it away from her body with two hands. "Is it loaded?"

"I'd never give you a loaded gun without telling you, but you should assume any gun is loaded." He showed her how to swing out the cylinder and load and remove bullets, how to cock the hammer, and how the back snap on the holster served as a safety.

"Pistols in movies aren't this big," said Harper.

"True, but they won't kill a grizzly bear either. Let's go to the range."

Snowball ran to the door, sensing they were leaving. "Not this time, boy. You won't like the loud bangs."

They backed out of the driveway, laughing at Snowball's paws pressed against the window as he barked at them.

Cooper drove to the park and turned left, past the covered stage used for the annual music festival, past campgrounds, and past two ATVs racing along the dike, a six-foot mound of dirt and gravel running the length of the park, which protected the town from flooding. Anders Fork had flooded during spring breakup in 1974, drowning First Street in two feet of water. The dike was built during that summer and had been a favorite speedway for kids and adults on ATVs and snow machines ever since. Jumping the dike—speeding up one side and catching air on the other—was a rite of passage for teens.

"Is that Kenzie?" asked Harper.

"And her boyfriend. Seeing who can catch more air jumping the dike. Kids do it all the time."

As Kenzie's Honda jumped, she threw up both arms and whooped, then bounced on the other side.

The trees lining the open field had recently sprouted leaves, fluttering in a rich unblemished green, lighter than the dour spruce needles nearby. For those who had endured the long winter, green-up was the most magical time of year. It was so hard to believe the world could regain its colors after six months of deep snow, but here they were, oozing out of the ground and branches so fast one could literally watch the world painted anew.

The road ended in a gravel turnaround and a log shelter facing two hundred yards of open field, backed up by a fifteen-foot tall mound of gravel. Fifty yards into the field lay an old truck covered with more bullet holes than metal. Parts of another vehicle were twisted into a parody of modern art.

Harper looked quizzically at Cooper. "What happened here?"

"Left over from the Memorial Day Machine Gun Shoot. Bunch of folks come out here with machine guns and cannons, even mortars, and honor our fallen heroes by shooting a junk car to pieces. Sounds like a little war when they're here."

Cooper pulled a target stand from his truck bed and walked twenty paces away from the shed. He set the target bullseye four feet high then walked back to Harper.

"Never put your finger on the trigger until you're ready to shoot. This thing kicks like a mother, so you need to hold it with two hands, like this. Equal force against the gun from both hands."

Cooper planted his feet just outside each shoulder, bent his knees, and leaned forward at the waist. "Lock your elbows and bring the gun sight level with your eyes. Pull back the hammer and squeeze the trigger. The recoil will make you jerk the gun up, so keep your wrists and elbows locked to keep the gun pointing where you aimed it after it fires. This is a very loud gun, Harper, so get ready for it."

"OK"

"Watch me. I'm going to shoot twice." He cocked the hammer and squeezed the trigger.

The world seemed to explode, but only a tiny hole appeared in the target.

"Shit!" yelled Harper, jumping backward.

"Get ready!" He shot a second time. This time Harper barely flinched. Cooper noticed one hole in the target was high, and the other was to the right of the bullseye. "Dammit. OK, your turn."

Harper walked over to the spot Cooper vacated.

"Take your stance, left foot slightly ahead of your right. Bend your knees."

He handed Harper the gun and positioned her two hands around the handle, left thumb forward along the barrel, right thumb up and to the left of the hammer.

"Lean forward. Lock elbows. Sight along the barrel. Got it?"

"I think so." Her voice quavered.

"Now think very strong and very firm. You are rock solid. Pull the hammer back and squeeze. Try not to flinch."

Harper shot. Her mark was high, but on the target.

"Damn good first try! Pull the hammer again and keep that gun down."

She shot again. The hole just nicked the right side of the eye.

"Great! Now try to take two shots in a row. It's double action, so all you have to do is pull the trigger twice."

Her first shot hit the eye, and the second hit just below.

"You're a natural, young lady. How do you like shooting? Oh, take your finger off the trigger."

She did. "Kind of fun, but I think I'd go deaf if I shot much more. My brain's ringing like a bell."

"I wanted you to get used to the noise because you won't be wearing ear protection in the bush."

"Bush?"

"Bush country. Boonies. Away from the craziness in towns. If we come out here again, I'll bring my earmuffs. I think I'll feel safe with you as my backup on our hike." Cooper smiled and took the pistol.

Harper folded her arms and looked hard at Cooper. "Had you always planned to teach me to shoot?"

"What do you mean?" He put the gun into the holster.

"You planned on driving me around town and planting flowers. Was shooting always on your list?"

"No. I wasn't sure how'd you react, but after watching you chase that bear this morning..."

He tried so hard to act happy and casual. But she knew why he brought her there. "And after telling me you planned to shoot yourself. That wasn't on your original list either."

"OK." He felt nervous under her gaze. "Why don't we...?"

She moved closer. "You said you never used it. Have you ever almost used it?"

Harper's eyes bored into Cooper. He stopped smiling and looked at the box of bullets he pulled from his pocket.

"Almost, when I was walking my old dog in the fog through the village. A two-year-old polar bear surprised us. I pulled the holster out of the pack, but Sonny Boy didn't bark. We just stood there, silent, until the bear walked off." He loaded the pistol.

"Any other time?" she pressed. He looked away. "Please tell me."

He snapped the barrel back. "Let's get back to the house before the bugs come out." He turned to walk towards his truck.

Harper held his arm. "Cooper, talk to me."

Cooper stared at her, seeing the fear in her eyes. Should he be honest? He had to. If what he feared might happen at some point, he had to be brutally clear. "Just before you came up here, I got the gun out and considered whether I could use it on myself. It was before you called. I honestly don't know what I would've done if you hadn't called me." He shoved the gun back into the holster. "There. You satisfied?"

"No! So now I'm supposed to shoot you if you can't?" Her face showed so much pain.

"No, Harper. That's not..."

"Why else would I have to shoot this thing?" Tears filled her eyes. "You taught me so I could shoot you!"

He panicked. Would she leave? Had he told her too much?

"No, I didn't and I would never ask you to do that." He scrambled for another reason to give her. "We could be hiking and a bear surprises us, and I can't remember anything! I blank out! I won't even know what a bear is! I didn't know who Snowball was a few days ago. That's when you have to use the gun! To shoot the bear!"

"The bear." Harper repeated numbly, shaking her head as she took a step backward.

She didn't believe him. "Yes, the bear." He thought she was about to walk away.

"Did you want me up here to take care of you or to kill you?" She sounded so sad.

"Neither one. When the time comes, I'll do it myself."

"Unless you can't!"

"Then I can't!"

"Then what do I do?" Harper wailed.

He pulled her head to his shoulder. "Just help me. I may need a little help is all."

Harper wept into his chest, while his tears fell into her hair. They held the same pose as last night at the airport, but now they felt no joy. After both stopped crying, they separated and stood looking at the target.

"Why didn't you call us?" asked Harper. "All those years. Didn't you ever think about it?"

"Many times."

"Then why didn't you?" she pleaded.

"I don't know. I guess I hoped Greg would call me. That he'd forgive me and not be so ashamed of me. I thought if I called him, he wouldn't answer the phone or hang up if he did. I didn't want to beg!"

"I begged you to take me."

He held her face so she would see his eyes. "The happiest day of my life, so far."

"Did you almost say no?"

"Yes. Thought I was being selfish to bring you here, but you were desperate, and I thought I could help."

"Why?"

He walked out to disassemble the target. "Because I couldn't do worse than I did with Heather." He unclipped the paper and began to roll it up. "And I had thought about everything with her over and over since she died. What I did wrong. What I could've done differently. How many times I said no when she needed me. I gave up on her and waited for her to die."

He stifled a sob, wiped his eyes, and undid the clips to collapse the target frame. "I thought if I had another chance, I could save her, but that could never happen. Then you called. I wanted so badly to help you, but now I've got this crap going on in my head."

"When did it start?"

He picked up the frame and walked back to his truck. "Not sure. Months ago maybe."

"Would you have shot yourself if I hadn't called?" He saw the fear in her eyes.

"I don't know." He tossed the paper and target into the truck bed. "I don't want to die, Harper, especially now, but blanking out forever is not living. Rachel's mother went through that." He looked at the gun. "I won't."

"Maybe you'll get better. You were lonely, and now I'm here, so maybe you'll get better." Her smile flickered. "I just got you back, and I'm not going to lose you." She reached for his hands. "I need my grandpa."

"You have another grandfather."

"John? After I was expelled from their school, he hardly spent time with me. He's ashamed of me. He cares about expanding his Christian store business, not about me."

"I'm sure he and Zoe love you."

"They love who they want me to be, not what I am."

Cooper hesitated. "And Rachel?"

"She's sweet and kind, but I'm not a little girl anymore. She can't give me dolls or read me books, so she doesn't know what to do. And PawPaw has been sick with cancer. He's in a lot of pain and on drugs all the time. I haven't talked to him in over a year. She's been like a ghost."

"Has she ever mentioned me?" He tried to hide the longing in his voice.

Harper looked at him and shook her head. "No."

Cooper nodded his head slightly and looked down the range toward the destroyed truck. "I'm sorry her father's having to go through that, and sorry Rachel has to see Jacob disintegrate. It's not really fair after what she went through with her mother. Years ago, when I still lived in San Antonio, one of our teacher friends' father got cancer. He knew he was going to die a slow, painful death. She went to check up on him after work one day and found his loaded shotgun leaning against his chair. She tried to take the gun. They struggled for it, but she won. Then she gave it to me to keep for her. He'd planned to shoot himself. Instead, he lingered on for months, full of drugs and barely conscious.

"He didn't die quietly in his sleep. He screamed and gasped then suffocated while his family watched. Later on she told us she wished she'd never taken away his gun. Why would anyone want their child's last memory of them to be a scream of pain, or in my case a crazy man who doesn't even recognize them?"

"You could get treatment," Harper pleaded. "Maybe the doctors could help you."

"There's no cure."

"I just got you back. I'm still getting to know you. I don't want you to leave!" She clutched him to her.

"I'll try my best, Harper. I can't leave just yet. I've got too many things to teach you." He walked toward the truck. "And you need to help me finish my book."

"How can I help you? Remember, I failed everything." She followed him. "How could I possibly help you?"

"Would you want to?"

"Yes, but I don't know how."

"You've already done the hard part—found something you want to do. Everything flows naturally after that." He opened the door to the backseat and laid the gun on the floor. "You want to sing?"

"Yes."

"Maybe write some songs?"

"That'd be cool."

"Then I'll help you." He opened her door, and she climbed in. "You're not a failure just because your teachers gave you bad grades. They just didn't find what you wanted to learn. Now we know you want to write, sing, and compose." He closed her door, walked to the other side, and climbed into his seat.

"When did anyone in your high school try to discover what your talents are and what you like doing?"

"Never."

"Because schools are more interested in producing kids with the same knowledge and skills than they are in fostering the development of individual talents and skills. Schools are factories when they should be imaginariums."

"You think kids should have to learn only what they like?"

"No, but if you can find something that hooks you first, then you'll be more willing to learn the corollary stuff that can be boring and tedious. I know you can sing and perform. You sang at the airport and people applauded, and you sang in my truck last night. You have talent. Lots of it. We're going to pursue that tomorrow and see how much you like singing. Then we'll work on the other things you like. Sound like a plan?"

She beamed back at him. "Yes."

"Good." He started the truck and shifted it into gear. He could feel her staring at him.

"Is teaching me what's keeping you alive?" He looked over at her. "Because there's so much I need from you. You'll need years to show me everything." He could see the pleading in her eyes and her shaky attempt to keep smiling.

"Whatever I can give you, I will."

"Promise me?"

"I promise."

Chapter Twenty-One

The sun, burning behind thin clouds, was still hours away from setting, casting a long shadow in front of the truck as Cooper drove out of the park. Harper reached over the seat to grab the jacket and sweatpants Cooper had brought last night. Dust swirled behind the truck, making the shooting range disappear, but Harper still heard the shots, the pleading, and the crying. She hoped she'd never have to fire the gun again but felt a foreboding now that she had.

She sat back down, pulling on the sweatpants. Was she cold or just anxious?

Cooper noticed and rolled up his window. "I feel a little chilly myself."

Could they both keep their promises? He'd stay alive as long as he could help her, and she wouldn't abandon him if his mind faded. No, that was a lie. She'd promised to help him die. She remembered seeing him standing outside, absently pulling his ear, not knowing the phone was ringing. What would she do if that happened again, and he couldn't snap out of it?

Why couldn't she have come sooner? How different would her life be if she'd known him sooner? Before Zachary. Before the expulsion.

The sun glared through Harper's window, forcing her to shade her eyes.

She was here now. She had to make the most of the time she had. He said he was in a rush. Now she understood why because she was, too.

"When can we start singing?" she asked.

"Maybe tonight."

Cooper turned from his driveway into his large parking area. Kenzie walked away from the front door and waved. Snowball's paws pressed against the window as he barked.

"I believe Kenzie is here to see you," said Cooper. "Today was the last school day. Kids must be planning a party." He looked at Harper with cocked eyebrows. "You could meet all your future classmates."

I don't have time for parties, Harper thought. "Probably not. I thought we'd start later."

"Whatever you want to do." He parked the truck.

Harper opened her door and jumped out. "Hey, Kenzie. Give me a second. I'm going to let Snowball out."

Harper opened the door, and Snowball barreled out, running to Cooper, then back to Harper, then over to Kenzie who jumped onto her Honda. "Oh, my God!"

"Snowball!" yelled Harper, who kneeled on the grass and opened her arms. Snowball crashed into her and licked her face repeatedly as Harper squealed.

"He's crazy," said Kenzie, standing on her Honda.

"He's the best," said Harper as she stood up and walked over to Kenzie.

"I need to pee," Cooper announced as he walked towards the house, "so I'll leave you girls alone."

"Saw you catching air on your ATV," said Harper once Cooper was inside. "Looked like fun."

"ATV?" She laughed. "Everybody calls them Hondas."

"I'd like to try jumping sometime."

"I'll take you. It's really fun in winter on a snow machine."

"I hear school's out for summer," said Harper as her brain scrambled through her options for dispensing with her stash. Would Kenzie tell her, or would she have to ask about drugs?

Kenzie sat on her Honda seat, trying to block Snowball's sniffing nose.

"Yeah. Last day." Kenzie cautiously rubbed Snowball's head. "Bunch of us are meeting at Jordan's in an hour. I thought since you're new you'd like to meet all the kids. Not much to do around here during the summer 'cept hang out." Snowball pushed his nose between her legs, and she batted him away. "Stop it, Snowball!"

"Thanks for thinking of me." Harper had learned how to identify kids who liked to party. Like a sixth sense. She had guessed wrong only twice, both at TCA. Of course, her father got called, and Harper had to pretend she was just trying to identify trouble-makers at their good little school. "Just trying to protect TCA, Daddy." She didn't think she was wrong about Kenzie. She had enjoyed being stoned way too much.

"Of course, the big blowout will be after graduation on Friday, but you and Cooper will be at the park, so I thought I'd ask about going tonight." Snowball lifted his paws onto Kenzie's chest. "I swear this dog's a pervert!"

Harper smiled and lifted Snowball's legs off Kenzie. "Just a puppy wanting attention."

"Yeah, well now I got bruises on my boobs." She rubbed her chest and straightened her shirt. "I could drive back in an hour and pick you up."

Harper cocked an eyebrow. "How do kids from Anders Fork hang out? Do you do anything exciting?"

"Probably not as exciting as...where are you from again?"

"San Antonio, Texas."

"Wow. Big city! I went to Seattle once. Malls, movies, clubs, restaurants everywhere. Sad to say we don't have any of that, so it's Netflix, video games, a little weed, and some beer if Andrew remembers to bring it."

Time to take the plunge. She raised her brows. "Weed gets boring. Got anything stronger?

Kenzie smiled. "Sure. Oxy's pretty common and meth."

Score another point for my ability to pick out the misfits, Harper thought. "Heroin?"

Her eyes widened, and she stood up. Harper gripped Snowball. "You got some? I never tried that."

Harper grinned. "I might have something I want to get rid of."

Kenzie almost stood on her toes, she was so excited. "Are you a dealer?"

"No. Just trying to stop bad habits. Who would I talk to if I had something to sell?"

Kenzie glanced around and then spoke quietly. "You can talk to me."

"Great." She had some leverage then.

"So do you want me to pick you up?"

Harper looked behind her and saw Cooper watching them from the window. "Think I'll pass. I had no sleep last night, and Cooper had me planting flowers all afternoon. I'm dead tired. But thanks for asking."

She looked disappointed. "Sure."

Harper put her arm around Kenzie and walked her slowly to the other side of the truck. "Also, Kenzie, I really love Snowball and Houdini, and I don't want anything to happen to them while we're gone. If I were you, I'd get my boyfriend over here and we'd party for a few days, but I don't want you to do that. Or smoke pot in the house. I don't want Snowball getting high and running off somewhere. And don't want you crashing at the parties Friday night and forgetting about them. So if you do a great job, when I get back I'll give you some stuff for free."

"What you got?"

"Don't worry. You'll like it. Deal?"

"OK."

"Great. I'm going to take a shower then sleep with my new boyfriend."

"Who is he?" she asked with a touch of worry in her voice. Harper hugged Snowball. "Oh, you mean Snowball. You expect me to sleep with him, too?"

"You'd better not!" Harper smiled and let Snowball lick her lips.

"Gross!" whined Kenzie.

"He only sleeps with me. See ya, Kenzie. Thanks for stopping by."

"See you Friday." She put on her helmet, started her Honda, and drove away.

Harper and Snowball went inside the house. Harper felt a bit lighter knowing she could get her cash for the abortion without having to spend precious time. Just one sale and done.

Cooper sat at the table drinking a beer. "So what's the plan?"

"No plan. I told her I was tired. Maybe next time."

"I wouldn't have stopped you."

"I know." Their eyes locked. "I'm sure I can find another party if I feel the urge. There's always a party somewhere. Besides, we have a date."

Cooper nodded. "Hey, I got some ice cream, chocolate sauce, and whipped cream. You want a sundae?"

"Sure. I'm going to change." She took off the baggy sweatpants and jacket and draped them on a chair. "Be back in a little bit."

Harper went to her bedroom and heard her phone vibrate on the dresser. She saw texts from Zachary.

Where are u?!

Prior to that: *U had better answer!*

Prior to that: *No way u get away with this! I have friends I can call!*

And then the first message sent earlier that morning: *Friend of mine contacted me from Seattle. Said u were flying to Alaska and that u said u weren't pregnant. That u lied to me to get free drugs. R u pregnant or not?*

U had better not mess with me, Harper. I have friends who can ruin u. Might check out YouTube and search for "High School Teen Dances In Sexy Negligee." There's plenty more videos and photos, none yet with ur name on them. U better contact me.

Harper gasped. Her stomach locked up, and her hands shook. She tried to calm down before talking to Cooper. She knew she had embarrassing photos on the internet, as did a lot of girls her age, but posting what Zachary had would be bad. Zachary had been the biggest mistake in her life, and though he was four thousand miles away, he was still interfering with her life. An abortion wouldn't fix that.

She walked into the kitchen where Cooper washed dishes. A chocolate sundae waited for her on the table.

She tried to keep her voice calm. "Cooper, can you text Dad and ask him for the password to his monitoring software on my computer?" She sat down and ate a bite of ice cream.

Cooper flung water off his hands then wiped them with a towel. "He bugged your computer?"

"Yeah, the day after he sent me to the suicide hospital then decided that would be too embarrassing to explain."

Cooper frowned. "There's a lot you haven't told me. You tried to commit suicide?"

"No. Look, I'll explain later. Can you ask him for the password? I need to use my computer and don't want him spying on me. Also, I need your WI-FI password."

"That's easy. 'Snowball&Houdini' with the ampersand. It's after midnight in Texas, by the way."

"He stays up late." She ate more ice cream.

Cooper texted by the sink while Harper connected her phone to Wi-Fi at the table. She kept the phone muted and went to YouTube and typed in Zachary's search phrase. And there she was—somewhat blurred to keep the video from being rejected by YouTube—dancing, shaking, bending, showing almost everything, laughing and looking so hot and happy. But she wasn't. She saw a girl desperate to be loved; those around her must have seen a wasted girl willing to screw anyone. Bystander faces were blurred, but the laughter and catcalls were loud and clear. The video already had hundreds of views.

Did she care? At home she wouldn't have minded as long as her parents never found out. But here was different. She wanted something else, though she didn't know what that was. When would the past stay in the past?

Cooper cleared his throat. Harper saw him wipe an eye with the dishtowel.

"Did he send it?" asked Harper.

"Yeah," he choked out, "after I threatened to get you another computer and change my phone number. I just sent it to you."

Cooper turned away from her, and she heard him cough. Was he crying?

She opened his text: *Heather071501*. "That couldn't be her birthday."

"No." Cooper turned around wiping his eyes. "The day she died. She was twenty-six."

"Why would he...?"

"Your dad is a very complicated man. I'm sure he uses that password for lots of things. That day nearly killed all of us. He disappeared for a while then came back angry as hell. Think he uses it to remind himself of what we all did wrong and why he needs to act differently. But it also shows how much guilt he feels, though he'd never admit that."

All her father wanted was to make sure she didn't ruin her life then die. He'd wanted to protect her, yet all she ever saw was a man disappointed in her, yelling at her. He didn't know what to do. He saw her turning into his sister, panicked, and knew nothing else but to yell louder. "And he's worried I'll turn out like her."

"From the day you were born. Parents always have mixed feelings about their kids. They want them to be like themselves in some respects, yet don't want them to experience any of the problems and mistakes. 'Course those are what made us who we are."

"It's kind of hard to avoid making mistakes," said Harper as the video played in her mind.

"And harder to put them behind you. The past is a wound which never heals."

Silence hung heavily until Houdini pleaded for food with a pitiful wail.

Harper finished the last bite of ice cream and stood. "Cooper, I need to take care of something."

"That's OK. I'm going to take Snowball for a little walk." Houdini whined again. "After I feed kitty."

Harper went back to her room, entered the password on her computer, and uninstalled the software. What would she say to Zachary? She was still pregnant and still planned to get the abortion, but he'd still threaten with the videos. She Googled paternity tests.

The side door opened and closed. Harper peeked out her window to see Cooper walking Snowball down the driveway. Grabbing her phone, she ran to the front of the house where she could see them walking away and punched in Zachary's number.

"Where the hell have you been?" yelled Zachary with a bit of a slur. He sounded drunk.

"My phone died, and I've been busy all day."

"What are you doing in Alaska?"

"I can't get an abortion in Texas. Alaska doesn't require parental consent. I'm staying with my grandfather."

"Are you pregnant or not?"

"Yes. I gave you the pregnancy results. My name is on the paper. Ted was acting like a dick, so I told him I wasn't. Look, asshole, I'm still getting the abortion. I don't want anything to remind me of you. I told you I'd send you a receipt when it's done."

"I'm not taking any more chances with you. Did you check out your video?" he taunted. "Everybody seems to like it. A lot."

Harper didn't answer. She hoped he couldn't hear her heart pounding her chest.

"I'm sure you did," he said. "That one is mild compared to others I have. Wait till the world sees the real Harper Lyons! If I don't have a receipt by Monday, your name will be tagged to that video and another one will be uploaded. Same thing happens on Tuesday. And Wednesday. I have a friend who does this stuff all the time and never gets caught." He chuckled. "Your name will be famous by the end of the week as will every other part of your body."

Harper forced herself to show no concern. "Guess what I took from your bathroom on Sunday? After you raped me for, what, the tenth time? Probably more."

"I never raped you!" he seethed.

That obviously hit a nerve, she thought. "I already told you. Consensual sex between a sixteen-year-old and a twenty-year-old is considered rape in Texas." *Here comes another lie.* "I took your toothbrush, Zachary, perfect for DNA tests, and I'm going to the troopers tomorrow. I'm going to tell them all about you and then get a paternity test to prove what you did to me. So add my name to anything you post and see what happens."

"You're bluffing."

"You'll find out soon enough. Whatever embarrassment you could cause me will pass soon enough. However, when the cops knock on your door with a warrant for your arrest, that won't pass. That's permanent." She was sure his very rich and influential father wouldn't want his son arrested.

"You got nothing on me!"

She smiled hearing how easy it was to rile him. "Really? I had to run to Alaska to get away from you. You drugged me up repeatedly. And gave me to your friends when I was unconscious. Even beat me."

"I never beat you!"

"Funny, I woke up Sunday with a fat lip. I got a picture of it. Where did that come from? This could be quite a story, Zachary. And then there's the drug dealing."

"That goes both ways, bitch."

"Already sold what you gave me before I left. You got nothing on me, except the money to pay the doctor. So if I were you, I'd just sit tight and be patient. I'll send the receipt as soon as I can. No way am I going to keep this baby."

"I'll wait a few days, but don't screw with me, Harper!"

"Never again, Zachary. Never again." She ended the call, dropped the phone, and used both hands to keep the tears inside her eyes. Houdini jumped up next to her, purring, dragging his tail across her face as he paced in front of her. Harper held the kitty like a baby in both arms, rubbing his tummy and ears like Cooper had showed her. Houdini closed his eyes and vibrated against her chest. The feeling calmed her.

For the first time Harper thought about the baby inside her and how holding it might feel. Houdini lay on his back against her arm totally relaxed, his paws curled forward, limp, blissfully trusting her. Harper rubbed her nose and lips across his head. As soft as baby's skin.

When she was younger, she'd held a few babies when she volunteered for daycare services on Sundays at her church. Supposedly, she had a knack for calming them down. She found herself smiling at Houdini as she walked around, bouncing him slightly.

Suddenly, Houdini jerked his head up and twisted out of her arms. He jumped onto a windowsill and gazed intently at a robin on the table outside.

For a few seconds she had imagined holding her own child. But she couldn't keep it. She had a plan and now a source of funds. She had to get on with her life and learn as much from Cooper as she could. How could she ever raise Zachary's baby?

Chapter Twenty-Two

Harper looked out the window to see if Cooper was walking back, then went to her bedroom. Opening a compartment in her pack, she removed the drugs she'd carried onto the plane. She needed to hide them before Kenzie had the house to herself. Now that she knew Harper had drugs, she might go through her things.

Harper decided to keep the two joints in her pack and take them with her to the park. She hadn't felt an urge to use since she'd been with Cooper. But a J might come in handy if hiking got boring. She pulled her bed away from the wall until she could reach the box spring. Using her pocketknife, she cut a tiny slit just under the corded seam and pushed each balloon inside. After pushing the bed back, she found a Corona Light in the fridge, opened it, and took it to the deck.

A rabbit posed in the yard while Harper drank a few sips. Two small bunnies hopped into view, stopping to chew the grass. Harper took another sip.

She couldn't stop thinking about holding Houdini. Would her baby weigh about the same? Would it be the same size? She absently twirled the bottle as she stared at the bunnies. Then reached for the bottle and noticed the warning label: "According to the Surgeon General pregnant women shouldn't..." She remembered a day in her freshman health class when the teacher showed photos of fetal development and the effects of alcohol on the brain.

She stared at the rabbits as they cautiously moved across the yard.

What did her use of drugs and alcohol matter? She'd get the abortion next week. Still. Maybe she should wait until after it was done. She set the bottle down on the table.

"Snowball!" yelled Cooper.

Harper heard the freight train rumbling across the deck then saw Snowball leaping in front of her onto the grass, chasing the rabbits into the trees.

Cooper stepped up on the deck and collapsed into a chair next to Harper. "I'm beat. I think the sleep I didn't get last night is demanding equal time."

Harper stared at the trees where Snowball and the rabbits ran.

"It sucks being a rabbit," said Harper. "Everybody is after you, and you can't fight back. Their only option is to run."

"They're a universal food source, especially the babies. Owls, coyotes, wolves, lynx, hawks, eagles—all eat them." Snowball pranced out of the trees, smiling. "Except for Snowball. You feeling sorry for rabbits?"

"No, for what they represent. The ones who can only run away or hope they're not abandoned." *Or removed*, she thought. She could see Cooper looking at her from her periphery as she stared into the trees.

"You let me know when you want to tell me what happened in San Antonio. Your thoughts are screaming at me, but I'm too tired to figure them out on my own." He stood and stretched. "I'm going to bed." He moved toward the door.

Harper stood. "I'm going in."

"You're forgetting your beer."

"No." She picked it up. "I just don't feel like drinking it."

They went inside, along with Snowball.

"Mind if I borrow one of your books?" asked Harper. "I don't think I can sleep yet."

"Which one?"

"The one that's going to be published. With the music."

"*The War Blog*. C'mon." He led her to the back of the house through the utility room and opened a door. "This is where I live. My own imaginarium."

Her eyes widened as she stepped into a large open room with one triple window facing the backyard, the side casements cracked open. A full-sized keyboard rested on a stand in front of the window with large speakers on either side. A stuffed leather chair was wedged into a corner with scratch marks everywhere—Houdini's work, most likely. Against the back wall stood a heavy desk, covered in papers with an iMac computer and speakers.

Two acoustic guitars and a banjo hung from the left wall near an amp and a microphone on a stand. Various cables ran along the baseboard or lay coiled in corners.

The rest of the wall was full of shelves and books. Other walls were covered in corkboards with music sheets pinned to them. Here and there were pictures of a younger Cooper with his family, pictures from the villages, etched baleen and carved whale backbone, certificates, and plaques.

Stunned, Harper drifted around the room, staring at each section.

"I had most of this stuff in the village when I taught music." He stood in the center, turning around slowly.

"This is amazing." She sat at the keyboard and placed her hands on the keys.

"That's almost new. You play? Let me turn it on." He pressed the power button and a central screen lit up.

Harper played a few notes. "I took piano lessons from five to fourteen."

"Let me guess. Bach. Beethoven. Chopin. Debussy."

"And hymns. That's why I quit. I wanted to play the songs on my phone." She began playing *Clair de Lune*, slowly, trying to remember.

"Do you know your scales and chords?"

Harper played four octaves of C major scale, arpeggios, and chords.

"This is going to be fun," said Cooper smiling. "I had no idea you could play. What was the song you sang in the airport?"

She thought back. "'I Will Not Bleed.'"

Cooper dragged his finger over the track pad, typed on his computer keyboard until the song poured out of his speakers. After the first verse and chorus, he stopped the song. "Tomorrow we'll start with that one and record you singing. That's a great microphone over there, and I have all kinds of software plugins. You'll sound great." He went to the bookshelf and pulled out *The War Blog.*

"I thought it was going to be released in the spring," said Harper, taking it from Cooper.

"It is. I bought a few advance copies." He gave it to her. "You're welcome to come in here anytime. Just don't move my papers. I know it looks messy, but I know where everything is."

Harper stood and walked around, her skin tingling. She touched the guitars, looked at books and held the microphone in her hand. "This is cool."

"Well, I'm going to bed. You can stay in here or come back later. There're headphones on the music stand in case you want to make some noise."

"Thanks, Cooper." She hugged him.

"You want banana pecan pancakes or Belgian waffles tomorrow?"

"Waffles."

Cooper walked to the door and looked back. "Did you say pancakes?"

Harper's eyes widened, and Cooper laughed. "Just kidding. Ha! Good night, Harper." He walked out of the room, chuckling.

Harper stood behind the keyboard and stared out the window. The tops of the tallest trees glared bright yellow as if spotlights were pointed at them, while a section of cloud to the southeast had turned a soft pink. The flowers seemed to have grown since they were planted just eight hours ago. Dragonflies darted low above the yard, gobbling up mosquitoes, as the rabbit family nibbled the grass. She heard owls hooting nearby and tried to resign herself to the loss of at least one of the baby rabbits during the night.

Harper plopped down into the chair and opened the book. She had read the first three chapters online at the airport. Two kids had been abandoned by their drug addicted mother years ago and were being raised by their grandparents. Though the kids had been told both parents had died, their father was alive and on his way to see them. But, he was an evil man, supposedly, and the grandparents weren't happy.

How do families become so separated, she thought, *so angry with each other? You'd think a reunion would be welcomed, but too much had happened in the past which could not be forgiven.*

Cooper and her Dad were like that. Her grandma and Cooper were like that. And she was well on her way to being like that too. Would she ever see her parents again? Alex? Jack? Maybe her parents would stop talking about her, and she'd be forgotten like Cooper had been. They'd clean out her room. Take down her pictures. Erase her from their lives. Would any of them fly up to see her, or would she wait for a call for years, staring at photos on the refrigerator?

She couldn't think anymore. Better to lose herself in someone else's complicated story. She found chapter four and began to read.

The next morning, rain pounded against the metal roof, as Harper gave her last bite of waffle to Snowball. Looking out the window, she noticed the rain wasn't as intense as the sound suggested. "If you didn't look outside, you'd think the rain would wash the house away," said Harper as she sipped her perfect three-squirt hazelnut latte.

"Goes to show you that troubles aren't as bad as they seem to be." Cooper carried dishes to the sink.

"That's not what your book says. Everything's worse than the characters imagine."

"Where'd you get to?"

"The pizza delivery." She stood and cleaned the table. "Pregnant mother drinking while her toddler walks around untended in a full diaper while the father is screwing another girl in the back room."

"All I can say is the reality in the village was actually worse."

"How could it be?" asked Harper as she scraped plates into the trash.

"Reality is always worse than fiction. People wouldn't believe the story otherwise. Books are supposed to make some sense out of life no matter how rough it is, but real life makes no sense, most of the time. No song is as sad as real weeping, nor as happy as a belly laugh because songs have a structure: verse, chorus, bridge, and the chords move in patterns. Real emotions hit you in the face out of nowhere."

Like finding out you're pregnant, thought Harper.

"Let's go sing." He closed the dishwasher and walked toward his studio. Harper followed. "First rule in this imaginarium is that no idea is bad, no melody is horrible, and no singing is awful. This is where we're free to make things without judgment. Editing comes later. Got it?"

"Yeah."

"Ready to try?" Harper nodded. He gave her the headphones. "Wear these so you can hear the singer on the track. Your voice along with the instrumental tracks will come out of this monitor speaker on the floor. Here are the lyrics. Have you had any training?"

She spread the pages across the stand. "Some. In choir."

"Just relax. It's going to take several times through before you can open up to the song. You might want to listen at first and just mouth the lyrics."

She fitted the phones to her ears. "Hey, I already did an a cappella version at the airport. Let her rip."

Harper stared at the lyrics and thought about Zachary, the house party, and the videos while her anger swelled. She swallowed to keep her throat loose and imagined her voice surging from her diaphragm through her skull.

The intro started and Harper jumped in on cue, full of emotion, angry at the man in the song who had used her. She felt such a release in singing, directing every word at Zachary.

You're a dirty fighter
You hit below the belt
Never cared what I felt

You're a sucker puncher
You cut my heart in two
While I smiled right at you

You played me like a game
All your perfect moves the same
A grandmaster lover man
You must be your greatest fan

Chorus
You knocked me down
But I'm not out baby
I'm off the ground and on my feet

What doesn't kill me makes me stronger
I try so hard to believe

The only thing I will remember
Is love is never free
The next time I love
I will not bleed
I will not bleed

"Damn, you sound good," said Cooper, stopping after the first verse and chorus. "You got the emotion of this song so quickly."

"I know what it's like to be hurt by that kind of asshole. This is a good song, Cooper."

"And you're a helluva singer. You could make a living at this or at least gain a lot of attention. Did you ever act in a play?"

"Once in a Nativity thing at church. In seventh grade I wanted to try out for *High School Musical II Jr.*, but my parents said no."

"Why?"

Behind a smug grin, she said, "I think they worried about me liking the spotlight and guys and using make-up. So keeping me out of that play obviously prevented all of that!" She laughed.

"That's a shame. But now you can sing as much as you want. I can set you up with some good online singing instructors."

"I'd like that."

"We're going to go through all the songs a few times. I'll record you then add enhancements and some tuning, and we'll both listen later on."

"Whatever you say."

"I can't tell you how much fun this is for me."

"Me too." Harper floated. She was energized and felt confident. She could do this! She'd never wanted to do anything so badly in her life. If her father came into the room right now to stop her, she wouldn't threaten to hurt herself nor throw tiny bottles. She'd bellow, "Yes, I will!" with such force he'd be blown out of the room.

For the next three hours, they worked in Cooper's imaginarium until Snowball scratched at the door and whimpered. Harper took him outside and ran around the yard with him before they wrestled in the grass. Panting, they came back inside where Snowball emptied his water bowl in seconds. Harper opened the fridge and reached for a beer, then grabbed the Diet Coke next to it. They both sat in front of the fan, Snowball panting on the floor next to an exhausted Harper.

Cooper walked into the kitchen. "I've got a couple you can listen to. You sound good, Harper. I think I'll send these to your dad."

Would he think she was good? Or just yell some more? "Only if he lets Alex and Jack hear them."

Cooper's phone rang. He pulled it out of his pocket and stared at the screen. "It's a 210 area code, but not your Dad's number."

Couldn't be Zachary's, Harper thought. His was 830.

"Hello?" said Cooper. "Hello?"

Harper saw Cooper's face turn pale. He swallowed hard. "Rachel, is that you?"

Harper stood.

"Is something wrong? How's Jacob? Harper said he was sick." He paused, his face became shuttered.

"Here she is." Cooper handed the phone to Harper. "Your grandmother." Cooper sat down, staring outside.

"Grandma?" said Harper.

"Harper, I have some bad news. Your PawPaw died this morning."

Her great grandmother had died years ago, and Harper felt clumsy then, not knowing what to say. She felt horrible that she hadn't seen PawPaw much during the last several months, that he'd been so far in the back of her mind. "I'm so sorry. Was he asleep?"

"No." Her voice quivered. "He was in a lot of pain, so they took him to the hospital. It was a pretty rough night, but he's finally resting."

"How are Mom and Dad?"

"I told them this morning after he passed. I didn't want them to see him like that. This past year has been very hard for him. He's finally at peace."

"I'm so sorry, Grandma," said Harper.

"He hated that I had to see him die. He wanted you to remember him when he was still his real self. So don't feel bad about not seeing him. That's what he wanted."

"OK." And she knew that's what Cooper would want after he died. "Grandma, how are you doing with this?"

"I'm fine. It hurts, but I'm glad he's finally at peace. Harper, I didn't know you were in Alaska. No one knew your number. I asked Greg for Cooper's number. Your father wouldn't tell me very much. I can't understand why they sent you up there."

"It's a long story, Grandma. I'm living with Cooper now." She saw tears dripping down his cheeks as he sat motionless, staring outside.

"When are you coming home?"

She walked over to Cooper and held his shoulder. "I don't know. Not for a long time." He reached up and held her hand.

"I want to see you. The funeral is Sunday. You'll be there, won't you?" Harper heard the pleading in her voice.

"No, Grandma. I can't leave now. We're going backpacking in the park this weekend. I can't go home."

"Certainly, you can. I know I've been busy with PawPaw for months, but I'm free now. I want to help you."

"I'm putting the phone on speaker now, Grandma." She pressed the speaker icon. "Cooper's helping me. We spent all morning recording his songs. Did you know he's a novelist, Grandma? And a composer?"

"No, I didn't. A novelist?" Cooper stared at the phone. "Where are his books?"

"Go to his website—cooperlyons.net. They're all there. And his music."

"OK. I will."

Harper saw Cooper smiling. She glanced at Cooper. "Why don't you come up here?"

Cooper opened his mouth in shock. Harper nodded.

"He'd love to see you," said Harper. "Alaska is beautiful, Grandma. You'd love it up here. After the funeral you could visit us."

"I'm not sure..."

"I am sure. You need to come up here. You two need to see each other. I'd really like that. And Cooper would too." She and Cooper locked eyes. Harper nodded, and he nodded back, trying to scrunch his eyes to block his tears. "He's got a big garden and beautiful flowers. Please."

She paused for several seconds. "Let me think about it. Can you give me your phone number?"

"My phone is dead. I'm hoping Cooper will get me another one, but that'll take several days, so just call through his phone. He won't mind." Harper smiled at Cooper who shook his head. Maybe amazed at her quick thinking, or possibly shocked by her ability to lie so easily. But it was for his benefit.

"Are you sure you're all right?"

"I've never been better, Grandma. Cooper saved my life."

"Can I speak to him?"

"Sure." Harper handed him the phone. "All yours." They smiled at each other.

Cooper tried to clear his throat. "Hello, Rachel. I'm real sorry about Jacob. He was a good man."

"Thanks, Cooper. He always liked you. Is Harper OK?"

"She's great. And she got that wrong about who saved whose life. She saved mine."

"I don't like all this talk about saving lives. Sounds dangerous to me."

"We're both doing just fine," said Cooper. "And, Rachel, what Harper said about you visiting. That would be fine with me. I know she'd love to see you, and...frankly...so would I." He looked up to the ceiling and closed his eyes.

"Well, I might come up there just to make sure you're treating her right."

He opened his eyes. "You're welcome to do that. Any time."

"Is...is there...anyone else up there?"

"Nobody, Rachel. Just me, Snowball, and Houdini, who used to be my pets until Harper stole them."

"No one stole them, Grandma!" Harper shouted. "They think I smell better!" Harper laughed and pointed at Cooper, who sniffed his armpits and scrunched his nose as he waved his hand to get rid of the smell. Harper laughed louder.

"It's that tangerine wash you use," said Cooper. "Maybe I'll get me some."

"Don't think it'll help!" Harper laughed louder.

"That girl has always been a loud one," said Rachel, chuckling.

"You should hear her sing," said Cooper. "She has an amazing set of pipes. I'll send you a recording of her when I get it done."

"Thanks for taking care of her, Cooper."

"You're welcome. I'm sorry for the reason you called, but I'm sure glad you did."

"Goodbye, Cooper. And tell that granddaughter of ours I'll talk to her soon."

"I will. Goodbye." Cooper sat back in his chair and smiled at the ceiling.

"What?" asked Harper.

"She called you 'granddaughter of *ours*.' Isn't that something?"

"You didn't mind me asking her to come visit?"

Cooper stared blankly at her. For a second Harper thought he'd blanked out. Then he blinked and stood up. "She can't come up here. What was I thinking?"

"Why?"

He stood up and paced. "Because of my head! She spent years taking care of her parents. She's not going to want another invalid in her life. How could I be so stupid?"

"You're not an invalid. You should've seen your face when you talked to her. I bet she feels the same way."

"I can't allow her to come up here without knowing the truth."

"You let me. Knowing wouldn't have changed anything. If you found out she had the same disease, would you tell her to stay in Texas?"

"No, then you'd have two old invalids to deal with."

She grabbed his hands and looked up into his eyes. "We're all invalids in some way, Cooper. We all need someone to help us out."

"I don't want to lie to her again. I don't want to have to hide anything. Somehow, we have to be able to tell each other the truth."

Harper knew she still hid so much from him. She wondered if there would ever be a time when she could be entirely honest with him or her family.

"Just so you know," she said to change the subject, "I think she wanted to talk to you as much as you wanted to talk to her." She winked.

"Why do you say that?"

"She could've had Dad call us with the news about PawPaw. She could've told him to have me call her. Now that her father has died, she's free to do what she wants. I think she wanted to see how you'd react."

"Never could understand women. You really think so?" He looked like a little boy who just been told a girl had a crush on him. So cute!

"I know so. Make the sandwiches. I'm hungry." They smiled at each other, then Harper went back to her room to check her phone.

Zachary had left a message. Her heart raced as she began reading: *Guess what? I went to the Spring Branch Post Office today and the guy mentioned seeing u on Tues mailing crates to Alaska. He remembered u cuz u r so hot. So I figure u mailed my smack that day, which means u lied once again. And I'm not missing a toothbrush. I use an electric, and it's still here. Which means u have no way of charging me with anything. Too bad! My friend has already tagged ur video with ur name and added a couple more. He also sells videos to porn sites and those won't be blurred at all. My plan is the same. No receipt, more photos uploaded with ur name. Oh, did I ever tell u I have a camera in my bedroom? I'll look for a receipt on Monday.*

A camera in his bedroom? Why? So he could have leverage over any girls or just for personal jollies? Or was he lying?

Panicked, she jumped off her bed and tried to lift the lid on her laptop. Who knew what he could've posted. Her last fake nail popped off. After logging in, she Googled Harper Lyons images, and there she was. Another dancing video of her grinding against a blurred man, and most of the last nudes she had sent Zachary.

He knew the crates contained the drugs. Maybe he or someone else had tipped off the police. She'd have to be careful when they arrived.

"Harper, your sandwich is ready," called Cooper from the kitchen.

"Coming." She pushed the computer lid down and tried not to cry. Even if she never Googled her name again, others would. How many times had she searched a name? It was as common as breathing. She'd just started singing again. How could she hope to become a singer with those pictures out there? Her life was totally screwed.

Chapter Twenty-Three

Cooper stared at Rachel's photo on the fridge after he put all the items on the counter to make sandwiches. It was her yearbook photograph from a year before Heather died, free to staff members, so most had theirs updated. The bright-eyed smile with the little dimples she always had was still there, though the stress of Heather's increasing problems had deepened lines around her eyes and lips. Eighteen months later he'd betray that smile with a younger teacher.

That evening in the theatre flashed through his mind.

During a ten-minute break from rehearsal, Ellie called him to the control booth. Younger than he, pretty, a new teacher who had volunteered to help him with his plays. Their affair had started weeks earlier when his pain from Heather's death nearly killed him. Ellie became his outlet.

"What do you want to show me?" Cooper asked as she stood, leaning through the doorway. "You said you were working on a new light sequence for the opening." He smiled, knowing that was not the reason for her summons. They'd met there several times.

Ellie looked both ways, put her fingers behind his belt buckle, down his pants, and pulled him closer. "I can't show you out here." She pulled him inside and closed the door.

The room was dark. She pressed her body against his.

"What am I looking for? I can't see anything," he said. He felt the intense warmth of her body and breathed the infatuating scent of her skin. Every nerve tingled.

"Then you'll have to feel your way around," she said, her lips touching his, kissing as she spoke. She unbuttoned her top and placed his hands on her chest.

"Ellie." He sighed and squeezed tentatively.

"Silly." She pulled his face down.

Somebody pulled the booth door open. Cooper jerked his head up and saw Victor, a student in the play, staring open-mouthed at them. Ellie covered herself. They heard a girl's voice outside. Cooper's muscles locked tight.

"C'mon, Victor, go in. We just have a few minutes," Laila laughed. Another student in the play and Victor's current girlfriend.

"It's occupied. I know another place." Victor closed the door, but both Ellie and Cooper knew he'd seen them.

"Occupied? Who was in there?" asked Laila as her voice trailed away.

"He saw us!" said Cooper in a loud whisper. "We need to get out of here."

She pulled him back to her. "Victor's cool. He won't say anything." She tried to reassure him.

"Maybe I should go talk to him now."

"I think he'd rather have time with Laila." She pulled him to her again and purred. "See if you can find where I dabbed my perfume," she teased.

Blanking out his panic, just like he'd blanked out his daughter's death, he allowed Ellie to make him forget, if only temporarily. "I'll conduct a thorough search," said Cooper. She giggled as he explored. He wished he could feel that level of excitement. He wished he could feel anything .

For the next few rehearsals, Victor never spoke about the incident, though he smirked more than usual. He knew Victor would wait for an opportunity. Then one night after another break, Victor came back with Laila from outside. They reeked of marijuana as they passed Cooper.

"Victor. Where were you?"

"Outside. Me and Laila wanted some fresh air." They were both giddy.

"That air reeks, son. You both need to stay inside during breaks." He hoped by giving him a break, Victor would give him a break.

"Maybe we'll go to the control booth next time." He winked as they moved by him, toward the stage.

Later at the end of rehearsal, Cooper knew he had to talk to Victor. He couldn't allow a student to think he had condoned marijuana use at his rehearsal. He pulled Victor aside. "You're my lead actor. Everyone in this production depends on you doing your best. If you can't give them one-hundred percent of your effort and talent, then let me know so I can find someone else who will." He put on a stern face, hoping he could hold it, and Victor would respond appropriately.

Victor smiled, meeting his challenge. "You won't do that. I don't think Ms. Ellie would want that either." He winked, and Cooper's chest hurt.

In retrospect, that's when he should've replaced Victor and accepted the consequences of being caught with Ellie. But he didn't.

"No more weed during rehearsals. Is that clear?"

Victor's smile widened. "Sure. No problem."

The next evening, he saw Victor and his girlfriend go outside during a break and followed them. He heard them in the bushes and then smelled the smoke. He saw the security officer a few hundred yards away. He should've called the officer over, but he succumbed to denial and a foolish hope that no one would find out. He said nothing and went back inside.

A few minutes later, Victor burst into the theatre, holding a burning joint, pulling Laila down the aisle. Cooper smelled marijuana smoke.

"Victor!" Cooper stood up and yelled. "Come here! Right now!"

"Later, dude!" Victor ran down the aisle, pulling a giggling Laila into the hall.

Several kids laughed. One said, "What have they been doing?" More laughter.

The security guard ran in. "What's going on here?" He walked briskly to Cooper. "This theatre reeks of pot."

Cooper pointed at the exit door a few rows away. "They ran out there." The officer took off. Cooper learned later that he caught them exiting the boys' restroom. Evidently, Victor had flushed the joint down the toilet.

The kids were busted, Victor told about Ellie and Cooper, and all hell broke loose. He claimed that Cooper gave him the pot to keep him quiet about Ellie. Victor's parents sued.

When the dust settled, Cooper kept his teaching license but lost Rachel. He pleaded for forgiveness, told her he was just trying to escape the pain of losing Heather. Even that excuse sounded stupid to him. Rachel wouldn't forgive. Maybe she thought if he left, she could forget about Heather's death. He asked her to go with him, to start anew, far away from Texas, but she said no.

And now here he was in Alaska having spoken to Rachel for the first time in over sixteen years. She didn't sound angry at him. She might even visit.

All because Harper had contacted him. Maybe he and Rachel could at least be friendly.

Cooper finished making the sandwiches and called for Harper. After a minute, she trudged into the room, sat at the table, and put her head down. He brought the sandwiches over and sat with her. "What's wrong?"

"Everything." She blew out a breath. "Promise me you'll never Google my name."

"Ah. I know that feeling." He raised a brow. "What would I find?"

She sat up and stared at him with blood-shot eyes. "Nude pictures, probably having sex with one guy, maybe more videos of me dancing in a see-through negligee." Her chin quivered.

Cooper was shocked. There was so much he didn't know about her. "Who's uploading this stuff?"

"My former boyfriend."

"Why?"

"It's complicated. He wants to control me so I'll do something he wants. Are you embarrassed? Ashamed of me?" She wiped away tears.

Cooper saw such pain in her face, her hands clutching the computer. "No, but I can see you are."

"How could I not be?" He saw her wet chin quiver. She wiped her running nose. "I'll wonder if anyone I talk to or sing to has seen those photos. That's all they'll be thinking about when they look at me. Boy, Tommy's going to be in heaven! And Alex? What's she going to think of me? This morning I thought maybe I could be a singer, and now this happens. How can I do anything?" She covered her face with her hands.

"This guy is an asshole for exploiting you like this. No one deserves that. This doesn't have to define you, Harper, and despite what may be going on between you, this boy doesn't control you. You're too good for that."

He sat down across from her. "Before I left San Antonio," he continued, "there were all kinds of embarrassing stories on the internet about me. For years I never Googled my name. The first school that hired me was desperate for a teacher and didn't bother to check my past. I worked there for a few years, then was offered a job here in Anders Fork. I bought this house. But the Board President refused to approve my contract because he Googled me and believed all the crap online. So no job, but I'd already closed on the house.

"I found another village, and every once in a while, a kid would say something or ask me an odd question. I used to have panic attacks worrying about this crap. Until I decided to fight it. I wrote a book and created a website. I got reviews. I blogged. I entered contests and won a few awards. Pretty soon the first ten items on a Google search were about all of that and not about smoking marijuana with students."

"Did you smoke with them?"

"No." He told her what happened at rehearsal, about Victor's lies, and his parents' lawsuit. "I was negligent and irresponsible, but I did not allow or promote or participate in smoking pot. Rachel divorced me, and I went to Alaska. You can still find something online about the incident if you search hard enough. But most people don't, and I don't care anymore.

"So, what I recommend is to hold on to that bravery in you, like when you fought that bear yesterday. You can definitely create more buzz on the internet with your talent than those photos and videos will produce. And I know there are people who can help get that stuff taken down. You're a minor for God's sake. Let me look into that. Embarrassment is not a requirement. You choose to feel embarrassed because that's what you think you should feel. You have to choose not to. Don't let him have power over you. There is so much more special about you than a few photos can reveal." He gently lifted her puffy face. "You hear me?"

She wiped her eyes and sniffed. After a few deep breaths, she nodded and choked out, "Yes."

"Good girl. In the meantime, we should eat our lunch, take Snowball for a walk, and then get back to the studio. Deal?" He held up his hand.

"Deal." She slapped his hand then pulled him into a hug. "Thanks."

• • • • •

After lunch Harper went to her room and threw her pillows against the walls. She wasn't going to allow Zachary to ruin the rest of her life. She wanted to hurt him, to make him fear her. She refused to let him think he'd hurt her.

She sent him a text. *Tell you what, asshole. I've decided to keep this baby and sue you for child support. I'll show these messages to the troopers tomorrow and have you arrested for posting child pornography. Then when you upload a video of us having sex (You pervert! What, you watch these clips when you're not getting any?), that along with your texts will be proof of rape. You and your "friend" are such idiots!*

She wouldn't really keep the baby. Another lie. Would she ever be able to tell the truth?

She and Cooper went to his studio. He had finished mixing three songs from their morning session and wanted Harper to hear them herself. She couldn't believe how good they sounded. Cooper let her hear how different plugins enhanced her voice, and she chose which one she liked best. His original vocalist had added several harmony lines, but she wasn't ready to try those yet. Even without them the songs sounded great.

"I'm going to send these MP3 files to your father."

She didn't know why Cooper was wasting the effort of including her dad. "Why? He'll probably just delete them."

"I don't think so. Even he won't be able to deny your talent. I guarantee you he'll be pleasantly surprised."

That would be nice. "Send it to Grandma, too. Make sure they know these are your songs, and give them your website address."

He sent the files and hooked up Snowball for his walk to the river park.

"Tell me how you started writing books. Did you start with a real story or make up something entirely new?" Harper asked as they walked along a trail full of flowering rose and raspberry bushes.

"A little of both. Most everything in my books has happened in one form or another, but I've changed the context or the motivations or the timeline. There's some amount of truth on every page, but it's altered. And when the story is finished, it's more real than the supposedly real events and people who spawned it. The first book was the hardest. I had only a vague notion of where the story was going. Wrote lots of words then cut a bunch of them, then an editor told me what she thought my theme was, so I rewrote and focused the plot. It took forever, and I deleted ten times as many words as stayed on the page. The second and third books were easier."

"What are you working on now?"

Snowball stopped in front of them, looking to his right, ready to pounce on something. They came around the corner and saw a large porcupine waddling into the brush. Cooper pulled hard on the leash just as Snowball lunged forward.

"No, Snowball! You don't want to mess with that!" Cooper kept pulling until Snowball got back on the dike and walked in front of them.

"You were about to tell me what you're working on now."

"I'll show you when you're ready."

"And when will I be ready?"

"When you can't stand not knowing." He smiled. "Or when you figure it out on your own."

"Fine. Be mysterious. I don't care."

They walked in silence for another minute.

"Is the guy who posted the photos the reason you left San Antonio?"

Harper didn't want to tell him she was pregnant. Not yet. She wasn't sure what he felt about abortion and still worried what he'd think about the parental consent issue. She didn't want to hurt him. But she could tell him everything else. Where to start? Being twelve with Luke or the night at the hospital? She was afraid he'd never think of her the same regardless of when she started.

"Promise me you'll still love me when I'm finished."

Cooper stopped and looked at her. The wind pushed his wispy hair into his face, across the bags drooping under his eyes and a nose a larger version of hers. "I couldn't stop loving you if I tried. I promise, Harper."

She'd never heard more sincere words in her life. "I love you, too." She pulled him to her.

He stroked her head. "No one's told me that since you left ten years ago. It feels good to be loved again. That's the best feeling anyone can feel, Harper. Better than anything. I hope you learn that."

"That's the first thing you taught me."

They started walking.

"When I was twelve, Chris had a friend over. He kept sneaking looks at me, smiling at me. I could feel him staring at me as I walked by. He bumped into me on purpose and brushed his hand across my butt. I couldn't believe he was interested in me. I was twelve, but I looked older. Just before going to bed, I stood in front of my mirror and undressed, wondering if he'd actually like me. And then he opened my door, and I couldn't move."

Harper continued her story as they walked to the river, saw Denali's peaks barely visible above the surrounding clouds, then turned around. Snowball tried once again to lunge into the brush where the porcupine had been before, then stopped at the end of Cooper's driveway, watching a rabbit sitting motionless on the edge of the gravel. Harper hadn't stopped talking until that moment when they all stared at the rabbit.

"And the reason you felt you had to leave was...?" asked Cooper.

"Zachary didn't care about me, and my parents would never forgive me. And I didn't want to ruin Alex."

"As much as you've told me, I think there's more."

Does he suspect? "There's always more. You told me about Victor, but you haven't said why you cheated on Grandma. How that got started. And what happened to Ellie?"

Cooper's phone rang. He showed Harper the screen. Her father was calling. He punched the speaker button.

"Hello, Greg. So what do you think of Harper's singing?"

"That was so cool!" shouted Alex.

"My sister is a rock star!" shouted Jack. Their phone was evidently on speaker as well.

"Hi, Alex! Hi, Jack!" shouted Harper. She waited to hear her parents. Surely, they'd say something.

"Harper," said Greg, "your mother and I are very impressed."

Harper beamed. Cooper held out his hand, and she slapped it hard.

"We're stunned," said Natalie. "And, Cooper, you wrote those songs?"

"Yes, I did. I had them produced by a very talented man, but I wrote the melodies and lyrics."

"Your songs are good, Dad," said Greg.

Harper thought he sounded fake, like her mother had told him to say this. With Alex and Jack listening, she wasn't going to call him out on it.

"Well, thank you, Greg." He looked at Harper and raised his brows, like he detected some insincerity as well.

Greg continued, "We looked at your website, and your books seem very interesting. We'll definitely spend more time looking them over. How long have you had the site?"

Interesting? thought Harper. Like the comment you make about a bad Christmas present. *He's just saying the words.*

"Started it six years ago," said Cooper. "I sent the URL with my Christmas cards when I launched it."

"We're sorry we didn't pay more attention," said Natalie.

"I'm going to play your songs at school tomorrow," said Alex. "You should make videos and put them on YouTube!"

"We'll get that done in a few days," said Cooper.

"OK, kids, say goodnight and go to your rooms," Greg commanded. "We need to talk to Harper and Grandpa for a little bit. We'll be there in a few minutes."

Harper heard the hidden edge in his tone. Something was wrong. Alex and Jack whined, shouted their good-nights, and left. Suddenly, Harper knew what was coming, and she wanted to run.

"A guy called the school today and spoke to Mom," said Greg. "He asked if we'd seen your photos and videos online."

Harper started to run, but Cooper held her arm. "We'll get through this," he said to her. Harper looked at him, tears beginning to form.

"We know about those," said Cooper.

"How long have they been online?" asked Greg with more edge to his voice.

"I'm so sorry, Dad," cried Harper. "Zachary uploaded them today." *He must have called the school after I sent him that last note*, she thought.

"Where did he get them? How could you have put yourself in that position?" His volume increased. "What were you thinking?"

"Greg, we agreed not to shout," Natalie hissed.

"I'm going to contact a company to get them taken down," said Cooper. "At this point, it doesn't do any good to blame Harper."

"I'm so sorry!" Harper shouted. "I thought he loved me. I had no idea he'd do this to me." The only thing that kept her from running was Cooper's arms.

"Even if they're removed," said Greg, "the damage has been done. Kids have seen them. Someone evidently left flyers on the way to school. After we got the message, I caught kids gawking at their screens then shut up when I walked by. I heard your name mentioned more than once. I've already had phone calls. Can you give me some kind of explanation that might help me out?"

Harper felt her tears evaporating from her face as it heated in anger. She took the phone from Cooper. "I was wasted and drunk. I was probably raped. I sent him nudes to make him like me, like thousands of girls do. He played on my emotions to make me think he loved me, when all he cared about was another score. I regret every moment I spent with him, and I'm trying to deal with the fact that thousands of horny guys are beating off while watching me on their computers and phones. I appreciate your concern for the embarrassment this has caused me." She paused, waiting for a response. "It's always job first for you, isn't it Daddy?"

"I won't have a job after this, Harper!"

"Or a daughter!" She ended the call and stomped toward the house.

Chapter Twenty-Four

Harper didn't care that she'd left Cooper behind. She needed to vent and to curse. It was better he hadn't heard her. Once again she was honest with her father, and he wouldn't listen. He was more concerned about his job than her pain. As she threw open the door to Cooper's house, she heard the phone ringing and found it in her hand. She hadn't realized she'd run off with Cooper's phone. She saw a number with a 210 area code and thought it was her father calling back.

"Hello!" she barked, ready to give him hell.

"Hello, Harper," said Rachel. "What's wrong?"

"Oh, I'm sorry, Grandma. I thought you were Dad." She wiped away some tears.

"Sounds like you two had a fight."

"Yeah." She yanked a chair away from the kitchen table and plopped into it.

"He's always been too negative with you. I've told him that a hundred times."

Harper never knew. "Seems that's the only way he can deal with me." She wiped a napkin across her nose.

"Your songs are beautiful, Harper. Where have you been hiding that voice?"

Cooper opened the door and walked in with Snowball, who lifted his paws onto Harper so he could lick her face.

"I'm so happy you like them, Grandma," said Harper, trying to keep from squealing as Snowball licked her ears.

"Your voice is so powerful, so emotional," said Rachel. "I just can't believe it's you singing."

Harper beamed at Cooper and punched the speaker button. "They're great songs, Grandma. It makes it a whole lot easier to sing."

"They are good! I can't believe Cooper wrote those. And his books. I read a few chapters. He's really talented."

Cooper looked stunned, staring at the phone.

"Yes, he is. He just walked inside." She stood and smiled at Cooper. "Why don't you tell him yourself?" She gave the phone to Cooper, who sat down at the table.

"Hello, Rachel. So you liked Harper's singing?"

"I'll be in the studio," whispered Harper as she walked out of the kitchen.

One of the few times she had received praise from her parents, and it had to be ruined by Zachary's photos. She was sure he'd called the school. How could she help her father out of this one? Write another note? She wanted to fix this, but she couldn't figure out what to do. She could understand his anger, but once again, he'd expressed no sympathy for her. She was the cause of all his problems and would probably get him fired. How would her parents live? And what would that do to Alex and Jack?

Maybe if she'd told Cooper the truth yesterday and had the abortion, this could've been prevented. Zachary would have his receipt. No videos or photos on the web. But now, it was too late. Even if they disappeared tomorrow, the damage to her and her family had been done.

So like Cooper had told her, she had to stiffen her spine and define her own presence for the public. She wanted to sing and maybe write her own songs. Harper looked through the papers pinned to cork boards in Cooper's studio. She found the sheet music for "I Will Not Bleed" and set it on the stand above the keyboard. Her fingers moved tentatively at first, but she was up to speed by the end of the song. Then she tried playing chords only and singing along but realized that was difficult. Playing and singing simultaneously was not as easy as musicians made it look. Either her lyrics were too slow or she played the chords too fast.

She searched for other music on the board until she found what looked to be a song in progress with a chord progression, a melody, and a few lyrics—scratch outs and scribbles on the side. She changed two lines:

You put a hole in my heart changed to

You burned a hole in my life

And ripped my life apart changed to
Left a scar I cannot hide

Then she sang the chorus:
I still dream of you
My memories won't release you
You burned a hole in my life
Left a scar I cannot hide

Cooper walked in and sank into his leather chair. Harper saw tears on his face, but he was smiling.

"How'd that go with Grandma?" she asked as she penciled in another change.

"Good. Very good. Still not out of the woods yet, but we're talking again, this time without the yelling and the anger. I told her about the photos, and she said something surprising. 'John will fire him, and they can finally get away from that school.' She thinks your parents made a mistake working for John. Besides putting you and your siblings into the awkward situation of having your father be the big boss on campus, she said John is too much God's law and not enough God's love."

"I wish she'd told them that four years ago."

"She says she did, but Greg wouldn't listen, as usual, and Natalie has difficulty saying no to her father."

Harper perked up. "Is Grandma coming up?"

"Maybe." He got up and reached for his lyrics page. "I like the changes. I've been having trouble with this one. Can't decide if it should be a slow, simple ballad or have a beat."

"You have a rhythm in mind?"

"Possibly." He hit some buttons on the keyboard until a straight eight beat emerged. He played the melody while Harper tried the lyrics. He tried a country waltz rhythm then a reggae style. He pulled his Guild guitar off the wall and tried a few strum patterns. For the next hour, they worked on the song until they had a verse and chorus.

This was fun even though she had to concentrate continuously. Time flew by without her noticing. When they found something good, they cheered. Cooper showed her different rhyme patterns and how to vary the chorus from the verse. He liked her suggestions! As they sang and played it together without stopping, Snowball came in and collapsed onto the floor.

"Jeez, what time is it?" asked Cooper. He checked his phone. "Eight o'clock. Snowball's hungry, and I forgot about dinner. Sounds like a chicken potpie night. I'll feed the puppy, you find the pies in the freezer.

"Sounds good to me."

After dinner Harper walked Snowball while Cooper worked on his computer. He told her he wanted to get her photos off the web and find a new job for Greg. He was still busy when she returned, so she climbed into bed with Snowball and began to read the second half of Cooper's book. She did not charge her phone. She wanted nothing more to do with Zachary.

The next morning Cooper woke her up early with a latte and a breakfast taco. "Eat it quick. I need you to help me hook up the trailer."

"What trailer?"

"My camper. The one we're sleeping in tonight before we head out to the bush."

Ten minutes later, she stood by the trailer tongue waving her hands in various directions as Cooper backed up his truck. She noticed his rear bumper was full of dents and figured she couldn't screw this job up more than he had on his own.

"How much farther?" Cooper asked, sticking his head out of his truck window.

"Not much." She waved him to keep going. She held up her hands about two feet apart.

"Left or right?"

Harper looked down at the trailer tongue, which was to the right of the truck ball. "Left."

Cooper turned the wheel to the left and backed up.

"The other way!" shouted Harper.

"I went left, Harper." He sounded frustrated.

"The trailer needs to go left."

"I can't move the trailer! Just the truck."

"OK, go right."

He turned the wheel the other way and backed up.

"Stop!" The bumper crashed against the trailer tongue. *Oh no! He's going to be mad!*

He jumped out of the truck and walked back to see the damage. "Harper, I can do this bad on my own. You're supposed to keep me from banging my bumper."

She blinked at him, stunned. "That's the first time you've yelled at me."

"I didn't yell!"

She raised her brows and folded her arms across her chest.

"I did not yell," Cooper repeated more quietly.

She squinted at him in the sun. "Are we having our first fight?" she teased.

"It doesn't count unless you yell back."

"I'll save my yelling for later if you let me drive and you do the wavy hands thing." She hopped into the front seat and slammed the door. "You're my guide. That's the way this relationship is supposed to work."

She moved the truck forward and followed his hands and voice until he could drop the tongue directly onto the ball.

Harper leaped out of the cab and watched Cooper hook the chains. "Perfect. We are such a team." She smiled down at him.

"Now I'll worry when you're going to lash back at me. I imagine you're a hellcat when you're angry."

"Ask Daddy."

"Speaking of which, I completed applications for him last night. There are still some principal positions open in the villages. If he needs a job soon, he should be able to get one."

Harper was stunned. Had she ruined his career? "Why would he work in a village?"

"He may have no choice."

"He hasn't done anything wrong. Why couldn't he get another job?"

"Because another school won't want to deal with his baggage. He can claim he resigned because of disagreements with his father-in-law, but your photos and past text messages are going to undercut him at any school he applies." He hooked the chains onto his truck. "Why would a superintendent choose him over another candidate who doesn't have his background?"

Harper stared at Cooper then looked away. "Can you get the photos off the internet?"

Cooper leaned against the truck and wiped his forehead with a bandana. "A company is working on that. Supposedly they can, but it'll take some time. They said everything's already been downloaded hundreds of times by now."

Harper tried to hide the horror she felt.

"They'll get them down," he said gently. "It'll be OK."

"Do you think Grandpa will fire him?" So much regret flooded into her.

"Rachel thinks so. Maybe when John knows you're in Alaska, he'll give Greg more time, but on the other hand he might think you being with me makes it worse."

She wiped a tear off her cheek. "Can I do anything?"

"I don't know. Talk to Greg after we come back from our hike. See what he says."

"OK."

"Come help me with the packs and gear."

She followed him inside the house where he took her to a closet crammed with camping equipment. He pulled out two backpacks already stuffed and ready to go and a new Helly Hansen rain jacket with the tags still attached.

"When did you get this?" She tried it on. "It fits perfectly."

"That was supposed to be Harold's, one of my students, along with the pack and bag. I bought them three years ago. He was going to visit me after graduation so I could take him into the park. I had everything ready for him, and then he died in an accident."

"What happened?"

"He got drunk with his friend then raced around the village until he slammed his Honda into a telephone pole."

"I'm sorry."

"I was, too. I really liked that kid."

"Why didn't you return everything?"

He shrugged a shoulder. "Seemed wrong, I guess."

"Maybe it was meant for me."

Cooper raised his eyebrows. "If that's what you want to believe."

"You don't believe in fate?"

"I believe that people try to make sense of things after the fact by believing someone or something planned it before the fact. Seems convoluted to me. Does it comfort you to know that God made Harold die in an accident, so all his stuff would be here for you? I could've bought all of this tomorrow."

"Or returned it, but you didn't. Besides, it'd still be here even if he'd used it. I'd like to think there's a master plan working somewhere. Just feels like too much coincidence you had this gear in my size. Some things have to happen for a reason. Without all my screw-ups, I wouldn't be here with you. And now Rachel might come see you. And even the rest of my family! Wow! This all makes sense! If Luke hadn't been a pedophile, and I hadn't been boy-crazed at twelve, you might have ended your life. Now, you're going to see everybody. Pretty amazing, huh?"

He shook his head, bewildered. "So I'm saved by sex, which is what put me up here to begin with."

"It's what put all of us here." She realized she was having a conversation about sex with her grandfather, and yet she didn't feel awkward. It felt so good to be able to talk about anything with him.

Cooper laughed. "The source and ruin of everything. Yes, it's a helluva plan, Harper. Everyone's going to live happily ever after at the end of this."

Then reality hit her hard. *Not everyone*, she thought. Without thinking, she had put her hand on her abdomen. *And where are you in this plan?*

"Let's get all this gear out to the trailer. And don't forget your clothes."

As they walked through the mudroom, Cooper said, "Grab the pack if you have a free hand."

Harper lifted the pack with two fingers and felt the weight of the gun inside. She wedged her way through the door, trying not to drop anything, and reached back with her foot to swing the door closed.

Harper could barely see in front of her, depending only on gaps between the stuff she carried to guide her way when Kenzie drove up in her Honda.

"Hey, Kenzie," said Cooper. "I've got everything ready for you. I'll show you inside as soon as I stow all this." Cooper tossed his load into the trailer and took Harper's gear, a few items at a time.

Kenzie walked over to Harper after Cooper disappeared into the trailer. "I didn't know you were such a wild girl," said Kenzie with some edge to her voice. "My boyfriend won't stop looking at your photos and videos. Or his friends. You're quite the dancer."

Harper bristled and felt her pulse quicken. "My ex-boyfriend uploaded those to punish me." *And now I'm being gawked at by guys from Texas to Alaska and beyond. Great!*

"Why?"

"Because I left him to come up here. I'm not happy guys are gawking at me."

Kenzie laughed. "You kidding? You're walking around and dancing in practically nothing at a big party with guys everywhere. And you don't want them looking at you? Give me a break." Kenzie shook her head and almost sneered.

Harper wanted to scream and to cry, but she had to control herself. She needed Kenzie's help. "I was wasted at the time, and my boyfriend made me walk around like that. I'm sorry, Kenzie. I won't be doing that up here. I'm trying to start over, which is why I want to get rid of some drugs. You remember our deal about taking care of Snowball and Houdini?"

"Yeah."

Cooper emerged from the trailer. "Come inside the house, Kenzie, so I can show you everything. Harper, why don't you take Snowball out before we leave?"

Harper opened the deck door and called for Snowball. He ran full speed around the garden boxes then stopped to lick Harper's face as she sat on the deck.

"I'm going to miss you," said Harper, hugging his big neck. "Please don't do anything stupid while we're gone." She led him back inside and found Houdini flopped on the floor. Harper cuddled with him as he purred. She knew she could never hold him again without thinking about her baby, or condition, or whatever it was to her now.

Harper walked to the kitchen where she found Cooper going through his typed instructions and pointing at food cans and kibble he had lined up on the counter. Kenzie stood nearby with her arms crossed and tapping her foot, seeming confused and impatient.

"You've got my cell number," said Cooper. "We'll be back around eight or nine on Sunday. You good?"

"Sure," said Kenzie.

Cooper bent down to hold his pets one more time then walked outside.

Harper looked at Kenzie, trying to smile. "Please take good care of them."

"Hey, I've got an incentive," said Kenzie with a smirk. "Can't wait to see what you're gonna give me."

Harper didn't like the look in her eyes, but what choice did she have? Kenzie had watched them before, and Cooper trusted her. But that was before Harper screwed everything up with drugs and photos. She climbed into the truck.

"Let's go camping!" shouted Cooper as he drove down the driveway. "We're stopping at the post office. Maddie called and said two crates were waiting for me. I thought maybe you mailed some extra clothes."

Most of her clothes were in those crates, along with shoes and hoodies, which she could use right now. As Cooper pulled into Main Street, she looked around and thought she saw a trooper car behind some trees to the side of the post office. After calling the school and her parents to tell them about the videos and pictures, it wouldn't surprise her if Zachary had called the troopers to tip them off about a drug delivery. Her stomach fluttered, and her mouth went dry. Cooper pulled the trailer along the edge of the post office lot then parked it. They walked inside.

"Hey, Maddie," said Cooper.

Harper studied Maddie's face and thought she was avoiding eye contact. This was a bust waiting to happen.

Cooper found some letters in his box, including the yellow card for packages. He flipped it on the counter. Maddie picked up one of the crates and set it in front of him. "Lots of tape on these."

Cooper stared at the crate and said nothing. For a second, Harper worried that Cooper was having another episode, but then he rubbed his eyes and said, "Zip ties work better."

"We don't want to accept delivery," said Harper.

"We don't?" asked Cooper.

"No. I think those are from my ex-boyfriend." She pointed at the return address. "That's his address. I don't want anything from him." She tried to hide her nervousness behind her anger with Zachary.

Maddie seemed surprised and maybe a little relieved.

"You heard the lady," said Cooper. "We refuse delivery! First time I've ever done that."

"You could've refused me," said Harper, trying to be funny and reduce tension.

"And miss all the fun we've been having? Send it back, Maddie!" He laughed and patted Harper's shoulder.

"OK," Maddie smiled. "They'll go back to the return address."

Good, thought Harper. *Maybe they'll bust him.*

Cooper held the door open for her as they exited the building. "Harper," said Cooper, quietly, "you have good survival instincts."

Harper stopped and looked at Cooper standing outside the doorway. *He knew*, she thought. "Maybe, but I'd like to do more than just survive."

"I know, but survival comes first," Cooper said as she walked past him. They both got into the truck. "I saw the trooper car, which I'm sure you did, too. And Maddie was nervous as hell. Some stuff you decided you didn't need after all?" Cooper looked at her, both eyebrows lifted.

"Yeah, I don't even know why I mailed them up here in the first place. Just wasn't thinking right." Cooper pulled the trailer onto the road. *The story of my life so far*, she thought.

She could return those crates but couldn't rewrite the past. Now she had no way to pay for an abortion without asking Cooper for money. Would she ask? Did she still want to go through with this?

Chapter Twenty-Five

Maddie had given Cooper a heads up about the crates. She wasn't sure what was going on, but the trooper seemed way too interested in two plastic crates. Cooper figured Harper had mailed more than extra clothes in them. He'd decided to stop and give Harper a chance to make her own decision. Had she changed since she came to him? Whatever her decision, he had planned to refuse delivery, but when he saw the duct tape, he froze. He remembered the last birthday card Heather had sent him. She claimed she'd found it in a dumpster and patched it up with duct tape just like her Pops had taught her. Smiley faces, some smeared, covered the patches. Cooper's use of the tape was a running joke in the house. Two months later, Heather was dead. The card remained on his refrigerator.

Cooper looked over at Harper sleeping, her feet propped up on the dash just like Heather used to do. And then he remembered a conversation with Ellie. Teacher in-service for the new school year started soon after Heather's death. Cooper sat at his desk in his classroom at the end of one session thinking about his daughter, crying. After a knock, Ellie walked in. She was a new teacher at the school, younger than Cooper by a few years, and pretty. Cooper tried to wipe his eyes while standing up and banged his legs on the desk.

"Oh, are you all right?" Ellie ran over to him and put her hand on his back.

"Yes, thank you. Just stood before pushing my chair back."

"I'm Ellie." She shook his hand. "I hear you're a fabulous director, and I want to work with you. I can do your lights and sets and even your costumes, if you let me." She paused, looking at his face. "Is something wrong?"

"My daughter died two months ago. I was just thinking about her."

She grabbed a tissue and began to dab his cheeks. She looked into his eyes with such sympathy. "I'm so sorry." She dabbed his face some more. A spasm of pain shook through Cooper's chest, and he covered his face, crying again. Ellie hugged him. "You poor, poor man." She rubbed his back. She felt so warm, so soft. After she held him for a minute, he hugged her back and cried some more.

That was the day his new relationship began. She talked and listened and touched his hands. During the next few days, she came after school to talk to him, to comfort him. There was so much tension at home between him and Rachel fed by an undercurrent of blame and deep, deep pain. It felt good to receive Ellie's sympathy.

Ellie shared her own problems, talked about her recent divorce, how her husband had run off with some trollop in her twenties. He gave her amazing advice about what she might do with her life, now that she was free to seek new opportunities. She thought he was such a caring man, one who wasn't afraid to show emotions. No one had praised him like that before. She began to sit with her feet up on a student desk, her dress falling back, revealing a lot of her thigh. At the end of each visit, she hugged him. Soon the hugs lingered, their bodies pressed together, their hands moved beyond each other's backs, and then he kissed her.

Why? He'd tried then to justify his betrayal by blaming Rachel and their strained relationship after Heather's death. Ellie was a release, an escape, something fresh and new who kept him from drowning in sorrow and anger at himself for his daughter's death. Ellie made him feel like the most handsome, most caring, and most talented man in the world. And soon he was the most amazing lover as well.

The sedan ahead of him swerved sharply to the left to avoid a moose but hit its leg with its right front fender.

"Damn!" muttered Cooper.

The car slowed and pulled over to the shoulder.

Cooper looked in his rearview mirror and saw the moose on its side in the road, kicking its legs, trying to get up. Cooper eased his rig off the road and stopped behind the sedan.

"Harper, wake up!" He shook her shoulder before opening his door.

"Wake up." He got out of the truck and walked up to the car. Five tourists were standing on the road, two talking into their cell phones. One of the women was crying and being held by another.

"Anyone hurt?" asked Cooper.

"No. Everyone is OK," said one of them.

"Is someone calling 911?"

"Yes. Right now."

Cooper turned around and saw Harper standing outside the truck. He walked past her toward the trailer. "They hit a moose, but it's not dead."

She followed him. "What does that mean?"

He opened the trailer and went inside. After a few seconds, he emerged holding his pistol. "It means we're going to have to shoot it. C'mon."

"What?" asked Harper, walking quickly to stay up with him.

Cooper decided Harper should shoot it. This was the perfect opportunity for her to gain experience should she ever have to use a gun. He didn't want her scared to shoot if the need arose.

They saw the moose flopping on the road as several cars moved slowly past it, having to cross the yellow line into the other lane. "Can't someone fix him?" asked Harper.

"No, and it's a female. She's suffering, Harper. This needs to be quick." He gave her the gun.

"Why me?" She looked horrified.

"Because you know what to do, and I need to keep the cars away. Walk within five feet and aim just above where the front leg attaches to the chest, about six inches to the left. Get on her leg side so your gun is pointing off the road. I'd have you do a head shot, but she keeps jerking her head around."

"But I don't want to shoot her!" She tried to hand the gun back.

"She'll die slowly and painfully if you don't. You can do this." He looked directly into her eyes. "Be strong. That moose is suffering."

Cooper walked down the road with his hands up, waving at the cars. One car passed him, but the others stopped. He looked over his shoulder and saw Harper standing a few feet away from the moose's legs. "Harper! Do it now!" *Come on, girl. You can do this.*

She positioned herself and held the gun in front of her, pointing down. The moose raised its head and bleated in gasps. She took a step back and looked into the bushes then back at Cooper. Then she squared up, aimed, and shot. The moose moved one leg slightly then lay still. Blood pooled onto the asphalt as Harper lowered her gun and backed away.

Cooper went to the first two cars and asked the drivers to help him pull the moose off the road. The three of them walked back toward the moose. Cooper took the gun from Harper's shaking hand.

"You did good. I know it hurts, but it had to be done." He gave her a quick hug then walked toward the moose.

One of the men pushed the back of its head with his boot. "Probably dead," he said.

"I'm going to give it a head shot to be sure." The men backed away a few feet. Cooper aimed at the ear and fired. Harper flinched and turned around. The moose did not move.

The men grabbed its hind legs and pulled, dragging the carcass slowly onto the shoulder and into the grass, leaving a smear of blood back to the road. Cooper thanked them, and they walked back to their cars.

Cooper found Harper, who rubbed tears from her eyes. He put his arm around her, and they walked slowly back towards the truck.

"That's the second time I've ever shot an animal," said Cooper. "And I probably didn't have to. I think your shot went through the heart. A good, quick kill, like it's supposed to be."

"What will happen to her?"

"Someone will come out soon to harvest the meat. The troopers will call from a list of people who've signed up to harvest road kill moose. Probably be here in less than an hour."

"I saw another moose in the brush."

Cooper stopped and looked back. "Maybe a calf. How big?"

"Smaller than the mother, but not too small."

"Probably from last year."

"Will it live?"

"It could. Depends on so many things."

Harper looked back towards the dead moose, tears in her eyes. "So both will die?"

Cooper held her shoulders and spoke gently. "Those tourists killed the moose. It couldn't walk. It would've starved or been eaten by a wolf or bear. People would've driven by it as it suffered until somebody with sense and a gun stopped to shoot it. She was lucky we were right behind those tourists. Maybe that's your fate working. You OK?"

"No." She breathed, then met his eye. "You said that's the second time you shot an animal. When was the first?"

A very painful memory flashed through Cooper's mind. He sighed and looked away. "I had to shoot my Sonny Boy in the village. One month before I retired, he got sick and couldn't walk. Could hardly breathe and was in a lot of pain. He was an old dog. Couldn't send him to Fairbanks because fog had shut down the airport for days. The clinic up there had no doctors, just aides. That was hard."

Harper held his arm. "You OK?"

Cooper looked at her. "Not when I think about it." He hoped she would understand. "Killing is a horrible thing, Harper. Sometimes it's an act of love. Sometimes it's an act of selfishness. Either way, a little of you dies, too." Cooper saw her eyes open wider.

"Does the hurt ever leave?"

"Not yet. I think when it's for love it hangs on longer." For some reason she looked scared.

"If it's not for love, what happens? Does it ever leave?"

"I don't know. I've never been in that situation."

Harper gave him an odd look, then turned to walk back to the truck. Maybe he shouldn't have given her the gun.

Cooper called the troopers and gave the moose's location so they could make their calls. The tourists said their rental car was still drivable. He told the tourists they could leave, that no trooper would come by because the moose was dead and off the road. Soon after they left, Cooper pulled onto the highway and headed south for the park.

• • • • •

Harper could still see the moose lifting its head and peering at her then twisting farther to look back into the bushes. She knew her calf was out there. Did she want to see it one last time, or did she want it to stay away? When the mother bleated, the calf moved back into the brush. She wanted to see her child and to protect it at the same time. The mother had to know she'd die.

If the calf had been hurt instead, what would the mother have done? The calf would call for its mother even if it meant putting her in danger. That's what kids do. They think of themselves. Mothers think of their kids. Would she have charged out of the brush and chased them away from her calf?

Probably. Even if it meant both of them dying, because a mother protects and is willing to die, if necessary.

Cooper would do that for her. And she believed now she'd do the same for him. Though she still thought of herself as the injured calf on the road, screaming for help. Was she ready to be the protective mother, willing to sacrifice herself? She wasn't sure.

She didn't want to deal with this question. It was too hard. Killing a suffering moose was one thing. That was an act of love. But...the other? She placed her hands on her abdomen. She bit her lip and felt a flutter in her gut.

They drove into Healy, past a cafe and a gas station. She saw a sign for a clinic and panicked. Could she get her abortion there? She felted both excited and scared. Maybe it would be easier to get done than she'd thought. "Cooper, turn left."

"Why?"

"There's a clinic. I need to stop there."

Cooper slowed and turned on his signal. "Are you hurt?"

"No, but I need to check on something."

He turned down the road and found the clinic. "I'll only be a minute." She jumped out of the truck before he could say anything else and looked at the clinic door. She had to deal with this, one way or another.

She walked in and saw a mother trying to control her two kids. An elderly man walked slowly through the door behind the counter then shuffled over to the nurse. He said he needed to make another appointment. Another nurse came from the back to the counter—kind face, about forty years old. Harper walked quickly to her.

"Can I ask you a question?"

"Certainly."

Harper looked around. She could hear the old man talking and the woman behind her, telling her kids to sit down. "Do you have something to write on?"

The nurse looked like she was going to ask a question, then said, "Sure," and found a pad and pen.

Harper quickly wrote, *Do you perform abortions here?* She handed the nurse the note.

The nurse shook her head. "Closest place is Fairbanks."

The door opened behind Harper, and she turned to look. A tall young man with blonde dreadlocks, a beginning beard, and a big smile walked in with a box, which he put on the counter next to Harper. He wore a cap with the letters EMT across the front, dark blue cargo pants— pockets full of various items—a t-shirt, and a jacket with some kind of logo. Harper stared, mouth open, at his dark blue eyes. He was gorgeous.

"Hey, Laney. We took what we needed. You can have the rest." His voice was smooth, almost lyrical.

The nurse smiled at him. Who wouldn't smile? "Thanks, Gabriel."

He noticed Harper staring at him. "How're you doin'?"

Finally, Harper took a breath and closed her mouth. "Good. How 'bout yourself?"

"Not bad. I haven't seen you around here before."

"That's probably a good thing, considering..." She motioned to the clinic waiting room.

"Right." His grin turned wry.

Do his eyes really sparkle, or is it the track lighting on the ceiling? He looked away from Harper toward Laney, then back to Harper.

"I just moved in with my grandpa. He's out in the truck. We're going backpacking tomorrow." Her heart pounded.

He stared at her a little too long before saying, "Sounds like fun." His eyes never left hers, like he was stuck. No up and downs, no leers. So different than anyone else had looked at her.

He waved at Laney. "Later." He looked at Harper. "See you around."

"Sure." She watched him open the door and bang into it with his shoulder, as he stumbled out. Maybe he was nervous because of Harper? Or maybe just clumsy. Either way, it was cute. She looked back at Laney.

"He's a cutie," said Laney, smiling at Harper. "Just graduated from the high school and is working with EMS this summer."

Harper smiled. "He seems like a nice guy."

"One of the best." She held up the note. "Do you need to talk to someone about this?"

"No. That's OK. Thanks." She opened the door and looked for Gabriel. Maybe he was still around. Then she saw an ambulance turning onto the road. Too late! She trudged back to the truck and got in.

"What was that all about?" asked Cooper.

"Just had to check on whether I could get birth control pills there. Since you're so nosy, my periods are irregular and painful, but if I take pills they're not so bad."

Cooper blushed and looked out the windshield. "Oh. Well. Can you get them there?"

"Yeah, but they asked me about health insurance, and I didn't bring my card with me." Another lie. "Did you see that boy with the blonde dreads?"

Cooper chuckled. "He kinda stands out, doesn't he? Nice looking guy. Wish I had all his hair, but I wouldn't tie it up in knots."

"Yeah." Harper put her feet up on the dash and leaned back. "Laney said he was one of the best. Just graduated and working as an EMT. Kinda makes me want to have an accident or something." She sighed, and Cooper laughed.

"Maybe just a little one." He winked.

"No. Something serious. Like I'm dying unless he gives me mouth-to-mouth with his beautiful lips." She looked at Cooper. Was he blushing? She couldn't believe she and her grandpa had just talked openly about him. That had never happened before. "Guess you never thought of a woman like that?"

"Oh yeah. But not since I've been in Alaska. Just haven't had any interest."

And she shouldn't have any interest, but here she was replaying every moment in the clinic after he entered. She saw the slight shade of difference between his hair and his beard, the curly fuzz on the sides of his neck, dimples which rose above his beard line, and the impossibly long, thick eyelashes. Was he a great guy...or just another Zachary hidden behind a beautiful smile? The nurse thought he was a good guy. Which is why he'd have no interest in her. She was pregnant, a party girl with photos and videos all over the internet, with two joints in her pack and a stash of heroin in her bed. If he knew all that and still had an interest in her, then she should avoid him because he was like all the others.

What kind of guy would be interested in her except for the Zacharys?

"Still thinking about him?" asked Cooper.

"Yeah. Thinking of all the reasons he'd have no interest in me, but I'll never see him again anyway."

"You never know. This is a big state with a small population. You'd be surprised how many times I've run into old friends or met somebody who knew a friend of mine. Lots of interconnections here. Like a small town stretched over thousands of miles."

"Why'd you have no interest in hooking up with another woman up here?"

"Cause the last one was such a bust, and it ruined my marriage."

"Rachel should know you've had no relationships since you left her. She hasn't been with anyone since either. At least I've never seen her with anyone." She knew he still loved Grandma, and she hoped her grandma would love him again if she spent time with him. They needed each other.

"I'll tell her if I have the opportunity."

The truck rose over a hill, and Harper saw a stoplight stretched across the road.

"Here's the Gulch," said Cooper. "We'll come back here to get your clothes and eat something after we get our campsite."

To the right Harper saw rustic resort hotels made of logs and timbers, all covered with dark red metal roofs. To the left, she saw wooden restaurants and shops, signs advertising t-shirts for $1.99, an ice cream shop, even a Subway. Hundreds of people, mostly middle-aged to elderly, walked around on elevated boardwalks or crossed the highway, many carrying bags for the souvenirs they had bought. Then after a few more traffic lights, it was all gone, and the road curved over the Nenana River and through trees again. After a quarter mile, Cooper turned right and passed by a sign for Denali National Park, blocked by tourists taking selfies and group photos.

They stopped at the Wilderness Access Center to pick up their various forms and tickets and to watch the required orientation videos for travel in the backcountry—how to cook and store food, cross rivers, leave no trace, and deal with animals. They also got their bear can, a plastic container for their food that bears couldn't open.

They walked across the parking lot back to the truck. "The park's divided into forty-one sections," said Cooper. "Most accept only two or three hikers, but ours takes four. Each section is thousands of acres, so we won't see anyone else, just a bunch of bears and caribou."

"So, just us two in the middle of a bunch of bears and caribou? Seems dangerous to me."

"That's the point. The excitement of seeing a bear in the wild and never knowing when one might come out of the bushes is addictive. Better than any drug you've used. And it lasts the whole time you're out there."

Why would anyone enjoy feeling danger? She realized that was part of the drug lifestyle, though she'd never thought about it in those terms. Hiding, keeping secrets, defying rules—these had defined her life before coming to Alaska. Now Cooper claimed she could feel that same excitement, even better, by walking through the middle of nowhere. Maybe she'd like this hike.

They picked a drive-through spot in the Caribou Loop of the Riley Campground, unhitched the trailer, and headed back to the Gulch for clothes and food. He pulled up to the Mountain Shop and led her inside. The store was small but packed with clothes and gear. A young man wearing a North Face light fleece and a Life is Good cap approached them.

"Can I help you?" His eyes lingered on Harper, but she went to a nearby rack and looked at price tags.

"Where's Isabelle?" asked Cooper.

"Hey, you old coot!" Harper heard a woman shouting from behind the counter.

"Hey, girl!" said Cooper as he walked over to her. "I want you to meet my granddaughter."

Harper held up a pair of nylon pants and saw Cooper turn around, looking for her.

"Well, she's here somewhere. She needs boots, pants, long underwear, fleece, hat, and, well, you know what she needs. We're going into seven tomorrow, for one night. Already have her jacket, pack, pad, and bag. Can you help her while I check out all your new gadgets?"

"Sure, Cooper. Your granddaughter, huh? You never mentioned any family."

"Kind of a surprise, but a very welcome visit."

Harper walked over to Cooper. "Here she is. Harper, this is Isabelle. She's going to help you gear up."

"Nice to meet you, Harper." They shook hands.

Harper pulled Cooper aside. "Do you know how much this stuff costs?" whispered Harper.

"Sure, I do. Isabelle gives me twenty percent off."

"But still, a shirt and pants will cost $200."

"Hey, you need the clothes. We're going to be doing this more than once. I haven't bought you anything for years. So let a grandfather indulge his granddaughter a little bit. OK?"

"OK."

"Nothing but nylon and spandex, Isabelle."

"Don't I know," said Isabelle. Harper looked at her questioningly.

"Cotton will take days to dry out there," said Isabelle to Harper. "You don't want to put on wet clothes in the morning. Let's get you fitted into some boots."

She took her to the back of the store and measured her feet, then pulled out a few different brands for her to try on.

"I've known Cooper for ten, maybe twelve years," said Isabelle while she laced up a pair of boots. "He came to my store and said he wanted to backpack before he was too old to try it. He'd never gone before. So I sold him gear, and off he went." She put the boots on Harper's feet and tightened the laces. "He came back a few days later and said that was the best time he'd ever had in his life. How do those feel?"

She stood and walked around. "Good. Has he always gone by himself?"

"I think so. Try walking up and down this hill." Harper walked up a simulated rock incline then started going down. "Stop. Do your toes hit the front of the boot?"

"Nope."

"Good. You don't want your toes jamming when you go downhill."

"Why by himself? Seems pretty sociable," said Harper as she removed the boots.

"He is, and I know lots of people who'd love to go with him, including women, but he likes the danger, I think."

Harper heard Cooper laughing loudly from the front of the store.

"Danger from bears?" asked Harper.

Isabelle pulled pants from the rack and a couple of shirts. "Some, but when you're alone in those mountains, you have to make lots of decisions, and staying alive isn't guaranteed. You can buy all the right gear, but you still have to cross a river or deal with the weather. And when you're miles away from the road, you can't just quit and expect someone to come save you. You have to finish what you start." She handed the pants and shirts to her. "Go try these on. You want them comfortable, not pretty, though anything you'd wear would look attractive on you."

Harper went into the dressing room and removed her pants and shirt. She looked at herself in the mirror and remembered all the times she'd posed as an imaginary model, always finding new ways to look more sexy and alluring. Mirrors were her friends, the eyes of every hot guy focused on her. But she didn't pose in front of this mirror. She saw an amazing body which came to her suddenly at twelve with no warnings or instructions, a magnet for every eye, begging to be touched, giving her power with no effort, pulling her inevitably toward events like water finding the easiest path downhill. She wondered how her life would've been different if she were less attractive or at least if she'd developed more slowly like most of her friends.

She wrapped one of the shirts around her and held it closed with one hand as she peeked out the door. "Isabelle? Can you get something for me?"

Isabelle came to the door. "What do you need?"

"Do you have a sports bra? Something plain?"

Isabelle looked into Harper's eyes. "You ever worn one?"

"No. Wasn't my style in Texas. Trying to find a different one here."

Isabelle nodded her head as her eyes shone with kindness. "I'll bring you some underwear, too. Not stylish, but comfortable and easy to wash and dry."

Harper tried on the pants and forced herself to pick the most comfortable, though her butt looked so much better in the smaller size. Isabelle handed her packages and told her to try them on. After a few more minutes, Harper emerged from the room in her new clothes, feeling more rugged than pretty. She liked this.

Isabelle told her to squat and do lunges to make sure nothing pinched her. "You'll rarely be standing up straight out there. Clothes got to fit when you're moving."

She gave Harper a bright orange Bana bandana for her head. She tried it on. With her hair back, the color made her face glow. Harper looked at herself in the mirror and knew it was perfect. She also saw the North Face sales guy staring at her from behind. *Creep!* She was doing nothing to attract attention, and still... His problem, not hers.

Isabelle put her arm around Harper and said, "The only thing you could do to keep from turning heads is to wear a burka, dear. Now let's find you a fleece jacket."

As Isabelle looked through a rack, Harper moved closer and almost whispered. "I've never hiked before, much less carried a pack. What if I'm out there and can't do it?"

"Don't you worry. Cooper will get you through it. A few years ago, Cooper had hiked into Section 6 and was just about to turn toward Section 7 when he saw a family trying to cross the Teklanika. They'd linked arms and were trying to walk through high, swift water. He saw two of the kids break away and start to float down the river. He got to them as fast as he could, but they were all soaked. All their food and gear was wet, and the youngest wouldn't stop crying. Cooper cooked them his food and helped them back to the road. Took hours, but he did it. That was six *cheechakos* he saved. He can surely handle one."

But that was before his episodes, thought Harper. *What will happen if he has one out there?*

"Cheechakos?"

"A newbie to Alaska," Isabelle clarified and then piled the clothes onto the counter. "I think we're done, Harper."

Harper tugged on her shirt. "Can I keep these on?"

"Sure. Go get your other clothes, and I'll give you a bag for them." Harper retrieved her clothes from the dressing room.

"Hey, Cooper!" shouted Isabelle. "We need your credit card. You might need two!"

Cooper held a few items he'd found when he walked up to the cash register. He saw the large pile of Harper's clothes. "My God, woman, is there anything you didn't sell her?"

"She's wearing some things I couldn't carry. And just because I like that girl, I'm going to give you a bigger discount."

"Thanks. Maybe I won't have to take out a second mortgage." They both laughed.

Harper watched as Isabelle scanned item after item. "Cooper, you sure you can afford this? We're only going to be out there for two days."

"Don't worry about my money. Besides, you can wear these clothes most of the year here. I like your outfit, Harper. I'm going to be proud hiking next to you. Oh, Isabelle, throw in some moleskin. She's not going to have time to break in those boots."

"Already did. You make sure you take good care of her and bring her back to me afterwards. I want to see how she liked it."

"I know that's a ploy because you want to see me again." He laughed.

She slapped his hand as he picked up his card. "You can stay in the car, for all I care. Just send her in."

"Say whatever you want, but I know the truth!"

"Sorry you have to put up with him," Isabelle said to Harper. "Have fun, and I do want to see you again." She extended her hand.

Harper shook it. "Thanks."

They left the store and put the clothes in the truck.

"Let's get ice cream," said Cooper. "They have great huckleberry and a decent waffle cone."

They walked along the boardwalk past various stores. One sold Christmas items. Another sold amazing Alaskan photography. And another had a bear fur thong hanging in the window. Harper stopped to look.

"Always wanted to buy that," said Cooper.

"What would you do with it?" asked Harper through her laughter.

"I'd send it to Greg as a Christmas present, of course. Natalie would love it."

"Or to Grandma. You could send a selfie with the caption, 'Your mountain man awaits you.'"

"Now that's an idea worth exploring!"

They laughed and kept walking, not paying attention, when Harper heard, "Hey."

Chapter Twenty-Six

She stopped and saw Gabriel standing outside a coffee shop, holding a guitar, his case on the deck with cash scattered inside.

"Hey," said Harper. Gabriel smiled, deepening his dimples. "Thought you were an EMT."

"That's my real job. The one that makes money."

"Looks like you're making money here," she said, gesturing towards his case.

He looked around, making sure no one else would hear. "That's my own cash. Makes people think they're supposed to tip."

"Does it work?" asked Cooper.

"Most of the time," said Gabriel.

For a moment, he just looked at her intently as she smiled at him. "Play something for me," said Harper.

He stared back. "What would you like?" he asked a little breathlessly.

She stared at his lips. She tried to imagine what the combination of his plump, soft bottom lip and whiskers would feel like if she kissed him. "Something slow and sweet. With some love in it."

"OK. This is for you." He started picking Jeff Buckley's version of "Hallelujah."

"Oh, I love that song." Harper sat on the table against the rail, watching him.

Still picking the strings, he said, "You never told me your name."

"You never asked. It's Harper Lyons. And this is my grandfather,

Cooper."

"Nice to meet you, sir. Harper." He nodded at both while he continued to pick the intro. "My name is—"

"Gabriel," she interjected. He raised his eyebrows, and she felt herself blushing. "Laney said your name when you brought the box in."

A few people stopped along the boardwalk and watched the show. Then he began singing with a beautiful, high-pitched voice, better than Buckley's, all the time looking at Harper. She saw nothing but the blue of his eyes, darker around the edges with light blue around the iris. Beautiful and pure. The way he watched her, intent, but warm and inviting, made her both excited and comforted. The longer she stared into his eyes, the harder it became to breathe.

After the first verse, Cooper suggested to Harper, "Sing with him."

She looked surprised. *Would he want her to?*

"You can do it."

She looked at Gabriel, unsure.

He nodded and said, "Please."

She jumped in on the chorus, watching his face. Their voices blended perfectly, hers starting softly, rising in volume throughout the second verse. She had a vague sense that more people stopped to listen. She felt her body floating and swaying to the song and at times a rush of excitement. When they hit long notes together, especially the high ones, she felt...she couldn't describe it. She felt totally engrossed, focused, separated from everything else, watching his face, like sharing a beautiful dream with him. That was it. Dreaming together. By the time they got to the final hallelujahs, they were harmonizing, sometimes battling to see who could hit the higher note, until Gabriel conceded, singing the lower harmony for the last measure.

The applause was unexpectedly loud. She hadn't noticed how many people had gathered around them.

Cooper tossed in a couple of five-dollar bills. "That was amazing, young man. Great guitar! And what a voice!"

Others dropped in bills. A few onlookers went into the coffee shop. An elderly couple handed Harper cash. "Beautiful! Beautiful!"

Harper thanked them and dropped the money into Gabriel's case.

Gabriel accepted more kudos and cash until the crowd had fully dissipated. "That's the most money I've made after one song. Actually, in a week of doing this."

"Maybe we should pair up," said Harper, smiling at him. His eyes widened a little and she couldn't tell if she shocked him or awed him.

"Maybe," replied Gabriel, averting his eyes.

Was he nervous or did she overstep?

Gabriel turned his eyes toward her again. "You're a really good singer," he said, shyly, then shifted his eyes away.

Her smile turned amused. His nervousness was cute. "I think you're better."

Cooper watched them both for a few seconds. "I'll get some coffee. Harper, I know what you want. Gabriel, what can I get you?"

Gabriel turned to Cooper. "A plain latte. Thanks, Cooper."

"You both save a table. I'll be back in a few minutes." He entered the shop.

Gabriel looked at her again, then down.

"Is there something wrong?" She touched her face. "You keep looking away."

"No. You're perfect. I mean...it's hard to look at you...not hard. It's easy, but you're pretty. And your voice is beyond beautiful."

"Yours is pretty good, too. And if I'm pretty then you're gorgeous." He looked away. She touched his chin and lifted his face to look at her. "Please don't look away."

"Trying." He grinned.

How can your eyelashes be so thick and long? "How long have you been busking?"

"Did a little last summer. Then started up again once school let out." He turned to lean his guitar against the wall when a big gust of wind blew bills out of his case.

"Crap!" He slammed the case, put his guitar on top of it, and jumped over the rail.

"I'll get the ones up here!" yelled Harper. She grabbed what she could, bumping into other people as she scrambled along the deck. "Sorry! I'm so sorry!" Some of the adults helped her until she thought she had found them all. She walked back to the case, her arms holding a wad of cash, and met Gabriel walking up the stairs. He opened the case, and they dumped everything inside. They laughed as they leaned up against the coffee shop wall, legs stretched out across the deck boards.

"Thought for a second we'd have to do an encore so I can buy gas,"

Gabriel joked, still trying to slow his breathing.

"Wanna do one anyway? What else can we sing?"

He arched a brow. "You really want to?"

"I can't think of anything I'd rather do." *Well, other than kiss you,* she thought. "Do you know any duets?"

"I know 'You Are The Reason.' I always sing it solo, but we could divide up the verses." He reached into his case and pulled out pages of lyrics. He found the song he wanted and placed it on the boardwalk between them. They leaned toward each other. "You could start the first verse, and I'll do the second. We could go to that corner and practice a little."

"Sure. I used to sing this while driving to school." *Thinking about Zachary,* she thought. *How stupid.*

"Where was that?" He picked up his case and guitar.

"Texas."

"That's a long ways to go to find a singing partner." He smiled.

"If I had known you were available, I would've come sooner."

She thought he blushed a little. He seemed awkward at this banter. It was obvious he wasn't comfortable picking up girls. How could someone so good-looking not be a pro? Another endearing feature of his. Along with his blushes. She enjoyed making him blush and stammer. So cute!

They moved to the farthest table and sat down, backs to the boardwalk. Gabriel added a capo to his guitar neck. "I usually play it here, but you might want it a little higher. We could sing all the verses together for now."

He started strumming, and then his clear, high voice filled the space around them. Harper joined him after the first line. They started softly but grew louder as they both succumbed to the song's emotion. When they got to the second chorus, Harper belted out the main melody while Gabriel did the harmony and the background voice. As they finished, they heard a burst of applause. Turning around they saw several people standing along the rail bordering the deck, as well as Cooper holding a tray of drinks. The applause grew as the crowd saw their faces.

Gabriel smiled. "We were just practicing."

Someone said, "I think you've got it down. Sing it again!" Others agreed.

Gabriel raised his eyebrows at Harper, who stood and nodded. He held her hand as they moved closer to the rail. How could holding hands feel so electric? When was the last time she held hands with a guy?

"You take the first verse, and I'll do the second," said Gabriel close to her ear. "Then we'll both do the rest." She nodded and still felt his whiskers barely kissing her skin.

Cooper saw what was about to happen and quickly placed the tray on the table, took out his phone, and moved to the side to record.

Harper saw all the faces smiling at her, wanting her to amaze them. Not with her body or her dancing, but with her voice. She flashed back to the tour boat and once again felt no fear. She felt alive. Coming to Alaska had definitely been one of the best decisions of her life. She wished she would've done it sooner.

She started singing, all the while staring at Gabriel. When he sang the second verse, she moved closer to him without being conscious of effort, just pulled to him. After the last stanza, she felt bubbles of joy erupting around her and without thinking she quickly kissed his lips. Immediately, she covered her mouth in shock and backed away. His face turned deep red while the crowd erupted, clapping and cheering.

"Kiss her, man," someone said.

He looked down at her, reached for her hand and slowly touched his lips to it.

The crowd cheered. Cooper put away his phone, grabbed the case from the table, and opened it on the deck beside them just in time to catch the bills launched toward it.

"Sing another!" someone shouted.

"Give us a few minutes," said Gabriel. "We just met. We'll be back in a while. Thank you!"

Cooper closed the case and carried it back to the table. Harper stuck by Gabriel as they thanked the last of the crowd.

Harper turned toward the table, but Gabriel held her arm. "That kiss was brilliant. At first, I didn't know what to do. But then they screamed and threw money."

Harper felt numb. He thought the kiss was fake? Just for the show? Her smile dimmed. "Yeah, I...I've never sung with anyone before. I was floating in your voice."

"Yeah. I almost forgot to breathe."

That she wasn't the only one affected gave her some hope that her interest wasn't one-sided or that he was just going to use her for pulling in more tips. She knew what she was saying was crazy and vulnerable, but she couldn't help but share her feelings with him. "I know you have no reason to trust me, and we don't know anything about each other, but I'm excited to be here, and you're the reason for that. I've never been happier than when we sang together."

He moistened his lips. "Neither...neither have I."

His deep-blue eyes reached into her, gazing at her soul and still smiled. How could he see inside her and still smile? She'd always known what guys were looking at, what they saw and wanted, and how her looks turned them to jelly. But this boy was different. "What do you see?"

He looked away then back. "Everything."

He reached for her hand and looked at it in his then lifted it, placing his palm on hers. He spread his fingers. She did the same, both looking at their hands. His fingers were an inch longer than hers. He placed the tips of his fingers on the tips of hers and pressed slightly. She trembled.

The warmth pouring through his skin shocked her. He pushed his fingers between hers slowly then barely touched his palm to hers. So gently, teasingly, excruciatingly slow. She gasped and found his eyes focused intently on her fingers. He stroked the back of her hand, covered it entirely with his then gracefully pulled it back until just their tips touched.

Harper's mouth opened, and she whimpered. How could this feel so good? She couldn't take the electricity sparking between them anymore, and she grabbed his hand in both of hers and pulled it to her face, breathing heavily, trying to keep her knees from buckling.

"I owe you a kiss." She kissed one of his fingertips. She kissed the other tips. "You have a beautiful hand." She gave it one more squeeze, then pulled her hands away. She had never felt more intimate with anyone, and all she'd done was touched his hand.

She took a few breaths, grappling for a subject change. "So...why the dreads? I mean I love them, but they seem out of place on you."

He laughed. "Allison did it to me a week ago."

A tightness settled in her chest. *Allison?* "You didn't want her to?" She tried to smile.

"I fell asleep on the couch and woke up the next morning with these. All I can do is keep them or shave my head. I'll get her back." He chuckled, reached for her hand, then stopped and gently held her arm as he led her back to Cooper at the table.

"Is she your girlfriend?" Her heart pounded.

He laughed. "No. My foster sister. I've been in a foster family for a few years. Laney's my foster mother. You met her at the clinic."

Harper's heart skipped a few beats. *She knows I'm pregnant. She'll tell Gabriel. He won't want to be with me when he finds out.* She knew this was too good to be true.

He pulled out a chair for her and leaned his guitar against the wall. Harper saw the phone in Cooper's hands.

"Did you take our picture?" asked Harper as she sat in the seat.

"Damn right I did. Several of them. And recorded your whole performance. When you guys become famous, you'll appreciate the amazing trailer I'm going to make of your beginnings."

Gabriel sat down. "I can't believe this," said Gabriel, counting the money. "I sang that same song two days ago and got a good response, but nothing like this. You should take half the money."

"No way," Harper said. "This is your gig. I'm just tagging along." But she couldn't help but think that two or three days singing with him would raise enough money to pay for her abortion, but she had such doubts now. Would she actually go through with it? She tried to push all of that out of her mind, though she knew he'd find out about her, the real her, as soon as he went home.

"When I was inside," said Cooper, "I talked to the manager about hiring you two. He'd set up a small stage inside for weekends during lunch and let you use electricity outside, so you can plug in an amp and microphone, maybe a keyboard. You both could make some decent money, and I'll bet you'd get other offers as well."

"I'd love to," said Harper, all of her senses sparking.

"Maybe you could come out to our house," said Cooper to Gabriel. "I have a studio. And a portable keyboard Harper can learn to play."

"Plus, he writes amazing songs," said Harper. "We could record our own singles."

"Wow," said Gabriel. "That sounds cool. I'm working all day tomorrow and Sunday at the fire station, but I could come by on Monday."

Cooper pulled out a pen and drew a map to his house on the back of a napkin, along with his phone number. "What's your number, Gabriel?"

A phone rang with a siren ringtone in Gabriel's pocket. "I've got to go." He fished the phone from his back pocket and looked at the screen. "I'm on call today. I need to get to the clinic. Sorry."

Cooper scribbled quickly on the paper. "We're in Caribou Loop at Riley

Campground. Site number..." He blinked and glanced at Harper with a furrowed brow. "Harper, do you remember the site number?"

"112."

"Yes, 112. Come by later if you can. We're in a green trailer." He gave him the paper.

Harper stood, glancing out at the parking lot as rain began to fall. "Can you call later?"

"Sure. I got to run." He took a few steps then turned back to grab his guitar. Took a few more steps then came back for the case, which Cooper had opened on the table. Gabriel yanked the case off the table, almost left, then stopped.

The rain was heavier and the wind had increased.

"My truck is down a ways. Hang on to this for me." He put the case on the table. "I'll come by sometime tonight." Then he looked at Harper, who took a step toward him, looking at his lips. He reached for her hand and squeezed it for a second, then jumped down the stairs, his feet splashing in the water running down the hill toward the road.

Harper stood in the rain watching him as water ran down her face. Cooper pulled her arm. "Let's get inside." They found an open table and sat down.

A waitress came over wearing black jeans and a black t-shirt tied at the waist. "Saw you with Gabriel."

"You know him?" asked Harper.

"Yeah. We graduated together." She rolled her eyes. "He's really shy around girls. He doesn't party or do anything. How'd you get him to hold your hand?"

"We like singing together."

"Nobody thought of trying that, I guess. What can I get you?"

After she took their orders and left, Cooper turned to Harper with raised brows. "Do you always fall so quick and so hard?" asked Cooper.

She thought for a second. "Yeah, one of my many faults, but he's different. Singing with him is like nothing I've ever felt before. Like a total connection. And as gorgeous as he is, he seemed surprised I'd be interested. But I should have more sense by now."

"Maybe he has enough sense for both of you. Why is he different?"

"Because he wanted to touch my hand. Just my hand. I almost died, it felt so good. And his voice. I'll never forget that voice. Valerie, my counselor at the hospital, pointed out I chase older guys who are experienced with girls. Gabriel is certainly not experienced. I'm probably scaring the crap out of him. He's not going to be interested in me when he finds out everything."

"I think it depends on how he finds out."

She looked at Cooper and nodded. She'd have to tell him when he came by the campsite. Better to hear it from her than see it on the internet.

After dinner, they drove back to the campground, where Harper helped Cooper set up a tarp over the picnic table. She loved being there. Except for the narrow road looping through the sites, trees covered the campground, giving it a comfortable, secluded aura. Campfires flickered and popped here and there, yielding a pleasant smokiness to the air. A few kids ran around playing hide-and-seek, sometimes admonished by parents.

"This place is pretty cool," said Harper.

"Too many people crammed into too little space for me," Cooper grumbled. "Tomorrow you can look for miles and see no one. We're taking the seven o'clock Camper Bus tomorrow, so we need to get up early. I'll make coffee, and we can take some cereal bars." He hauled out their packs and showed her where to put her sleeping bag and pad.

He gave her a compression bag for her extra clothes—underwear, socks, thermals, and nylon shorts—and a zippered bag for her toiletries. He'd carry the tent, while she'd carry the food can. He helped her put on her pack and adjusted all the straps.

"Doesn't seem very heavy," said Harper.

"Wait till you're climbing to the ridgeline. You'll be pretty sore on Sunday and Monday."

"How far will we hike?"

"About twelve miles."

"Six miles a day doesn't seem too hard."

"Except most of those miles are either up or down on squishy tundra. You will definitely feel it, but the views are absolutely priceless."

They stowed the packs in the truck and played some cards under the tarp as they drank spiced tea. Harper kept looking around, hoping to see Gabriel's truck. Would he come? "What time is it?" she asked for the twentieth time.

"About nine thirty. He'll be here."

"I guess so. We have his guitar and money."

"I'm betting he'll want to see you more."

What if Laney had already told him? Why would he want to be with a pregnant girl? What if he didn't believe in abortion? She wished she hadn't talked to Laney, but then she wouldn't have met Gabriel. Would he have spoken to them as they walked by the coffee shop if he hadn't seen her first in the clinic? Probably not. He seemed too shy to say "hi" to a girl he'd never seen before.

She wanted to sing with him, to feel that magic again.

Cooper's phone buzzed with a text from Gabriel. *Almost there.*

"I'll heat more water," Cooper said then entered the trailer.

Harper's heart beat faster as she stood to look up the loop. She saw headlights, then his truck, and ran to it as soon as he stopped.

"Hey," she said, searching for any sign of upset with her.

He smiled and climbed out. His smile wasn't as big as when he left her on the boardwalk, and her worry festered.

"Hey," he said as he shut the door. She wanted him to reach for her hand again, but he didn't. She walked by his side as they headed toward the table.

Cooper brought out a steaming kettle. "Would you like some tea or coffee?"

"Whatever you're drinking would be fine." Gabriel rubbed his neck. Harper studied him, taking in the deep frown line around his mouth, the shadows beneath his eyes, the way he sunk into the seat beside her with slouched shoulders.

"You look tired," said Harper.

"Yeah. There was a bad wreck south of the park. One had to be airlifted to Anchorage." He picked up the tea Cooper offered and sipped.

"You hungry?" asked Cooper. "I have a beef stroganoff pouch. Would take just a few minutes to heat up."

"No, I'm good. I stopped at my house and grabbed a sandwich."

Harper felt like someone had slugged her. How could he not know about her being pregnant and asking for an abortion?

"Have you figured out how to get back at Allison yet?" she asked, pasting on a big smile.

"Actually, I'm beginning to like them." He shook his head. "I don't have to do anything with my hair."

She played with his curls. "How long was your hair before the dreads?"

"Past my shoulders. I used to wear it in a ponytail. You never gave me your phone number, by the way."

"My old phone is broken," she lied. Not broken. Just connected to a life she never wanted to see again.

"I ordered a new one," said Cooper. "It should be at the house on Monday."

"Thank you," she said. She couldn't stand the tension. Did Gabriel know about her or not? She couldn't stand not touching him and grabbed his hand, holding it with both of hers. "My hands are cold," she explained at his questioning look. She figured if he knew the truth, he would've pulled away. But he placed his other hand on top of hers. She scooted closer to him, feeling so much relief.

"I think I'll get ready for bed," said Cooper, taking the hint that they needed some time alone to talk. "Or actually the tiny booth I'll have to squeeze into. You get the bed, my dear. I'll turn on the noisemaker so my snoring won't bother you as much. Good night, Gabriel. Very happy to have met you." He shook Gabriel's hand, smiled at her, then walked inside.

It's supposed to rain for the next few days," said Gabriel. "You're going to get wet out there."

"Have you ever gone backpacking?"

"No. I always worked in the summer. My foster father, Noah, took me hunting once, but I didn't like it."

"Camping out or shooting?"

"Both, I guess. Up until three years ago, I always lived in abandoned shacks or smelly trailers so I didn't see the point in roughing it when I didn't have to. Noah doesn't see the point in going out in the bush if he's not hunting. 'Why would you go walking around just to look at animals?' he's said to me many times. Lots of people around here think that way. And I don't like killing things."

"I had to kill a moose this morning, and I can't get it out of my mind."

"You killed a moose?" He looked at her in shock. "Why?"

Harper explained what had happened. "She had a calf. I hope it lives."

He stared off into the darkness, like he was trying to find a way to say something difficult. Her nerves fluttered in the silence.

"Our waitress at the coffee shop said she graduated with you," Harper blurted out. "Do you miss high school?"

"Not really. I spent a lot of time by myself."

"Why?"

"I worked jobs as soon as I could, so I didn't have much time. Besides, hanging out usually meant drinking beer at the gravel pit or smoking dope at the lake. Or worse. That's not really my scene." He let go of her hands and grabbed his mug for a few sips. "My parents were drug addicts, and they killed my little brother."

Her stomach dropped. "What happened?" She put a hand on his back.

"They left me at home while they took him to the store, supposedly. He was two years old, in a car seat. They stopped off at a friend's place on the way and smoked meth. They forgot he was in the backseat and ended up partying all night. It was late September, so the temperature fell past freezing. James died sometime before morning, or whenever they decided to check the car. They're both in jail, and CPS put me with Noah and Laney."

"I'm so sorry."

"I'm not sorry to be away from them. I like my foster family. James was a meth baby. He cried all the time. He was really messed up." He took a sip. "CPS should never have given him back to my parents." He stared off into the darkness again. "I asked Laney why you were at the clinic. She wouldn't tell me, but she said I should ask you." He looked at her with frightened eyes.

Harper was so tired of hiding both her past and her present. She wanted for once in her life to be honest and find someone she could tell the whole truth to without worry. He'd told her about James. Maybe that was his way of telling her she could be open with him.

"Can we walk?" asked Harper.

"Sure."

The air was wet, but there was no rain. They zipped their jackets. The campground was mostly quiet now except for a few people sitting around their fires, talking. They passed another couple walking their dog.

"Before I tell you something, Gabriel, I want you to know..." She worried about his reaction. No, she was scared to death. *Please don't run away.*

"Know what?"

"I'm in trouble, and I need help. I thought going inside that clinic would solve my problem, but it didn't. And then I met you. We sang and I felt so happy, and I can't remember a time when I was that happy. And when you touched my hand..." She reached for his hand, placing her palm against his. "No one has ever touched me like that, and I...I'm going to mess it up because..." She collapsed against him, crying.

"Talk to me." He held her. "I'll listen."

She took a deep breath and pushed herself back so she could see his face. "I'm pregnant. I went into the clinic to ask about an abortion. Cooper doesn't know."

Gabriel closed his eyes.

She started crying again, thinking he'd surely walk away. "I'm not even sure I want an abortion. And I don't have anyone to talk to about this. Anyone who'd understand and know what to do, 'cause I don't know. I don't know what the right answer is. It seems like no matter what I choose, someone is going to get hurt."

After a moment, he put his arm around her. "You can tell me."

As they walked, she told him about Zachary, the drugs, the videos, and her father. All of it. She told him how much she loved Cooper and didn't want him to think the reason she came to Alaska was so she could get an abortion there.

"When my mother got pregnant with James," said Gabriel, "I thought she should have an abortion because they were using all the time. Then after he was born, Child Services took James away from them. They had to take a class and pass drug tests. Which they did. At the time it gave me hope they'd change, but as soon as they got him back, they started using again. I tried to take care of him. The poor kid just wanted love and attention. And to live. I was happy she had him even though they were worthless.

"That night they wanted all of us to go to the store, but I had a bad feeling. They seemed stoned already. I told them I'd keep James with me and stay home. My dad got mad and said I'd stay home by myself, that I wasn't telling them what to do. If I'd just kept my mouth shut, I would've been in the car that night. James wouldn't have died." He stopped and looked up, sighing heavily.

"Oh, Gabriel," said Harper, hugging him to her.

"I guess you have lots of reasons to not want a baby, but I keep thinking about James. Nothing they did was his fault. You can blame yourself for lots of things, but whoever's inside of you is innocent. I mean, it's your decision, Harper. You do what you need to do to."

The mist began to drip on them. Both their faces were wet, tears mixed with rain.

"I don't think it's fair that this baby won't have a chance because of all I've done," said Harper, "but I'm scared. I'm sixteen. Pregnant. I have no family now except for Cooper. And I just met you." She saw such sweetness, such understanding in him.

"I'm glad we met," said Gabriel. "Kids need people who'll love them. You being pregnant doesn't bother me. It just makes you more special."

"I'm glad we met, too. You're the most beautiful boy I've ever known, and I don't mean just your looks. You're kind. Every boy I've ever known just wanted sex. I've practically thrown myself at you, and you haven't taken advantage of me. That's all guys have ever done with me."

He held both of her hands. "You have a good heart. Anyone who sings like you do has to have genuine feelings for people. You've just been with the wrong guys."

Harper held his hands and looked up at his face, tears dripping down her cheeks. Her nose snotted, but she didn't care.

"I'd love to kiss you, Harper. I've never wanted to kiss anyone more than you, but I don't want you to think that's all I see in you. Being with you and singing with you is plenty good for me."

She grabbed him, and pulled him in for a hug. He hugged her back with no hesitation. She began to sob.

"I'll help you, Harper. I'll do whatever I can."

She lifted her head off his chest and held his face. She kissed him, and he kissed her back fiercely, before placing soft kisses along her cheeks and her eyes and then moving back to her mouth again.

"I don't even know your last name," she said breathlessly.

"Light." He kissed her again. "Gabriel Light. And I already thought of our stage name—Lyons & Light."

"I like that."

I like you. The words were on the tip of her tongue, but she didn't want to say them out loud, fearing she was moving too fast, and she'd ruin the moment.

They finished walking the loop until they returned to the trailer.

"You need to get some sleep," said Gabriel. "Please be careful tomorrow."

"I will. I'm finally doing good for someone else, Mr. Light. And you are the reason." She started singing, but he put his hand over her mouth. She held it to her lips and kissed his fingers.

"Shhhh," he said, laughing. "Everyone's asleep. We'll sing on Monday."

"Promise?"

"Promise. Goodnight." He kissed her again, walked to his truck, waved as he got in, and then started to back up.

"Wait! Your guitar." She ran to Cooper's truck, pulled out his case, and took it to him. "You can't forget your money."

"It's our money. We'll split everything we earned today and in the future."

She laughed. "OK. It's our money. Lyons & Light."

He kissed her through the window. "Lyons & Light." He smiled then drove off.

She placed her hands below her waist, closed her eyes, and hugged herself. For the first time, she had hope. Real hope. If she could sing with Gabriel and make some money, maybe she could do this. Maybe she could have her baby and take care of it. Maybe she could finally turn things around for herself. Would Gabriel stay? He said he'd help her, but could he some day love her? Could he love her child? Is it just because James haunts him that he is doing this for her at all? Maybe. But the story of James's life had affected her, too. He wanted to live and be loved. So did her baby.

She opened the trailer door and found Cooper curled on his tiny bed, snoring softly. She hung up her jacket and removed her boots. Changing in the bathroom, she dried the tears and rain off her face and hair. She looked at herself in the mirror and smiled. Her eyes were puffy and her face needed a good scrub, but she had never been happier with how she looked. Everything had led to this moment. All the crap she'd done, all the heartache she'd caused and felt was OK because it had given her Gabriel and Cooper. She opened the door and found Cooper sitting up.

"You're supposed to be asleep," she said.

"So are you."

She plopped onto the bed and bounced. "This is comfortable."

"This isn't. You seem happy."

"Never been happier. Love you, Cooper." She kissed his head. "You made me sing again. Without that, I wouldn't know Gabriel. You're a very special grandpa. And you're my Grandpa from now on."

"I'm trying to be, and I love you, too. I like Gabriel. I guess I'm going to be seeing a lot of him?"

"Lots." She turned off the light above her bed and lay down, watching the video of them singing together in her mind.

Chapter Twenty-Seven

Cooper awoke just before his alarm sounded, a weird habit he'd developed since he retired. When he knew he had to get up at a certain time, he woke up several times during the night, not just to pee, and looked at the clock. Without an alarm set, he woke fewer times.

Harper slept, facing the rear of the trailer, hugging her pillow, undoubtedly a substitute for Snowball. Cooper had already dressed, so Harper could have the bathroom as soon as the kettle whistled.

She squirmed and opened one eye. "It's too early."

"Yes, it is, but you have to get up, nevertheless. The bathroom is yours."

"Is your phone charged?"

"I left it in the truck last night, and I have an extra charger, but we won't get a signal out there."

"I know. I just want to be able to look at the video and Gabriel's photos." She walked into the bathroom and shut the door. Cooper raised the table that was his bed and sat down to drink his coffee. After a few minutes, Harper emerged wearing yesterday's clothes. She sat down, and Cooper scooted her coffee over to her in a thermal cup.

"Sorry you don't have a latte this morning. Just Starbucks instant, what we'll have out there."

"Good enough for me." She took a sip and almost danced in her seat.

"You're too happy for this early on a rainy morning."

"Yes, I am."

They both heard the squeal of brakes.

Cooper stood. "That's the bus. Take the coffee. I've got our breakfast."

They left the trailer and gathered their packs from the truck. Cooper held Harper's up until she put her arms through the straps.

She frowned. "Ugh! Feels heavier this morning."

Cooper pushed a wisp of hair out of his face. "That's the lightest it will feel all day."

"Great."

As they walked, Cooper handed her an empty zip-lock and a package of tissue. "Put this in one of your pockets."

"What's it for?" asked Harper.

"We pack out our tissue paper and trash."

"Tissue for wiping your nose?"

"No, for wiping your butt."

Harper stopped. "Are you kidding?"

"Nope. Dig a hole to do your business, use your tissue, and put the paper in the bag. Then cover the hole." Harper stared at the bag and then back at him. "C'mon, the bus is waiting."

She started walking. "Couldn't you find colored bags, so we don't have to see each other's...dirty tissue?"

"Sorry." He chuckled. "I've never backpacked with anyone, so never had to worry about this. I imagine the experience will only bring us closer together." He walked on.

"Either I don't wipe my butt, or I hold it until we get back!"

He turned around but kept walking backward, laughing. "I guarantee when you get out there, the possibility that someone will see your poopy paper will seem unimportant."

They walked down the loop until it emerged next to the bus stop where a green bus was parked. People sat inside the open-sided log shelter, their packs leaning up against benches. A few drank from insulated cups. Several slept. Cooper walked to the front and knocked on the hood, gaining the attention of the driver, who smiled and opened the double side doors.

"Hey, Cooper!" The driver seemed to be Cooper's age with gray hair hanging under a wide-brimmed hat.

"Hello, Gary! I can't believe they still let you drive." He chuckled.

"I can't believe you're still able to carry a backpack!" His eyes shifted to Harper and widened a bit. "Who's this?"

"My granddaughter, Harper." Cooper put his hand on her shoulder. "I'm taking her out on her first hike."

"Nice to meet you, Harper." He held out his hand for a shake. "I've known your grandfather for about ten years. First time I've seen him hike with anyone else, so you must be special."

"He's more than special." Harper beamed up at her grandpa.

"Aww, she likes you, Cooper. How'd you manage that?"

"She doesn't know me very well." They both laughed.

"Come around the back and hand me your packs."

A crowd had gathered behind the bus. Cooper was by far the oldest. Most were 18 to 35-year-old males with large packs and hiking poles. But there were a few women with packs and one young couple with a nursing baby. He carried the gear pack, while she wore a baby-carrier backpack.

Gary opened the back door. "Hello, folks. Cooper, hand me your pack. Where are you going?"

"Six then seven." He lifted Harper's pack from her and handed it up. "We'll be out until tomorrow."

"You should see lots of wildlife," said Gary.

Cooper and Harper walked to the front of the bus and entered, sitting in the front row across from the driver's seat. Harper asked for Cooper's phone as she pulled her earphones from her pocket. Once he handed it to her, she leaned against the window, watching Gabriel and her sing.

The couple with the nursing baby entered the bus, attracting Harper's attention. She looked at Cooper and raised her brows.

"I've seen it before," said Cooper.

The couple sat down behind Cooper and Harper, who couldn't keep her eyes off the baby.

Cooper turned around. "This is my granddaughter, Harper. This is her first backpacking trip."

"Oh, you'll love it!" said the woman. She wore her hair in braided pigtails hanging over her headband. The man leaned against the window and tried to sleep.

"Boy or girl?" asked Harper.

"Girl. Six months old."

Harper watched the baby nurse. The woman covered herself and put the baby on her shoulder, lightly tapping her back. Harper heard the burp and chuckled.

"I can't believe you're taking her camping with you," said Harper.

"We took a two-day trip earlier this summer. She did great."

"Where're you headed?" asked Cooper.

"We're going to Section 10. We'll be out four days."

"Wow," said Harper.

"At least you don't have to carry extra food for her." Cooper chuckled.

"Nope. Just a little cereal."

Thunder rumbled above them, and the rain began to fall. Everyone else hurried to get inside the bus. Gary took his seat and started the bus.

"So where are they putting the animals at night, this year?" Cooper asked Gary.

Gary gave a side-glance to Cooper and smirked. "I hear the rangers and environmentalists came to an agreement that the bears and wolves would stay in the big pen in Section 8 while the ungulates would stay in 11."

"Well, that seems reasonable," said Cooper, trying to keep a straight face.

"The negotiations got a little rough at times. Couple of environmentalists attacked the wolves, and you know how that ended up." Gary shook his head soberly.

"Is that for real?" Harper asked. "They actually move the animals at night? How?"

Gary stopped at the intersection and looked at Harper. "Gotcha!" He smiled.

Cooper turned toward her and quietly said, "Just kidding. Gary gets a lot of crazy questions each season. Our running joke."

Harper shook her head. "Men." She plugged in her earphones and watched the video again.

After a few more minutes, Gary turned the bus onto the park road. Just after the Savage River Campground, someone yelled, "Moose! Three o'clock!" Gary stopped. Though half the bus was asleep, others dropped their windows and aimed cameras at a huge bull moose chomping on willow leaves. Harper looked outside then went back to the video.

"You don't want a picture?" asked Cooper, kneeling on his seat.

"Not of a moose. I don't think I can ever see one again without remembering what happened yesterday. Do you think her calf is still alive?"

He was confused by the desperation he saw in her face. "Might have been more humane to shoot it, too. It could starve or be attacked."

"But it could also live!" she snapped.

Why is she angry? "Yes, it could."

"Then it deserves a chance to try." Harper shot him a harsh look.

Cooper sat back down. He frowned. She'd never spoken to him in that tone. "What's wrong, Harper?"

She told him about Gabriel's little brother James and his parents and how he'd wanted his mother to get an abortion then was glad she didn't.

"That's a hard story," said Cooper. "Poor kid."

Gary drove the bus down the road while Cooper thought about his last conversation with Ellie. After their affair had been exposed, he and Ellie hadn't seen or talked to each other for several days. Rachel stopped speaking to him, the lawsuit had been filed by Victor's parents, and his job was in jeopardy. Then Ellie called him.

In a cold, angry tone of voice he'd never heard from her before, she snapped, "I'm pregnant, Cooper. About ten weeks."

Cooper's stomach flipped, and he tried to think how he'd raise another child. This would definitely kill his marriage. He'd probably have to move.

"Ellie, I know we weren't expecting this, but I'll do everything I can to be a good father..."

"Are you kidding?" she chuckled. "I'm not keeping it. I have an appointment on Friday. It will cost $500."

His heart pounded. "You want an abortion?"

"Yes. What else would I want?" she scoffed.

An abortion would certainly keep his problems from escalating, but he'd never forgive himself for this. He was perfectly willing to accept any consequences. He deserved them. But his recklessness would affect an innocent being that he caused to live only to be eliminated after ten weeks.

His mouth went dry. "If you don't want the baby, I'll raise it."

"This is not your decision, Cooper." She sounded so angry.

"But I'm responsible," he pleaded.

"Which is why I need the money."

The next day, he slipped an envelope into her mailbox at the school containing five one-hundred dollar bills. He felt numb. Ellie never spoke to him again. Just before the end of the school year, Cooper entered the staff lounge and found the football coach pouring coffee.

"Did Ellie hit you up for $500, too?" the coach asked with a smirk.

Cooper just stared. His heart raced. How did he know?

"She got the same from me. Frankly, I don't think she was even pregnant. She's transferring to Crockett next year. I've already called their coach and told him to be careful." He smiled, patted Cooper's shoulder, and left.

Was she really pregnant? He'd never know, but he vowed never to put himself in such a situation again. Or take a chance that he'd conceive another child, which might then be aborted. He wasn't interested in any more relationships.

"Cooper!" shouted Gary, snapping Cooper out of his thoughts. "Why are you so quiet? You're normally chewing my ear off."

"Sorry, Gary. Think I dozed off. I'm not used to getting up so early."

"Neither is she, evidently." He nodded to Harper, who slept against the window. "Where is she from?"

"San Antonio. Just got here Wednesday morning."

"For a visit?"

"For a life. I want to show her why it's different up here."

Gary pulled into the Teklanika Rest Stop, usually crowded with buses but empty at this time of day. "We'll be here for about ten minutes," Gary announced.

Cooped nudged Harper. "Hey, time to pee. This will be your last real restroom for two days."

Harper stretched and looked outside. "I'm already missing a bathroom, and we haven't even started yet."

They walked outside and each found an empty cubicle. After a few minutes, Cooper saw Harper emerge from a stall while he was talking to the backpacker couple with the baby. She jogged over.

"Can I hold her?" She held up her arms ready to receive the baby.

"Sure," said the woman as she carefully handed the sleeping baby to Harper.

Cooper was amazed at how happy Harper looked. "You look like you've done this before."

"At the church on Sundays, when I was younger. I could always get the crying ones to calm down." She touched the baby's cheek. "So soft." She beamed. "Even softer than Houdini."

After all that Harper had gone through, Cooper was amazed she could still look so young and innocent with a baby. So much love there needed a good outlet. *Sure hope you find it.*

Gary walked past and entered the bus. "Everybody ready?"

Harper handed the baby back. "Thank you."

"You're very welcome," said the mother.

Cooper and Harper plopped into their seats. "How'd you like the bathroom?" asked Cooper.

"Smelly and nasty. I think women are messier than guys. I decided to wait to dig my own hole."

Cooper laughed. "So now you're happy I gave you that bag."

"I still don't understand why we can't bury the paper. Whose job is it to walk around the tundra searching for dirty tissue paper? How will anyone know what I put in the hole?"

"I won't tell."

"You'd better not." The bus moved toward Igloo Canyon.

About a quarter mile after Igloo Campground, someone shouted, "Bear! Five o'clock!"

Gary stopped, and most of the passengers got out of their seats and walked to the back of the bus. Windows were opened. A large golden sow lumbered across the road behind the bus, then two brown spring cubs bounded after her, only to stop in the middle of the road, wrestling like kids. One stood on its hind legs until the other knocked it over.

"They're so cute," said Harper, holding Cooper's phone up to take a photo. "Even the mom is cute. How can they be so dangerous?"

"They can bite through your skull and rip your face off with their claws," said Cooper.

Harper looked back at him in shock. "But the cubs are like puppies."

"Maybe so, but there is nothing more dangerous than a mother grizzly protecting her cubs."

They sat down and the bus continued. "Drop us off at the trail, Gary," said Cooper.

"OK, but keep an eye out for that sow."

The bus climbed out of the canyon toward Sable Pass and pulled over just before a wooden sign full of nails.

"What's with that sign?" asked Harper.

"The nails keep the bears from eating it. Go to the back, and I'll drop the packs to you," said Cooper.

Harper stood and looked back at the couple. "Wish my parents had taken me out here as a baby. Have a good trip." She jumped to the road and walked toward the back of the bus.

Cooper opened the back door and handed her each pack. He closed the door and walked back to the front.

"Maybe I'll see you tomorrow evening on the way out," he said to Gary.

"Have a good hike, Cooper. Take care of that girl."

Cooper left the bus and joined Harper. Gary drove the bus away.

"How will Gary know when to pick us up?" asked Harper.

"Buses drive this road both ways all day and into the evening," said Cooper. "We can hop on any green bus if they have room. You usually don't have to wait more than thirty minutes to get a ride." He stared at her. "You ready for this?"

Harper put on her pack and looked over the edge at the steep trail to the creek below. "We're going down there?"

"And out there," he pointed toward a hump between two ridges. "A couple of miles before we take a right. This first part is easier because of the trail."

"Looks easy enough."

The wilderness deceived all the time. The scrub was deeper, the distance farther, and the cliffs steeper than they appeared. But Cooper realized the wilderness was the one telling the truth. It was the eyes of the beholder that lied, and saw what they wanted to see.

"Looks are always deceiving, Harper." Cooper removed the gun from his pack and gave it to Harper. "Hold this a second." Cooper noticed her flinch slightly when she took the gun. He hoisted his pack onto his back, buckled up, then took the gun and wrapped the holster flap around the pack strap so it rested against his ribs. "Got your binoculars?" She lifted them from around her neck. "You ready?"

"Lead the way."

They descended the hill fairly quickly, walked through the brush along the creek until they found a shallow place to cross, then picked up the trail on the other side.

"How are you doing?" Cooper asked. "Are those straps pinching your shoulders?"

"They were, but I lifted the pack a little higher and tightened the belt, so it's OK."

"Good girl." He stopped and scanned ahead with his binoculars, looking for animals. Then they moved on.

Clouds covered the sky in layers of gray, some thin and translucent revealing bright light behind, while others gathered dark and thick. The colors on the mountains were saturated greens, yellow, and orange. Most of the vegetation hugged the ground and looked uniform until you stood right above it and noticed the flowers scattered throughout—bluebells, purple orchids, forget-me-nots, and yellow dwarf daisies. Part of the trail dipped through scrubby trees and brush then rose again to bare rock.

Cooper stopped and pointed to the right. "Look! Halfway up that ridge. The blonde lump. You see it?"

Harper lifted her binoculars. "Yes. It moved! Is that a bear?"

"That is a bear," he confirmed.

"What's it doing?"

She sounded so excited. "Looking for food."

"Do we need to worry about it?"

"No. It's going the other direction and is pretty far away. But we know it's there, and we'll keep an eye on it. Are you tired?"

"Not really. Just thirsty."

"Then let's drink." They pulled out their water bottles and drank.

"What happens when we run out of water?"

"We get more. I have a filter. No shortage of water around here." He pointed to his left at a creek. "See that?" He turned and pointed toward a large pond to the right. "And there."

Harper turned toward the lake, her hand shading her eyes. "Is that the road?"

"Yes. That's a bus. You can see the dust plume behind it. What do you hear?"

She listened, then smiled. "Nothing."

Cooper beamed. "Exactly. Isn't that wonderful? In about thirty minutes we won't even see the road."

"At my parents' house, you could hear the cars on 1604 all night long."

"So this is pretty cool, huh?"

"Very. Thanks for taking me." She gave him a side hug.

"Hell, we haven't seen any of the good stuff yet. You'll run out of words." Cooper handed her an energy bar. He'd worried she might not like this trip, but she seemed to be having fun. "I'm going to walk behind that bush and pee, if you don't mind."

"I'll turn around. You don't have to walk anywhere." She turned back towards the road and watched the bear moving slowly down the hill. "That bear is going to cross the trail we left behind about an hour ago. We could have run into it."

"Always like that out here," said Cooper over his shoulder. "Got to always be looking." He zipped up his pants. "I'm done. Forgot to tell you that one of the great joys of backpacking is peeing openly while looking at all the scenery. No one can see you except the mountains and the animals."

"So that's the real reason we're in the middle of nowhere?" She smiled. "Grandpa, you might be a little too preoccupied with peeing."

"For one, I'm 65 and grateful for all my working body parts. For two, you come from the land of euphemisms where basic human behavior is hidden behind a lingering Puritan blanket still covering this country with hang-ups and guilt. First time I went backpacking, I'd hide behind a bush and look all around before dropping my pants. I even scanned the area with my binoculars. Such foolishness. Society's rules may make some sense when millions of people live on top of each other, but you're in Alaska now, the real Alaska. We're free to walk and camp wherever we want and to pee while watching the sky or the mountains."

"Makes me want to drop my pants and wet the ground right now." She laughed.

"Always the smartass. Let's move out."

Chapter Twenty-Eight

They headed toward the hump in the distance, past two lakes. A few Dall sheep high on Cathedral Mountain followed a steep trail across scree that only they could traverse. Finally, Cooper and Harper reached the summit of the saddle and could see the braids of the Teklanika River glistening as they churned through the gravel.

"Water level is high for this time of year," said Cooper.

"Looks like skinny little creeks from here. How can you tell?"

"By the color, and there're more braids than normal, running closer together. The water's full of silt. Usually doesn't look like that so close to the source."

The glacier, shrouded in diaphanous dark clouds, fed the river. To the left were miles of riverbed and the east face of Cathedral Mountain, a huge mass with spires like a freeform Gothic church. Between the columns, one could see hanging alpine valleys of green, nestled beneath yellow and orange volcanic rock.

"Wow," said Harper.

Cooper scanned the ridge to the right. "We're going off the trail now and climbing that ridge. If you can hold it until then, I'll show you a great place to expose yourself to the mountain."

"You seem a little obsessed with that, Grandpa."

"Do it once, and you'll be obsessed, too."

They left the hard-packed, rocky trail and started to slog through the tundra, which was really a soft, miniature rainforest full of an amazing variety of plants. Cooper always compared it to stepping on deep marshmallows. He told her to find rocky outcroppings to step on for easier walking. From a distance this ground looked flat, almost velvety, but it was a universe in itself, more varied than the larger landscape surrounding them. One could lie down and pick through a few square feet of plants, finding wonder in each inch.

But their goal was the ridgeline.

About halfway up, Harper stopped, breathing hard. "I want that trail back!"

"No more trails until tomorrow. We'll just stop every few minutes, rest, and look around."

They were higher than any trees or scrub bushes. Water ran in rivulets everywhere, soaking the outside of their leather boots. The breeze whipped harder as they climbed, and the views expanded beyond imagination. They approached a different world, a deceptively barren landscape just beneath the clouds. And they were totally alone. They could see no one and hear nothing but the wind.

After reaching a few false ridgelines, they found the top and stopped, mouths agape, turning slowly in a full circle.

"This is unbelievable," said Harper, breathing hard.

"Few things in life make you feel like this, Harper. Up here, you learn what's really important. At some point I won't be able to walk this ridge, but I'll always remember what it's like. I wanted you to experience this, and there's still more to see. C'mon."

He walked along the ridgeline toward the mountains until they could see the gorges made by old glaciers and the tributaries of the Teklanika. The clouds dropped, hiding the peaks, increasing their height in their imaginations. The mountain rock was almost black, highlighted by wedges of ice and snow. The sight was both foreboding and magical. Surely, dragons lived there. Or nothing at all.

"Take off your pack," said Cooper, as he removed his.

Harper unbuckled her waist strap and dropped her pack. "Oh, my God!" She raised her arms. "I feel like I'm floating!" She ran into the wind, arms stretched until she reached the edge and stood with her face pointing to the sky.

"No greater feeling than dropping a pack you've carried all day," said Cooper, wishing he could drop his disease, his loneliness, and regrets so easily. He had walked this ridgeline many times and miles beyond, searching for...what? He'd always hiked alone. Why? Because he'd been alone, trapped by his past and estranged from his family. Because hiking alone was more dangerous. But nothing scared him anymore, including death. Perhaps, in some ways, he'd already died years ago, at least a part of him had. He came here each summer to prove he could face death. He was rugged and isolated like these rocks, still standing, still meaningful, and able to take whatever life could throw at him.

Or had been. Now his brain crumbled like the scree on the steep slopes, ready to slide at any second. Before Harper arrived, his only concern about dying was the fate of Snowball and Houdini. Now that concern intensified because of Harper. He looked at her face enraptured with wonder and awe and knew he'd given her something she would never forget, something stronger than all her city substitutes. She smiled at him.

"Don't move," he said. He took her picture, then a 360° video. He walked toward her. "See that ledge?"

"Yes."

"That's where you pee or whatever. I'll move back into that dip over there and start some water boiling for ramen and tea. Take your shovel and tissue paper. You'll love it. Even if you don't have to go, strip off some clothes. No one will see you."

She removed her hand shovel from the top of her pack and walked down the hill. Cooper picked up both packs and carried them thirty yards away into a depression, providing a slight break from the wind. He removed his stove, covered it with an aluminum shield, and filled his pot with water.

• • • • •

Harper reached the ledge and removed her jacket, weighing it down against the wind. She kneeled to dig a hole below the rock protrusion, pulled her pants down to her ankles (resisting the urge to look around) and sat on the ledge. "Ouch!" The rock was rough, so she placed her coat arm under her tailbone. She stared at the mountains, sitting on her natural toilet, began her own little river, and laughed.

She scooted back on her elbows, spread her jacket under her, lifted her feet onto the ledge, and lay down, looking straight up at the clouds roiling above her. She unbuttoned her shirt, lifted her bra, and spread her arms.

Grandpa was right. What an amazing feeling! Naked at the top of the world. No rules, no hang-ups, just absolute and total freedom. A little sunshine broke through to warm her, and the wind caressed all of her skin. Then a cold gust whipped against her, and she screamed in surprise. The harmony was deafening.

She breathed deeply and slowly and tried to endure the cold, ignoring the goosebumps contracting her skin, drying painfully and turning numb from too much sensation. The sky and the mountains were not interested in her skin or her looks, which she'd revealed to Luke and many other boys afterward, thinking she'd capture their attention and love, only to discover they cared nothing for what lay beneath her physical beauty.

And what lay beneath? What was in her soul? The sky searched, rummaging around with cold fingers, then held it up to her: a fiery ball of light and heat. Passion. Love. Boundless creativity. Unrestricted by anyone's limits. What she was and could become. She placed her hands below her waist over the seed growing inside, her child and her destiny. And then she sang the chorus of one of Cooper's songs:

Be the star that you are
And shine your light
For the world to see.
The stars above are shining for you
A Heavenly family.

She stood, facing the mountains a little longer, trying to etch every sight and feeling into her brain, then pulled up her pants and put her clothes back in order. She covered the hole and put her wet tissue into the bag.

Feeling so happy and confident, Harper climbed up to the summit and saw Cooper pouring water into cups. She was hungry and would love hot tea.

"I see by the smile on your face that you liked it," said Cooper offering her a cup of ramen.

"I loved it! Do you think other people do that, or are we both pervs?" She sat down on the edge of the depression.

"I think others do it and don't admit it. Go into any tourist shop, and you'll find stickers and placards with 'Hike Naked' on them. So someone does it."

"I'm going to bring Gabriel up here and we're doing that together."

"Ah, I can hear it now: 'I know a place where we can pee together in the mountains.' He'll marvel at your romanticism."

"So will Rachel when you invite her."

"Now that's a beautiful thought to kick around. We never went backpacking, but I bet she'd like it. When you finish that, make yourself some tea. It's my turn." Cooper stood up, grabbed his shovel and paper and walked over the ridge.

Harper gobbled her ramen, rinsed her cup, dropped in a tea bag, then poured the water, already cooling in the wind. She knew why Grandpa wanted her here. This was the apex, the measure of all things. How could anyone experience this place, especially with a loved one, and not realize how traffic jams and long commutes and scrambling for more and more money and worrying about acceptance and approval were meaningless?

That couple with the baby knew the truth and wanted to imbue it into their child even before she was conscious of the event. They wanted her to know that these sights and sounds should be the baseline on which to judge everything else. She'd do the same with her baby.

She looked back from where they came and saw a sow and cubs on the saddle they had recently left. This peace wasn't without danger. In fact, the continual contrast heightened her senses, so that every glance and every sound was crucial, not to be ignored or unappreciated. In the middle of nowhere, life was at its most intense.

She would never leave Alaska.

"Glorious day!" said Cooper as he came up behind her.

Harper pointed toward the bears. "We have visitors."

"Those are two-year-old cubs," said Cooper. "Let's mount up. There's a place where we might see a whole congregation of animals."

He packed the stove and clipped their cups onto carabiners. They lifted their packs onto their backs and moved west. The land bent down steeply to a draw full of brush and a creek. On the other side, another ridge had to be climbed. At each ridge, they scanned the valley for sleeping bears, which would force them to detour. Fortunately, they saw none and made decent time. After three ridges, their descent was more gradual, broader, leading to a plateau on the other side of a creek lined with dwarf birch and greyleaf willows, three to five feet tall, perfect for hiding bears.

"We need to make a lot of noise while I fill up our bottles," said Cooper as he removed his pack and located his water filter.

"How do we make a lot of noise?" shouted Harper.

"Keep doing that," he chuckled as he tossed in the sponge float at the end of the tube connected to his pump. She watched him work the pump several times before adding the filtered water to their bottles. "And keep your head on a swivel."

She lifted her gaze and looked around. "Just want you to know that I love it here. I'm never leaving Alaska, so you're stuck with me."

Cooper nodded. "I know exactly how you feel. I said the same thing sixteen years ago. It'd be kind of hard going back to the city, wouldn't it?"

"Even Mexican food isn't worth the trip. Taco Cabana, I forsake you!"

They chuckled as they stashed two liters of water each into their netted side pockets. "I hate to carry this extra weight, but we'll use the additional water soon for lunch," said Cooper.

They walked up the sloping plateau, which extended south to another gorge. Animals were everywhere, though hundreds of yards away.

After thirty minutes they reached an outcropping of rock, not too close to the bushes, and far enough away to give them time to move if anything emerged from the creek area.

Cooper pointed toward the upper slope of the plateau. They both peered through binoculars and saw another sow with cubs, several caribou in two groups, and a bunch of sheep. They scanned all around them and discovered more bears, none close to them, but still, a dozen bears within sight was nothing to scoff at.

"How can there be so many?" asked Harper.

"Most every time I'm here, I see animals. This is a hidden oasis. If we kept moving up the plateau, by the time we got to the gorge, all the animals would've moved on. They know we're here and don't want anything to do with us. Let's eat lunch."

He pulled out the stove and set it up behind the rock out of the wind. Harper opened the bear can and pulled out two food pouches. "Do you want lasagna or stroganoff?"

"I'm partial to stroganoff, but whichever you want is fine."

She returned the lasagna pouch to the can and fastened the lid.

"Tea or coffee?" he asked. "I brought creamer."

"Coffee would be nice." She kept standing, looking for bears, while Cooper kneeled by the stove. After a few minutes the water boiled fiercely.

"I love Jetboils!" He opened the pouch, poured in the water, and resealed the package. Their meal would be ready in fewer than ten minutes. Cooper stood and handed Harper a cup of coffee and a baggie of creamer. "When we eat, we'll sit back to back. It's more comfortable and there's less area each of us has to watch."

"What do you do when you're by yourself?"

"I'd never eat here. I'd find a larger open area and stand with my pouch. It'll be nice to sit for a change."

They drank their coffee and watched the animals move slowly. A single male bear would get too close to a sow, and she'd move on with her cubs. Then the caribou would drift to another spot. Every movement caused a counter-movement. It was like watching a slow-motion dance.

They sat down with backs touching, Cooper facing the creek and Harper facing the next ridge, a quarter mile away. Cooper scooped out half the stroganoff into a nifty, collapsible bowl he'd bought yesterday at Isabelle's store and gave the pouch to Harper. They began to eat.

"This is really good," said Harper around a mouthful.

"I know. When they're on sale, they're cheaper than regular food. I could eat these at home every day and never have to wash a dish."

They ate in silence. Harper watched the animals and sipped her coffee, munching on noodles and meat every once in a while. She was in total awe.

After several minutes, she offered the rest of the pouch to Cooper. "Hey, I'm full. You want the rest?"

Cooper didn't answer. She held the pouch over her shoulder and shook it. "Free food if you want it. Better eat it, or we'll have to carry it out."

He still didn't answer. She realized what had happened and turned around.

Cooper sat upright, but the bowl had fallen to the ground. His hands were in his lap.

Three bears were seventy feet away walking ponderously from the creek. The sow was huge, a darker brown than the ones she'd seen earlier in the day, with golden tips on her thick fur. The cubs were much larger than the ones she saw on the road with long, sharp claws pointing toward her.

Her legs tightened, and it took all her will power to keep from running. "Grandpa! C'mon, I need you!" She kneeled down beside him and shook his shoulders. She lightly slapped his face. "Grandpa!" He stared blankly ahead.

Her chest pounded as she stood and remembered the backpacking videos they had to watch. She couldn't allow the bears to get food from them! She picked up his bowl and her pouch. She lifted her arms over her head with both items and waved them back and forth. "Hey, bear!" Her voice quivered. "Just us humans. You can turn around now."

One of the cubs stopped and stood on its hind legs. The sow turned sideways and woofed.

"Shit! Anytime, Grandpa!" She tried to open the bear can, knowing it contained a white garbage bag. After fumbling with her nickel, trying to twist open the screws, she finally got the lid open. She tossed the food pouches onto the ground and pulled out the bag, throwing in her pouch and Cooper's bowl. She pushed the unopened pouches back into the can and sealed it. She stuffed the can into her pack and lifted it onto one shoulder. The stove and utensils went into Cooper's pack.

The cub had moved closer, sniffing the air. The other had now turned toward them.

"Hey, bear! Time to leave, guys!" She closed Cooper's pack, leaned it against the rock, then tried to stand on floppy legs.

Cooper turned his head a little.

"Grandpa! Get up! Please!" she begged.

She stumbled toward him, put her arms under his shoulders from behind, and tried to lift. She screamed with effort and felt a twinge in her lower abdomen. She tried again and felt a sharp pain that buckled her knees, which smashed onto the rocks. "Goddammit!" she cried.

The two cubs had moved closer, and the sow was now facing her, lowering its head.

"Grandpa!" She slapped his face. "Grandpa!" Another slap.

He blinked his eyes. She faintly heard, "The gun."

"Shit!" She'd forgotten they had a gun. She pushed herself up, feeling a sharp cramp in her gut, and moved to his pack, ripped off the holster, unsnapped the back, and pulled back the hammer. "OK, assholes, you need to leave right now!" she yelled, pointing the barrel towards the nearest cub.

Cooper lifted his arms slowly and moved them awkwardly side-to-side.

Harper waved her arms. "Can you get up, Grandpa?"

"Trying." He pulled one leg under him and tried to lift himself. He reached out his arm. Harper kept the gun in her left hand while she grabbed his left arm with her right hand. She pulled and screamed with effort. She let go and grasped her gut. Cooper slowly moved onto his knees and finally stood up, breathing heavily.

"Let's back away, Harper, slowly. Don't look them in the eyes. Look to the ground and talk to them. We're just passing through, Mrs. Bear. We'd like to get on our way." He walked backward.

"Yeah, you piece of crap, you can back off now."

"Gentler, Harper." He pulled her back and took the gun from her.

She limped backward until her boot hit his pack. She tried to lift it, but she hurt too much. "Help me!" He turned and lifted the pack from her, inserted his arms into the straps and buckled it. He then reached around her shoulder and pulled the strap of Harper's pack, still hanging off one shoulder.

"Buckle up and walk backward." He grabbed the white trash bag off the ground and looked around for anything they might have left. They kept walking backward, talking softly, until the bears began to move down the plateau, perpendicular to their path.

After another twenty yards, they turned around and walked normally, glancing over their shoulders. "Keep a slow, steady pace."

Harper limped along until she had to stop, pressing her hands to her lower gut. *Damn! This hurts!*

"What's wrong?" asked Cooper.

"I think I pulled a muscle trying to lift you up."

"Here." He pulled a baggie out of his jacket and gave her two pills. "Acetaminophen. Here's some water."

She took the pills and hesitated. She remembered her mom avoiding pain pills when she was pregnant with Alex and Jack. "I don't feel like swallowing pills. Maybe later." She put them in her pocket.

"You sure?"

Gritting her teeth, she nodded.

"I'm so sorry, Harper, but you did everything right. You got the food, you got the packs, you didn't run."

"I think if I'd remembered the gun earlier, I would've shot them."

"It's better you didn't. Bears don't want to attack. The cubs were curious, is all." He looked at her with tears filling his eyes. "I'm so sorry, Harper. I completely failed you." He looked to the sky, gritting his teeth. "Goddammit! Why?"

She held him. "I'm fine, Grandpa. Nothing happened."

"You're hurt."

"I just pulled something. I'll be fine. You got us out of there. We're OK."

"I can't be doing this anymore. I shouldn't have come out here, but I wanted to show you this place. I think you know why now. We should've eaten farther up the hill, and I should've stood up like I normally do. I'm getting old and lazy."

"I'll remember that." She straightened up and looked around. "What's the shortest way back to the road?"

"Keep going. We're about halfway and after this next ridge, the walking is easier than what we already did. We have to finish what we started."

"That's what Isabelle told me. You can't quit out here and call for a lift."

"We're miles from the road, and the only way back to it is on our own two feet. Can you walk?"

"I'll do my best. Need to stop more often, though." She tried to tighten her waist strap, but that hurt. *Hope you're OK down there*, she thought. She cupped the sides of her pack and lifted it a little. That felt better, but how long could she hold it up?

"Think we ought to go as far as we can today," said Cooper. "Tomorrow you'll be sore. I know a good place to camp if we can get to it." He held out the trash bag to her. "Tie this to my pack. I'll deal with it later."

Harper tied the bag, and they started walking. Her limp gradually lessened as her cramp loosened up. A light rain began to fall, so they put their pack covers on. Twice they walked over a ridge and saw grizzlies running down the hill ahead of them. The bears had been digging for squirrels and heard them coming.

As she walked, Harper kept her mind off the pain by thinking of Gabriel and singing Cooper's songs—more like gasping and mumbling them.

After another two hours, Cooper pointed to a clearing across another valley then up a gentle rise. "If you can make it, that's a good spot. Water's nearby without high bushes."

Harper had bent over, panting, massaging her left lower side. "Yeah, I can get there. I'm so looking forward to taking off this pack."

"You can take it off now for a few minutes."

"No, when I take it off, I want it off until tomorrow. Lead on."

After another hour they reached the clearing. "Are you sure...this is the spot?" She panted for breath. Her shoulders ached, and her arm muscles felt like jelly from having to hold the pack up.

"Positively. And the rain has stopped. Drop it, girl."

Harper unbuckled her waist and chest straps, loosened her shoulder straps, and let the bag fall to the ground. "Oh, does that feel good." She held out her arms, closed her eyes, and felt the tingles running through her shoulders.

Cooper dropped his pack and removed the tent. They positioned the ground cloth, connected all the bungee poles, pushed them through the grooves and snapped the pole tips through the straps at the bottom. Cooper pushed in the stakes, and buckled the rain fly while Harper dug out sleeping bags and pads. They both blew up their pads before shoving them inside the tent.

"We're going to be crowded," said Cooper, "but I think this is my limit on carrying weight."

"The two pads fit, so we should be fine. Just keep your butt on your own pad."

"Ditto to you, young lady." They laughed.

They grabbed the stove bag, bear can, trash bag, and their toiletry pouches. "I always cook over there and then store everything over there," he said, pointing to two small rock platforms, corners in an imaginary triangle. "Each is more than the required hundred yards from the tent, but they're the best spots."

They walked to the first rock and set up for dinner. Cooper got the water cooking while Harper rearranged the bear can to accommodate the leftover lunches. They ate and drank standing, watching two three-year-olds, probably siblings, moving across a hill a few hundred yards from them.

"Bears are going to be walking all around here at night, aren't they?" Harper asked nervously.

"Generally, but they usually avoid the tent. The good smells are with the can and the cook site, so they're more likely to sniff around there. I've never had a bear bother my tent before."

"Yeah, well, after what happened at lunch, that's not very comforting."

"Are you worried?"

"Some. But it's also weirdly exciting." She grinned at him. "Just so they don't pay us a visit."

After dinner and drinks, they walked to the other rock and placed the bear can lid down in a little depression, along with a dry bag containing the stove, utensils, and toiletries. They walked back to the tent, which had two vestibules, one for each pack. After removing clothes from their packs and light sandals, they climbed inside.

"Oh, does it feel good to take off these boots," said Harper. She tossed them onto the tundra inside her vestibule.

Cooper sat on the other side, rubbing his bare feet. "Yes, it does."

"I'm going to change clothes, Grandpa, so unless you want to see what the mountains saw today, keep facing your end."

"Ditto for you."

Harper removed her shirt, bra, rain pants, and hiking pants and replaced them with thermals and her shorts. "How cold will it get?"

"High 30s, probably. Good sleeping weather in these bags. You done?"

"Done."

They turned around.

"Can I have the phone?"

He handed it to her. "And I brought the noise-maker." He turned it on. "I like the white noise, but if you want something else, just push the button. Good night, Harper, and thanks for saving me from the bears."

"We're even now, huh?"

He chuckled. "I guess we are." He lay down and soon fell asleep.

Harper lay back on top of her bag and watched the video of Gabriel and her several times, listening through her earphones. After thirty minutes, she felt a gurgling and knew the dam was about to burst. She opened the fly and found the poop kit. It was still bright enough outside that she could see all around her. After a quick check for animals, she looked for a bathroom. A small earthen ledge stood twenty feet away. She trotted over, feeling another twinge, and quickly dug a hole. Her thermals went down and her butt barely covered the hole when her intestines erupted. Did she make the hole large enough?

She looked down between her legs and saw blood. Confusion filled her mind at first. Why would she be pooping blood? Then fear flashed through her, and she gasped. *My baby!*

Her hands shook trying to open the tissue pack. She dabbed it between her legs and raised the tissue up, bloody, like her period had started. Her eyes teared up. She thought she'd pulled a muscle, but this was something else. Could she be having a miscarriage? She couldn't lose her baby!

She pulled out more tissue and tried to wipe her butt. Her hands still shook as she opened the zip-lock. She started to put the poop paper inside, then stopped. She'd save any bloody tissue so a doctor could check it. She threw the first bloody piece inside the bag and shoveled dirt over the hole. She pressed another wad of tissue between her legs for a few seconds then lifted it to the light. More blood. *No! No! No!* How much blood had she lost? Did she feel light-headed, or was she just nervous?

Gasping for breath, she tried to think of what to do when a cramp squeezed her insides, and she felt blood trickling down her leg. *Is this my period? Why would I have a period now?* She couldn't. This was a miscarriage. It had to be. *Think! Think!* Water. She needed to drink some water. She unscrewed the cap to her bottle and lifted it to her mouth, spilling water all down her top. She needed to calm down. How do you stop a miscarriage?

Marijuana. Smoke some pot and lean back with her feet on the pack. She found the joint and her lighter, dragged the pack and her jacket to the dirt ledge, and leaned back against the dirt while propping her legs up on the pack. She lit the joint and inhaled, holding the smoke as long as she could. Her heart slowed. Another toke and she felt mellow. *Stay inside me. Please, stay inside*, she thought. After another toke, she felt better and closed her eyes, imagining the little baby in her arms at the rest stop. She touched her tiny face and smiled. *Stay inside. Stay inside. Please, stay inside me.*

• • • • •

Cooper dreamed of that night at the theatre with Victor and Ellie. He saw Victor running down the aisle holding the joint. He never knew why that kid had run back inside.

He woke up, needing to pee and thought he heard Harper singing: "I will not bleed, I will not bleed, I will not bleed," and he smelled marijuana. *What the hell?*

He rolled over, seeing the empty pad next to him. A jolt of panic struck through him, settling heavily in his stomach. "Harper? Where are you?"

Harper sang. "*You knocked me down, but I'm not out, baby. I'm off the ground and on my feet.* Well, I'm not on my feet, but I'm not out!"

He scrambled out of his bag, unzipped the tent, put on his sandals, and unzipped the fly. "Where are you?" he yelled as he stood up. He looked all around, then saw her lying on the ground. He walked over as she took another toke. "What are you doing?"

"Trying to keep my baby inside me."

"What?" He dropped to his knees beside her. "What's wrong?" He thought maybe she was hallucinating from the weed.

Harper turned her head, tears dripping off her cheeks. "I'm pregnant. When I tried to lift you, I felt a cramp. I'm bleeding, Grandpa. I don't want to lose it!" She sobbed.

"Oh, no." He stroked her head. "Just calm down. Smoke some more and calm down." He covered her with her jacket. "We'll get you back. We just need to get to the road, hail a bus, and they'll send an ambulance."

"Gabriel!" Her eyes lit up. "He'll come."

"Yes, he will. He'll save you, too. We'll save your baby, Harper. I'll get you home."

She smoked the roach until ashes fell from her fingers.

"Just breathe, Harper. Nice and easy."

"Give me some tissue."

He pulled some tissue from the pack and handed it to her. She pulled out the waist of her leggings and reached in with the paper. After a few seconds, she pulled it out. She showed the tissue to Cooper. "What do you think? Am I just bleeding, or is that my baby?"

Cooper looked closely and didn't see any clumps of tissue. "I think it's just blood, like a period. Years ago, Rachel miscarried between Greg and Heather. Doctors looked for clumps of tissue. I don't see any." He found a micro fleece towel in his pack and cut it in half with his pocketknife. He handed one piece to Harper. "Use this to absorb the blood."

She put it between her legs.

Cooper looked all around. He knew the myth that bears were supposedly attracted to menstrual blood. No studies had ever proven such a connection, but here he was in the middle of nowhere with his bleeding, pregnant granddaughter who'd left his tent to sing and smoke weed—and he'd barely woken up. He should never have taken this trip in his condition. Facing danger on his outings made him feel more alive, more jazzed, replacing his loneliness with thrill and adventure that stoked his energy through the cold, dark winter. Now, the danger made him question himself and worry. Did her bleeding increase their danger?

He couldn't think of what to do. His phone didn't work. There wasn't anyone else out here for miles. Their only option was to walk out tomorrow morning.

"Harper, why didn't you tell me you were pregnant?" He knew he'd asked too loudly, like he was mad at her.

Harper's chin quivered as she looked at him. "I didn't want you to think I came to Alaska so that I could get an abortion."

"What?" That wasn't the answer he'd expected.

"Texas requires parental consent. I never told my parents I was pregnant. I don't need consent in Alaska. I stopped at the clinic earlier to ask if they did abortions. I'm so sorry." Harper wept. "Even if you had lived in Florida, I would've come to you. I love you, Grandpa. I would never hurt you."

Cooper knelt by her. "No, no, no, Harper. I'm not mad at you. How could you hurt me?" He stroked her hair. Now he understood why she had to leave Texas. "Even if you'd told me you were pregnant, I would've wanted you with me. You poor thing."

"Gabriel helped me decide to keep my baby."

"Good for him. Harper, if I'd known you were pregnant, I wouldn't have taken you out here. Well, I probably would've since my judgment has been crap about everything else. My head and your baby. Not the best combination."

"What are we going to do?"

"We're going to get you to a doctor tomorrow."

"I'm so scared. I can't lose my baby now."

Cooper knew he had one job in his life now—save Harper and her baby. "You won't. I promise, but you need to calm down. You need to get rest before tomorrow."

"How am I going to sleep? I'm too worried." She pointed at her pack under her feet. "In the top there's a breath mint case with another joint. And a lighter."

"I'll get them." He dug through the compartment until he found them.

She flicked the lighter and sucked on the joint until the flame caught then inhaled deeply, holding the smoke in until her body relaxed. She exhaled.

"Besides several pills my doctor prescribed," said Cooper, "he said marijuana might help my dementia."

"Really? Why haven't you tried it? Here." She handed him the joint. "Take a toke. Would do you good." She laughed as Cooper inhaled. "I want to say I smoked pot with my grandpa in the mountains before he saved me and my baby." She giggled. "When's the last time you smoked pot?"

Cooper exhaled the smoke and coughed a little. "Wow, this stuff is powerful. Always heard that today's weed was more potent than what we had in the 60s." He handed her the joint.

"Were you a hippy?" She inhaled.

"I guess so. A long-haired, weed-smoking, war-protesting hippie."

"Cool. Please tell me you wore tie-dyed shirts."

"I still have one, with a peace sign on it."

She breathed out the smoke and offered him the joint.

He waved her off. "I don't think I should smoke anymore. My head's already swimming."

Harper laughed. "Grandpa is stoned!" She handed him the joint. "Take one more."

He took it and inhaled again. "Whoa," he said, letting out the smoke.

"Are bears attracted to weed?" Harper asked, then drew another toke. "Sure hope not, because I ain't moving. They can find someone else to scare the crap out of. I left a big pile of poop in a hole up there." She pointed vaguely upwards. "That's all the poop I got. So watch out bear, or you'll get shot. Hey, that rhymes!" She sang the words a few times then took another toke.

"That's how I wrote my first song, getting high with friends at a house with a piano. I sat down and began playing the blues. Another fella made up lyrics to my melody."

"Really? You don't smoke now when you compose?"

"No way. Weed nearly ruined my senior year in college. If I tried to play my keyboard now, I'd hit one note and listen to it over and over. 'Wow, man, listen to that music,'" he said like a stoner. "Never smoked since."

"And this is my last toke," she inhaled and let the ashes fall to the ground. "I'll never use drugs again. Not good for me or my baby." She looked down to her stomach. "Sorry, little one. I know weed is bad for you, but I needed to calm down so I wouldn't lose you."

"You ready to move back into the tent?"

"I think so." She looked at Cooper, her chin quivering a little. "I'm sorry I never told you about being pregnant. I thought you wouldn't want me. I was going to get an abortion but changed my mind because of you and Gabriel and Snowball and Houdini and the rabbits and James. You saved my baby's life."

"I wouldn't have rejected you for any reason. Let's get you to the tent."

He moved the pack from under her legs and helped her stand. "Whoa. What a rush!" she said. Carefully walking to the tent, she held onto Cooper. Before she climbed into her bag, she pushed more tissue into her pants then lay down and found her pillow. Cooper moved her pack into the vestibule and zipped it up. By the time he'd moved into the tent, she was asleep.

Cooper pushed her hair out of her face then got on his knees. He folded his hands and looked up. "Please, God. Help us tomorrow. Help her keep her baby. I know I haven't prayed to you and never really believed in you, but you have to exist to help her. It's my fault she's here and my fault she got hurt. I'll try extra hard to believe in you; whatever it takes, I'll do. Just help us out tomorrow. Save the baby. Please. Amen."

He lay down, letting his tears flow down his cheeks, and tried to sleep. His gun was next to his head, ready if anything bothered them during the night. With him and God and his gun, Harper would be safe.

Chapter Twenty-Nine

Cooper had decided that Harper wouldn't carry a pack for the rest of the day. He would leave their sleeping bags and pads stuffed into her pack and hide it. He'd carry the food, stove, clothes, and tent. By the time Harper woke up, he'd already stuffed his bag and rolled his pad.

"How are you feeling?" he asked as she stretched herself awake.

She flinched. "Still sore. I'm going to pee, so I'll see whether I'm still bleeding."

"I'll stay in the tent and get your gear ready."

She climbed out carefully through the vestibule.

Cooper rearranged the gear in each pack before shoving them out of his vestibule. He heard Harper's footsteps, so he climbed out.

Crying, she held the rag out to him, now completely bloody. He opened the zip-lock, and she dropped it in, looking pale and haunted. "It's gone, isn't it? My baby is gone."

"We don't know that. We're leaving your pack here. You're not carrying anything today."

"Is that OK?"

"The ranger who goes around picking up poopy tissue will probably find it someday. Or someone else will carry it out. It was never going to be used until you arrived, so it's no great loss. You can use mine in the future. I won't be needing it after today." He handed her the other half of the towel. She put it in her underwear.

Harper started to bend down to help him with the tent. "I'll take care of it," said Cooper. "You should wear your pants over your thermals today. I think it's going to be colder and wetter."

Harper put on the rest of her clothes. Cooper caught her grimace when she lifted her foot to put on her boot. "Easy, girl. Lean against that ledge to put on your boots and breathe slow and steady. I'm going to fetch the food and stove."

He trudged up to the rock and found that the bear can had been moved. He looked around but saw no bears. After ten minutes he returned to Harper. "You want tea or ramen?"

"Can we get started and stop later?"

"Sure we can." He pulled an energy bar out of his jacket. "Take this. You should probably drink some water."

He moved Harper's pack behind the ledge, anchoring it with some rocks. He stuffed his pack with the tent, can, stove, and their extra clothes. "You ready?" he asked as he buckled his waist belt and adjusted his straps.

"Yeah." She tried to smile.

"We'll move at your pace. Any time you feel pain, tell me."

"OK."

"We'll get through this. I promise."

They walked slowly up the incline as a light rain began to fall. When they gained the summit, they could see the groove cutting through the land from left to right indicating the East Fork of the Toklat River up ahead, though they couldn't see the water. Just a couple of ridges lay between them and the long slope down to the riverbed. Cooper knew that once they got to the river, the walking would be easier. However, he was worried about how close the Toklat had cut to the small cliffs along the east bank—and how full the river was. Rain had been falling off and on for several days, and now the rain became steady.

After an hour, they stopped for tea and ramen, huddling against some rocks, holding the hot water close to their faces to feel its warmth. Harper showed him the rag. It was bloody but not soaked yet. They moved on. The vegetation became larger and taller as they moved closer to the river—more places for animals to hide. Cooper stopped frequently to scan ahead. As they moved downhill, they saw another sow and cubs blocking their path, so they had to backtrack a ways before continuing toward the river, now shrouded by rain and low clouds.

They walked down a narrow strip of land toward the mile-wide riverbed. Finally, they were walking on flat, hard ground, such a relief from constantly sinking in the sponge of the tundra. Brush and trees rose around them.

"I need to pee," said Harper.

"I need to do more," said Cooper. "I'll go behind that rock. Why don't you go to the other side of those bushes? And make some noise."

"OK."

"Feel all right?"

"So far."

They moved their separate ways. What Cooper needed to do was pray. He looked up and folded his hands. "Thank you. Just a little farther. Please keep her safe." He tried to imagine God carrying them to the road. Then he heard Harper scream.

"Get away! Grandpa! Help me!"

He grabbed his pack and tried to sling it over his shoulders as he ran toward the bushes.

"Moose! Grandpa!"

Harper stumbled toward him, a huge bull moose standing right behind her. Cooper grabbed her arm and pulled her through the bushes. "This way. We have to run."

Harper gritted her teeth and screamed as they ran. Cooper zigzagged between bushes and trees until they reached a narrow rivulet of water moving through rocks. He stopped and looked back.

Harper bent over. "It hurts! Dammit! I can feel blood dripping down my legs." She pulled out her rain pants. "And there's blood on my pants."

Cooper dug out a nylon t-shirt from his clothes bag. "Here." Cooper handed it to her and put the fleece towel in the zip-lock. She looked at him, so worried. "Your baby is still there."

"Are you sure?" She shoved the shirt into her pants.

"Sure. I think we lost the moose. Try to walk with me." He held her arm as they moved slowly through rocks, angling back toward the edge of the river where the ground was flat.

"I peed my pants," said Harper. "I'd just pulled them down when that bastard walked right in front of me." She laughed a little. "I need to sit a second."

Cooper helped her to the bank ledge and gave her water. "You're not leaving my sight anymore."

The raindrops splattered against the pack cover and their jackets, forcing them to talk louder.

"How much farther?"

"Several miles, but it's all like this until we get close. Then it depends on the river. It's flowing pretty high."

"Is that a problem?"

"We'll see. Ready?" She stood up with a grunt and limped beside him.

They trudged on for another hour, then stopped for lunch. Cooper made her elevate her legs while he fed her lasagna. He saw Harper check the bloody cloth. "How is it?"

"I don't see any tissue. Just blood."

They moved on.

The roar of the river grew as they got closer.

Cooper dreaded what he expected to see as they walked around the finger of land jutting out from the bank. They stopped when they saw the main channel of the river ripping toward the cliff bank with standing waves. The water was full of silt, churning yellow-brown about fifty feet across. They walked until the water cut into the side bank.

"Where do we go?" shouted Harper, trying to be heard above the river and the rain.

"We have to climb some." He pulled on branches to help him up the slippery bank, then reached back for her. "Let me pull you. Try not to tighten up."

She raised her boot about a foot and pushed on a rock. Cooper pulled with all his strength with one arm as he hung onto a branch with another. "A little farther. There's a trail up here. Hold this branch and let me move up." Once he gained higher ground, he reached for her again.

They moved along the trail, darkened by the dense bushes on either side. Cooper pushed back branches stretching in front, held them until Harper passed, then repeated the process over and over. The trail traversed the cliff, most of it about a foot wide and flat, but they came to a steep scree slope that Cooper knew was coming. He'd hoped they could walk closer to the water, but the river had drowned that part of the trail. The only available path across the slope was just a scratch across the rocks.

"How do we walk across that?" asked Harper. "Looks like a goat trail."

"It is. I should've brought a rope," said Cooper. They both looked down to see deep, roiling water. If they fell, they'd likely be swept downstream. He considered his options. They could backtrack upstream and find places to cross the river—maybe— but that would require another several miles of walking. They could backtrack and get out of the riverbed, but that route was full of draws and more strenuous. Harper needed to get to the clinic soon. They had to chance the trail.

"I'll go across and leave my pack on the other side, then come back to get you."

The rain fell harder, blurring their vision, hiding the landscape behind a gray veil. They could see rivulets running down the slope, taking small rocks to the river. Cooper crossed, his foot slipping only once. He dropped his pack and crossed back.

"Be calm. I want you in front. Just look across the slope and keep your weight on the upside of the hill." Cooper knew she was scared. Her lips were turning a little blue, and her teeth were chattering. He guided her to the trail, hands on her waist.

She moved slowly and looked down.

"Look across, Harper. Don't look down. You can do this."

She started walking in small baby steps, scooting one foot ahead and dragging the other up. About halfway across she stopped. "I'm scared. I feel blood."

"Keep going, Harper. You're strong. You're going to be a good mother. You need to get your baby to those bushes. Walk, honey. Just walk."

She moved her feet and covered the path inches at a time. About five feet from the bushes, she tried taking bigger steps and crossed her front leg with her back, then slipped. She fell to her side, screamed, and started a slow slide to the river. Cooper ran across the trail, grabbed a willow branch, and reached down to grab her arm.

"Reach for me!" he yelled.

She was on her side, heading toward the water. "I can't stop!" She tried to push her boot up the scree, but it slipped, sending rock skidding into the river, now roaring like a train against the cliff. Her boots disappeared into the water, then her knees. She screamed and turned onto her stomach and reached up with her hands. The river pulled her legs away from her.

Cooper bent his knees, extended his left leg down the slope and lunged for her upraised hand. He hit it but couldn't grasp it. He tried again.

This time he caught her wrist. "Don't let go!" he yelled. He pulled the branch and pushed with his downhill foot. He grunted, "Push your feet, Harper. Help me!"

She pulled her feet out of the water and tried to walk up the hill while pulling on Cooper's arm. She screamed as he yanked her up to the trail and into the bushes, collapsing onto her back against the brush in tears.

"You did it! You did it! Just rest a little. Not much farther to go," Cooper panted as he tried to catch his breath.

After several minutes, Harper reached for him. Cooper leaned over her, scooted his hands underneath her back and pulled her up to sitting. "Can you stand?"

"It really hurts!"

"I know, Harper, but we got to get moving." He bent down and put his arms underneath her shoulders and pulled her up. She didn't stand straight. "C'mon. There's a cabin up a little ways, then a driveway up to the road."

They walked slowly. After thirty minutes the trail moved downhill toward a gently sloping area where the river curved and spread out. They'd reached a ranger patrol cabin for winter use. Though they couldn't go inside, they could find relief from the steady rain on the porch under an overhang. Harper shivered, entirely wet.

"Let's get you in some dry clothes." He removed his pack and dug out their clothes bag. He'd brought an extra pair of thermals, socks, and a small body towel. He found an extra pair of her underwear. "Unzip your jacket."

She tried, but her hands shook too much.

He unzipped it and checked her shirt. Wet from the waist down. He removed it and slipped on his thermal top over hers. He unbuttoned the sides of her rain pants, pulled the zippers, and took off the pants. "Lean back against the wall."

She did, and he lifted her boot, untied it, slipped it off, and removed her socks.

"I need to change your pants." He thought she nodded, but she was shaking so much he couldn't tell. He pulled down her pants, wet from water and blood, and pulled them away from her feet. "Can you change your thermals? Harper?"

She shivered vigorously and hugged herself. "No, you do it. Please."

He pulled down her thermals and her underwear. "Sorry, honey, but you need dry clothes."

"It's OK-K C-Cooper. Any ex-excuse to see me na-naked." She tried to laugh, but it sounded like a bark.

"Always the smart ass," he said as he quickly wiped water off her skin with the towel. "Turn around."

"Not smart. Just damn cold." She shivered.

Cooper pulled up her dry clothes then rinsed out her rag in the rain. "*You* can put this in."

"Coward!"

"It's going to be cold."

"Ya think?" She grabbed it and shoved it between her legs. "Damn!"

He shook out her rain pants, turned them inside out, wiped them with his towel, then readied them for her to step into. She did and he pulled them up then zipped and buttoned them.

Cooper did his best to dry her boots. He put new socks on her feet, then the boots. "Let's get to the road."

They walked behind the cabin until they found the road access. Harper struggled a little, trudging up the steep incline, needing to stop several times. Finally, they reached the road. Cooper looked both ways but didn't see a bus. The rain would hide a dust cloud signaling its approach.

"Sit down and lean against this rock." He helped her down then took off his pack. He knelt on the gravel shoulder, lifted her legs, and scooted the pack beneath them. "A bus will come soon. It'll be warm inside. The driver can use his radio to call headquarters."

He stood up and listened. He thought he heard the rumbling of an engine. Then he saw a bus round the corner coming from the park entrance, not the way they needed to go. Waving his arms, he ran out and hailed it to stop. The driver opened the doors, and Cooper walked in, dripping. The female driver was about Cooper's age, a small, wiry woman who sat on a thick cushion to help her see the road.

"Please call an ambulance. My granddaughter is possibly having a miscarriage."

"Oh, my gosh!" she said. She pulled a clipboard with a bus schedule from a compartment and lifted her glasses as she held it close to her eyes. "I can't turn around here but another bus should be coming the other way any minute. They can take you out."

"Tell the ambulance to meet us at the Teklanika Rest Stop."

She pulled her radio to her mouth. "I'll do it right now. Good luck!"

Cooper went back to Harper whose eyes were closed. He shook her shoulder gently. "Stay with me, Harper! Don't go to sleep on me."

Her eyes fluttered open . "I'm really cold."

"I'm going to sit you up." He reached behind her and pulled her up. He unzipped her jacket, then rubbed his hands vigorously across her back outside her thermal top. "Lean against me, girl."

"That feels good, Grandpa. Thank you." She clutched him to her. "You saved me again."

He heard the roar of an engine in the distance. "I think I hear the bus. I'm going to pull you up. OK?"

"OK."

He pulled her up to a standing position. "Zip yourself up." He walked out to the road and looked down the gravel bed. Soon, a bus appeared from around some dense trees. He waved his arms, and the bus rolled to a stop. The doors folded open.

"What's wrong?" Gary asked.

Cooper ran back to get Harper. He brought her to the step and yelled, "I need some help here."

Two guys jumped out of the front seat and helped Harper up the steps while Cooper retrieved his backpack. When he climbed in, the two men had put Harper in their seat. Cooper handed them his pack, and they moved to the back. "Thanks."

Gary studied Harper with concern. "Is she hurt?"

"I was hoping it'd be you. She's bleeding. She may be having a miscarriage. The other bus called an ambulance. Can you call to check on it and get us to Teklanika? We should both get there at about the same time."

He nodded and grabbed his radio.

Cooper took off his jacket. A lady to his side took it from him and draped it over the bar in front of her. He unzipped Harper's jacket and pulled her up to remove it. "How are you doing?"

Her teeth still chattered. He lifted her legs across the aisle and onto the seat. The two ladies seated there moved over. "Can someone give me their jacket, so I can drape it over her?"

A man in the seat behind him stood and removed his jacket. Another came up the aisle and gave him his. Another pair of men offered their seat and moved down the aisle. Cooper scooted in and leaned over the seatback to cover her with the coats.

"Warmer?"

"Mmmm," she groaned.

"About forty-five minutes to the ambulance, then an hour and a half to the clinic." He felt her head for a fever. She seemed normal, and her lips were turning back to pink.

She held her hand up for him to hold, and he did.

He had caused this, or rather his disease had caused it. If she lost her baby because of him, he'd...what? Put it on the long list of things he'd never forgive himself for? He could never backpack again. He could never put others in danger, and he surely couldn't go alone. To never be in those mountains among the animals again, to never feel that freedom and that danger, the intensity of pure feeling—how could he live without that opportunity every summer? The list of things he could never do again was getting longer. If her baby were saved, how could he help her raise it? She could never trust him to be alone with it, or even to carry it. He needed help, and she needed her family, now more than ever. He had to fix this soon before he wasn't able to.

At least he got to experience the mountains with Harper and give her something only he could give, something she would seek out again. Maybe she'd come back here with Gabriel, or her parents and siblings, hopefully with her child. God, he loved her, and he hated himself for putting her in danger and possibly causing her to lose her baby.

The bus climbed toward Sable Pass. Someone yelled out, "Bear!" but Gary kept the bus moving. After another thirty minutes, the bus descended toward Igloo Canyon and toward the rest area. Before they reached it, Cooper saw flashing lights.

"The ambulance is here, Harper. We're almost there."

She smiled. "Gabriel?"

"I don't know. Gary, can you contact that ambulance and ask if Gabriel is one of the EMTs?"

"Sure." Gary called and waited for the response.

"Gabriel Light here," came out of the speaker. "How's the patient?"

"Tell Gabriel that Harper is on her way with a possible miscarriage," said Cooper.

Gary repeated the message.

Cooper stroked Harper's hair. "Gabriel's waiting for you, honey. He's there."

She closed her eyes and smiled. "Gabriel."

Chapter Thirty

On Sunday, five days after Harper left for Alaska, Greg stood next to his mother, staring at his grandfather's casket resting on a gurney in the shade of a funeral tent. The air was thick and hot, causing Greg to sweat. He wiped his forehead, marveling at his mother, standing erect and calm, not a bead of perspiration on her. He thought she looked better today than earlier in the week.

"He wanted me to have him cremated," said Rachel, "but my mother had wanted him next to her. She wanted to be buried here under these oak trees, so they bought this plot years ago. Toward the end, Dad complained about spending any money on his funeral. He just wanted to die so everyone else could get on with their lives."

"What are you going to do now?" asked Greg.

"I want to see Harper."

Greg jerked his head in surprise. "What about Dad?"

"Well, he'll be up there, but I mainly want to be with Harper."

Greg's mouth dropped open as his brain stuttered. "Mainly? Does he know?"

"He invited me." She looked at her son's face and smiled. "You look shocked, Greg. Harper invited me, then he agreed. I think I'll try to call her tonight."

"Our last conversation didn't go very well." He hadn't told his mother about her granddaughter's photos. "She yelled at me then hung up."

"Let me guess. You yelled at her first?" She looked at Greg who looked to the ground. "Thought so. You need to call her again. Tell her you love her, no matter what."

Greg sighed. "Yeah."

He looked back at the coffin. Harper had made him angry, so he'd yelled. But she made him feel like such a failure. He shuffled his feet over the green carpet covering the grass and dirt. Not true. He knew he had failed her, and that made him angry which he took out on her.

And there was his grandfather in the casket. He'd failed him, too. He knew he should have made more of an effort to spend time with Jake, but he was so sick, and Greg had so many problems of his own. Now it was too late for Jake, but not for Harper. He had to find a way back to her.

Beyond the tent poles stood his father-in-law, glowering at him. John signaled with his hand that he wanted him to follow. *Is he angry?* wondered Greg. *Surely, he's not going to bring up Harper now. If he does, I'm going to be ready.* He would not allow that man to ruin him. He took out his phone and pressed the record button before placing it in his suit pocket.

"Excuse me, Mom. I need to speak with John." He walked toward the man: tall, thin, dark suit, looking every bit the cartoon undertaker, not the leader of a Christian business empire.

Natalie and the kids stood away from the tarp with Zoe, who wiped her eyes with a tissue. She was actually a caring woman, at least when she was away from John.

"I thought the service went well," said Greg. "Are you going to the reception?"

"Why don't we walk over to the bridge?" John strode slowly around several graves until they reached a beautiful creek, shaded by large trees, spanned by a white, arched bridge. John stood with his back to the crowd and stared out over the field of grave markers and fake flowers on the other side.

"Where's Harper?" John asked. "I thought she'd be here."

"She's with Cooper in Alaska."

"Really?" John turned his head toward Greg. "Why would she go there? And, more importantly, why would you let her?"

Greg looked away. "She's had problems..."

John scoffed. "That's an understatement."

"She wanted to get away for a while, and we needed her to sort things out away from Alex and Jack. She was destroying our family."

John squinted his eyes. "And why would you send her to Cooper? There are plenty of facilities that deal with troubled kids."

Damn him! Always challenging my parenting. He locked eyes with John. "She didn't give us that option."

"Didn't give you that option? Who's running your house?" He glared at Greg. "Who paid for her plane ticket to Alaska?"

Greg squirmed. "We did."

"Why? Why couldn't you send her to a facility with real professionals, rather than to a disgraced old man?"

"Harper is doing fine in Alaska." He hoped.

A hint of a smile spread across John's face. He licked his lips. "Really? Yet, since she's been there, photos and videos of her naked, even engaging in sex, are all over the internet."

Greg knew that John had no concern for Harper's whereabouts, just the damage she might cause the school's reputation through her connection to him. "How would you know that unless you've looked at every photo and video?"

Slowly, and with no effort to hide his disdain, John asked, "What did you say?" He tilted his head forward, glowering through his deep-set eyes at Greg.

With a tight smile, Greg looked back at him. "You heard me." It was about time he gave it to that asshole. "I know about those. They were taken before she left for Alaska by her boyfriend who decided to punish her. How many have you looked at? And how many times? And why did you have to watch any of them? Somebody called the school and told Natalie about them and somehow got the word to the students, but neither of us have opened any files. How many have you opened?"

Hatred burned in John's eyes. "You're fired."

Greg smiled. "Really? I'm fired because my daughter is naked on the internet, and you've seen the files?"

"You're fired because she accused you twice of inappropriate behavior with her, sending her claims to hundreds of students and parents. She was obviously abused. Her wild behavior is a classic sign. You're not fit to be around children at The Cross Academy." He turned to walk away.

Greg held his arm. "What wild behavior are you referring to?"

John swatted away Greg's hand. "The videos!"

"You've seen these?"

"You expelled her for drinking alcohol on a school trip."

"She possessed a bottle of beer which some girls gave her. She never drank it. Maybe you're referring to the video that the girls shot of her in the bathroom which no one but them ever saw."

"I saw it!"

"Oh, that's right. You told me she'd make hundreds of dollars in tips at the Palace Gentleman's Club because you'd watched her dance. She was a pro, you said." Greg saw a flicker of fear cross John's face.

"She was! And is! Now she's dancing in a skimpy negligee, surrounded by men."

"You saw this?" *Say it, asshole!*

"You're damn right I did! You would not believe what else she's doing."

Greg kept calm. "I haven't seen them, but you have. In fact, I'll bet they're on your phone right now. She's sixteen, John, a minor. You have child pornography on your phone. I'm going to call the police and make a complaint."

John's face turned red, and his jaw clenched. "What are you insinuating?"

"Their coach told me in October that you wanted the girls' phones, to check them out. She said you had those phones in your office for over an hour. Why? They were full of nude photos and my daughter stripping. You looked at all of them. You downloaded them to your phone."

"You have no proof. No one will believe you."

"Maybe, but they'll believe this." He pulled out his phone. "I've been recording since we started talking."

John grabbed for the phone, but Greg stepped back and spoke calmly. "What other photos do you have on your phone, John? You can't delete all of the evidence. Forensics can always recover files."

Greg saw hatred in John's eyes, but he also saw fear.

"This is what will happen. Natalie and I will resign, effective at the end of the month. You will continue to pay our salaries and health insurance through the end of August. You will write a letter of recommendation for us both, thanking us for our service, which we have regretfully terminated due to irreconcilable family problems between you and me. You'll respond to any future phone calls asking for a recommendation or explanation of the letter with the same words. We have personal issues totally separate from my work as Headmaster. Considering your position on the Board, I could no longer work at TCA. If you don't agree to these conditions or ever try to ruin my reputation, I'll send this recording to the police, the other board members, and to all the staff at the school. Do you understand?"

John continued to glare but said nothing, obviously running through all of his options in his mind.

Greg knew he'd never escape the texts Harper had sent to others and that any future employers conducting any decent background check would learn of them and probably his daughter's online photos. Greg could deal with those, but he couldn't deal with a vengeful John trying to ruin him. Through her photo blackmail of him and Natalie, Harper had shown him the way to protect himself and his family. He now understood how angry she must have been at him. Just like her, he'd had enough from this man and needed to strike back. He saw a caged animal in front of him, his eyes darting around, trying to find a way out.

"I always wondered why Natalie never allowed our kids to spend the night alone at your house," said Greg. "She'd claimed she always worried they'd misbehave, but now I think there were other reasons. Maybe someday she'll tell me what they were and why she worried about you. I know there's a story there, something similar to the time you slapped her then threw her out of the house all night for backtalking until she memorized Bible verses."

"I'll have the letter ready as soon as you and Natalie clear out your personal items by the end of day tomorrow," John growled. "And you will tell curious staff members that you and I had a falling out and that you can no longer work under me, despite our continued professional respect for each other." He walked away.

Greg stopped the recording.

He noticed a text message from an unknown number with a 907 area code, from Alaska.

I have reviewed your application and would like to speak with you ASAP regarding a principal's position we have open. Please message me if you are interested and provide a time we can talk.

Greg stared at the screen for a moment, baffled. He'd never applied any...Dad. He sighed. What had the old man gotten him into now?

He typed in a message to Cooper: *How is Harper? Please contact me when you have returned from your backpacking trip. Also, I need to ask you about a message I just received concerning a job in Alaska. What's going on?*

• • • • •

Harper saw the flashing lights reflecting on her window as Gary parked the bus next to the ambulance and opened the door. Gabriel walked inside and found Harper. She reached out for him. "Gabriel!"

"How are you doing, Harper?" They hugged, and Harper felt her body flood with warmth.

"She hiked twelve miles, mainly in the rain," said Cooper. "Started bleeding after bears surprised us while we ate. Bears left without incident, but she was scared and tried to lift me up. Strained a muscle and caused her to start cramping. She's been bleeding ever since. She got pretty cold and wet today."

"I'll take care of you," he said as he lifted her out of the seat.

Gabriel carried her out of the bus, through the rain and into the back of the ambulance. She lay on the gurney with her head propped on a pillow while Gabriel began to take her vital signs. He strapped on a blood pressure cuff and pumped it.

A moment later, Harper heard Cooper through the window. "I'm here, Harper. Thanks, Gabriel."

After a few more minutes, Gabriel said, "Pete, I'm ready."

The ambulance pulled out of the parking lot and headed for the park entrance.

"Do you have any pads in here? I'm tired of this rag," said Harper as she pulled it out of her pants.

Gabriel's eyes widened a little. He opened a bag for her to drop it into and sealed it. Then he gave her two pads.

"You're seeing me at my worst, Gabriel Light. If you still like me tomorrow, I think you're a keeper."

"Walking twelve miles in the rain, bleeding and cramping. You might be a keeper yourself."

She smiled at him and held out her hand, spreading her fingers. Gabriel placed his tips on hers and pressed gently. Their fingers interwove with each other's as they both stared transfixed at their movements.

"I think my hand likes yours, Gabriel." She saw his blues eyes raise toward hers.

"I know mine does." With his other hand he lightly touched her cheek, her ear, then her eyebrow. "What happened out there?" he asked.

She told him about Cooper's spell and the bears. Trying to lift him up and pulling something. Then the continual bleeding and falling into the river, only to be saved by Cooper.

"I think lots of women bleed during pregnancy, especially at the beginning," said Gabriel. "I remember my mother having to go to the emergency room a couple of times when she was pregnant with James because of bleeding. Of course, she was using drugs all the time, but she didn't have a miscarriage."

"Maybe the drugs I used are causing this." She was so scared.

"My mother didn't miscarry. Just bled. You'll be OK."

"I panicked last night when I saw the blood. I couldn't calm down. I smoked some marijuana." Would he forgive her?

"Did it help? Did you calm down?"

"Yes. And I went to sleep. I don't think I could've slept otherwise."

"Then you did the right thing. You needed your strength for the hike out today." He kissed her hand. "I'm proud of you."

She pulled his hand to her cheek.

"A miscarriage isn't the same as having an abortion," said Gabriel. "There's nothing you can do, Harper."

"It'd still be my fault." Tears formed in her eyes. "I want to make something live. All I've done is destroy things and cause pain."

"That's not true. You saved Cooper from the bears. You pushed yourself to get here and to get help. Others would have given up. I think you'll be OK. We'll deal with whatever happens."

"Thank you, Gabriel."

"Try to sleep. I'll be here when you wake up."

She closed her eyes while still holding his hand.

Harper heard the back door open and saw Gabriel jump out. He and Pete put the gurney on the ground and pushed it into the clinic while Cooper stopped at the desk to talk to a nurse and fill out paperwork. A nurse took a blood sample. Gabriel stood beside her holding Harper's hand.

After a few minutes, Cooper entered her room. "How are you feeling?"

"I'm worried about my baby."

"The nurse is coming. We'll know soon."

The nurse wheeled in an ultrasound machine. "I'd like to do a sonogram of your uterus. Would you gentlemen wait in the lobby?"

"They can stay, if they want." said Harper.

"OK." She pushed back Harper's top and pulled down her pants slightly. "Your blood test shows you're pregnant, and the blood on the cloths you brought in look like menstrual blood. So we should be seeing an embryo and hearing a heartbeat."

Harper felt a surge of happiness. "My baby is still there?"

"Let's make sure." She moved the probe on her lower abdomen as she watched the screen. "Can you see?" She adjusted the screen so Harper could watch. Cooper and Gabriel moved behind Harper. She held both of their hands. "There it is." The nurse adjusted the sound level, and they all heard the rapid heartbeat of a fetus.

"Oh, my God," cried Harper. "My baby's alive. It's OK."

Gabriel bent lower so his face was next to Harper's and kissed her cheek.

"Can you take a picture, a video so I can hear the heartbeat?"

Both men held their cameras pointed at the screen while Harper smiled through tears. Harper saw Cooper pan over to get her and Gabriel beaming together.

"The baby looks to be about nine or ten weeks," said the nurse.

"Nine and a half," said Harper.

"What caused her to bleed?" asked Cooper.

"It's called breakthrough bleeding. Some women, especially those who've had irregular periods before pregnancy, have bleeding during the first trimester. It doesn't affect the fetus."

"Could fear or heavy lifting bring it on?" asked Cooper.

"No. Those events just happened to coincide. She would've bled regardless."

"But she felt pain and cramping."

"She probably did strain something trying to lift you, plus carrying a pack all day for the first time. But the cramping was caused by the bleeding. Were your cramps bad before you got pregnant?" she asked Harper.

"The worst!"

"These will be the same."

"How long will this continue?" asked Harper.

"Maybe a couple of days. Depends. I think we're done, Harper. I'll bet you'd like a good hot shower tonight." She put the ultrasound machine back together.

Harper sighed. “I’m going to lie in the tub for an hour.”

“First, we’ve got to hook up the trailer,” said Cooper, “get something to eat, and get home. Can you stand?”

Gabriel helped her off the gurney. Harper felt a little wobbly, but otherwise, she was fine.

“Any pain?” asked Gabriel.

“Hardly. It’s amazing how good happiness feels. It makes everything better.” She hugged Gabriel.

“Gabriel, could you give us a lift to our campsite and help me hook up to my trailer?”

“Sure.” He held the door for them both as they left the building.

“Harper’s gifts don’t include giving directions,” said Cooper, “just so you know.”

“Or taking them, just so you know,” she added with a smile.

“Well, I can tell you’re feeling better, because you’re back to being a smart ass,” teased Cooper. He helped her into Gabriel’s truck, then climbed in and shut the door. As soon as Gabriel got behind the wheel, she snuggled up next to him. They drove back to Riley Campground and hitched up the trailer in a few minutes.

“You coming to see me tomorrow?” asked Harper.

“Damn right.”

“I’ll smell good and have on clean clothes, maybe a little lipstick. You might not recognize me.”

Gabriel hugged her. “I’m kinda partial to the waterlogged, stinky, blue-lipped version.”

“We’ll see.” She snuggled against his neck. “I’m going to knock your socks off. You’ll be speechless.”

“I don’t wear socks.”

Harper’s eyes widened. “What else don’t you wear?”

He backed away, laughing. “Guess you’ll have to wait and see.” He waved to Cooper. “Tomorrow!” He climbed back into the truck and drove off.

Harper watched after the truck until it disappeared. She turned and saw Cooper smiling at her. “What?”

“I’m happy for both of you. He’s a good young man.”

She rushed over to hug Cooper. “You’re a pretty good man yourself.”

“And you’re the best granddaughter I could hope to have.”

“You think all of our trips together will be as exciting?” She laughed.

"God, I hope not. Let's go home."

They climbed into the truck and pulled out of the campsite. As he waited at the highway intersection for two motorhomes to pass, he hit Kenzie's number and waited for her to answer. After many rings, he hung up. "Damn. Where is that girl?"

"Problem?"

"Yeah. Tried calling her an hour ago and she didn't answer then either. I wanted to tell her we'd be a little late. I hope Snowball and Houdini are OK."

Harper remembered she was supposed to give Kenzie heroin when she got back home. What was she thinking? She should've flushed her smack down the toilet.

"As soon as we passed the dog kennels, my phone buzzed with messages from Rachel and Greg wanting to know how you were. I didn't tell them about any of this. Just said we were still in the park and couldn't communicate much now. I think you should be the one to talk to them."

"OK." *Something else for Dad to yell at me about.*

"Are you hungry?" asked Cooper as they stopped at a light in the Gulch.

"A little, but maybe just grab a sandwich?"

"I'll stop at the grocery store in Healy. I need gas anyway."

Cooper's phone rang. He grabbed it quickly and punched accept. "Kenzie, is that you?" Cooper asked.

Harper looked at Cooper.

"Oh, hello, Rachel." He glanced over at Harper who smiled back at him. "Kenzie is a high school kid house-sitting my pets, and I haven't been able to reach her. We're heading back to the house right now."

He paused, listening.

"Sure you can. She's right here." He handed the phone to Harper.

"Hi, Grandma."

"Would you still like me to visit you?" Rachel asked.

She caught his eye and smiled. "How soon can you come?"

"In a few days. I'm trying to decide whether to get this house ready for sale first or do that after I come back."

"Do it after. Come up now."

"Is there something wrong?"

Could she tell from my voice? "No, nothing's wrong."

She looked at Cooper who mouthed, "Tell her."

Harper nodded. *How do I do this?* "I'm going to send you some videos, Grandma. I want you to look at them and then call me back."

"Videos of what?"

"You'll see." She saw Cooper frowning at her. "I'm going to hang up, send them, then you call me back after you've watched."

"OK." She ended the call. Harper selected the video of Gabriel and her singing and the one Cooper shot at the clinic.

"You could've just told her."

"I know, but I want some time to think." She wanted Grandma for Cooper's sake, but she also needed her for the baby. Grandma was always great with babies. She couldn't decide whether to tell her about Cooper's problems. Maybe he should be the one to tell, but she was tired of hiding secrets. Her baby needed a family, a complete family.

Cooper pulled into the store parking lot and headed for the gas pumps. Harper saw him insert his credit card into the pump then reach into his pocket to pull out his phone. Harper opened the door and got out.

"Hello Rachel," said Cooper, as he looked back at Harper.

She stood by her grandpa. He put the phone on speaker.

"Yes, and she's very happy she is," said Cooper. "We had a rough time on our backpacking trip, and for a while we thought she might have lost it."

"Who's the boy? Is he the father?"

"No. Harper met Gabriel two days ago. They're good friends. I'm going to give the phone to Harper in a second, but I want to ask you something. She's going to need help with her pregnancy and the baby, help I can't provide for her. She needs you here, Rachel, not just for a visit, but to be with her."

He paused, looking at Harper, who mouthed, "Tell her."

Cooper nodded and turned around. "And I need you. I'm sorry for being such a stupid fool. I never blamed you for divorcing me. I deserved it, but I never stopped caring for you. I..."

"Nor I, you."

"What did you say?"

"The worst mistake in my life was kicking you out. I realized what a fool I was the day after you left. I've...I've missed you."

Cooper broke down sobbing. Harper hugged him from behind.

"Cooper? Are you there?"

He wiped his nose. "I'm here, Rachel."

"I'll fly up there as soon as I can."

Cooper turned around to face Harper and hugged her. "Thank you." He gave her the phone. "Here."

"Cooper? Are you OK?"

"Grandma, he's crying because he's so happy you'll be with us."

Cooper wiped his eyes and held out his hand for the phone. Harper gave it back to him. "Rachel, I need to tell you something. I don't want you flying up here not knowing the truth about me. I have early-onset dementia. I have spells where I blank out and can't remember anything. Hell, I almost got Harper killed yesterday in the mountains because of it. I don't know if it's going to get worse or how soon. You don't have to worry about having to take care of me, like you did your mother, because I won't let it get that far. Maybe if both you and Harper are with me, I'll get better. The best day in my life so far was when Harper came to see me. The next best day would be when I pick you up at the airport, if you still want to come."

Harper rubbed his back.

"Nothing could keep me from it," said Rachel. "Sounds like both of you need me, and there's no better feeling in the world than being needed. Now, let me talk to Harper."

"OK. Here she is." He gave the phone to Harper. "Fill the tank up, and I'll get us something to eat."

Harper kissed his cheek. "Go. Get me turkey if they have it." She watched him walk off, slowly at first, then a little faster. He threw out his arms, looked up, and shouted, "Yes!" then almost skipped the rest of the way to the store.

"Grandma, I'm here." She put the gas nozzle into the truck and pulled the handle.

"Do your parents know you're pregnant?" She sounded like she was crying.

"No. Are you all right, Grandma?"

"Yes, dear. Cooper's not the only one who cries, you know. He's always been emotional." Harper smiled. "Do you want me to tell them, or do you want to?"

"I don't know. The last time I talked to Dad, I hung up on him. He's pretty mad at me, and I don't blame him."

"Your father resigned today."

Harper felt weak. "Oh, God. Because of me?"

"No. Because of John's anger at you. I think your father finally realized he should never have taken that job."

"Maybe you should tell him about the baby."

"I will. Tell me why you went to Alaska."

"Because I was pregnant, and I was scared how they would react. I thought I wanted an abortion but I needed parental consent in Texas. Alaska doesn't require it. And Grandpa was so loving toward me. I didn't tell him I was pregnant until last night. I should've told him sooner, but he showed me the most amazing place in the mountains. We want to take you there. And he saved my life, Grandma. More than once. I would have drowned today in the river, but he pulled me out."

"You almost drowned?"

"I could've if he hadn't grabbed my arm and pulled me out."

"Why did you fall into a river? Oh, never mind. Who is Gabriel?"

She felt so excited to tell her about Gabriel. "He's an EMT and a singer. We're going to sing together for money! He's so amazing and singing with him is magic."

"Slow down, Harper. Slow down. Why did you change your mind about the baby?"

"Lots of reasons, but mainly because I was responsible for making this baby, and it deserves a chance to live and be loved. I've been selfish all my life. I need to help someone else."

Rachel paused, then spoke slowly. "Raising kids is hard. Your whole life will change, and they don't always turn out like you hope."

"Like me? Like Heather? But you know what? I'm doing better since I've been with Grandpa. I love him unconditionally, and I know he loves me the same. We can talk about anything without embarrassment. I'd never hide anything from him. He's always on my side, and I'm always on his. If I can convince my child that I feel the same way, maybe things will turn out OK."

Rachel sighed. "I think he and I fell apart because we stopped talking and having fun together."

"He still loves you, Grandma. He's so sorry for hurting you. But if you hadn't thrown him out, he wouldn't have been here to help me. If you come back to him now, I know something new and strong will grow among all of us. I want that for my baby."

"I'll be there, sweetheart. For all three of you. Now I'd better think about how I want to talk to your parents."

Harper felt a deep ache in her gut. She wished they'd give her another chance. "Please tell them I want to see them. And...I'm sorry."

"I will, Harper."

"OK. I love you, Grandma."

"I love you, too. Take care of that big guy until I get up there."

Harper smiled. "I'll do my best."

Harper ended the call. The sky was beginning to clear and brighten. She saw the sign for the clinic pointing across the highway. Two days ago, she'd wanted to destroy something else in her life. She thought she had to cut everything off from the past to start over. Now she knew that creating her new life didn't require destruction. Just a new perspective, like discovering freedom and harmony in the mountains, like finding joy in the sound of a heartbeat, like caring for someone more than herself.

"Harper!" She turned and saw Cooper trotting back to the truck, panting, and out of breath. "Kenzie got hurt Friday night. She's in a hospital in Fairbanks. Nobody's been taking care of Snowball and Houdini for the past two days!"

Chapter Thirty-One

Cooper's truck roared out of the lot and onto the highway, his trailer rocking and squeaking. As soon as he reached the 65 mph sign, he pushed the accelerator until he got to seventy. Harper knew Kenzie's accident was her fault because she was high on Harper's drugs. She felt a painful lump in her throat.

"Kevin and his family were in the store. I said 'hi' to him, and he asked if I'd heard about Kenzie and her boyfriend. After the graduation party Friday night, a bunch of Hondas were jumping the dike. Kenzie's bounced when it landed and threw her off. She wasn't wearing a helmet. Supposedly, they were stoned or high on something."

Harper groaned. "Probably on my heroin. I'm sure she dug through my room until she found the balloons I brought up. Dammit!"

"Why would she search your room?"

"Because I told her I'd give her something extra if she took special care of Snowball and Houdini. I brought up a few heroin balloons on the plane. And because I had stupidly sent up smack in those crates, I thought I needed to sell all of it to pay for the abortion. She said she'd buy it, so she probably thought I had it hidden in the house. Just when I think I'm doing good, something from the past comes back to bite me. I'm so sorry." She slumped into her seat.

"Not your fault she stole from you, and we don't know that's what she did. She was crazy on that Honda before you came along."

"What about Snowball and Houdini?"

"They'll be hungry and thirsty, and the house will be a mess. But they should be OK."

Harper had begun to feel happy with herself—Grandpa, Gabriel, her baby, and Rachel—and thought she had turned herself around. She knew what was important and what was not, or was beginning to recognize the difference. But she hadn't reconciled her past. Her mistakes still affected her and others.

"Daddy quit his job. Rachel told me."

"I need to talk to him, maybe tonight. He mentioned something about a job offer from a school in Alaska." He pushed the accelerator to the floor and passed a slow-moving pickup.

"How could he get an offer?"

"Because I completed an application on ATP's website for him. The state has a centralized education job site, so it's easy to see what jobs are available, and districts are able to find applicants. I answered all the questions I knew, made up some answers, and wrote his philosophy of education essays."

"How could you do that?"

"Because Greg agrees with everything I know about village schools. How could he not?" He glanced over at Harper with a smirk. "Besides, he mentioned me a lot in his essays. Gave me credit for piquing his interest in Alaskan Native culture." He laughed. "So somebody's interested in talking to him. If Greg will listen to me, he could get a job and be a good principal."

"You think he'll come up here?" *Would he want to? Would he hate me forever if he had to?*

"He might not have a choice. I didn't, but it turned out OK for me."

"I need to talk to him."

"And to listen."

She snapped her head toward Cooper. "And he needs to listen."

Cooper raised his eyebrows at her.

"OK," said Harper. "We both need to listen and to apologize."

"Eating crow can be the best meal of the day. The sooner you chew and swallow, the happier you and everyone else around you will be. Better you learn that at sixteen than wait until you're sixty-five like an old buzzard I know. Is Rachel going to tell them about your baby?"

"I asked her to."

"Good."

Harper looked outside and recognized where they were. Up ahead, she saw the gut pile of the moose she'd shot under two ravens picking through it. Another mess she'd caused. Harper replayed past events from Texas in her mind, now seeing them differently. She sank lower and lower in her seat so when Cooper pulled up to the house, she could see only the roof through the windshield.

They both leaped out of the truck. Snowball's big paws banged into the kitchen window, and he barked repeatedly. Cooper fumbled for his keys to unlock the door. Harper turned the handle, and the door opened.

"She left it open!" cried Cooper.

Snowball ran outside, unable to control his happiness. He ran in crazy circles, divots of grass flying behind him. He jumped onto Cooper and smothered Harper in kisses. Cooper ran inside then ran out with an empty water bowl, a food bowl, and two cans of food. He put the water bowl on the ground outside and filled it with a hose. Snowball lapped it up almost as fast as Cooper could fill it. Then he scooped out two cans of food.

"Watch him while I check the house." Cooper hustled inside, closing the door behind him.

Harper could hear him hollering for Houdini from throughout the house until he came back outside. "I can't find him, and his litter box has barely been used. He's outside. Dammit!" He trotted away. "Houdini! Houdini!"

Harper pushed herself up and walked gingerly toward the deck, calling for Houdini. She found a half-eaten vole near the back door and a dead bird on a chair. Cooper walked behind the garage calling his name. Harper walked down the path into the woods past where the bear had been hiding, calling his name gently.

She heard a long meow and saw a very ragged kitty in a clump of Labrador tea. "Come here, Houdini," she said softly, lowering to her knees and leaning forward.

She could hear Cooper calling frantically from the back yard.

"Come here, Houdini," she said as she reached out her hand.

He slinked toward her furtively, almost touched her hand, then darted to her side. He meowed again, almost sorrowfully. He moved closer, and Harper could hear him purring. He pushed his nose against her hand, purring louder. Harper stroked his back while the kitty lifted his head then his tail in response.

She picked him up and cradled him on his back in the crook of her arm, like a baby. Harper rubbed her nose against his face. "Soft as baby's skin.

Hope you didn't kill every bird and vole outside."

She walked slowly toward the house. Cooper sat in a deck chair, his face in his hands, crying.

"Hey, look what I've got."

He looked up. "Bless you!"

She moved toward Cooper then gave him the cat. Cooper kept him cradled, hugged him, then scratched his tummy until the purring became ridiculous.

"The house is a little smelly," said Cooper. "I'll clean it up. You get in the tub. Thanks for finding Houdini."

"He's my baby substitute. Holding him started changing my mind about keeping my baby." Harper scratched his ears.

"C'mon, Snowball. Let's get inside."

They all went in through the deck door. Harper walked back to her room and found her bed turned on its side and the bottom of the box spring cut open. Drawers were left open. A burnt spoon and straws lay on the dresser. "Took an advance. Good stuff! Thanks!" was scrawled in lipstick on the mirror.

Harper had acted just as crazy in the past, and it was only luck she'd survived her escapades. But she'd ruined her parents' jobs, started Alex on the same path, ruined any good reputation she had, and gotten herself pregnant. Then fed her baby heroin, weed, and beer. She couldn't make any more mistakes, and she hoped that the "fun" she'd already had wouldn't hurt her baby. She could try to comfort herself into thinking that all her mistakes had led to her reawakening and to Cooper and Gabriel and even reuniting her grandparents, but so much destruction lay in her wake.

Surely there had to have been an easier path.

She knew if she'd stayed in Texas, she would've turned into Heather. Kenzie was already transforming, stealing drugs when she could've waited two days and been given everything Harper had.

Her phone sat in the windowsill. She turned it on and found a message from Zachary. *Expect to hear from u tomorrow.*

Harper texted back. *I miscarried today while crossing the East Fork of the Toklat River in Denali Park. Our mistake is now flowing north toward the Yukon River. It hurt like hell, but I'm sure you're happy to hear this. I'll never speak to you again.*

He could react however he wanted to. He would never know the truth.

The contrast between Zachary and Gabriel, between Gabriel and every guy she had known made her gasp. How different would her life have been if Luke hadn't groped her butt and barged into her bedroom? She was twelve! Just boobs and ass was all he'd cared about. And then all she cared about. She'd learned to think of guys in the same terms as they'd thought of her. And now at sixteen she was pregnant and could never experience the innocence of a first kiss or exploring skin for the first time in nervous wonderment. Her encounter with Luke in the bathroom was basically a rape she thought she'd wanted.

She'd kill any boy who did that to her sister.

She couldn't go back or pretend she could recover what had been lost. And she couldn't stop thinking of Gabriel's lips and his scent—sweet and woodsy. She could imagine the joy they both would feel having sex—no, not just "having" sex. No, fully and completely loving each other, a melding of souls. That was the difference. She wanted to share her soul with Gabriel through her body and her mind and her voice and every ability she had—especially her heart, which had been cheated and broken so many times looking in the worst places. She hoped to find a different world through him and with him. Her past couldn't negate her desire for sex with Gabriel or shame her into thinking she was wrong to want him. Her desire now was for entirely different reasons than those in Texas. And the culmination would result in much more than feeling good for a moment.

She'd try to take it slow, but knew she'd fail. She just hoped he wouldn't run away.

She felt a cramp twisting inside, making her want to puke. Grabbing some clothes, she went to the bathroom and stood in the shower to wash off the blood. Then she filled the tub. A few hours ago, she was hanging from Cooper's wrist above a raging river, worried she and her baby would die in the middle of wilderness. Now, she was about to take a hot bath and wanted to play Cooper's keyboard later that night. Danger and comfort lived side-by-side in this state, which created its own addictions.

• • • • •

"Greg, we just got home from our trip into the park," said Cooper into his phone as he sat in the kitchen. "Everything is fine here."

"How is Harper?"

"She's taking a bath. I know she wants to talk to you tomorrow."

"Well, something's up. Mom is over here. She says she needs to talk with us."

Yes, she does, and I hope you listen to her. "How can I help you, Greg?"

"I resigned from TCA today. John was going to fire me, but we came to an agreement, so I can possibly find another school. Then I got a text from somebody in Alaska about a job."

"When I talked to your mother a few days ago, she thought you'd get fired, so I started an application for you on our state education website. I know I should've asked you first. I'm sure I got some things wrong on the app, but you can make corrections. I was trying to help you out." *Please understand, Greg. Let me help you.* "Thought you'd have trouble finding something in San Antonio. The jobs are hard up here, but the pay is good, and I know you can find a position." Cooper waited for the blast.

After a good pause, Greg cleared his throat then spoke calmly. "Thanks, Dad. That might be an option we'd have to consider. Don't the applications up there require more than name, address, and work history?"

"Sure they do. I wrote a bunch of paragraphs and essays to show your deep understanding of rural education in Alaska. You'll be impressed with how much you know."

He heard Greg chuckle slightly.

"I'm going to send you your account info and password, so you can access your application. Read it over tonight, and we'll talk tomorrow...if that's all right."

"Sure. I'll do that."

Cooper felt such a relief. "I'll send it as soon as we hang up. You should go listen to Rachel now." Cooper ended the call and typed in Greg's ATP account information, then sent it.

Snowball pawed at the bathroom door. Cooper knocked. "Hey, Harper, your favorite dog wants to visit. Can I let him in?"

"I'm in the tub. The door's unlocked."

Cooper opened the door a little, and Snowball scrambled inside. He heard Harper squeal as he closed the door.

For the next hour, Cooper cleaned the floors where Snowball had peed, brought in their gear, then parked the trailer behind the garage. Afterward he sat in the kitchen and drank a beer, thinking about the promise he'd made last night when he prayed for Harper. He'd try his best to allow faith to break through his reason. He had always wanted to believe in the existence of a power for good in the world, but too many events seemed to contradict that possibility. Maybe his disease would make it easier this time.

When Harper came out of the bathroom, he was kneeling on the floor, his hands clasped, looking up to the ceiling. She knelt next to him, put one arm around him, and said, "I didn't know you prayed."

"I'm trying to learn. We got a lot of extra help recently."

"It's been a long time for me. I'll pray with you." She folded her hands. "Thank you, God, for saving both of us and my baby, and for keeping Snowball and Houdini safe. Thank you for Rachel's understanding. And especially for my grandpa and Gabriel. Please help my parents forgive me. I'd really like to see them again. Amen."

"Amen."

Chapter Thirty-Two

"You two need to sit down," Rachel commanded Greg and Natalie. "I've got a lot to say to you both."

Greg knew better than to argue with his mother when she took that no-nonsense tone. He and Natalie sat at their kitchen table. He felt his palms moistening.

"I talked to Cooper and Harper yesterday evening after they left the park and the clinic."

"Clinic? Who got hurt?" asked Greg.

"They're both OK. Your father pulled your daughter out of the river and took her to a clinic. They were trying to get to the road when she slipped on a rocky slope in the rain mainly because she was having cramps and bleeding."

"Bleeding?" asked Natalie, her eyes widening.

"At the time she was worried she was having a miscarriage."

"Miscarriage? She's pregnant?" shouted Greg. His insides froze.

"Oh, my God," said Natalie. "Is she OK? Did she lose the baby?"

Rachel continued calmly. "Her baby is fine. She left home to be with her grandpa, but also because she was too scared to tell you about her pregnancy."

"Dammit! Was it Zachary?" Greg slammed his hand on the table and stood. He knew that kid was trouble, but this? If he ever saw him walking down the street he'd strangle him! That Harper ran to Alaska and not to Zachary's told him all he needed to know about the guy.

"I didn't say you could get up, Greg. Please sit down."

"How long have you known she was pregnant?" asked Greg as he sat, his chest heaving.

"I just found out. Now hear me out." She moved to the table and sat across from them. "Harper was scared because she had no one to talk to except for Cooper. She thought she wanted an abortion but was scared to tell you."

Greg grabbed Natalie's hand. He felt his own pulse in his throat.

"She planned to get an abortion in Alaska but changed her mind. She wants to take responsibility. She said her baby deserves a chance to live and be loved. I'm going up there to be with Harper and to be with my Cooper." Rachel wiped her eyes. "I should never have divorced him. I realized some years ago that if the roles were reversed, he would never have thrown me out. He made mistakes, and I made mistakes. And the biggest was not talking and not listening. I let my pride get in the way and was angry with him, but also with myself, which is exactly the mistake you both made with Harper."

Greg stared at his mother, felt a chill in his gut, and nodded his head.

"When Cooper and I needed each other most after Heather died, we stopped talking except for blaming each other. No wonder he turned to someone else, and then I threw him out." She stood. "That big guy was the best thing that ever happened to me, and I decided I couldn't be embarrassed by him. I made him run off in shame to Alaska. I spent years missing him, and I know now he spent those same years missing me. Now, Harper has given us a chance to get back together." She put her hands on the table and leaned toward them. "And she wants her parents. She wants her family. When's the last time you heard that from her?"

Greg's mouth dried, and he couldn't swallow. He coughed. "I don't know, but I can't remember the last time I told her I loved her or that I was proud of her. All I'm able to do is ridicule her. That's why she ran away from me."

Natalie pulled him to her. "We both did this, Greg. We both drove her away."

He had to make this right. Harper needed his help. "I'm going with you. When do you leave?"

"As soon as I can buy a ticket." She pulled her phone out of her purse that was sitting on the table. "Now I want to show you two videos Harper sent me."

• • • • •

Harper moved the lip-gloss across her lips as she stared in the mirror above her dresser. She couldn't help but be reminded of that night weeks ago when she did the same thing before hoping to see Zachary. She had much less make-up on now, but she still wanted to impress Gabriel. Her outfit had changed several times from skimpy to covered to something in-between. If she looked too sexy, he might see her as a party girl, jumping from one bed to the next, now trying to hook up with a father for her baby. But she so wanted to see his eyes pop when he saw her. Of course, that's what she'd wanted from Zachary, and what did that get her? So, just a little lipstick, a little liner, and a suggestion of color above her eyes. She wore a tank top with lining and jeans. She'd washed her hair, fluffed it out, and added some tiny braids in a few places.

"Coffee's ready!" shouted Cooper.

"Coming." She walked down the hall and entered the kitchen. Cooper turned around to hand her a mug and stared.

"You look beautiful, Harper. You're not being fair to the boy."

She took the coffee. "I was trying to be subtle! Did I do too much?"

"I don't think you need to look like a movie star for Gabriel to care about you."

She sipped her coffee. "Do you know I've never held hands with a boy before Gabriel? Everything is totally different with him. He knows more about me than anyone else ever has, and he still wants to be with me." She took a sip. "I don't understand why."

Cooper sat down next to her. "Because he sees what I see in you: a loving, extremely talented, fun, determined girl who was forced to grow up too fast, but who's used all her trials to become a better person. You're pretty special, kid. Don't you ever think otherwise."

Harper grabbed his hand and kissed it. "Thanks, Grandpa."

"I talked to Rachel this morning. Your parents now know about your baby. She said they took it better than she expected. They understand why you were scared to tell them and thought you had to leave. They want to FaceTime today."

"Understand" and "my parents" should never be used in the same sentence. "After Gabriel gets here. I need him with me, and I want them to

meet him. What else did you and Rachel talk about?"

"She missed me, and I missed her. We cried a lot. I told her about life in the villages. She thinks I lived a much more exciting life than she did...and she wished she could've been a part of it." He wiped a tear.

"Do you wish that?"

"Sure. I wanted her to come with me. I should have called her. We both should have contacted each other. There's a lesson there, granddaughter. Say what you feel, especially if it's love."

Harper nodded her head. "Always."

"Oh, and this was on the deck this morning." He handed her a box from Apple.

"My phone!" She opened the box and began to set it up. "Thank you!"

"Also, I got a text from Greg." Cooper cleared his throat and began to read. "*Spent a long time going through the application and what you wrote for me. I feel like the kid who had his parents write his college application essay for him. You obviously know what you're talking about. It's such a different way of approaching education in a village than what I'm familiar with, and truthfully, I like your ideas. You made me out to be a child-centered educator and administrator, and I know that's a lie. But I believe that's what kids need and what I need to become. I filled in the items you couldn't know and made some corrections, but otherwise you did a great job for me. Thanks, Dad. I need to talk to you about what I should do next. Text me when you have time.*

Harper saw a few tears in her grandpa's eyes. "Do you think he'll come up here?" she asked.

"He'll have to if he wants that interview. Maybe he can fly up with Rachel. I'd sure like to see him." Cooper wiped his nose.

Do I? she thought. Grandpa deserved a family, and she wanted hers whole again. But she worried over how he'd react to Gabriel and how much of the past he wouldn't be able to let go of. How much could she let go?

Snowball began to bark as they heard tires rolling over gravel. Gabriel's truck turned into their driveway. Harper stood and started to run out the door, but Cooper held her arm.

"Let him breathe a little." He smiled. "Don't treat him like guys have treated you."

Harper tried to calm down. "I promise to walk outside and try not to attack him." She opened the door just a little bit before Snowball pushed his way through and ran towards Gabriel as he emerged from his truck. He wore a blue bandana around his forehead, a tank top t-shirt with an open denim shirt on top, cargo shorts, and sandals. Harper nearly swooned just as Snowball barreled into him.

Gabriel laughed, knelt and vigorously rubbed Snowball's back as he licked Gabriel's face.

"Should I stand in line?" said Harper and she walked toward him, trying not to sway her hips too noticeably.

Gabriel stood up and smiled. "The line starts with you." He walked to her.

She held out her hand as if to shake. "Good morning, Gabriel Light."

He drew closer. "Good morning, Harper Lyons."

She held up her hand, palm toward him and smiled. He pressed his palm against hers and then folded his fingers through hers. She held up her other hand, and he did the same. They both watched their fingers and hands stroking each other.

Almost gasping, Harper said, "I just wanted to make sure I didn't dream this last night. Your hands are magic."

For several seconds they stood with their hands clasped by their sides, their faces an inch apart, and their eyes wandering, memorizing each other's features.

"I could get used to this," he said. He reached for one of her braids and smiled. "You didn't need to do anything special for me."

"Neither did you, but you did anyway." Her fingers danced through his beard, around his earlobes, and through his curls.

"Are you feeling better?"

"Now? I'm floating."

"You know what I mean. Are you OK?"

She shrugged a shoulder. "My cramps are better but still there. Anything else you want to ask me about?" She moved closer. "Temperature, blood pressure? You are my EMT, after all."

"How's your baby?"

She took his hand and placed it on her lower stomach. "What do you think?"

He breathed faster. "I think it's perfectly fine."

She removed her hand from his, still on her stomach, and looked into his eyes.

"You sure?"

They stared at each other.

Finally he realized where his hand lingered, and he jerked it back.

"Sorry."

"You're going to meet my parents today."

His eyes widened and he stepped back, buttoning his shirt as he scanned the yard and looked over her shoulder at the house. "Are they here?"

She laughed and reached for his buttons. "No, they aren't. They're going to call." She unbuttoned what he'd buttoned. "I like it open." She stared at his chest. "I really like it open."

He smiled and took another step back. "But I should button it for them." He started to button his shirt.

"Stop it." She grabbed him and unbuttoned his shirt while he laughed. "I think we should go inside before Cooper thinks I'm trying to undress you in the driveway."

"OK." He walked back to his truck and pulled out Cooper's backpack. "I picked this up for Cooper. Gary dropped it off in lost and found." He grabbed Harper's hand, and they walked toward the house.

Cooper opened the door. "I'm not even going to ask what you two were doing out here."

"If you don't want to see it, don't look," said Harper.

Gabriel held out the pack. "I believe this belongs to you."

Cooper grabbed the top strap. "Hey, thanks for fetching this!"

"You're welcome."

"You hungry?" asked Cooper.

"No, I'm good." He glanced at Harper. "I made a prenatal care appointment for Harper tomorrow at the clinic. Nine o'clock, if that's OK. Laney wants to meet you for real this time."

"Thank you, Gabriel," said Harper, shocked by his thoughtfulness. "I was going to call later. Grandpa just got me a phone."

"I thought I could drive you. Maybe see the doctor with you." He looked at Harper's eyes. "If you'd want me to."

Harper was stunned by his offer. No other boy had ever been this kind to her before. She never knew such guys existed.

"Yes, I would." Tears moistened her eyes. "I can't believe you."

"I told you I'd help you."

"You're going to be making two trips from here to Healy?" asked Cooper.

"That's a lot of driving. Why don't you stay with us? We've got a spare bedroom; that is, if you don't think your foster parents will mind."

"No. I'm eighteen. Technically, I could stay with them longer, but I was planning to find my own place by the end of the summer after I earned enough money."

And now I'm taking half of your money, she thought. She'd have to make sure they made more than double what he expected to make. She could think of nothing more enjoyable than working hard with Gabriel.

"You can stay here anytime you want," said Harper as formally and sternly as she could while keeping a straight face. "And I for one will control myself. I trust you'll do the same."

"Certainly," said Gabriel as he started to button his shirt.

"No!" Harper lunged at him and hugged him.

"You two do need to work some, you know," said Cooper. "You have a show to prepare for."

"Then we should get to work," said Gabriel.

"Can't wait!" Harper said as she hugged his arm.

"Well, we'll see how much work we get done," said Cooper with a little chuckle.

"I'm ready when you are. Where's the studio?"

Cooper's phone rang. He fished his phone out of his back pocket and glanced down at the screen. "Your parents," he said to Harper. "You ready?"

She took the phone and grabbed Gabriel's hand. "Come with me." She hurriedly pulled him to the deck. Cooper followed. She sat down, Gabriel beside her, trying to button his shirt. She accepted the call and propped the phone against the umbrella pole on the table.

Her parents' smiling faces appeared on the screen. Harper covered her mouth, trying not to cry. She'd missed them. Gabriel squeezed her arm. "Hi, Mom. Hi, Dad."

"Hi, Harper," said Greg.

"How are you feeling?" asked Natalie.

"Better." She tried to swallow. "Mom, Daddy, I'm so sorry for everything. I was a total ass to you. If you never want to see me again, I'd totally understand." Tears dripped from her chin.

"We're the ones who need to apologize," said Greg. "Especially me. I should've helped you rather than drive you away."

"I didn't give you the chance. I wanted to tell you, but I was worried how you'd react."

"You were right to be worried," said Greg. "You knew how I would've reacted."

"What have you decided to do about the baby?" asked Natalie.

"I...I want to keep it. I'm going to see a doctor tomorrow. Gabriel's taking me." She pointed the camera towards Gabriel.

"Hello, Mr. Lyons, Mrs. Lyons," said Gabriel. "Your daughter is an amazing young woman. I'll help her all that I can." Harper grabbed his hand.

"You have a beautiful voice, Gabriel," said Natalie. "How did you two meet?"

Harper jumped in before he could utter a word. "Outside a coffee shop where he sang for tips. He and Grandpa tricked me into singing with him, and people started throwing money at us. He decided to keep me. I'm his cash cow."

"That's not really..." said Gabriel, smiling.

"Actually, I'm going to be a real cow in a few months." She looked at Gabriel. "You still want to be seen with me when I'm fat and bulging out of my shirt?"

"You'll still be you," said Gabriel. Harper put her other hand on top of his, and his grin turned wicked. "As long as you can still sing."

"What?" Harper looked at Gabriel in mock shock. Cooper and Natalie laughed.

"I just want both of you to know that I do care for your daughter," said Gabriel. "I know we just met a few days ago," he looked at Harper, "but she's a loving, funny, very talented young woman. I'm not sure I can keep up with her, but I'm going to try as hard as I can."

Harper stared at Gabriel in shock, then bent over and kissed his cheek. "Thank you, Gabriel. I care for you, too." She turned toward the phone. "Just so you know, Gabriel is the kindest, most thoughtful boy I've ever known." She held up their clasped hands. "And all we've done is hold hands! Well, I just kissed his cheek, and..."

"We did kiss once on the lips at the campground...maybe twice..."

She turned to Gabriel and sighed. "Yes, that was wonderful." Then turned back to the camera, "But that was the only time. He's a very good man, and I'm very glad I met him."

Greg cleared his throat. "So, Gabriel. What is it you do?" He leaned closer to the camera. Natalie put her hand on his arm.

Oh, no! thought Harper. *Please be nice to him.*

Gabriel sat up straighter. "I'm not just a starving musician. I'm an EMT and I have a job at the fire station."

Greg frowned. "That's an interesting hairstyle for an EMT. I'm surprised they allow that."

"I have these dreads only because my foster sister ratted my hair when I was asleep. My supervisor has known me for several years, and he knows how crazy Allison is. Besides I'm one of their best technicians."

"Really?" asked Greg, not hiding his doubt.

"According to my evals. Yes, sir. I'm the youngest EMT the fire station has ever employed. I'm very good at my job, sir."

Greg nodded. "Good to know, Gabriel. Thanks for helping our daughter." Gabriel nodded back.

Natalie smiled. "I love your dreads, Gabriel. You should keep them."

"I do, too!" laughed Harper, twirling his hair around her fingers. "Um, Daddy, I'm sorry you got fired because of me."

"I wasn't fired. I quit. We should never have worked at TCA. I'm sorry I put you and Chris through that awkwardness."

"Grandpa says you can get a job up here, and...I'd like it if you and Mom were with us. I want you to be here when I have my baby." Greg's mouth fell open. Natalie wiped a tear away. "I miss you and Alex and Jack."

"We miss you, too, Harper," said Natalie.

"When can you move up here?" begged Harper.

"That's a big move for us," said Greg.

"Please, Daddy. I don't want to leave Alaska. You'd love it here. It's beautiful! We can hike in the mountains just a few miles away. There's no traffic..."

"And no fences," said Cooper.

"And your first grandchild is going to live here," added Harper.

"You'd want to go hiking with me?" her dad asked softly.

"Sure." She smiled. "I... I came up here to start over, and I'd like to do that with you too."

"I'd like that, too." He glanced at Natalie. "We'll talk about it. Who knows? You may have a child exactly like you. If that happens you're going to need all the help you can get." Greg laughed, as did Harper.

"Greg!" scolded Natalie.

"If he or she turns out like me," said Harper, "then I hope you're the same kind of grandpa your father is. If you are, then my kid will turn out all right."

"I'll try to be." He coughed. "Dad, are you there?"

Cooper quickly wiped away a tear. "Yes, Greg. I'm here." He moved behind Harper.

"Thanks for taking care of our girl and saving her life, twice from what Mom says."

"We have each other's backs. She saved me a few times, too. Greg, why don't you fly up here with your mother? You need to see my house and the state and maybe try out for that interview. Can you get up here in a couple of days?"

"I already decided I'd fly up with Mom."

"Thank you, Daddy," said Harper. *Maybe everything will work out this time.*

"Good," said Cooper. "Now I need to work with these two if they're going to perform tomorrow."

"Tomorrow?" asked Harper.

"Tomorrow. Might as well make some money since you'll be near the Gulch for the appointment."

"Sounds good to me," said Gabriel.

"Text me when you know your flight," said Cooper to Greg. "And I'll call you later to talk about jobs up here."

"Bye, Mom. Bye, Daddy. I love you!" shouted Harper.

"I love you, too, Harper," said Greg. "It's been a long time since we've said that."

"It's a good start." Harper smiled.

"Love you," said Natalie.

"Take care of my little girl, Gabriel," Greg warned.

Gabriel squeezed her hand. "I will, sir. Great to meet you both."

"Good bye," said Cooper and ended the call.

Harper sobbed, and both Gabriel and Cooper held her. "I have a family again. A whole family." She turned to Gabriel. "And you will, too. I can't believe you said all those things about me to them."

"I meant every word." He leaned in and kissed her.

"I think my lips like your lips." She kissed him again.

Panting, Gabriel said, "My lips definitely like yours."

"OK, I'm going to fix myself up a little," said Harper. "I'm not going all day with smeared eyes and lips. Show him the studio, and I'll be there in a few minutes." She ran to the bathroom.

Cooper set them up on separate mics and put a pick-up on Gabriel's guitar. They redid the songs they had sung on Friday, trying different harmonies. They picked out several new songs, including "Bless the Broken Road" and "Shallow," a perfect duet number for them. Gabriel couldn't read tabs easily, but he had a great ear and had no trouble following "how to" videos on YouTube. His memory was quick and sure.

They took Snowball for a walk around the lake and to the park. The sea of dandelions that Cooper had blanked out in a few weeks ago had now turned to puffballs and long grass. Snowball ran down the dike into the grass, snapping at the balls, and ran back up only to run down the other side. The rain of yesterday had turned to partly cloudy skies with thunderstorms building here and there to drop showers later in the afternoon.

After lunch, they worked for three hours straight in the studio, learning new songs, recording, and experimenting with different plugins. By the evening, their set included a few of Cooper's songs and ranged from sweet ballads to up-tempo hip shakers. Cooper would ride with them to the Gulch and take the mics, amps, and a mixer. They were ready for the next day.

Gabriel played some melodies he'd been working on.

"Those are beautiful, Gabriel," said Harper, "but so sad."

"I think maybe I can write some happier ones now."

Cooper translated them to the keyboard and showed Harper how to play them. She and Gabriel jammed, then Harper tried writing lyrics to his songs. Cooper left them to call Greg.

When he came back an hour later, Harper had straddled Gabriel on the floor, his shirt hiked up, while she softly dragged a fingernail across a special spot on his stomach. Gabriel wrenched with laughter every time she did it.

"He said he wasn't ticklish," Harper explained at Cooper's amused but bewildered look. "I found his spot."

"Get her off me, Cooper!" She slowly dragged her fingernail again, her smile almost evil. He writhed and yelled with mirth. "Aargh! Please stop!"

"You wouldn't believe how many places I had to check to find this one."

"Mercy!"

"OK." She stood up. "But now you know you can't challenge me and remain unscathed."

"Yes, Harper." He sat up and pulled down his shirt. "This girl can be wicked."

"You haven't seen anything yet, Mr. Light."

Cooper stood smiling at them. "How'd you do on the lyrics?"

"We finished." She gave him a paper. "You want to hear it?"

Gabriel picked a pattern of notes while Harper sang a sweet love song.

"With a little work, this would be a great song," said Cooper.

"See? You can leave the room without worrying about us," said Harper. "We work, then play."

"OK, kids," said Cooper. "I'm going to bed. Gabriel, Harper will show you to your room. I'm reclaiming Snowball tonight, so he'll be upstairs." He left the studio.

Harper took Gabriel to her room. "This is my room, in case you wanted to know." She pulled him down the hall and opened the door to the other bedroom. "And this is your room." She turned on the light and he peeked inside. They both stood in the doorway. She raised her right hand. "Goodnight, Gabriel."

He raised his hand to match hers. Soon they were caressing each other's fingers, hypnotized by the movement and the sensations.

"I turn to jelly just touching your fingers," sighed Harper. "I can't imagine touching the rest of you. How can you make me feel so good?"

"This is beyond good...but I think we should stop."

Hands still pressed together, they both panted. "Why?"

"Because I want to kiss you and touch you...and make love to you so much it scares me."

"Why are you scared?" She stroked his face.

"I don't want you to think that sex with you is all I care about. You're more special to me than that. We should wait."

Harper knew that any other boy she'd been with would've pulled her onto the bed if she hadn't pushed him there first. If Gabriel had given her any prompting, she would've made love with him right then. Warmth spread in her chest, welcoming and consuming. She knew he wanted her, but he made himself stop because he cared more for her than as a means to feeling good. Even beyond good.

And she liked that. Really liked that.

"OK," she said, pulling her hand away from his. "What do you want to do?"

"I already told you what I want to do. And what we should do. And,

Harper, you have to help me be strong with this because I don't think I can wait on my own."

She saw the pleading in his eyes. "I'll wait as long as you want to. I think if I made love to you now, I'd explode into a million pieces."

"I wouldn't want that." He gave her a wry grin. "I'm really bad at puzzles."

They laughed.

"We can still...?" She held out her hand.

He touched her hand. "Yes."

She kissed his lips gently. "And...?"

"Sometimes."

"Anything else?"

"Yes. I...I want to sleep with you, but just sleep. Clothes stay on. I just...I want to hold you."

Her mouth dropped open. She wasn't sure she could be that close to him and behave. But she told him she'd wait, and she meant it. "Just one night?"

"One night at a time."

She looked at the scruffy, beautiful face smiling at her through a tangle of blonde hair. "Deal." She giggled and pulled him back to her room. "Turn off the light."

He did. "The room isn't very dark."

"OK. Turn around. I'll take off my bra and put on some shorts. You do what you want to do."

Back to back they got ready for bed.

"Ready?" she asked.

"Are you wearing a shirt?"

"Yes. Are you?"

"Yes."

She pouted. "Bummer, but I can live with it."

They turned around.

Harper stared at him. "I knew you wore boxers under your pants."

"How would you know that?"

"Intuition." She raised her brows, laughed, and jumped into bed, holding the sheet up for him. "C'mon."

He climbed in, facing her, their noses almost touching.

"I don't trust my hands," said Harper.

"Hold mine." She did. "Goodnight, Harper."

"Goodnight, Gabriel."

Chapter Thirty-Three

When Harper awoke the next morning, she was spooning Gabriel's back. He'd clasped her hand against his stomach. For a few seconds she breathed in his aroma: the tang of fresh split spruce with a sweet, earthy background. She could get used to waking up like this every morning. She bent over and kissed his ear. "Good morning."

"Mmmm. That tickles." He squirmed.

"Found another spot."

He sat up. "Yes, you did," then kissed her lightly on the lips.

"I could look for others." She played with one of his curls.

"I think we should get up. We have a lot to do today."

She heard scratching. "Snowball!" She jumped up, climbed over Gabriel, and opened the door. The big dog jumped on her as she collapsed back onto Gabriel.

"Harper! Your coffee is ready!" yelled Cooper from the kitchen.

"OK."

"Where's Gabriel? I checked the other room."

"I'm in here, with Harper," said Gabriel.

"Oh," Cooper muttered.

"He's embarrassed," Harper giggled.

"Well, your coffee is ready, too," Cooper informed him.

Gabriel stood up and extended his hand. "Let's go get our coffee."

She grabbed his hand then hugged him. "You're staying?"

"If you want me to."

She kissed him. They walked into the kitchen and found a red-faced

Cooper trying to look calm. He held out their coffees.

"Guess what we did?" teased Harper.

"I...I'm not sure I want to know, Harper."

"Relax. We slept. That's all. Nothing else happened."

During their trip to the clinic on Tuesday, Greg texted Cooper he and Rachel would arrive at 2:00 am Wednesday morning.

"That's tonight!" said Harper. A week ago she felt her world had unraveled. Now her life had seemingly turned around.

Laney was very happy to meet Harper again and told Gabriel how proud she was of him, but she was sad when he told her he'd move more of his things into Cooper's house. Harper felt some sorrow for Laney because her love for Gabriel was obvious, but she felt more joy at the prospect of Gabriel staying with her longer.

"I'm so glad you decided to keep your baby," said Laney. "Did your meeting Gabriel have anything to do with changing your mind?"

"Yes. Not everything, but a lot. He's good at saving lives."

"I've never seen him happier." She looked deeply into Harper's eyes. "I don't think you two meeting in the clinic was an accident."

Harper had already decided she was meant to find him, that everything had happened for a reason. "I hope he feels the same way."

"Don't you worry."

The doctor told Harper the baby was doing fine and gave her a due date of January third, about thirty weeks away. How could she wait that long before holding it? Then she laughed at herself. She had much to learn about being a mother. She was already holding her baby every second of every day. She had to cherish this time because too soon she'd have to go longer and longer periods without touching it. How did any mother endure letting go of her child?

Harper and Gabriel sang on the deck outside the coffee shop twice then moved inside when it started to rain. While they played, Cooper drove around to the hotels and restaurants to promote Lyons & Light and book other gigs. At the end of that day, the two singers had collected $326 in tips.

They dropped by Laney's house and met Allison. She was Alex's age and crazy about her foster brother. She cried when he told her about moving his things.

"Can I visit?" she begged.

"Hey, I'm not leaving forever." Gabriel hugged her and wiped tears off her cheeks. "We'll still see each other."

"I have a sister your age who'd love to meet you," said Harper, hoping that Alex would soon join her. "If she comes up here, she'd love to have you spend the night."

Allison wiped her nose and tried to smile. "OK. Be nice to my brother."

"Always," said Harper. "We'll pick you up when we go to the Gulch for performances. You can scream and clap and keep the audience excited."

"Cool."

That evening, Harper and Gabriel walked Snowball by themselves while Cooper returned to the book he'd started weeks ago.

"Are you going back to school?" asked Gabriel as he sat on a campground table hugging Harper from behind, watching the wind blow through the trees. Snowball dug holes in the dirt.

"No, I want to spend all my time working with you, writing songs, and learning to play the keyboard. Grandpa wants to sign me up for online singing lessons and a songwriting course. You could do them with me."

"You sing pretty good now." He kissed her cheek.

"We could be better. He wants me to work on his book with him."

"What's it about?"

"I have no idea." She turned around, holding his hands. "He said he'd show me in a few days."

"Will you live in Cooper's house with your baby?"

"Yes." She searched his eyes. "What about you? What are your plans?"

"Lyons & Light. I think we're going to do pretty well."

She played with his earlobe. "Our gigs, or us?"

"Both," he said huskily.

He leaned in to kiss her, but before their lips could touch, Snowball saw a raven and took off, yanking Gabriel's arm until he stumbled. "Snowball! Stop!" he yelled.

"We should go back. I don't like leaving Grandpa alone for very long."

"When was the last time he...?"

"In the mountains, with the bears."

They walked along the dike back toward the house.

"Is your father going to accept me sleeping in your room?"

"I guess we'll find out. We're not doing anything."

"Still, maybe when he's here, I should move to the other room."

"That's where he'll sleep."

"Then to the trailer."

"No way! I'm not keeping secrets anymore. We are sleeping together, and I don't care who knows it. No more lies. Besides, you have my consent..." They both stopped, staring at each other. "Whenever we both feel...we should do anything...requiring consent." She nearly kissed him. "How much longer, do you think?"

"Weeks, months." He smiled.

"Months?" she whimpered. "How about days?"

"One night at a time."

When they arrived at the house, they saw Cooper standing on the deck rubbing his ear, looking lost. The back door was wide open.

"Run, Gabriel! Close the door before Houdini gets out!" Gabriel took off while Harper unleashed Snowball, so he wouldn't pull her down the driveway trying to race after Gabriel.

Cooper looked vaguely at Gabriel. "Hey! What are you doing? You can't go in there."

Gabriel had just closed the door and turned toward Cooper, who looked scared, backed away, then turned to run but stepped off the deck and fell onto the grass.

"Are you OK, Cooper?" Gabriel bent down to check on the man who was now crawling across the yard.

"Get away!" Cooper screamed, swiping his arm to ward off Gabriel.

Harper ran up and knelt beside her grandfather. "Grandpa," she said, calmly, quietly. *Please, snap out of it!* "We're here. Gabriel and Harper. Everything's OK." He looked up at her, his fear finally dissipating. She smiled and fluffed up his ponytail. "We just got back from walking Snowball." She called him, and the dog ran over to lick his face. "He wants you to pet him, Grandpa."

Cooper's eyes showed recognition, and Harper helped him sit up. Her heart finally started to slow down.

"Gabriel," said Harper, "go inside and find Houdini. He may have gotten out."

He nodded and walked into the house.

She picked some grass out of her grandpa's beard and hair. "You feeling better?" asked Harper.

He breathed heavily. "I was just thinking I hadn't had a spell since Saturday and thought maybe ..."

Her heart ached for him. "You're worried about seeing Grandma." She gave him her hand and helped him stand. "Maybe once she's here and everyone relaxes, you'll be fine."

Gabriel opened the door and carried Houdini in his arms. "He was sleeping on the washing machine."

His eyes showed fear. "Did I leave the door open?" asked Cooper.

"Yeah," answered Harper.

"So now I have to be watched all the time, so I don't let the animals loose?" He stepped onto the deck and pushed one of the chairs. "Dammit."

Harper followed him. "Rachel will be here."

Cooper jerked around. "Why would she want that job?"

"Because she loves you." She held his hand. "That's what people do who love each other. Watch them, help them find their way, save them. What you do for me and what I do for you. She won't mind."

He jerked his hand away from her and walked away. "She won't mind until I don't recognize her one day and scream at her. I looked up what happens to people with this condition. They get paranoid and throw tantrums, sometimes even get violent."

She followed him, refusing to let him give up. "I looked up some things too, and loneliness exacerbates dementia. You've been by yourself for sixteen years. Now you're going to have your family back. That will help you."

He sat down at the table and held his head in his hands. "God, why do I have this disease now? Just when things are finally getting better, I have to fall apart."

Harper sat beside him. "Why don't you ask for help? You've prayed for me and my baby, but I don't think you've prayed for you."

"I'll try." He stood up, Gabriel gave him Houdini, and he walked into the house.

"He doesn't believe?" asked Gabriel.

"I think he's trying to. Do you pray?"

Gabriel looked away. "Not after James died. I prayed all the time for my parents to stop using drugs, but they still did them. After he died I decided I needed to learn how to save people and kids, do something that worked." He sat next to her. "So I enrolled in an EMT program at school. Then once I turned eighteen, I took more classes. It was hard for me. I'm not a good student. I have trouble reading. But I kept at it and became an EMT. I've actually saved people, and that feels pretty good. I think it's better to use my hands for that than praying." He searched her eyes. "Do I have to pray to stay with you?"

She held his hands. "No. Just keep being who you are."

They found Cooper dusting the table when they went inside the house. "Grab a broom and sweep. We have guests coming."

Gabriel found the broom by the trashcan and swept the kitchen floor.

"Harper, dust what you can. I'm going upstairs to clean the bedroom and bathroom. Help me get this house clean, please." Cooper stomped hurriedly upstairs.

"He's nervous," said Harper.

"Aren't you?" asked Gabriel.

"I need to talk to Daddy alone. If we're really going to start over, I need to clear the air between us. I'll do it tomorrow when you're at work." The back of her throat ached. She needed to do this and hoped she could.

For the next two hours, they cleaned what they could. Cooper brought an inflatable bed in from the garage and set it on the living room floor.

"Who's that for?" asked Harper.

"For me. Rachel can have my bedroom. I'll sleep down here."

He walked around the room, straightening things that were already straight.

Harper followed him. "Would you like to be with her again?"

He stopped and looked at her. "Yes, but I'm scared. It's been a long, long time and the last time wasn't with her. We're different people now. We're not young anymore."

"Love doesn't have an age-limit, Grandpa. We have some time. Why don't you take a shower and fix yourself up? She might surprise you."

"OK."

"We'll finish cleaning things. Go."

Cooper walked quickly upstairs.

"Do you think Rachel will surprise him?" asked Gabriel.

"I hope so. If there was ever a man who deserved a second chance, it's Grandpa. I just hope his mind can hold up."

• • • • •

Cooper hated having to leave Snowball at the house while they drove to Fairbanks, but they didn't have enough room in the truck to accommodate his boisterousness and the five passengers who'd make the return trip. He knew Snowball would panic and think he was being left for days again.

Gabriel drove, with Harper leaning against him, while Cooper sat on her other side.

"I talked to Owen Henry," said Cooper, "the man in charge of the music festival, about getting you two into the show in late July. Sent him some recordings and references. He thought there was a chance. If Greg and Natalie move up here, everyone in the family could see you two perform. Wouldn't that be something?"

"That's a three-day event, right?" asked Gabriel.

"Yes. I'm not sure which day you'd play. The schedule should come out this week."

"How big is it?" asked Harper.

"A few thousand people attend over the weekend. Bands from throughout the state, a few from Outside. It's been a long time since anyone local or near local has played in our music festival."

"You should've been a band agent, Grandpa," said Harper. "You're good at this."

"Maybe, but I think anyone could sell you two. You don't know how good you are."

And I hope I'm around to see it, he thought.

Surely he could make it until then. He had to. Time was his enemy. No, his disease was his enemy, and the only weapon he had to fight against it was his sense of urgency. He had to do more in each day than he ever had before if he hoped to get those two launched toward a career and restore his relationships with his wife and family.

Though he yearned to be with Rachel, he was worried. Their conversations had been friendly enough. They'd talked through everything. She claimed she had forgiven him, but still—sixteen years was a long, long time. And then there was his disease. What if he screamed at her, not knowing who she was?

He looked at Harper snuggling with Gabriel as they drove though the hills north of Nenana. They could've been him and Rachel, but he'd driven this road by himself a thousand times. How he wished she could have been with him. Now he hoped they'd have the opportunity to drive together like that at least a few times.

A week ago he'd made this same trip with Harper. How life could change so quickly for the good, and for the worse.

"Hey, let's take a picture," Cooper suggested as they walked into the terminal. "I know how to do it now. Come here, Gabriel."

He waved him over and held up the camera while they all smiled. Cooper took several then flipped through them. "Which one, do you think?"

"Alaskans don't care how they look," said Harper. "Just send that one."

They waited downstairs in the baggage area, watching kids play with the toy dinosaurs in the stone sandbox as the first passengers trickled down from the upstairs gates. Cooper walked around, finding things to read to kill time.

"Here's a mint," Harper whispered conspiratorially. "She'll appreciate it when you kiss her."

Cooper took the mint. "I'm scared."

"Just do what you did with me." She hugged him. "Big hug and tears. Then kiss her."

"Aren't you scared a little?"

"Yes," admitted Harper. "I know what I want from Daddy, what I think I've always wanted. Just depends on him."

"He can't be a fool all his life."

Soon after, Cooper received a picture of Greg and Rachel with the message, *Almost there*. Cooper stared at Rachel's photo. He hadn't seen a picture of her for so many years. He wiped his nose. He noticed she'd put on make-up. She'd never spent much time fiddling with her face when he lived with her. Such a natural beauty needed no enhancements.

Did she dress up for him? Was she trying to impress him? His heart raced at the thought. Maybe there was still a chance for them. He hoped he wasn't reading too much into it.

Harper leaned over and looked at the photo. "Grandma sure looks nice. Is that for you?" she teased.

"OK, OK. Don't make me more nervous than I already am." He stared at the photo again. "She's still so pretty."

"You're not so bad yourself." Harper grabbed his hand and walked over to Gabriel, all three standing outside the glass doors. "There they are."

Rachel smiled and waved while Greg held her other arm as they walked down the stairs. They moved through the doors and stopped, each group staring at the other. Greg's eyes filled with tears as he looked at his daughter. She walked up to him, peering at his face.

"Daddy?"

He hugged her and lifted her off the ground. "Harper, I'm so sorry."

"I love you, Daddy."

"I love you, too, Harper," he said thickly.

Cooper walked up to Rachel slowly, amazed at how good she looked. Her peppered gray hair flowed over her shoulders. She wore a soft white, loose knit top, which hung over her bright paisley leggings. Leggings! And she looked good in them! Then he noticed her earrings, the gold and sapphire pair he'd given her for their twentieth anniversary after a romantic evening in the Hill Country. He knew then that she wanted their reunion to be as special as he did.

"Rachel...I've missed you..." he barely managed to choke out over the lump in his throat.

She touched his face and smiled. "You look so rugged, so Alaskany. When did you get curls?" She played with his ponytail.

"Once my hair grew past my shoulders. You're still as beautiful as you ever were."

"You know that's not true. I thought we decided we were going to be totally honest with each other."

"In my eyes, you are beautiful."

"Thank you, Cooper." She leaned forward and kissed his cheek.

Cooper's heart stopped, then pounded in his chest.

Her lips lingered near his cheek then kissed him again closer to his jaw, pressing her cheek against his lips. He kissed. She lifted her head, exposing her neck. He kissed again, then clutched her to him. "Rachel, I..."

She moved her lips so close to his he could feel her breathing. Then they both melted into each other.

• • • • •

Harper sobbed against her father's chest as he rubbed her hair and tried to wipe his eyes. She had longed for her father to hug her so many times, then when he didn't she had accused him of gawking at her, forcing him to avoid touching her. She realized she'd made it impossible for him to show affection toward her even when she'd wanted it the most.

Gabriel handed him a tissue from a small pack in his hand. "Thought somebody would need these."

"Thanks, Gabriel." Greg tried to wipe his eyes.

Harper grabbed Gabriel with one arm and pulled him toward her. She hugged them both. Gabriel wrapped his arms around both of them. Finally, they let go of each other and Harper saw Rachel and Cooper still embracing. He was kissing each eye and her neck while she giggled. Harper took out her phone and shot pictures of them.

"These are the first photos on my phone."

The two lovebirds kept kissing each other.

"OK, Grandpa, save some for later." She gently pushed herself between them. "I'd like to kiss her, too." She hugged Rachel and kissed her cheek. "I've waited my whole life to see you two together."

Cooper held out his hand to Greg, who smiled and grabbed it with both hands. Soon they hugged.

"Good to see you, Greg."

"Good to see you, Dad."

"And my whole life to see you two do that," said Harper, as she took a photo.

Harper grabbed her grandparents' hands and walked them toward the baggage carousel.

Greg and Gabriel got the bags and wheeled them to the truck.

"Is it ever dark here?" asked Rachel.

"Not in June and most of July," said Cooper. "Not as long as you're here, in fact."

They took the backseat. Harper sat between Gabriel and Greg in the front.

As they merged onto the highway, Greg turned his head to talk to Cooper. "I spoke to the superintendent of..."

"Let's talk about that tomorrow, Greg. Your mother and I are getting reacquainted."

"Sure, Dad."

Rachel laughed as Cooper said something to her. Then she squealed a little. Gabriel gave a side-glance to Harper, who smiled back. She grabbed his right-hand from the wheel and held it in her lap.

Harper saw her father gazing at her. She turned toward him and smiled.

"You seem pretty happy," said her father as he curled some of her hair behind her ear.

"I am." She felt energized and bubbly, even though it was 2:30 in the morning.

"What are your plans for the summer?" he asked.

"Singing, making some money, writing songs, playing keyboard, learning about music, taking online classes, helping Grandpa write a book, and trying to stay as healthy as I can for my baby. And being with my family." She grabbed her father's hand. "Have you thought about moving up here? Do you think you can?"

"We'd have to sell the house. Moving up here will be expensive. There are several teaching jobs available in Alaska, but few principal positions except for three villages, all several hundred miles from Dad's place. If I got one of those, then your Mom and I would be in a village for most of the year and not with you. And I'm not sure Alex and Jack should go to a village, especially when I'm the principal. I realize now it's not a good idea to have my kids at the same school I lead. It's not fair to them."

"They could stay with us at Grandpa's house. We have an extra room they could share, and there's a school a mile away."

"But your mother and I wouldn't see Alex and Jack, or you, for several months at a time, What's the point of moving up here, just to be separated? Besides, I'm not sure Dad would want a bunch of kids running around."

"Sure I would." Cooper chimed in. "My house could use more life in it. I have a spare room they can share. Harper has the other room and is sharing with Gabriel while they work on their music."

"Hold it," said Greg. "Gabriel lives with you? Dad, did you allow this?"

Here it comes. Harper braced herself.

"Sir," said Gabriel. "It's my fault. I wanted to take Harper to the clinic, and we needed to practice. I live in another town. Cooper offered to let me stay at his house for a couple of days. Now, I don't think I can stand being apart from her."

Harper grabbed his hand. "Yes, we share a room, Daddy, but just sleep together. We haven't had sex. We decided to wait."

"Sure!" scoffed Greg.

"Daddy, I love you and I want to start over with you, but the first thing you have to understand before anything can change between us is that I'm always going to tell you the truth now, whether you like it or not. I won't hide anything from anyone. Gabriel and I have held hands and kissed, but that's it. When we have sex, I'll be the first to tell you."

She saw a vein pop out on his forehead and readied herself for the explosion.

Just before Greg spoke in anger, Cooper cut him off: "Please don't say what just popped into your head, Greg." Cooper lowered his voice. "Please. Are you going to play the role of parent, or be a parent? Are you going to respond to Harper like you think you are expected to, or be the parent she needs?" Greg turned his head back to look at his father. "Gabriel is a fine, responsible young man. Harper is an amazing young woman. I couldn't imagine anyone better for either of them right now."

"Thank you, Grandpa," said Harper.

"Thanks, Cooper," said Gabriel.

After a few more moments of silence, Greg coughed. "I'm sorry, Harper. Gabriel, I'm looking forward to knowing you better. And if I could redo the last ten minutes of my life, I'd sure do it differently."

"You can't redo anything, Daddy," said Harper, "and it's pointless to think that way. I'm with my Grandpa and Grandma who are necking in the backseat of this truck, sitting next to the best guy I've ever known and looking forward to snuggling with him in bed, just snuggling, and you're sitting next to me, trying very hard to connect with me for the first time in years. I wouldn't want anything different."

"I just wish we could've come to this point without so many mistakes and so much heartache," said Rachel. "Life is too short for so many detours."

"Harper thinks everything happens for a reason, even the bad things," said Cooper. "I'd still be by myself if she hadn't gotten pregnant, she claims."

"Is that true or not?" asked Harper."

"True, but if one of my books had become a best-seller, you might have noticed my name and called."

"Is that why you began writing books?" asked Rachel.

"No, but after I did, that thought crossed my mind. But none of them were that popular."

"And I wouldn't have met Harper if she hadn't asked about an abortion at the clinic," added Gabriel.

"What made you change your mind about having the baby?" asked Greg.

"Lots of things," said Harper, "but talking to Gabriel and learning about James really changed things for me."

"Who's James?" asked Greg.

"He was my little brother," said Gabriel. "My parents killed him."

Gabriel told them about his life before meeting Harper, and Harper explained how talking to Gabriel had affected her.

In the spirit of confession, Greg told them about his encounter with John and why he resigned.

"What a creep!" said Harper. "He should be in jail!"

"I'm sure Zoe doesn't know," said Greg. "Or she may have suspicions but is scared to pursue them. I debated whether I should say anything to anyone about this, but then I thought back over the years and realized this wasn't isolated behavior. Your mother and I should've listened to Mom and never taken that job."

"Aren't you going to tell the Board about him?" asked Harper. "Who knows what else he'll do."

"I've talked to your mother," said Greg, "and we agreed to contact the other Board members before school starts up again."

"People who declaim the loudest about bad behavior in others often do so to hide their own worse behavior," said Cooper.

"How ironic that he wanted to fire you because of my false claims when he's guilty himself," said Harper. "Dad, I'm sorry I ever accused you. I knew it was never true." She leaned her head on his shoulder.

"I think I gave you the idea," said Greg. "Years ago I told you that Heather had accused Dad. I think it was soon after we returned from our last trip up here. You wanted to go back, and I tried to convince you why that wasn't a good idea. I'm sorry I ever told her that, Dad."

"I believe I gave Heather that idea," said Rachel.

"How?" asked Cooper.

"She was wild in ninth grade, as you know, sneaking out of the house, having sex, drinking, using drugs. I wanted to know why, so I made an appointment with a psychologist. He said she may have been abused, so I asked her. She laughed and said no. I told her the psychologist said she was exhibiting classic abuse behavior. Then I asked her specifically if there was any chance her father may have done something. I even suggested that maybe she had suppressed the memory. Her accusations started soon after. I never told you, Cooper. That whole ugly chapter was my fault, as if we needed more issues to deal with."

"Not your fault. She would've made the claim regardless of what you'd asked her," said Cooper. "Maybe there was an incident with someone that she never wanted to admit. She probably thought she was to blame and kept it hidden. I was a convenient target."

"She kept it hidden because sex is the taboo subject no one talks about," said Harper, noticing her Dad's cringe. Parents have 'the talk' with their kids—maybe— then say nothing else about it except wait and don't do it. When kids don't wait, they hide it from their parents even when they want advice or get pregnant. Under different circumstances, I'd be sneaking out of the house to meet Gabriel. But that's not happening anymore. I'll be totally honest with you, so I hope you can learn to deal with it."

"I'll try," said Greg.

Harper giggled. "Grandpa did a good job this morning when Gabriel and I walked out of our room together, but he did turn a little red in the face."

"I can't help where my blood goes," said Cooper, "but I didn't say a word to either of you."

"Which is what Cooper and I will expect from all of you when you see us leave of our room in the morning. I like this honesty and openness idea, Harper," said Rachel.

"Told you, Grandpa!" laughed Harper. "Grandma, please disregard the inflatable mattress in the living room."

"You expected me to sleep there?" asked Rachel.

Flustered, Cooper stammered a response: "No, I wasn't sure...I didn't know...didn't know where you would want me to sleep, so I...I put it there in case you wanted...some privacy."

"Where would you like to sleep, Cooper?" asked Rachel.

"With you, in my bed."

"Good. And just so you know, I don't want to hold hands. Life's too short."

"Mom!" said Greg.

"Go, Grandma!" shouted Harper.

Chapter Thirty-Four

The next day, Greg walked with Harper and Snowball to the park. He couldn't believe the difference between living in San Antonio and living here. He could hear the river through the trees and saw nothing but open field and forests for miles, framed by mountains to the south.

"I need to tell you some things," said Harper. "Stuff I lied about and kept from you."

Greg dreaded bringing up anything that could cause an argument. "You don't have to. We could just enjoy the walk. Feels so good out here."

"I want to. And I just want you to listen. I'm not blaming you or Mom for anything. I want you to understand what I did and why I did it."

She told him about Luke groping her then coming into her room. Later she'd opened her robe and made out with him in the bathroom. Greg breathed deeply, trying his best to keep calm, but his little girl had been assaulted in his house, and he'd done nothing except yell at her, calling her the worst names.

"When you yelled at me, I felt ashamed and hurt. I built up a wall of anger to protect myself. Then I got into drugs and dressed how I thought guys liked. I liked it at the time, or thought I did, but now I think I was lashing out at you."

She went through her secret meetings and dates with all the other guys before Zachary. Smoking marijuana and drinking beer. Spin-the-bottle and truth-or-dare games that got way out of control. Then Zachary, heroin, and the big party at his house. When she found out she was pregnant and the way Zachary responded.

Greg felt like dying. His daughter had been paraded around, photographed, then handed off to another man. He ached to know she'd been so debased, and he'd done nothing to defend her or comfort her. She'd cried alone in her bed under his roof while he did nothing to help her. "Zachary should be arrested. Everyone in that house should be in jail."

"Yes. There was at least one other high school girl there. I'm sure he had more parties after I left."

"When I get back home, I'll go to the police. The least I'll do is tell them what's going on at his parties. When did you find out you were pregnant?"

"The day you confronted me about my grades and the phone."

Greg winced.

She told why she'd mailed heroin to Alaska, her plane ride with Ted, and then the airport encounter. She'd believed she was nothing until she sang at the airport and found her grandpa.

Greg's guilt was a vise in his chest, clamping painfully around his heart. He'd made nothing better for her. He'd driven her away. He'd not said one good thing about her since...when? He knew what he would've said to her if he'd known about any of her problems. He couldn't imagine what would've happened to her if Dad had not offered his help.

He grabbed her to keep from collapsing and held her close. "I'm so sorry, Harper. I did nothing right." His voice cracked. "I only made things worse."

Harper swallowed hard. "I didn't do anything right, either. I'm sorry I haven't been a better daughter to you and Mom," her voice quivering

"You tried your best under the circumstances. We failed you. And I'm making the same mistakes with your sister." He wiped his eyes and looked up, gasping for breath.

"Just hug her and tell her you love her more than anything."

In almost a wail, he said, "She won't let me."

"She wants you to. I wanted you to. I always wanted you to."

They held each other and wept.

A few seconds later, Snowball saw a rabbit and took off, ripping the leash out of Harper's hands. It bounced behind Snowball, who headed toward the road to the river.

"Snowball!" yelled Harper as she ran after him, with Greg right behind her.

After a hundred yards, Snowball must have realized something was bouncing behind him and stopped to sniff at the leash handle.

Harper knelt beside him. "I don't know why you keep chasing rabbits. You never catch them, and even if you did, you'd let them go." She picked up the leash and led him back to the dike.

Rapid gunshots cracked through the sky, echoing like thunder.

"What's that?" asked Greg scanned the forest, suddenly nervous.

Harper laughed and kept walking. "Shooting range is down there. We hear shots all the time. Grandpa taught me how to shoot his pistol last week."

"Why?"

Then she told him everything that had happened since meeting Grandpa. Everything, including what had really happened on their hike.

"I love him so much, Dad, but I'm afraid he's going to die or shoot himself."

Greg stared at her for a minute, as he processed what she'd said. He averted his gaze. He'd finally made some peace with his father only to learn he was dying. He had failed him, too. His insides chilled. "Does your Grandma know?"

"He told her, but he hasn't had a spell in front of her. He seems desperate to teach me all he can like he could die any day. I keep telling myself he'll stay alive as long as I need him and that being with Grandma and the rest of his family will help him. You have to move up here! He needs all of us."

"I wish I had enough money that your mother and I could live with Dad for a year and worry about a job later. I don't want my job to get between us again."

"Grandpa said the sooner you get into the system, the more likely you can find a job closer to us after a year. You could leave Alex and Jack with us the first semester, come home for the holidays, and then decide what you want to do next. We can FaceTime every night and maybe come up to visit you."

"We'll figure something out. First, I have to be offered a job."

"You will," she smiled.

They stopped by the lake and watched a beaver swimming toward them until it slapped its tail and dove.

He sighed. "Still, I wish you weren't sixteen and pregnant."

"Then we'd be in Texas, and neither of us would have Grandpa. I used to think I started all this with my plan to sneak out with Zachary, but now I think I didn't start anything. I was part of a larger plan. I had to chase a bear and shoot a moose and meet Gabriel and hike through the blood and the rain to get everyone back together. Even Grandpa is beginning to believe in fate. And praying."

Greg stopped suddenly. "Praying? How did you do that?"

"I was pregnant and bleeding. He had to save me and my baby, and he knew he needed help."

"And he just started praying?"

"Yes, and we made it back. He's trying hard to believe."

Greg remembered his argument with his father on the tour boat when he had ridiculed him for not knowing God. His father claimed he had tried to believe but couldn't. Greg considered that another example of his many failings and had rejected him. Now his father had saved his daughter and was trying to save his career.

"Your grandpa is saving both of our lives. I need to thank him."

"Yeah, you do."

Greg spent the next two days interviewing with two different school districts. When he returned, they all went to the Gulch and listened to every performance by Lyons & Light. Greg marveled at both their talents, not just separately, but how well they worked together. On stage they seemed to be the happiest couple alive. Their adlib banter between songs was hilarious with Harper teasing Gabriel until he hugged or kissed her, or sometimes shot back with a funny comment. The crowds loved them.

"I've never seen a more talented couple on stage," said Greg, unable to hide his enthusiasm. "It's beautiful to watch. You two seem like you've been playing together for years."

"Thank you, Daddy. That means a lot to me," said Harper. "From our first song together we've had an amazing connection. Like magic." She reached for Gabriel's hand.

"All the best times in my life so far have been with Harper," said Gabriel.

She beamed at her boyfriend as Greg shook his hand. "I'm glad you found her, and she found you. And I'm sorry I barked at you a few times."

Gabriel smiled. "That's OK. You were just trying to protect your daughter. That's what dads are supposed to do."

Greg proudly introduced himself as Harper's father to anyone he could and Gabriel as her boyfriend. He sent videos to Natalie and Alex and FaceTimed them after the shows. Alex and Jack couldn't wait to see Harper and be with Grandma and Grandpa. But Alex especially wanted to meet Gabriel. "He's soooo hot! How can she stand it?"

That day Greg received offers from both districts. They decided to have a big family discussion with Natalie joining by phone after dinner about his options before Greg flew back the next day. That was the same night that Cooper wanted to say grace before dinner.

Cooper stood. "A week ago I was alone in this house except for my dog and kitty. And now..." He wiped his nose. "And now my house is full of people I love." He smiled at all of them. "So I want to give thanks."

"I heard you had started praying, Dad."

"I'm trying, Greg."

"I'm proud of you, Dad. Whether you pray or not, I'm very proud of you."

Cooper nodded, and they all held hands, but Harper and Greg and Rachel didn't bow their heads. They watched Cooper pray.

"I promised you I would keep praying and try to find faith. You've answered every prayer. You saved Harper and her baby. You brought back my family. I think my brain is better, or maybe Rachel makes me feel so happy I just don't notice blanking out anymore."

"Or maybe it's all the extra exercise you're getting," teased Rachel.

None of them could stifle their snickers.

"This is my prayer, Rachel," said Cooper, taking her hands in his. "So, God, you've done your part, and I'm trying to do mine. I couldn't be happier than I am right now, and I know it'll get even better when Greg and his family come up. Let me know anything you want me to do, and I'll try my best."

"Amen," said Rachel "God wants you to eat, Cooper, so let's eat."

"So God speaks through you?"

"Yes, she does."

"She? Maybe I need to change the image I've been using to pray to. What does she look like?"

"You will see the face of God later tonight." She kissed him.

By that time the only ones not crying in laughter were Cooper and Rachel. Greg pounded the table and tried to catch his breath.

"This house is a lot more fun than my last one," said Gabriel, his dreads bouncing on top of his head.

"I've got to pee!" Harper leapt up and ran out.

"I've never heard the word 'pee' said more in my life than in the four days

I've been in Alaska," said Greg. "Even during my meetings, people said they had to pee, or 'Sorry I'm late, but I had to pee.' What's with everyone here?"

"Welcome to Alaska: no fences and no euphemisms," boomed Cooper.

"I like it. Open and honest," said Rachel. "When Gabriel and Harper say they are sleeping together, they really mean sleep. Isn't that right, Gabriel."

Blushing, Gabriel replied, "Yes."

"When you decide to do something more, what will you call it?"

"Mom!" blurted Greg.

"About time!" shouted Harper as she reentered the room and hugged Gabriel's neck. "And you all will be the first to know."

• • • • •

Two nights later, Gabriel and Harper had just settled into bed when they heard screaming.

"Harper! Gabriel!" shouted Rachel. "I need you!"

They both ran upstairs to find Rachel crying in her bedroom doorway. Snowball ran into the room and jumped onto the bed.

"He's locked himself in the bathroom and won't let me in. He keeps asking who I am," she cried. They heard pounding from the other side of the bathroom door connected to one wall of the bedroom.

Harper approached and knocked. "Hey, Grandpa, let me in. Gabriel's hogging the bathroom downstairs."

"Who's that? Leave me alone." He sounded scared, the same voice he'd used when he tried to escape from Gabriel after falling off the deck. The first time he'd used it on her.

She spoke kindly and gently, trying to keep from crying. "It's Harper. You're my Grandpa. Rachel is right here with me. And Snowball wants to see you."

Silence.

Harper knocked again. "Grandpa, please open the door."

They heard crying muffled through the door, followed by a thumping against the wall. "Why does this have to happen to me?" he wept.

"We love you, Grandpa," said Harper, trying desperately to keep from falling apart. "Open the door and let us help you."

After another minute of crying, Cooper unlocked the door. Rachel opened it and saw Cooper sitting on the toilet with his head in his hands, disheveled hair draped over his face. Rachel knelt and held his head.

"I thought maybe it'd stopped." Harper's heart broke over how sad he sounded. "There's been nothing for several days. I've been so happy. But it's never going to stop." He opened his eyes. "I don't want you to go through this again."

Harper saw defeat in his eyes and gasped. *Please, no. Not now!* She buried her face into Gabriel's chest.

"I'll take any minute of being with you that you can give me," said Rachel holding his face. "You don't decide what's good for me, I do. And having a spell every once in a while doesn't lessen the joy I have with you the rest of the time." She kissed both of his cheeks.

He covered her hands with his. "You know it won't stay 'every once in a while.'"

"Then it doesn't, but until then I'll take anything you can give me. Now stand up and come out of there." She helped him stand. "Harper and Gabriel want to see you."

She walked him out, and Harper clutched him to her, crying into his nightshirt. "Please, Grandpa! Let us help you!"

"We're going to see the doctor as soon as we can," said Rachel. "No arguments."

Cooper sat on the bed and rubbed Snowball's tummy. "No arguments."

"You'll take the medicines he prescribes," said Rachel.

"Whatever he says, I'll do."

Harper hoped he was sincere, but she couldn't help thinking he was saying what they wanted to hear.

Snowball flipped over and stood on the bed, licking Cooper's face while he wagged his tail. The bed shook.

"You both go to bed. I'll be all right," said Cooper.

"You sure?" asked Harper.

Cooper nodded.

Harper kissed him good night then walked downstairs with Gabriel. He led her into the kitchen, sat her down, and heated water in the microwave.

She stared out the big window at the flowers already filling the planter boxes next to the garage. Changes were dramatic in Alaska, pushed by the significant gain or loss of light each day of the year. Every plant outside was in a race to grow and produce seed before the winter killed it. She had finally found some happiness yet now realized it could easily slip away. Nothing stood still or stayed the same here, which was why her grandpa was in such a rush the moment he saw her at the airport.

"This isn't going to end well, is it?" asked Gabriel, offering her a cup of tea.

Harper shook her head. "He wants me to write with him every day you're working. He wanted me to start writing down everything that happened since Dad and I had our big blowout. He's worried he won't finish in time."

Gabriel pulled a chair close to her. "Then work harder. Spend more time with him. You write, and I'll work on some songs. We'll stay up later and get up earlier."

She almost whimpered in helplessness. "How? We're working all the time now."

"We'll find the time. I'll help you."

He was her rock. "You always help me."

Gabriel leaned forward and held her hands. "That's what people do when they love each other."

Harper's heart stopped. They'd said many things to each other, but had avoided saying that one word. "You love me?" She stood, still holding his hands, tears gathering in her eyes.

"With no doubt in my mind or in my heart." He stood. "I love you, Harper Lyons."

She gasped then crushed his lips with hers, trying to breathe and drink him into her. Finally, she reached up to his face and held his cheeks. "I love you, Gabriel Light. Beyond words." They melted into each other. Soon they were watching their hands dance together in the tantalizing ritual they'd performed since they met.

"We're hardly going to have time to hold hands anymore," said Harper.

"We'll find time."

"Not enough."

Lowering his voice, he lifted her chin. "Maybe we should make better use of our time."

"How...?" She saw him smile and knew.

She slipped her hands under his shirt and gently explored the skin over his abs. "It's about time, Gabriel."

His hands smoothed around her hips and skimmed up the back of her shirt, kneading the muscles around her lower spine. "Are you sure?"

She giggled and squirmed. "Oh yeah."

After a few more seconds, they raced to their bedroom.

• • • • •

During the next few weeks, Cooper opened new venues for Lyons & Light. Besides playing at the coffee shop, they performed at two restaurants, two music festivals in neighboring towns, and a few hotels. Gabriel could've made more money as a fulltime musician and left his EMT job, but the Gulch would close in September, so Cooper persuaded him to take hours at the fire station when he could get them.

Cooper had more episodes, but they remained sporadic and short-lived. He and Rachel made doctors' appointments and tried medicines and dietary changes. He walked Snowball at least twice every day, sometimes with Rachel, who kept the house clean, prepared most of the meals, and tended the garden and flowers. He began to believe his disease had stopped progressing—still there, but manageable. The future seemed to flow along multiple colored strands, rather than drop into a black hole.

He raced against the limited time he knew he had. Besides writing his book, he recorded and wrote songs, established a media presence for Lyons & Light, and produced two music videos. He taught Gabriel how to use his music and video programs, how to build a website, and where to find music production services. Gabriel learned quickly and was soon enhancing Cooper's work with his own.

Harper, however, flourished beyond his dreams. Her passion for singing and creation seemed to grow each day. They spent hours together writing, bouncing ideas off each other, erupting into eureka moments of pure exhilaration. He knew she was pushing herself to her limit, but she seemed immensely happy.

He made legal arrangements to name Harper as the head of Cooper Lyons, LLC when he passed. He'd made good money working for village school districts, not only from teaching but with extra-duty contracts. He had few expenses during those years and had invested wisely. He also had a sizable life insurance policy. He was a fairly rich man who could take care of his loved ones. He wanted to give them the chance to be happy in their lives without having to sweat all the details, which so often consumed daily existence: money, security, shelter. Above all, he wanted everyone to find a purpose, a passion to live.

When Cooper bought his house years ago, it was too big for his needs, but was the only decent one available at the time. Now he wished it were larger. Of course, he'd never envisioned a time when it would need to accommodate eight people. He bought bunk beds, desks, and dressers for Alex and Jack. He ordered more dishes and utensils, more sheets and towels, and more food. He and Gabriel rigged up a curtained area in the living room to accommodate Greg and Natalie's bed. Whenever he needed to rest, he'd sit in the kitchen so he could see the entire length of his house and watch everyone move around doing things. Then he'd imagine what two little kids and two more adults would add to the view, and the noise level. He chuckled to himself, content, and trying to forget all those years of looking out at emptiness and photos, drowning in the silence.

• • • • •

Harper spent more and more time writing with Cooper, learning about novel structure, how to show rather than tell, reading books about writing, and writing lyrics to Gabriel's melodies. Online courses in singing and music theory also demanded her attention. She had never worked so hard in her life.

Sometimes she stayed up so late working with Cooper or by herself in the studio, that she climbed into bed to find Gabriel asleep. He never stayed asleep for long, however. Her brain was so wound up with plot lines and lyrics that she couldn't sleep without reconnecting with Gabriel. Faint light still shone into their bedroom during the early morning hours as they talked about their future, the baby (still not 'theirs,' though she knew he claimed it as such), and their family, then melted together with a passion so intense they still gasped in wonder at how all-consuming it was. Floating in their own afterglow, they fell into a deep sleep, breathing each other's soul.

During the now familiar drive to Fairbanks, Harper could barely contain her emotions as they headed for the airport to pick up her parents and siblings. After the initial hugs and kisses, Harper introduced Gabriel to her mother.

He held out his hand, but she pulled him to her for a hug.

Alex seemed to have added two inches in height. Her eyes bulged and her mouth dropped open when she saw Gabriel. She held out her hand then nearly swooned when Gabriel gave her a hug.

Harper did swoon when he lifted Jack onto his shoulders and jogged down to the end of the terminal to show him the moose on display. She couldn't help but think of what a good dad he would be some day. She placed her hand over the bump on her stomach, fantasizing about Gabriel putting her child on his shoulders and the things Gabriel could show him or her.

During the drive home, Harper gave the same narration her grandpa had given her weeks ago, supplemented by descriptions of their recent gigs and a lively rendition of a new song she and Gabriel had just finished. They arrived at the house just before four. When they drove up, Cooper and Rachel walked out of the house with Snowball bounding beside them.

Harper grasped Alex and Jack's hands and took them to Cooper. "This is Grandpa. He's the most caring, intelligent, and talented grandpa in the world. He saved my life many times. He loves me at least as much as I love him, and he'll love you the same way."

Jack's eyes were like an owl's as he stared at Cooper. "You saved her life? Wow!" Alex shouted, "Grandpa!" and ran towards him. Cooper dropped to his knees to hug her, then Jack walked over to him.

He reached for Cooper's hair. "Why do you have a ponytail?"

"Because there're no barbers in Alaska." He chuckled.

"Really? I'll grow a ponytail, too." He joined his sister hugging Cooper.

Snowball nearly knocked Jack down with his tail then licked his face.

"Is that a wolf?"

"That's Snowball," said Cooper. "He'll be your best friend if you let him. Actually, he'll be your best friend whether you want him to or not." Still on his knees, he looked at his youngest grandchildren, tears trickling down his cheeks. "I'm so happy you're both here. I can't wait to show you what it's like to live in Alaska."

They walked inside the kitchen. Natalie saw the photos on the refrigerator and looked at Cooper in shock. "How long have they been up?"

"Since I got your first batch."

Natalie cried and hugged Cooper. "I'm so sorry, Cooper."

"Nothing to be sorry about. Thank you for sending them every year."

"Why is Mommy crying?" asked Alex.

"Because he loved you even when you didn't know him," said Natalie.

Alex swooned when she first held Houdini. "How can anything be so soft?" She insisted he sleep with her that night.

Greg and Natalie slept on the inflatable bed in the living room behind surrounding curtains. Soon after the parents had settled down, Rachel stood outside the curtain, Harper by her side, and said, "Knock, knock."

"Mom. Dad. We have something to give you," said Harper, soberly.

"You can come in," said Greg.

Rachel pulled open the curtain and held out a battery-powered noisemaker. "Cooper got this for you. It's good at drowning out sounds which might disturb your sleep."

"Thank you, Rachel," said Natalie.

"And it will also drown out any sounds coming from you, should there be any. We're very modest in this house and want to make sure that appropriate decorum is maintained. And please do not say the word 'pee' for the same reasons." Not a muscle twitched on Rachel's face as Harper tried to stifle her laughter.

Confused, Natalie gave a little smile as she took the machine, while Greg, trying not to smile, pointed at his now laughing mother and Harper.

"Greg?" asked Natalie.

"Have fun explaining to Mom, Dad," said Harper as she hooked arms with Rachel and walked to the kitchen, slapping each other's hands.

Harper soon took Natalie on the same walk to the park she had made with her father, telling her everything. Natalie cried and held her daughter's hand throughout their journey.

"I'll make sure Alex will never feel she can't talk to me or to you about anything," said Harper. "And I'm going to talk to her about everything. Everything."

Natalie nodded.

"Same for Jack, though Gabriel will probably be better with Jack."

Her Mom took both of her hands. "I know it's no excuse, but I grew up in a very silent house. My father didn't want to hear anything except compliance and the Bible. You're so different than I was. I had no idea what to do with you. I'm sorry, Harper."

"Well, I never even asked you about your childhood or being a teenager."

"There's not much to tell you. I did everything I was told and tried my best not to make my Father mad."

"Didn't you ever get angry?"

"When I did, I prayed and kept it to myself. I used to think you were so much trouble, so outspoken, but now I admire you so much. You sing and write songs, you have opinions and you're not afraid to let the world know them. You made a decision to see Grandpa, and you did it yourself."

"And cost Dad his job and put you through hell," Harper muttered.

"Yes, but you showed determination and gumption. You can't teach that. I could never do what you did. When I was told no, I obeyed. When you knew what you needed to do to save yourself, you said, 'Screw you!' And did it anyway. You're going to do amazing things, Harper, and I can't wait to see you do it."

"Thanks, Mom." Harper laughed. She'd never heard her say that before. Harper squeezed her mother against her chest, hoping she'd feel her love flow into her.

"You always obeyed? Why?"

"I was scared of him." Her mom told her about the Bible verse incident.

"You never left us alone with him. I wonder how he would've treated me. Dad said Grandfather watched my videos." Harper pulled back and looked into her mother's eyes. "Did you know about that?"

Harper saw her mother's eyes quiver then look down. "Not until Greg told me after the funeral."

"Were you surprised?"

Natalie shook her head. "No."

"Why? Did something happen to you?"

After a moment, Natalie nodded her head and continued to look down. "I was fifteen when I was allowed to go to my first dance. My bathroom could be accessed through a bedroom door besides the one in the hallway. We always made sure to knock before entering, then to lock the adjoining door. I was excited about the party. I'd never danced before. I had a radio in the bathroom and was practicing in front of the mirror in my underwear. I don't remember the song, but it was fast, and I was trying to shake my hips. I'm not sure for how long, but my father had been watching me from the bedroom. I knew I had locked the door, so he must have opened it with a key when he heard the music.

"'Is that how you're going to dance at the party?' he asked. Scared me to death. I said, 'No, sir,' and grabbed a towel to cover me. 'That's how whores dance. Where'd you learn how to do that?' I said, 'That's how all the girls dance.' He said, 'Really?' Then he told me to do it again. He made me drop my towel and dance for him. I cried and begged him to let me go back to my room, that I wouldn't go to the party. But he said no. I was going to the party.

And if he heard from anyone that I danced like a whore, I'd never go anywhere again. He said if he told my mother what I'd been doing in the bathroom, she'd want him to whip me. I asked him why he opened the door. He said I had left it open, probably on purpose because that's the kind of girl I was. He glared at me and told me to be very careful what I said to anyone. We never spoke of it again.

"For years I thought it was my fault, but it wasn't. He's a sick man. I never allowed him to be alone with you or be in a situation where he could do anything to you or Alex."

Harper felt lightheaded. "Does Dad know?"

"Not yet. I was too embarrassed." She met Harper's eyes, then scoffed. "It was my fault, after all." She looked to the ground. "What would Greg have thought of me? Then you told me all that had happened to you. You were abused and taken advantage of, and we blamed you!"

She covered her face and cried. Harper held her as tears wet her cheeks.

Natalie lifted her head back from Harper's shoulder and placed her hands on Harper's face. "I realized what my father did to me was not my fault. What Zachary and Luke did to you was not your fault. I'll tell Greg. And Mom. Just not sure when."

Harper kissed her mother's cheek. "I was worried about hundreds of strangers gawking at me, but that's nothing compared to what you went through. I can't imagine Daddy actually doing what I accused him of. You must have died inside every time I accused him. Mom, I'm so sorry." Her shame burned her skin.

"I was scared of anything sexual for a long time. Your father's kiss was my first, if you can believe it. I was afraid to want him, afraid he'd think me a whore. He was very patient, and I finally loosened up. Your father has always been kind and loving to me. Has Gabriel always respected you?"

Harper nodded and smiled. "For days I thought too much. Then I realized why he wanted us to wait. He was showing me he cared more about me than himself. He'd sacrifice his own pleasure for me, and I began to feel the same way."

They took a few more steps along the trail.

"Are you still waiting?" asked her mom.

"No. And there's plenty of pleasure for the both of us." She saw her Mom blush and chuckled. "At least you don't have to worry about him getting me pregnant." Harper lifted her shirt. "Speaking of, I'm getting a bump!"

Natalie smiled and touched Harper's tummy. "Have you felt anything yet?"

"Maybe. Kind of a weird flip yesterday."

"Pretty soon you'll feel your baby move every day."

"It's due early January. You'll be back from the village for the holidays. I'll need you with me."

"Wouldn't miss it. We'll all be with you."

Harper smiled then looked down. Her voice quivered. "I'm worried about the drugs and the alcohol I used."

"It wasn't that frequently, and you stopped."

Harper looked up as her mom touched her cheek.

"Your baby will be fine, and nothing will change how much all of us will love it."

"I wish we'd been able to talk about this before now. Maybe you can with Alex?"

"Definitely. Would you help?" asked her mother.

"If you want."

Natalie nodded, and they hugged again.

They walked back to the house holding hands. Harper felt she had more than a mother now. She had a confidant and a good friend.

The next day Alex wandered into the studio as Harper and Gabriel worked. Harper saw the same expression on her face as when she used to watch Harper put on makeup.

"You want to sing with us?" asked Harper.

"Could I?"

"Anytime you want."

Gabriel started strumming "Hallelujah."

"This is the first song your sister and I sang together. Do you know it?"

"Yes."

"Sing with me," said Harper as she handed Alex the lyrics.

By the end of the song, Alex and Harper were adlibbing on the final "Hallelujahs," dragging them out ridiculously long until Gabriel broke down laughing. From that moment on, Alex spent many hours in the studio. Harper taught her to sing, and Gabriel taught her some guitar. Cooper spent a little time each day teaching her the keyboard.

After a week of practice, Alex accompanied Harper and Gabriel to the Gulch and actually sang with them in front of an audience. She loved the applause and asked when she could join the group. She thought Lyons² & Light would be cool.

Harper thought Alex's excitement about singing and performing was so much better than her impatience to look like Harper. How would Harper's pre-teen years have been different had she had such opportunities? Probably better, but how would one ever know? Alex could meet her own Zachary at some point. Harper had to prepare her for that.

At the end of July, Gabriel and Harper played Saturday afternoon for the music festival at the river park. They were the only local musicians playing amongst bands from throughout the state. Many in the crowd had never heard of them, but others had, either from the Gulch or online.

Harper smiled at her family sitting in the crowd on a warm afternoon as she walked to the microphone on the little covered stage. Alex held Harper's phone to record everything.

"Hello! My name is Harper Lyons."

"And I'm Gabriel Light," said Gabriel.

"We are Lyons and Light," they said together, holding their hands high.

Many in the crowd, stood up and applauded, but Harper saw only her family, hollering and cheering. She'd waited for this day her whole life.

"Gabriel and I live down the road at Cooper's house," said Harper. "He's my grandpa. The best grandpa in the world. He got me to sing again, and because of that I found Gabriel, who's the best boyfriend in the world. And because of him and my Grandpa, my baby is alive and kicking. See my bump?" She turned sideways, and many applauded. "So Gabriel, Grandpa and Grandma, and my wonderful parents, and Alex and Jack, you are the reason I'm so happy to be here today to sing for all of you."

They sang "You Are the Reason," then the rest of their set, ending with one of Cooper's fast country blues numbers. The crowd gave them a long ovation. Alex posted the video of the first number to YouTube soon after the song ended.

The next day, Harper noticed all the comments on her video. One in particular caught her attention: *Lies have consequences, Harper.*

Who else would write that except Zachary? But he was four thousand miles away, living in a world she cared nothing about.

Chapter Thirty-Five

Two days after the festival, Greg and Natalie had to leave to attend in-service for new principals. Cooper insisted he ride along with Gabriel and Harper to give his son more advice about life in the village. For most of the trip, he was turned halfway toward the backseat. Cooper had spent ten years saying nothing to Greg, and now he had so little time to be the father he'd wanted to be.

"Remember, Greg, you need to get to know your families and your kids in the village. Spend a lot of time walking around the place. See the locals in their homes. Be genuinely interested in their culture and lives. Make it clear you want to learn from them."

"I'm here to help them, not save them," said Greg. "I'll call you every night, tell you what happened, and you can tell me what you think."

Cooper wished they had always spoken like this. "I'd like that."

"I wish we could stay a little longer. We just got everyone back together, and now..."

"You'll be back in a little over four months. They'll go by before you know it."

"Hope so." He locked eyes with Cooper. "I need to see you again, Dad, so you listen to your doctors. You can fight this."

"I'm trying my best, son."

"Your whole family needs you now."

"Yes, we do," added Harper.

"I'm not going anywhere," said Cooper. "Don't you worry." He'd prayed, taken his pills, and done everything his doctors had told him to do mainly because doing so made everyone else feel better. But he knew gravity still worked, and he was racing the clock.

"There's a possibility that one of the schools in our local district will be looking for a principal next year," said Cooper. "I called the superintendent yesterday. You'll have more options next fall."

"That'd be nice," said Greg.

Gabriel parked the truck next to the curb outside the terminal, opened his door, then carried the luggage to the sidewalk.

"Gabriel," said Natalie. "Thank you for making Harper so happy. I hope you're still at the house when we come back." She hugged him.

"I'm not going anywhere unless Harper throws me out," said Gabriel.

"Never happening," said Harper who grabbed her mother. "I love you, Mom."

"Love you, too."

"Daddy?" Harper's cheeks were wet as she held out her arms toward her father. He held her close. "We'll take care of Jack and Alex."

"I know you will. I love you, sweetheart. Be good to Gabriel. And take care of Grandpa."

"I heard that," said Cooper. "Not too long ago you were asking me to take care of her."

"And she still needs you, Dad. At least for a few more years."

"More like decades," said Harper.

Cooper held out his hand to Greg, who grabbed his father into a bear hug.

"I love you, Dad. Thanks for everything."

Cooper touched his son's face and felt his heart flutter. "You're very welcome." He bent down to kiss Natalie on the cheek.

"I'm going to call you Dad from now on, if you don't mind," said Natalie as she hugged Cooper.

"I'd love that. Text us when you get there and send lots of pictures."

Greg and Natalie took their bags through the doors.

"See you at Christmas!" Cooper yelled after them.

• • • • •

On a Saturday in mid-August, just a week before Alex and Jack would start school, Gabriel called Harper about coming home late that evening.

"Another bad wreck south of the park."

Harper knew the world was safer with an EMT like Gabriel on the job, but she wished for more time with him. Snowball waited by the door for someone to take him for his walk. The kids were watching a movie with Rachel while Cooper worked in the studio.

"I guess it's just me, Snowball."

Harper got the dog's harness and leash. Snowball jumped up, wagging his tail, and stepped between the straps, which went around his front leg.

"Take the gun, Harper," shouted Rachel from the living room.

"Yeah, yeah."

During one of Grandpa's walks with Jack and Alex to the lake, they'd found wolf prints in the mud. Maddie claimed that someone saw a small pack of wolves moving along the train tracks, which ran between the town and the highway. Grandpa then decided anyone walking Snowball should carry the Mountain Gun.

As they left the mudroom, Harper grabbed the pack and slung it on her shoulder. It was a little breezy outside. Every day more leaves turned yellow. Some of the spent fireweed had already turned dark red. Mushrooms had sprung up everywhere: some gnarly, looking like solidified vomit; others, beautiful and large with bright orange heads covered with seeds. Harper and Snowball walked quickly down the driveway toward the street.

Just as she rounded the corner of the road to the lake, she thought she heard tires rolling on the gravel some distance behind her. She turned her head, but the curve blocked her view back up the road.

Snowball stopped to sniff along the alders bordering the gravel, looking for rabbit pellets.

"C'mon, Snowball, I have things to do. Let's walk quickly. OK?" She pulled him back onto the road and walked around the lake to access the trail. She loved watching Snowball's tail swish from side to side as he trotted down the path. Her best ideas often popped into her head as the graceful, hairy blur put her into a trance.

Tires biting gravel behind her ruined the spell, and she turned her head to see a new, compact car stop back at the lake's edge. Locals often drove out there to search for animals or to enjoy the view, but she'd never seen that car before. She hoisted her pack higher onto her shoulder and moved on.

Snowball tugged the leash harder, pulling her into the "tunnel," where trees had grown tall and thick on both sides of the dike. She followed

Snowball walking quickly from one side of the trail to the other, sniffing at moose droppings and scat piles, mostly from other dogs, but some looked like wolf droppings.

Snowball suddenly stopped and looked behind Harper, his head high and his tail stiffly arched.

A rifle shot ripped by them, cracking through branches until it stopped with a thud.

Harper screamed and jerked to her left as Snowball pulled his tail down and jumped toward the trees.

"Shit!" a man's voice yelled.

She knew that voice.

No. He couldn't be here.

Another shot whipped down the trail.

Snowball screeched, ran a few steps, yelped, and collapsed to the ground, kicking his front legs. A red gash dug deep across the dog's back.

"Snowball!" Harper cried out and jerked her head back toward the entrance to the tunnel.

A man rose from the ground, sneering at her, holding an assault rifle.

"Zachary!" A chill swallowed her body.

"Hey, Harper!" He lifted the rifle and aimed at her.

She lunged to the right, disappearing into the brush. The bullet shattered a tree near her leg. *What the hell is Zachary even doing here?*

Harper clambered through the trees and burrowed under dead limbs, trying desperately to ensure none of her skin or clothes were visible. But she couldn't block out the sound of Snowball's labored panting and whines. Was he dying? She gritted her teeth to keep silent.

She heard Zachary's steps pounding down the trail, then stop. "You're pretty damn lucky, Harper. The asshole who sold me this rifle said he'd sighted it. Fucking liar!"

His voice sounded shrill and too fast. He was on something besides heroin.

Her heart pounded in her chest so loud she thought he'd surely hear it. She tried desperately to calm her breathing. Slow footsteps approached along with a weird, incoherent mumbling. She heard a thud, and Snowball yelped again.

"Hey, Harper! Think your dog needs to be put down. He's in a lot of pain. Needs a vet real bad."

She heard a squirrel chitter near her then two cracks of the rifle, sending bullets ripping through the trees.

"I just got into town, and the first thing I see is your sweet butt swinging behind your dog. I always loved your butt. Too bad I'm gonna have to kill it. You lied to me, Harper! Miscarriage, my ass!"

He fired a shot, and Snowball yelped.

She flinched and gasped, and he shot again, the bullet breaking the strap on the pack next to her.

"I saw your stupid baby bump video! You just had to taunt me with it! You're just trying to get my money!" He shot again.

Snowball began yelping uncontrollably.

Harper couldn't stand the sound. Snowball's yelps ripped through her, boiling her blood and inflaming her anger. Zachary wasn't going to get away with this! She had to get out. She and her baby were going to live and be happy, and Zachary wasn't going to be there for any of it!

Clinching her jaw, she slowly moved her hand out to the pack. She had to get the gun.

"I'm going to keep shooting your dog, Harper, until you come out! You want that? Maybe we can work something out. I got a car. I can drive you to Fairbanks, and you can get the abortion you promised. I'm not paying for that kid!" Another shot echoed through the trees, followed by Snowball's shriek. "You're not holding a rape charge over me!"

"Harper!" A man's voice shouted in the distance.

Gabriel! She lifted her head.

"Who the hell is that?" growled Zachary.

He's going to kill him! Harper tried to peer through the leaves. She saw Zachary turned back toward the lake.

"Say goodbye to your boyfriend, Harper."

No! She grabbed the gun, leapt up, and ran out of the trees.

Zachary fired at Gabriel.

Without stopping, Harper held the gun in front of her with two hands, cocked the hammer, and pulled the trigger. Zachary's head exploded, and he dropped to the ground.

She turned back toward Snowball then bent down, crying, and put her left hand on his head.

"Harper!" Gabriel ran up to her and kneeled by Snowball, examining his wounds. "He won't make it."

"I know!" she cried. He was in pain. She pointed the barrel at Snowball's ear then convulsed in sobs. She couldn't. He was her dog. She couldn't hurt him like Zachary had. But she couldn't let him suffer, either. She tried to gather herself then pulled back the hammer.

Gabriel's hand covered hers on the gun. "He's dead, Harper." He took the gun and released the hammer. "He's gone."

Harper collapsed into Gabriel, shuddering, sobbing.

Gabriel held her. "I'm here."

After a few minutes, she lifted her head from his shoulder and looked at Zachary.

"Who is he?" asked Gabriel.

"Zachary. He saw the video from the festival. He thought I was going to sue him for child support. He said something about taunting him, like I was hoping he'd see the video. He was high on something."

She stood and couldn't control her rage. "Fucking piece of shit!"

She stomped on his back.

Then again.

"Don't!" Gabriel pulled her to him. "I'll call the troopers."

He made the call while Harper knelt by Snowball, weeping. He'd died because of her. Beautiful Snowball. She remembered her first night in Alaska, and the sweet, too-happy dog licking her face. How he'd run around the yard, kicking up grass, his big tail flying behind him, and tongue flopping out to the side.

Her fault!

"I'm s-so s-sorry." She collapsed on his broad chest, sobbing.

A hand gently touched her back. "I'm here, Harper."

She turned her head to see Cooper kneeling beside her. She rose and grabbed him. "I'm sorry, Grandpa. I couldn't save him."

"You did everything you could." He walked her back to Gabriel. They all stood in the trail, hugging each other until two troopers arrived, running toward them, with two EMTs close behind.

Harper told them what she could, going through her sordid past to prove once again how responsible she was for Snowball's death. If she'd never come here, he'd still be alive.

By the time the troopers were through with her, she was numb to the sounds and sights around her, unable to focus on anything except the horror show looping in her mind.

Gabriel picked up Snowball and put him over his shoulder. Cooper held Harper's hand as they walked back toward the trucks. Gabriel laid Snowball in the bed. Harper climbed in beside Gabriel as he drove back to the house. Cooper followed behind in his truck.

"I'm sorry I didn't get to you sooner," said Gabriel. "I just got home and heard the shots. They seemed too loud to be coming from the shooting range. I asked Rachel where you were. Then we heard another shot. She said you took Snowball for a walk."

"I saw a car parked near the lake," said Harper, "but I had no idea it was him."

"I raced to the lake and saw the car. I heard more shots and took off. Then I saw him point his rifle toward me, and you jumped out of the bushes. He fired, and I thought for sure I'd get hit. I heard the bullet whip past my head and everything."

She held Gabriel's hand. "He would've killed me if you hadn't come. You saved me and my baby. Thank you." She kissed his hand.

"I'll always be there for you, Harper."

As they parked in Cooper's driveway, Rachel and the kids opened the door. Harper held Alex and Jack and would not let them see Snowball.

"What happened?" asked Rachel.

"Zachary tried to kill Harper and killed Snowball instead," said Cooper.

"Zachary?" asked Alex. "The same Zachary from Texas?"

"Yes," said Harper. "The same one. He wanted me to have an abortion. When he found out I wasn't going to, he tried to kill me."

"You should take the kids inside," said Cooper.

"C'mon kids. Let's go," said Rachel as she ushered Alex and Jack inside.

Cooper opened the back of the truck.

"What do you want to do with him?" Gabriel asked.

"I got some wood in the back. Gonna build a coffin for him then put it inside another raised box. I'll set it on the edge of the yard by the trees. The water table is too high to dig a grave." Cooper pulled Snowball onto the dropped tailgate and paused. "Oh, Snowball." He leaned over and hugged his dog. "God, I'm going to miss you. Gabriel, get a bag from the garage. I don't want the kids to see him."

Harper reached out her hand and held one of Snowball's paws. She and Grandpa wept until Gabriel returned.

Harper walked inside and sat down at the kitchen table, put her hands over her face and cried. Soon after, Alex knelt and put her head in Harper's lap.

Rachel's phone rang, and she fished it out of her jean pocket and glanced at the screen.

"Your parents," she told Harper. "They want to FaceTime."

Harper looked at her grandma through bleary eyes then shook her head.

"Come here, Jack. Let's talk to your parents out here." Her grandma took Jack to the living room.

"Come on, Alex." Harper stood, held her sister's hand, and walked her back to Harper's bedroom.

They sat on the bed, leaning against the wall. Harper scooted down so her head lay propped on the pillow. Alex lay on Harper's chest.

"I'm going to tell you about Zachary and me. You probably won't like me afterwards, but you need to know. I don't want you to make my mistakes, but if you do, you're going to tell me about them. I'll listen just like you'll listen to me. Got it?"

"I'll always love you, Harper. No matter what you do or have done. I'll always love you."

"That's what we all need."

She told Alex everything that happened a few months ago before she left Texas. Alex cried and clutched at her sister. When Harper was done, both of their faces were wet as they sobbed.

"I love you, Harper. Always."

"I love you, too. Always."

Later that evening Gabriel opened the bedroom door and found Alex sleeping on Harper's shoulder.

"Shhh," said Harper. "She'll sleep with us tonight."

"I need to take a shower. Come with me."

They quietly left the room and went to the bathroom. When Gabriel closed the door behind them, Harper leaned against Gabriel, crying. "Will I ever stop hurting? How did you get over James?"

"Never have. It's like a cut that never heals. Sometimes it scabs over, but then it starts bleeding again. Being with you helps. You make everything better."

She turned to the wall and hit it with her fist. "No, I screw everything up."

"You did a good job of staying alive."

"Why did I have to show everyone my bump at the festival? That's the video he saw."

"You showed your bump because you're proud of it. I'm proud of it. I can't wait for it to grow."

"What he did to Snowball, what he did to me, what I thought he did to you. I can't stop seeing his head." Her throat burned, and her chest heaved. "Grandpa told me that whether you kill out of love or selfishness, a little of you dies."

"Did it?"

She closed her eyes and tried to find an answer. "The part of me he'd ruined. Maybe that's finally gone."

He knelt before her, holding her tummy. "What will you tell our baby?"

She held his head as she knelt. "Our baby?"

"Ours."

They locked eyes, and Harper nodded. "You're his father. His real father."

"I want to be, more than anything."

"At some point, we'll both tell him or her everything. I love you, Gabriel."

"I love you, mother of my child."

Later, they climbed into bed with Alex who'd rolled over toward the wall. Harper cuddled against her little sister, stroking her cheek, while Gabriel pressed against Harper's back, his hand on her tummy.

Harper tried to sleep but kept hearing shots and Snowball screaming. She tried to see herself jumping up from the forest floor and shooting the bastard through the trees.

She heard his words over and over*: taunting me, not paying for that kid, lied to me, rape.*

She did lie about the miscarriage. She'd threatened him with rape charges. She'd told him she'd have her baby and sue him for child support. She'd done everything he accused her of, but he'd twisted everything around as if she had a plan to go after him. In a sick way, he was trying to defend himself. He was desperate, obviously afraid of exposure and money. He must've been fried on drugs. And she'd killed him, her baby's...

How would she ever explain that to her child?

How long would she see Zachary's head explode?

Why couldn't she have told him the truth? She'd have her baby, and she wanted nothing from him. Her baby would never know he existed. Would he have believed her? She beat herself up with questions most of the night until she realized she should have died.

Why didn't she? Snowball took her bullets. What was meant for her went to him. She was saved once again. How many times was it now? And for what purpose? The question hung in front of her, teasing her, demanding she find the answer. And then the light broke through: To rid her of her past, to cleanse her mistakes. She'd always be grateful to Snowball.

She placed her hand over her stomach. Her baby was a blessing, unifying her family, together finally in love. Her new life grew inside her, protected by Gabriel and her family. This was the plan all along. She pulled Gabriel's arm tighter to her belly, hugged her sister, and finally fell asleep.

• • • • •

The next day Cooper talked to the troopers and showed them Harper's old phone. She'd turned it on that morning and found Zachary's messages. Harper had lied about the abortion, that she'd sent the crate back on purpose to taunt him. She'd called the cops to raid his house twice. She was just another bitch after his money, and his father was going to cut him off if he had to deal with another bitch demanding money. And finally, *Get an abortion or else.*

Before they left with the phone, the troopers said the case would be closed soon.

Cooper showed everyone the hair he'd cut from Snowball's tail and the feathers behind his legs. He wanted to keep some and scatter the rest in Section 7 along the ridge. He'd always wanted to take Snowball there, but park rules wouldn't allow that. Now, a part of Snowball could live there forever.

When Cooper asked Isabelle to take care of Alex and Jack for two days, she said yes before he finished his question. They'd see the sled dog demonstrations, ride the shuttle bus to Eielson Visitor Center deep inside the park, pick blueberries, and visit all the tourist shops. Houdini would stay at Isabelle's house.

Cooper bought clothes and gear for Rachel and Gabriel and a new pack for Harper. Rachel wanted poles to hike with, and Gabriel bought an orange Bana bandana to match Harper's. They looked so cute together that Isabelle took photos to use on her store window. She also shot Rachel and Cooper's picture for advertising flyers—"Hiking's Good at Any Age!"

Cooper decided they'd pitch their tents in Section 6, then day hike up to the ridge overlooking the Teklanika Gorge. That way, only Gabriel would have to carry a pack holding the bear can and stove on the long walk to the top. Cooper had planned to make this smaller trip with Harper weeks ago, but all the spots in Section 6 had been taken. Now he believed it was God's plan all along for Harper and him to trek through Section 7 and face all their trials. How else would he have learned to pray?

Gary still drove the seven o'clock Camper Bus and dropped them off at the social trail down to the creek. The day was perfect—just a few clouds and not too warm. Rachel walked slowly but steadily along the trail. They saw a bear in the distance and a marmot chirping from the rocks above them. After two hours, they lost sight of the road and stopped for water.

"I need to pee," said Rachel. She dropped her pack.

"Do you need help?" asked Cooper.

"I saw the video. I know what to do."

"You can go over to those bushes, Grandma," said Harper. "I'll come with you."

"Bushes? Hell no. Who knows what's hiding in there?" She walked a few feet away from them toward a small outcropping of rock and dropped her pants.

Harper laughed. Gabriel blushed deep red and turned around.

"Give us some warning, woman!" said Cooper.

"Nothing you haven't seen before." After another minute, she said, "Bring me some tissue, Harper."

Harper, still laughing, brought her tissue and an open zip-lock bag. Rachel wiped, dropped the tissue in the bag, stood, then bent down to pull up her pants.

"You're mooning all of Alaska, Rachel!" laughed Cooper.

"Alaska is too big to care about seeing my butt."

They pitched their tents just behind the saddle, ate lunch, and then began their walk up the slope. Rachel dropped to her knees frequently to show everyone the beautiful flower she'd discovered or the amazing colored lichen pattern on a rock. All those years without her, Cooper had simply walked over these areas, heading toward the summits. Besides missing her, he'd missed her eye for the little treasures in life and her love of small, cute things. She plucked a few purple flowers and pushed them into her hair.

"Smile, dear," said Cooper. "You're my flower girl."

She laughed. "Maybe flower old lady."

"Still look like a girl to me."

"Lucky your eyes have aged at the same rate as my face."

He took her picture, then he got down with her, looking for plants and flowers he knew she would like. Cooper took pictures of everything she found and lots of selfies of him and Rachel. Their walk was a slow, joyous procession of discovery and amazement at every sight and sound.

Finally, they gained the summit and stood speechless, staring at the mountains, the gorge, and the shining river braids.

"Looks so much brighter and friendlier than when I was here last," said Harper. "Even the wind is just a kiss today." She grabbed Gabriel's hand and held it to her tummy.

"You've been here often, Cooper?" asked Rachel.

"At least twenty times, but this trip is the best."

"Because of the weather?"

"Because you're here to share it with me." He put his arm around her and pulled her close. "I thought I'd never get to see this again. A perfect day for Snowball."

Cooper removed the bag of Snowball's hair from his jacket. "Snowball, I would've loved to see you running along this ridge. Maybe your spirit will get to. No happier dog ever lived. Love you!" With tears in his eyes he held some hair above his head and let them drift. He passed the bag to Harper.

She held it to her heart and let her tears flow. Then she dropped to her knees. "Sweet Snowball. I'll return every summer and see you again with Gabriel and our baby. I'll miss your kisses and your floppy ears. Thank you for saving me. I'll love you forever!"

She held the remaining hair above her head and gifted it to the breeze.

The hair floated, swirled a little, dropped to the ground, then spiraled up again, dancing with the wind as if Snowball stood next to them, shaking himself in slow motion. They stood watching his hair twirl around them for one last embrace before taking flight, sparkling in the sunlight.

After a few moments of silence, Cooper approached Harper. "Harper, on your first day in Alaska you asked me what the point of living is. Do you remember my answer?"

"You said that's what I'm up here to find out."

"And have you?"

She held up her hands to Gabriel as he lifted his, barely touching hers. "Yes. Passion. For those I love, but especially for what I can create with my body, my mind, and my soul. It's not enough just to live a life. I have to make a life, create it myself, reshape sounds into my own songs, turn events into my own stories, and ideas into my own poetry. But mainly, I have to help others find their own passion, like you helped me."

Cooper and Rachel watched the two lovers sharing their souls through their hands.

"What can't you live without?" asked Cooper.

Harper turned her head toward Cooper. "Huh?"

"Knowing what to live *for* also means knowing what you can't live *without*."

"The passion I feel inside me, that you and Snowball and Gabriel and everyone helped form, that will last even after those I love leave me." She pulled Gabriel to Cooper and Rachel. "But no one is leaving me any time soon."

She held out her arm to embrace Cooper, who did the same with Rachel, who reached for Gabriel. They moved in close and bowed their heads until they touched.

"Next year I want everyone to come here: all of us, my parents, Jack and Alex, and our baby."

"I'd love to," said Rachel.

"Count me in," said Gabriel.

"Grandpa?"

Cooper looked up to find Harper's eyes pleading with him. "Yes, Harper."

"You promise?"

"I promise." He tried to give her a smile, but he could only stretch his mouth halfway.

"And what can't you live without, Cooper?" asked Rachel.

These memories, he thought, but he knew they'd fade from his mind soon, kept alive only in the words he and Harper would write. He saw Harper's eyes stay fixed on him, underneath the beginnings of a frown.

"Cooper?" said Rachel.

"I can't live without showing you a special place." He winked at Harper.

"What special place?"

"Just a beautiful place for you and me to be totally free and exposed to nature. It's just over this ridge. Harper, why don't you and Gabriel get water going for tea?"

Harper gave Cooper a quick kiss on the cheek. "We will. And take your time. Enjoy the sun. Gabriel and I will do the same."

Cooper nodded.

Both couples walked in opposite directions away from the ridgeline. The sounds of their joy and laughter rose into the sky, dancing with Snowball's hair still drifting in the wind.

Chapter Thirty-Six: Harper

That was the last scene I wrote with Grandpa for this book, which we finished in late October. After all the geese and ducks headed east then south for the winter, and bright yellow and red leaves had faded on the ground.

After the first snow had drifted down in big flakes, landing on Alex and Jack's tongues as they ran around, squealing in delight.

After the next snow covered the flower boxes, gardens, and Snowball's grave.

After an eight-week-old white puppy named Sundance joined our family.

After Gabriel and I finished our first album of original songs.

After he asked for my hand in marriage, and I cried, "Yes!"

After Grandpa struggled to remember what we wrote the day before.

We'd raced through our memories, trying to make sense of them, arranging and rearranging the puzzle pieces until the story left us panting for breath, laughing out loud, and crying onto our keyboards. I felt the deadline approaching as his eyes became more desperate, his words and hands trying to teach me everything he knew before he forgot it all.

After we finished our book, he tried to read it from the beginning, but kept losing his place until he gave up. So I read it alone in the studio all day and most of the night. Gabriel finally came in and carried me to bed, where I cried in his arms.

Grandpa continued keyboard lessons with Alex until she asked me what was wrong with him. His brain was dying, I told her, but his heart was growing. He showed his love for us every second he could. He held our hands, gave us hugs and kisses, and expressed joy at everything we'd accomplished, for every moment he could share.

He spoke to Daddy almost every night, helping him, suggesting alternative approaches and praising him. But there were times he blanked out and dropped the phone, when he called the puppy Snowball, and when he forgot who we were.

Still, he was with us more than not, and we made the best of those times.

On Thanksgiving Day, we all stood around the table full of food and the joy we'd shared in preparing the dinner. The wood stove pushed warmth to every corner of the house. Grandpa wanted to give the blessing, no longer an unusual request. He'd prayed openly among us for weeks. He'd even prayed for Sundance to hold his pee until we could get him outside.

We held hands and bowed our heads waiting for his words.

But they never came.

Jack pulled on his hand and said, "Grandpa. Grandpa."

Grandpa jerked his hand away. "Don't pull my hand!"

Jack was stunned. Grandpa yanked his other hand away from me.

Rachel began walking toward him. "Cooper. Let's go sit down."

He had the most scared look on his face as he stumbled out of the room. We followed, calling his name. He acted like we were ghosts, shaking in fear, backing into a corner, then screaming and running out of the room. He bolted outside into the twenty below night, lurching into the snow. Gabriel followed, but Grandpa ran away until he fell, crying.

Gabriel carried him back inside where he continued to struggle against us as we tried to warm him up with blankets.

At least one of us stayed with him all night, even after he fell asleep.

Friday he acted the same.

On Saturday he woke up and complained of a headache. He was thirsty and hungry. After a couple more hours, he became Grandpa again.

He was so embarrassed and sorry. I hated seeing him like that. How much of his life had he spent feeling sorry? Too much. He deserved better than this, and it made me angry and helpless, as it did for him as well.

The next afternoon he found Gabriel and me in the studio. He carried in folders of documents. He told me he had made all the arrangements weeks ago and needed to explain everything while he still could. His business was now in my name, in Rachel's trust until I turned eighteen. He'd also set up accounts for Rachel, for me, and for Greg and Natalie. Gabriel and I would have plenty of money. We could do what we wanted with our lives. We could write and perform and compose without having to worry about taking other jobs to pay our bills. The house was now mine and Rachel's.

He told us we were the most important students of his life, the ones he could be proudest to have helped. We'd given his life meaning because he knew he would live on in us.

We cried and laughed, played songs together, and even started writing a new one.

He never entered his studio again.

A day later, he had another paranoid episode lasting three days. It passed, and he finally slept, but later that night I found him walking around the kitchen. He looked at each photo on the refrigerator door, now even more crowded with recent additions.

"Why aren't you sleeping, Grandpa?"

"Why aren't you?" he shot back.

"I heard you and wanted to make sure you were OK."

He hugged me, now having to curve his body over my swollen tummy. "You know I'll never be OK. And what's the point of being just OK? You were never happy with that, and neither was I. It's time, Harper."

My blood chilled with fear. I clutched his back. "I don't think I can stand losing you."

"You couldn't lose me if you tried. I'm as much a part of you now as that baby. Our book is our baby, and I'll be part of every new one you write. I would've died long ago without you calling me. Knowing you gave me such a joy. I couldn't stand not knowing you. You have to learn to focus on the knowing, not the losing."

I could barely breathe. "I don't want you to leave me. We could find a way..."

"To do what? Keep watching me? Keep me medicated so I don't run off? No fences in Alaska, sweetheart. Never let them build one around you."

We stood as one, his chin on top of my head, each of us trying to squeeze one more beautiful moment from the other, my baby pressed between us. His tears dripped into my hair; mine onto his old flannel nightshirt. Just like the first night we met. But this time, I was scared to let go.

He smoothed back my hair with both his hands and lifted my face. "Years ago, you jumped onto a table and demanded a sleeping world wake up. Jump while you can, Harper, and stomp hard on every table. The world needs you." He kissed my forehead and then walked upstairs.

The next morning he tried to make all of us one of his famous breakfasts, but he struggled to keep from burning the bacon and eggs. The multitasking required in cooking had become an increasing challenge to him. He frothed extra milk and put it into two bowls for Alex and Jack so they could feed Houdini and Sundance their own lattes with their fingers. But he couldn't coordinate the espresso drip and frothing, so all of our drinks had either too much coffee or too much milk. He forgot to add eggs to the waffle mix.

He smiled as he sat down with us, but he looked the same to me as he had during our first breakfast, worried about his failures. This time, though, he couldn't think of a story to deflect attention away from everyone's awkward attempts to eat and smile and pretend all was well.

I reached for his hand and squeezed it. "Thanks for breakfast, Grandpa."

"It sucks, doesn't it?"

"You made it for us, so it's wonderful," I said, hoping my big smile would cheer him up.

"Yeah, well, the list is getting longer," he growled.

"What list?"

He paused, scrunched his eyes, then shook his head. "I don't remember."

After breakfast, Gabriel and I left for Fairbanks. We had a gig, and our marriage license was ready. When I'd asked Mom and Dad to give their consent for my marriage to Gabriel, they did not hesitate. We'd be married in Healy on December 22nd in front of family and a few friends, the day when the sun began its climb higher in the sky for the next six months.

Gabriel and I returned home the next day to learn that Grandpa had died of a heart attack near Snowball's grave. Alex and Jack had just returned to school after lunch. EMTs had taken his body away by the time they came home.

"A heart attack?" I asked Grandma, peering into her bloodshot eyes.

She nodded behind an inscrutable face. "Heart attack. That's our story." My chin quivered, and I hugged her. "Thank you, Harper, for bringing us back together."

Later, I checked the pack hanging in the mudroom.

I never saw the Mountain Gun again.

That night, after the kids cried themselves to sleep, I walked upstairs and found Grandma sitting on her bed in tears. "Please, tell me."

"Last night he had a spell after we got in bed. He didn't recognize me. He told me to leave before his wife got home. Later, I found him downstairs trying to call Heather."

"Heather?"

"He'd kept all her old phone numbers and addresses in his wallet. He must have tried every one of them. A few people answered and cussed him out. He yelled at them to put Heather on the phone. I finally got him back to bed, but this morning I woke up to the sound of a shovel scraping across the driveway. He was outside pushing the shovel back and forth while the snow fell. Alex tried to get him inside, but he snapped at her. After the kids went to school, I brought him in for coffee. He was freezing.

"I told him we needed to see the doctor. He looked scared and said he didn't need to go and went upstairs. When the kids came home for lunch, they asked about Cooper and whether he was still acting crazy. Alex thought he needed to go to the hospital for a few days. Cooper heard them. I saw him standing at the bottom of the stairs, listening, just before they left.

"A little later, he came back downstairs, gave me a hug, and kissed me. He said he was sorry for scaring the kids. Then he went outside to shovel the driveway.

"I heard the shot about ten minutes later. I ran out and found him collapsed on Snowball's grave. He'd shot himself in the heart."

We sat in silence for several minutes.

I had missed his last day. Maybe I could've stopped him, helped him. But he'd purposely waited until Gabriel and I and the kids were out of the house.

"I don't blame him for doing it," said Rachel. "I tried to convince him I'd take care of him no matter what, but he said he knew what I'd gone through with my mother. Toward the end I was never sure whether the fear I saw on her face was due to imagined demons or the horror she felt at having me see her that way. I asked him what he'd do if our places were reversed. Would he understand my wanting to kill myself, or would he beg me to stay alive?"

"What did he say?"

"He said he'd fire the gun himself if that's what I'd wanted."

"I kept worrying he'd want me to shoot him. I promised him I would if he couldn't return from blanking out."

"Would you have?"

"It would kill me, but I would have."

Rachel stared at me in horror or surprise or maybe confusion. "Alaska changed him," she said.

"It's changed me and will change you. Once you get used to freedom, it's hard to give it up. He was a teacher and a creator, but above all, he loved us all with everything he had. He knew the pain we'd feel as long as he was trapped inside his head. I think he wanted us to see his death as his final act of love for us. When I begged him not to leave me, he said I needed to focus on the knowing, not the losing. I never knew anyone so completely in my life. I'll always know him, and so will you."

"Yes. But I'll miss him so very, very much." She leaned against me and wept.

I stayed upstairs with her that night.

I thought I'd never stop crying, but two days later in the cold, clear, silent darkness of early December, we all stood outside watching the aurora shimmer above our house, pulsing in red and green strands, like a sound wave from heaven. I recognized the rhythm—one of Grandpa's. I could almost hear him laughing as I smiled and waved.

Grandpa's body was cremated. The next June we would all hike to the ridge and spread his ashes among Snowball's hair.

Mom and Daddy's return to our house during Christmas holidays was both joyous and sad. Alex and Jack jumped into their arms at the airport and wouldn't let go all the way home. Mom and Daddy were so glad to see trees covered in snow after months of watching blizzards blow over tundra and build concrete dunes against the snow fences. Several gentle snowfalls with no wind at our house had piled up delicate, glistening snowflakes on every exposed branch, impossibly high. They had wanted to fly back when they heard the news about Grandpa, but a blizzard had shut down their airport for a week. So they waited a few more days for the holidays to start.

I'd called them many times during their absence, talking about what had happened in Texas, how they'd felt and what they'd thought. We'd become so close and yearned to be together. They knew Grandpa and I were writing our book. Soon after they arrived, I gave them a copy.

Daddy missed talking to Grandpa. He said Grandpa was right about everything in the village, that he couldn't have survived there without Grandpa's help. He stood in front of shelves in the living room, teary-eyed, staring at the photos we had framed of Grandpa and Grandma's selfies on their hike. "I never had a photo of him in Texas," he cried to Natalie.

"You're going to have to take his place," I told him. "You'll be a grandpa soon."

"I'm not ready."

"I didn't think I was ready to be a mother, but I believe I am now. It helped when I decided to be honest with everyone about my past."

Zoe made a surprise visit. She wanted to see the wedding, her grandkids, and the birth of her great grandchild. We asked Zoe about John.

"I've left him," she said. "I don't want to say any more."

She shared Rachel's room and asked later if she could stay indefinitely.

Our wedding was small but perfect. Laney, Noah, and Allison joined Isabelle, Maddie and my family watching Gabriel and me sing Grandpa's "We Could Be Lovers" for our wedding vows. We alternated verses then sang the chorus together:

If my smiling face
Warms your heart every day
If my spirit moves you
More than looks could ever do
If you're my best friend
Forever now and then
Then we could be lovers
Yes, we could be lovers
To the end

Our house was ablaze with lights on Christmas Eve: decorating the tree, trimming the windows, and wrapping around a few tree trunks. The full moon reflecting off the diamond flakes of snow made the forest glow on a cloudless night. Sundance ate all the low-hanging ornaments, while Houdini jumped onto branches, swatting baubles onto the floor with his paws.

Gabriel and I invited everyone into the studio to hear us sing some new songs we'd written. Afterward, Dad asked Zoe to take Jack to the kitchen while the rest of us remained.

"I want to tell you about your Aunt Heather," Dad announced.

For the next two hours, he told us everything he could remember about their adolescence, how he blamed himself for introducing Heather to drugs, how he could just as easily have died from using as she eventually did.

"When I went to college, I was still wild, drinking, smoking weed, using crack. I was a mess with no ambition or purpose. Then I saw your mother sitting in the library one night, staring at me as I cried. I hadn't even noticed tears were dripping down my face. I was supposed to be studying but couldn't stop blaming myself for Heather living on the street somewhere." He held Mom's hand as tears wet his cheeks.

"She came over to me and started talking. She was at peace with everything, so calm, so assured, so empathetic. Her face radiated love. I asked her why, and she told me about her faith. I fell in love with her and with God and then blamed Dad for not teaching me about the church because I thought if he had, Heather and I wouldn't have had so many problems. I screamed at him about that on our boat trip then tried to wipe him out of my life and your lives.

"And all that time, he kept loving me and Heather and our kids, unconditionally. My father's grace had to wait until Harper could see no other option than to find him and bring him back to all of us. I'm so sorry for being such a fool and hope you can forgive me." He held his head and wept.

All of us comforted him, crying for his pain and for our loss.

"You're ready to be the grandpa my kids will need," I told him. "Thank you for being my Dad."

Epilogue

Gabriel brought home fireworks for New Year's Eve. We launched bottle rockets from the backyard on a clear night, brightened by a full moon and whipping ropes of yellow aurora lights. Alex and Jack chased each other through the trees, holding sparklers while Sundance hopped through the deep snow, yapping.

My contractions began at nine and soon became regular.

"We need to go! Now!" I shouted, holding my tummy, while trying to breathe through the tightening.

"I've never driven on snow-covered roads before," said Daddy, as he helped both grandmas and Mom into Grandpa's truck.

"You have 4-wheel drive and good tires," said Gabriel. "The road's been plowed. You'll be fine. Just stay with me."

"What about Sundance?" asked Jack.

"Damn!" I shouted. "We can't leave him here. Daddy, get one of your suitcases. We'll use it to smuggle him into the hospital." Jack and Alex held Sundance in the backseat of Gabriel's truck. Daddy followed with everyone else.

"Are you timing them?" asked Gabriel as he turned onto the highway.

I held up my phone then arched my back as another contraction began. "Ouch! These things are starting to hurt! That one lasted twenty seconds and was four and a half minutes from the previous one. Maybe we should hurry?"

My back ached! I thought about all our baby had been through, how he

(I knew by then it was a boy) had stayed with me through so much, and now I worried that he'd jump out too soon. But I so wanted to see him! "You do know what to do, just in case?" I asked Gabriel.

"I had some training, but never any experience. But I'm good with my hands." He looked over and smiled.

"And other things. Aargh!" Another contraction began.

"I know what you're talking about," said Alex.

"Good." I panted and watched the timer on my phone. "But knowing is not the same as doing, little sister, and we need to talk about that difference. Ouch!"

"OK. Can Chase be with me when we talk?"

"That one was thirty seconds and four minutes apart. Who is Chase?"

"Seventh grader. I got him to kiss me last week. It was cool."

"Gross!" said Jack.

Gabriel looked at me as I shook my head. I almost barked at her but then realized if I did, she'd hide her relationship with Chase from us. So I smiled. "I'll bet it was, Alex. We'd like to meet Chase. Why don't you invite him over in a few days?" I looked back at my beaming sister.

"Cool. I will."

"Can't wait to meet him," I said.

My little sister, now in sixth grade attending a K-12 school, had started to fill out in all the right places. Or wrong places. *Grandpa, please help me,* I thought.

By the time we reached the hospital, my contractions were forty-five seconds in duration and two minutes apart. Gabriel stuffed Sundance into the suitcase and rolled it upstairs. Nurses flew into action, wheeling in monitors and stands full of instruments, as they positioned me on the elevated bed. One of them noticed Gabriel taking the suitcase into the bathroom and looked at me oddly. Then he pushed Jack inside to play with Sundance and try to keep the puppy quiet.

I started pushing at two-thirty in the morning, New Year's Day, almost exactly the time I first met Grandpa. Rachel and Zoe held hands and smiled at me as the nurses positioned my feet and the doctor put on his catcher's mitt.

"Alex, film this! And everybody watches. Argh! I want to see all of your faces. I need you! Mom, Daddy, hold my hands."

Alex held up my camera as my family laughed and chanted 'Push!' over and over then gave me pep talks between pain attacks. I felt like my insides were being ripped apart!

Sundance started barking.

The doctor and nurses looked around, but I screamed and got their attention back to me.

Jack brought Sundance out of the bathroom and held him to his chest as he stared with big eyes over the doctor's shoulder. When I heard Jack exclaim, "Gross!" I knew it was close. My lips curled back from my teeth as I pushed.

"Almost there, Harper!" shouted Gabriel. "Another big push, and our baby is born!"

I saw all the faces in front of me: excited, smiling, cheering me on. I felt so incredibly happy.

Everyone cheered as Gabriel took our swaddled baby from the doctor and showed him to me: a beautiful, healthy boy, staring open-eyed up at me with the beginnings of a smile.

I felt Grandpa's loving arms around Gabriel and me as we presented Cooper Lyons Light to the world.

The End

Acknowledgements

I acknowledge some fences exist in Alaska, but so few that when I see one it looks artificial against the vast, beautiful landscape. I remember my first drive into Alaska from the Canadian border, hauling a trailer because our Jeep was full of seven cats, passing through miles of incredible scenery unmarred by people or fences. I still remember the awe I felt, wondering how there could be so much open land with no structures, no roads, and no domesticated animals. From my house in Anderson, I can walk miles and miles freely in almost any direction. What defines Alaska more than anything else to me is its freedom. Pick a direction and go as far as your desire takes you. Or stay put and live as you please. My first debt of gratitude is for this amazing state. Once you truly experience its lifestyle, being anywhere else is mere existence.

Once again I wish to thank Reagan Rothe, the head of Black Rose Writing, for his continued faith in me as a novelist, and his staff of Christopher Miller, David King, and Justin Weeks for their great help in bringing my books to the public. Additionally, kudos to Cherie Chapman for her great cover design.

I began *No Fences in Alaska* in late April 2018 and finished my first draft at the end of August. Rewrites continued into February 2019 with the help of several beta readers and editors, including Jerrica McDowell, Ellie Firestone, and especially Elisann Grant. I also want to give special recognition to Melissa Kaye, an outstanding developmental editor and writing coach. All of them helped me improve my ability as a writer and the story of Cooper and Harper. Any shortcomings I still have are due to my own stubbornness.

Many years ago, I took a girl parking. My lack of experience at this activity showed in many ways: I parked the car near a street light where cars drove by frequently, and I parked near the runway approach at our airport, so the screaming jet engines could set the romantic mood. I don't remember kissing her, but I do remember touching and stroking her amazingly soft, warm hand for possibly an hour. Pam still has the most sensuous hands I have ever felt. (Those who have read this book will understand this vignette's significance.) Despite my mistakes and lack of experience, she married me 44 years ago and continues to be with me despite all the time I now spend writing (and walking the dogs). I couldn't do this without her support.

Those who have lost a child understand the ache that never disappears as well as the countless "what-ifs" that haunt forever. Maybe if Cooper Lyons had existed for Jenny, she would still be alive today. This book would not exist without her life and memory.

NOTE FROM THE AUTHOR

Word-of-mouth is crucial for any author to succeed. If you enjoyed the book, please leave a review online—anywhere you are able. Even if it's just a sentence or two. It would make all the difference and would be very much appreciated.

Thanks!
Glen

About the Author

Glen Sobey lives in rural Alaska with his wife, three dogs, and a forest cat. He plays several musical instruments, hikes, kayaks, catches fish (sometimes), builds things, repairs more things, gardens, shovels lots of snow, splits too much wood, enjoys his family, and writes as often as he can. *No Fences in Alaska* is his second novel.

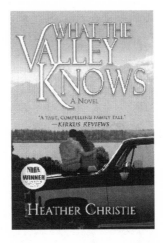